Tinsel Tidings 2025
An Anthology

Bookish Nerds Publishing LLC

Proofreaders

Ivy Graves

Sylas Seabrook

Cover Artists

Faith Sloan

Sandra Lynn Williamson

Contents

Foreword

Earlier this year, we embarked on a journey to give you twenty-five December holiday-themed short stories written by authors of genres ranging from light and dark romance, cyberpunk, horror, fantasy, and many more! For your convenience, we've put them in order from lightest to darkest themed. Please enjoy!

1
Saving Meri Christmas
Vanessa Williams

I wish for you
        to meet me
For a holiday party
on top of the Christmas tree.
It will be the rest of the cottage and farm creatures, you, and me.
Once the clock strikes midnight
Under the sparkling star's light
Let me meet you on this magical night.

Drew kissed the love poem and tucked it in his front jacket pocket. They'd been watching each other through the kitchen window with binoculars for a few days. Finally, he would get a chance to meet her.

He packed two bottles of wine from his cellar to gift to the party and was on his way across the large field to the pond between his tree and the house. When he got to the boat rentals by the pond, he was met by Fredrik, who was slithering around.

"Hello..." Fredrik hissed.

"I would like to borrow a boat, please."

"For how long?" Fredrik flicked his tongue as he slithered in front of the desk.

"Just across the pond and back."

"Where's your boating license?"

Drew reached his hand into his pocket and pulled out a wrinkled piece of paper. He hesitantly handed it over. Fredrik retrieved it with his mouth and set it on his desk. He inspected it with his monocle, which had been neatly tucked into his vest pocket.

Fredrik flicked his tail to point at the expiration date on the paper.

"Your license has expired." Fredrik slowly stuck the monocle back in his vest, then slid out of it. "And now you will too."

Fredrik coiled up and opened his mouth wide to show his two fangs, which were almost as long as Drew's tail.

Drew turned to run, but made it less than a foot before he found himself inside Fredrik's mouth, his left side pierced by the sharp tooth. He thought this was the end. When suddenly the snake's mouth sprang open! A brave toad had jumped on his head, shocking him into snapping his jaws open.

Drew mustered all his strength and rolled out of Fredrik's mouth. He hit the mud with a thud. The toad then leaped on top of him and faced Fredrik.

"Well, well, well, if it isn't my venomous friend Ribbit. Here to play the hero?" Fredrik began circling the duo, letting out a long and intimidating hiss. "Just because I can't consume you, doesn't mean I won't crush you like a grape."

Ribbit didn't hesitate. He spit venom straight into Fredrik's eyes.

"Do you trust me?" Ribbit asked, looking at Drew.

Drew didn't know if he trusted this toad, but he knew he had no choice. He nodded his head yes.

"Then get on my back!"

Drew grabbed Ribbit's shoulders and pulled himself onto the toad's back. Ribbit wrapped his tongue around Drew's wound and hopped into the boat. Fredrik sprang at them, digging his fangs into the back of it. Drew smacked him on the head with an oar, knocking him out, and the two began paddling with all their mite across the otherwise still pond

Water was gushing into the boat through the holes Fredrik made with his fangs.

"We need to patch the holes!" Drew's voice echoed off the water.

Drew remembered the wine in his bag. He quickly popped the bottles open and stuck the corks in the holes.

They looked at each other with meaning in their eyes. *We need to get out of here,* they thought at the same time. Then they began paddling as hard as their little bodies would allow.

After paddling a few miles, they stopped for a moment and Ribbit put his tongue back in his mouth to remove his shirt. He used it to make a tourniquet, which stopped Drew's bleeding pretty quickly.

"Have a few sips of that wine for the pain," Ribbit croaked.

Drew laughed in response but took the wise toad's advice.

Just as they began to relax, Ribbit peeked over his shoulder. He saw two eyes popping out of the water and heading for them at a hastened speed.

"It's Fredrik! He's coming!" called out Ribbit.

Fredrik's muscley form moved with purpose toward the boat, skimming the water's surface.

"What are we going to do?" Ribbit hollered.

"I've got an idea. Hold on tight!" replied Drew.

Drew rushed to the back of the boat. He stuck his tail in the water and began spinning it like a propeller.

Fredrik sped up, trying to catch the boat. His body moving in an S-shaped motion. His tongue sticking out. He was gaining on them.

Drew and Ribbit paddled to the edge of the lake and quickly jumped out of the boat.

They ran and hopped in between some tree roots far too small for the giant snake to slither in.

"Stay quiet," Ribbit croaked.

Fredrik slowly approached the tree, using his tongue to sniff around it. Ribbit and Drew held their breath, not wanting to make a sound.

"I know you're around here somewhere," Fredrik hissed. "I can smell you both."

Some dirt fell on Drew's nose. He tried to hold it in, but it was inevitable. He let out a loud sneeze.

"Gotcha!" screamed Fredrik.

The next thing Drew and Ribbit saw was Fredrik's big green eyeball peeking through the tree roots.

Fredrik used his sharp fangs to cut through the underground branches. He sprang his body backward, preparing to strike.

Drew and Ribbit squeezed each other. They knew this was it. This was the end. Drew let out a loud squeak as he squeezed Ribbit's hand. A calm passed between them as they shared this traumatic moment.

Like a bolt of lightning, a hawk struck down from the top of the tree. His sharp talons grabbed the snake's thick body and flew high in the sky, far away from the petrified duo.

The two adventurers stared at each other as they watched the hawk fly away with the snake.

"I'll get you two thieves!" Fredrik yelled from afar. "If it's the last thing I do!"

Drew and Ribbit giggled as they climbed out of the hole in the ground.

"That was a close one," they said in unison.

The rest of the journey was short and easy. A marked path took them through the trees straight to the old-timey cottage. They walked around the back of the home, and behind a hedge was a small door with a sign that read, "Meri the Mouse's House".

"Here it is," Drew said as he eagerly knocked on the door. It opened a crack.

"I guess that means we can go in!" Ribbit said matter-of-factually. He pushed the door open, and the new friends walked inside.

The door slammed heavily behind them, and the room was pitch black. Ribbit tried opening the door, but it wouldn't budge. Drew dug a match out of his chest pocket and lit it. In front and all around them were hard metal bars. They were in a locked cage.

"Hello?" called a soft woman's voice.

"Who's there?" called Drew.

"I'm Meri. This is my father, Lucas the Monitor Lizard."

"Meri? I got your invitation. What happened to the party?" asked Drew. "Where are we?"

"I didn't send that invitation! It was the evil Ferret Crel! He kidnapped us and locked us away. He's in love with me and saw you and I making eye contact through the binoculars. He became enraged with jealousy and sent you that invitation to lure you here and do... I don't know what. I haven't figured it out yet."

Footsteps sounded down a concrete staircase. Everyone turned their heads and Drew lit a new match. A bright lantern illuminated at the bottom of the stairs and everyone looked at the mangled ferret standing before them.

"Well, well, well," stated Crel. "If it isn't my arch nemesis, Drew."

"Arch nemesis? Why? We've never met!"

"I've seen you eyeballing my bride-to-be!"

"But, Crel, my dearest friend. How could you betray us this way?" said Lucas the Lizard.

"Psh. Friend? How could you call yourself my friend after you came into my home and stole all the attention from my family? The children never play with me anymore. Your daughter, Meri, denied my proposal and you sided with her! I don't know why they would rather play with a reptile like you rather than a furry critter like me! But here we are. And when the townsfolk voted *you* into office as mayor instead of re-electing me? That was the final blow! I had to kidnap you all, kill you, and reclaim my title of mayor of this cottage! Then the children will love me again and everything will be right!"

Crel held his cape up over his mouth and stared everyone down with his big red eyes before turning to head back up the stairs. They were left completely in the dark besides Drew's bright matches.

Ribbit listened for a guard. He heard someone standing in there besides them. He could feel their presence. He let out a heavy croak.

The guard quickly rushed over. "Hey, you, keep it down!"

Ribbit could now see the guard through the bars because of the light illuminating from Drew's match. Ribbit made eye contact with the guard.

"What are you looking at, punk?" asked the large black crow guarding them.

Ribbit's eyes began swirling green and yellow. The crow's attention couldn't be brought to anything else. Ribbit began whispering to him. "You will unlock the cages and set us free," Ribbit repeated this phrase three times as the crow smoothly followed his commands.

"How are you doing that?" asked Drew.

"Shh, don't talk to him," said Meri. "He needs to concentrate."

"What is he doing?"

"He's magic. He has hypnotic powers."

"How do you know?"

"My father is the mayor. It's my job to know everyone in and around this cottage. Including you," she smiled.

Lucas interrupted, "A smooth-talking bachelor who has many female friends, but never keeps one more than a night. You only look out for yourself. You have the largest wine cellar in the city, larger than mine, which means I'll bet you're a drunk. You're certainly not good enough for my daughter, Meri."

"We don't have time to talk about that now! We need to get moving. How do we get out of this place?" Drew begged.

"The crows will be monitoring the outside perimeter. Crel promised to kick out the wild forest animals if everyone followed him instead of me," Lucas explained. "I'm sure some of them are still on our side, unless they've all been captured like us. But we don't know which of the birds can or cannot be trusted."

"What else do we need to know?"

"There are four humans. Two adult males, one boy, and one girl. They don't have a tolerance for rodents in the home that aren't Crel. They love him more than he admits," Lucas said with a sigh.

"Don't forget about—," Meri began.

"About the cat." Lucas interrupted. "Anubis is the human's security system to try keeping the rodents out. I bribe him when the humans feed me meat, and he leaves Meri alone. But any other mouse, rat, or bird caught in the walls of this cottage are toast if Anubis catches them. That's why you must be very careful not to let him see you."

"Is Anubis working for Crel?" asked Drew.

"Anubis works for himself," Meri answered.

"How long will the guard stay this way?"

Ribbit croaked at them, "I'll stay here and hypnotize him long enough for you all to get away. Then I'll fight him off. I'll be fine!" Ribbit's eyes never left the guard.

Up the steps they ran one by one, the wood creaking with each critter's jump. Up, up, up, the steps they mounted, each step one lifted the next, Drew being the last to go. He looked down and saw Ribbit fighting the crow. By the looks of it, Ribbit was losing.

They reached the top step and scaled each other to reach the door handle, Drew being the one to turn the knob. When the door cracked open, he rushed everyone out.

He rode the guardrail down the stairs to fight off the crow, but he was too late. Ribbit lay there defeated. The crow who committed the sin stood there grinning with his sword.

Lucas and Meri hustled down the hall, looking for a hole to escape out of.

"Why... hello." Anubis jumped in front of them. His large green eyes stared into their souls. "Where are you two rodents heading in such a hurry?"

Without thinking, Meri hesitantly looked back at the door to the basement. Lucas quickly snatched her cheek and turned her head.

"Oh? Something is in the basement, huh? Perhaps a small snack awaits me down there?"

Anubis darted toward the basement door, his fur standing up making him appear to be twice as large.

"No!" Meri screamed. By the time she caught up to Anubis, he was at the bottom of the stairs, and she was still at the top. She covered her mouth as she looked down the now lit-up staircase.

Meri was surprised to see a little girl hovering over Ribbit. The human scooped Ribbit up and held him like a baby. She carried him up the stairs. Everyone stared in awe as the child took him to the kitchen. The whole crew followed behind her. The adults were snoring in the bedroom so all the animals decided to follow the little girl. The little girl grabbed some moss and a wet washcloth and wrapped them around Ribbit.

Crows jumped up into the window seals and watched from outside. Anubis even looked in amazement. Drew jumped onto the kitchen table where Ribbit was lying. A single tear from Drew landed right in Ribbit's cheek, waking him.

"Hello, my friend," he croaked.

Drew let out a heavy laugh.

"Don't you all see?" Drew began. "If a human was willing to help Ribbit, then why aren't we willing to help each other? The forest animals that want to come inside should be just as welcome as the house pets or spiders born in and around the cottage! Why do we treat each other differently just because of where we're born?"

The crows all gave each other embarrassed looks. "I can't believe we fell for Crel's game," said one crow, letting out a caw. The other gathered crows made sounds of agreement.

"We should've listened to Lucas. You'd think with how much this ferret talks, he's actually a weasel," squawked another crow.

Lucas got up on the table. "Drew is right. We must be a community and care for each other. If an animal is freezing outside, we need to welcome them in and around the cottage! Not turn them away. There's enough space in the walls, shed, and barn for everyone."

The crows began to cheer.

"No! I won't let this happen!" screamed Crel. Crel jumped on Drew and pulled a dagger. He held it up to Drew's neck.

"No!" screamed Meri. Everyone held their breath.

Out of nowhere, Fredrik slithered in.

"My best friend, Fredrik!" yelled Lucas. "I'm so relieved to see you."

Fredrik grabbed Crel with his tail and wrapped it around him tightly.

"You're coming with me," hissed Fredrik.

Then off he slithered back to his lake house.

Drew smiled at everyone around him, then he locked eyes with Meri. Drew pulled the fake love poem he had received from Crel out of his pocket. He handed it to Meri. She gave him a crooked smile.

Everyone ran to the Christmas tree and danced around the top all night under the sparkling star.

They ate the popcorn garlands off the tree, the cookies left out for Santa, and the carrot left out for the reindeer. They drank Christmas cranberry punch until their bellies were full. They exchanged gifts like bags of peanuts. Some twirled around each other. Some watched out the window for Santa's sleigh while others roasted marshmallows on the fire. There was finally peace in the cottage, and Christmas was saved.

"It turns out there's more to you than I thought," Lucas said to Drew, raising his glass and shouting, "Hip-hip-hooray!"

Everyone cheered in unison and lived happily ever after.

2

The Heart of Winter

Faith Sloan

Trigger Warning
Death of an old person (old age)

P ip's breath came out in tiny puffs of silver as he stood at the edge of Frostveil Lake, its surface gleaming like polished obsidian under the winter moon. His delicate wings, usually shimmering blue-white, had dulled to the color of old snow—a sure sign his magic was fading.

"Are you certain about this?" asked his older sister, Sage, her voice tight with worry. She hovered beside him, her own wings still bright and strong. "The water nymphs haven't spoken to our kind in decades. And the lake ... Pip, it's been frozen for three winters straight."

Pip nodded, though his small hands trembled as he touched the wilted frost-flower pinned to his chest—their grandmother's last gift before she'd begun her final sleep. "Grandmother Neve said the Heart of Winter is the only thing that can wake her. I have to try."

In the fairy village of Icicle Hollow, their grandmother lay in her crystalline bed, growing more translucent each day. The other elders whispered that she was simply growing tired, that old winter fairies eventually became one with the snow itself. But Pip refused to believe it. Not when there was still hope.

"The Heart of Winter," she had whispered to him just yesterday, her voice like wind through pine branches. "A perfect snowflake, preserved forever in ice ... deep beneath Frostveil Lake, in the realm of the water nymphs. But the cost, my little frost-wing ... the cost is always dear."

He couldn't lose her, not when he was able to do something about it. His grandmother and Sage were all he had left after a storm had taken his parents. He'd have given anything to save them; there's no way he was going to back down from saving her.

Now, standing before the frozen lake, Pip understood what she meant. To reach the water nymphs' realm, he would have to break through the ice. Even though he was a winter fairy, being in frozen water for too long would eventually hurt him too. This was going to hurt.

"Let me go instead," Sage pleaded. "Me and my magic are much stronger than you—"

"No." Pip's voice was small but firm. "Grandmother chose me. She gave me this." He touched the frost-flower again. "She said I would know why when the time came."

Taking a shaky breath, Pip closed his eyes and remembered his grandmother's stories. She had been the youngest winter fairy ever to create a blizzard. How she had once saved their entire village by weaving a protective dome of snow during the Great Thaw. She had loved them more fiercely than the winter wind itself.

"Love makes us brave," she always said. "Even when we're afraid."

I can do this, he said to himself.

Pip spread his wings and rose into the air, moonlight catching the few remaining sparkles along their edges. Below him, the ice stretched endlessly, beautiful and forbidding. He flew to the center of the lake, where the ice was thickest, and began to sing.

It was an old song, one Grandmother Neve had taught him—a melody of winter's first kiss, of snowflakes finding their way to earth, of the deep quiet that comes with the season's turning. As he sang, his magic flowed out of him, what little remained, and the ice began to glow with soft blue light.

The surface cracked.

Then shattered.

Pip plunged into the water below.

The water was impossibly cold and yet burned like liquid flame against his skin. His wings, so delicate in the best of times, felt as though they might dissolve entirely. But he forced himself to dive deeper, following the trail of blue light his song had created.

Down, down, down he went, past schools of silver fish that glowed like living stars, past forests of kelp that swayed in underwater currents, past his own pain and fear. His lungs screamed for air, his magic guttered like a candle in the wind, but still he swam deeper.

Finally, he reached a grotto carved from pearl and moonstone, where the water itself seemed to sing. There, on a throne of living coral, sat the water nymph.

She was ancient and beautiful, with hair like flowing seaweed and skin that shifted between pale green and deep blue. Her eyes were the color of the deepest ocean trenches, and when she looked at Pip, he felt as though she could see straight through to his trembling heart.

"A winter fairy," she said, her voice like the sound of waves on distant shores. "In my realm? How curious. How ... painful it must be for you, little one."

Pip tried to speak but only managed to produce a stream of silver bubbles. The nymph smiled sadly and touched his forehead with one graceful finger. Suddenly, he could breathe the water as easily as air.

"Better?" she asked.

"The Heart of Winter," Pip gasped. "Please, I need—my grandmother—she's dying, and the elders say only the Heart can wake her, and I know she's given so much to everyone, saved so many people, and I just ... I can't lose her. I can't."

The tears that rolled down his cheeks turned to tiny pearls in the water, drifting away like falling stars. He thought that if he could plead to her for help, maybe she would understand and have mercy on them.

The nymph studied him for a long moment. "The Heart of Winter," she said finally. "Yes, I know of what you speak. But tell me, young fairy—do you know what it truly is?"

Pip shook his head, sending more pearl-tears spiraling through the water. He didn't know, and he didn't really care. Not if it could save her.

"It is a sacrifice," the nymph said softly. "Love given freely, without thought of return. Your grandmother knew this. She has been preparing for this moment for many seasons."

From the depths of her throne, the nymph drew forth a sphere of perfect ice, no larger than Pip's small fist. Within it, suspended like a moment caught in time, was the most beautiful snowflake he had ever seen—six-pointed, intricate beyond imagining, unique in all the world.

"This was created by the first winter fairy ever to love someone more than herself," the nymph explained. "And it has been waiting for another such fairy ever since."

"I don't understand," Pip whispered.

The nymph's smile was infinitely gentle and sad. "To wake your grandmother, the Heart must be given willingly by one who loves without condition. But the giver ... the giver takes her place in the long sleep. The young for the old, the future for the past. This is the way of things."

Pip's own heart seemed to stop beating. "You mean ... I would ... "

"Sleep the sleep of stones and snow, yes. Until someone who loves you more than themselves comes seeking your return."

The grotto fell silent except for the distant whisper of underwater currents. Pip stared at the Heart of Winter, at the perfect snowflake trapped forever in ice, and thought of his grandmother's face. Her kind eyes, her gentle hands, her laugh like silver bells in winter air.

He thought of all the stories she had told him, all the magic she had taught him, all the love she had given so freely. He thought of how she had held him during thunderstorms, how she had shown him how to paint frost on windows. How she had believed in him even when his magic was the weakest of all the fairy children. How she had cried when they told him this might be his last winter too. Without the surge of magic given from fairy parents until the children reached a certain age...the child would wither away. Sage had been just old enough when they had passed. Pip had not been so lucky. He wasn't going to last anyway, he could do this for her. He could make his life matter.

He thought of Sage, waiting for him above the frozen lake. Sage, who would understand. Who would forgive him, even as her heart broke? She would...wouldn't she?

"Will she remember me?" he asked quietly. Even though he had decided, his stomach was twisting in knots.

"Love like yours is never forgotten," the nymph promised.

Pip reached out with trembling hands and took the Heart of Winter. It was warm to the touch, though it was made of ice, and it pulsed gently like a living thing. Like a real heart.

"Thank you," he whispered.

The nymph nodded solemnly and touched his forehead again. It was almost lovingly, like his mother would when she'd kiss him goodnight. "Go swiftly, little winter fairy. And know that your sacrifice honors all who came before."

Pip clutched the Heart to his chest and swam upward, his remaining magic carrying him faster than he had ever moved before. The journey back felt endless—his small body exhausted from the deep dive, his wings waterlogged and heavy—but now he barely noticed his fatigue. His heart was too full of love and sorrow and terrible, beautiful purpose.

He burst through the surface of the lake just as the first rays of dawn painted the sky pink and gold. Sage cried out in relief and joy, flying down to help pull him from the water. But when she saw the orb in his hands, She reached out to try to touch it but he snatched it away.

"You can't touch it. It might think I'm giving it to you and then not work."

Her brows scrunched together as she crossed her arms over her chest. "Well, what is it? How does it work?"

"It...trades my life for hers. Then, you both can finally be ok."

Sage's eyes widened in dawning horror, and she took a step back.

"No," she whispered. "Pip, no, there has to be another way."

"There isn't," he said gently, his voice already growing distant and dreamy. "And it's okay. Really, Sage. I'm not afraid anymore."

They flew together to Grandmother Neve's crystal bower, where she lay so still and pale she might already have been a sculpture of snow and starlight. Sage was crying openly now, her tears freezing into diamonds that chimed softly as they fell. She'd tried the whole flight there to convince him to find another way. That their grandmother wouldn't want to live if it meant he would die, but Pip wasn't listening.

Pip placed the Heart of Winter on his grandmother's chest, directly over her heart. The moment it touched her, the orb began to glow, and warmth spread through her translucent form like sunrise breaking through winter clouds.

Her eyes fluttered open—bright and blue and full of love.

"My dear ones," she whispered, but as she saw Pip placing the Heart of Winter on her chest, her expression changed to one of horror. "No! Pip, what have you done?"

She pushed the glowing orb away from her, and it rolled across the crystal floor, its light dimming. "I won't accept this. I won't let you trade your life for mine."

"But Grandmother," Pip said, confusion clouding his small face as his form remained solid, unchanged. "You were dying. I had to—"

"Everyone has their time," she said firmly, though her voice was weak. "This is mine. I've lived long and loved deeply, and I am ready. You have your whole life ahead of you—your magic to discover, adventures to have, love to find."

Sage flew to the Heart of Winter and picked it up, its glow flickering uncertainly. "There has to be another way," she said desperately.

"No," Grandmother Neve said gently but decisively. "Some things cannot be changed, my dear ones. And they shouldn't be. I love you both too much to let either of you sacrifice yourselves for an old fairy who has already had her time to shine."

She struggled to sit up, reaching for both children. "Pip, my brave little frost-wing, your love means everything to me. But true love sometimes means knowing when to let go. It means accepting that endings, even sad ones, are part of life's beautiful story."

Tears streamed down Pip's face as he realized what this meant. "But I don't want to lose you."

"You won't," she said softly, gathering him close. "I'll be in every snowflake you create, every winter song you sing. Love doesn't end when life does—it transforms into something even more precious. Memory. Legacy. The love you pass on to others."

Around them, the other winter fairies began to arrive, drawn by the commotion. They formed a gentle circle, their wings catching the early morning light, and began to sing—not a song of deep winter sleep, but a song of celebration, of a life well-lived and love freely given.

"Promise me," Grandmother Neve whispered as her breathing grew shallow again, "promise me you'll live fully. Both of you. Promise you'll be brave enough to love, knowing that all beautiful things must someday end."

"I promise," Sage whispered through her tears.

Pip nodded, unable to speak, but his promise was written in his eyes.

As the sun rose fully over Icicle Hollow, Grandmother Neve smiled one last time. "That's my brave ones. Remember—love makes us brave enough to live, and brave enough to say goodbye." She picked up the Heart of Winter and touched it to Pip's chest. His eyes widened as it began to glow. The magic and light remaining from his grandmother flowed into Pip. In moments, his wings were fluttering and shining brightly with pulsing magic and he felt a surge of energy unlike any he had ever felt before. Tears streamed down his face as he realized what this meant. His grandmother had given the last bit of her life force for him.

"I love you both. Take care of each other." She said, her voice bursting with love. And with that, she closed her eyes and became one with the eternal winter, her body transforming into a thousand glittering snowflakes that danced up toward the sky. The two of them joined hands with the other fairies, tears streaming down their faces. Sage sang brightly, more accepting of her grandmother's passing. Pip, however, couldn't believe that he had failed. What was he supposed to do now? Just move on and accept that his grandmother had given her life for his?

Suddenly, he felt a warmth blooming in his chest. He looked down to examine the feeling and was surprised to see a light spreading. For the first time in his life, his heart glowed with an inner fire, like the others. His heart fire matched the color of the heart of winter, and his grandmother's eyes. The tears came stronger then, and he realized something. She had become a part of him, and she always would be.

Sage gripped his hand tighter, pulling him to the present. They smiled at each other, and he finally joined the other fairies in song. He was part of them, at last.

Pip and Sage lived for many seasons after that, their magic growing strong, their love deeper for having learned that some gifts are too precious to accept. They told Grandmother Neve's story to every child in Icicle Hollow, teaching them about love that honors life by acknowledging its natural rhythms.

"She was right," Pip would say gently. "Sometimes love means knowing when to let go."

And sometimes, on the clearest winter nights, when the aurora painted the sky in ribbons of green and gold, they would see familiar snowflakes dancing among the lights—six-pointed, intricate beyond imagining, unique in all the world—and know that love, once given freely, never truly ends.

3

Peetie's Christmas Vacation

Sylas Seabrook

Sunshine dug into Peetie's feathers, warming his skin. He poked his beak up at the sun and ruffled his feathers, basking in the light. He felt good, so he chirped pleasant little tweets that almost made a song. This was a magnificent morning, a sign of a day that was going to go great.

Trib, Peetie's owner, whistled at him. "Come, Peetie."

Peetie hopped around on the windowsill, turning his budgie body to face Trib, and leaped into the air, spreading his wings and flying the short distance between them. Trib extended his arm in his six-foot frame, and Peetie landed near his elbow, then used his beak to dig into Trib's Inves bodysuit and inch up to Trib's shoulder. Trib reached up and dug into the back of Peetie's neck, scratching an itch that did not exist, but giving a joy that was much loved. Peetie lifted his head to let Trib's fingers really dig in.

"Trib, you made breakfast again?" Liv, Trib's wife, had her hands on her hips, staring at the kitchen. Her eyes went wide, then she reached out and rubbed her tummy.

"She's kicking again?" Trib said. "I want to feel."

He rushed over without thinking about Peetie being on his shoulder, so Peetie hunkered down and extended his wings enough to stabilize himself. It was a short distance, so Trib was delicately touching Liv's belly before Peetie knew it. Peetie was a good bird, so he let Trib spend time with his wife, even though Peetie wanted the attention.

"Baby come?" Peetie squawked.

Liv shook her head. "Not yet, Peetie." She was overdue but insisted on a natural birth.

Trib marveled at Liv's womb like it was a magical place, then stood and kissed her. Fortunately, Trib was tall enough that she put her arms around him from below instead of over his shoulders—that would send Peetie scurrying for safety.

"Hungry?"

"Ravenous." Liv pulled her Inves top over her tummy and sat at the dining room table.

"One ham omelet coming up!" Trib hurried back into the kitchen, plated two meals, and served breakfast.

Peetie turned around and buried his beak in his feathers. Now was a good time for a nap.

Trib stood, startling Peetie. The Transformer Adori, a mechanical pet turned into a semi-living being, fluffed his wings and squawked. Trib ignored him, picked up the plates, and washed them in the kitchen sink. He dried his hands off and returned to his recliner in the living room, propping his feet up and turning on the visisheet.

"Are you going to watch the news now?" Liv was standing right next to Trib and sounded exasperated.

"Sure. Why not? I'm the CEO of Ementhe Enterprises. I have to know what's going on in Myeinth."

Liv shrugged. "As soon as it's over, I want to talk to you. I have an idea."

Trib nodded, then she leaned down and kissed him. She headed off, and the news of the day played on the visisheet. There was a gang forming. They called themselves R's, the *r* signifying rebels. The news host theorized that a new rival gang would appear on the world stage anytime. There were numbers about Ementhe Enterprises and a clip of Trib saying something. It ended with a story about a young boy who helped an elderly woman.

Trib flipped his feet down, locking the recliner in place, stood, and stretched, forcing Peetie to climb around to the back of Trib's neck. Trib's stretch was a little too good and his head started to push Peetie off, so Peetie climbed up Trib's head and stood on top while his owner finished stretching.

"Peetie!" Trib laughed. "Get off my head!" He reached up and put a finger out, prompting Peetie to step on it, then swung his arm around and let Peetie back onto his shoulder.

"I see you're done," Liv said, appearing from nowhere.

"Yeah. That's right. Your idea."

She smiled and put her hands on her hips, leaning back to relieve some of the stress of a tummy on the brink of bursting. "I was thinking we could give Peetie a vacation. He's always around us, but he must want to do something on his own. You can always hear him through the connection I created for you."

Trib rubbed his chin, but Peetie got to thinking and almost immediately decided against it. Trib nodded and reached up, extending his finger for Peetie, so the budgie hopped on and waited while Trib brought the bird around to face him.

"What do you think, Peetie?" Trib was enamored by the idea. "Do you want to go on a vacation?"

Peetie's squawk of displeasure made Trib take a step back. "Whoa! Why not?"

"Peetie good bird. Peetie vacation, not see Trib. Vacation bad."

"And they say a dog is man's best friend." Liv came up and scratched that nonexistent itch. It relaxed Peetie.

"Well, do you want to see snow?" Trib said.

"Peetie not know snow."

"Well, you're gonna. It's time to go to work."

One hundred and fifty stories above ground, Trib and Peetie stood in Ementhe Tower looking out a window at Myeinth. Trib was loved by the citizens for freeing them from the Corporations' rule. Trib was glowing blue, with little wisps of blue vapor zipping off his skin. It meant he was full of pure Ementhium vapor, a vapor that gave him magical powers to do almost anything. Peetie could use vapor, but not like Trib.

"This city has never seen snow. The weather is controlled, raining only when needed to clean the streets. It's never too hot or too cold. We're going to give them something to remember."

Who was Trib talking to? Sometimes he talked to Peetie. Was he doing that now? Peetie chirped to acknowledge Trib, just in case.

Trib thrust his hands out, and a vibrant blue stream of vapor erupted from his prosthetic fingertips. It flew through the window as if it weren't there, curved up, and formed a cloud in the sky. The cloud spread until it covered the city, a breeze whipping up as evidenced by the lighter city trash tumbling through the streets. The clouds stopped growing but churned with ominous undertones, thunder rumbling though no lightning striking.

It began raining little white dots. Peetie zoomed in with his Eye of Ra sight on the little dots. They were geometric disks tumbling down. Is this what he meant by snow? The little white flakes collided with the ground and dissolved into micro-puddles. People began wandering into the streets and holding their hands up, shivering against the cold. They started appearing with thin jackets on—probably the thickest they had—and the snow started sticking to the ground, creating a thin layer of beautiful white across the city.

Peetie cocked his head to the side and stared at the wondrous sight, but Trib lowered his arms, stopping the stream of vapor and causing Peetie to lose his footing. He gripped onto Trib's Inves to steady himself and righted his head, giving a squawk to show his lack of appreciation for the sudden movement.

"Sorry." Trib reached up and scratched Peetie's perennial itch. "It's going to last for a day. I'd have to add more vapor to keep it going, but I think that's a good enough treat for the city."

The day at the office over, Trib headed home. This gave Peetie a chance to try pecking the falling snow. It disappeared under the clamp of his beak, which seemed odd. Why would something vanish like that? Did it not like being bitten? And why did it have to be cold? It was so cold that it got deep below Peetie's feathers to his flesh. He wanted to shiver just to get some warmth going on, though that wouldn't really work for him. He did have some Ementhium vapor in his stores, so he released a little bit using a heating pattern to keep him warm enough to function.

They arrived home, and Liv had the house at a comfortable temperature with food ready. Trib, like always, put his finger up for Peetie to climb onto and sent Peetie flying toward his open cage. There was a nice wooden bar there with a sphere that rang little metal balls when Peetie fought with it. One day, he would get those little bells and catch their ringing once and for all. It looked like it was asking for it now, so Peetie pecked at the thing. It swung back and forth and started chiming. He was right. It wanted it, so Peetie stood tall and pecked violently at the ball. Maybe today would be the day he got to those bells. In the background, Trib and Liv talked, ignoring Peetie's battle with the ball.

The two of them ate their food, leaving Peetie to tend to his cage. Peetie got bored with the toys and decided to shut down, so he buried his head in his feathers and powered down to a ready state, ears listening and touch sensors activated. Trib disturbed Peetie's rest with a gentle neck scratch just before they went to bed. Tomorrow was Christmas, and the house would be full of activity.

A clickity clack clack crash on the roof triggered Peetie's ears. What was that? Did snow make sounds on the roof? Peetie wasn't sure, so he decided to investigate. He flew up the unused fireplace chimney, stirring the snow at the bottom, and burst out the top. He stopped mid-air and hovered, not flapping his wings—that was an advantage of being a Transformer. A large man in a red and white outfit kneeled behind a reindeer with a bright red glowing nose.

"Oh, Rudolph. You're going to be okay," the man said with a jolly but concerned voice. "Let's get you into the sleigh."

He lifted the reindeer up, and Peetie saw an ankle positioned at a weird angle. It must be broken. He carried the reindeer to the back of two rows of reindeer and set him down in the seat the man must use. He grabbed a soft, red velvet bag and rummaged through it.

"I know I have something that can fix you up in here." He pulled out box after box wrapped in pretty paper and ribbons, setting them down on the roof.

Peetie was tempted to go peck at the ribbons. They looked like they were begging for it. Instead, he remained hovering and observing this odd scene.

The packages piled up to a mound that was larger than the bag itself, making this all more curious than before. Something wasn't right.

"I must have left it at the North Pole." The man pursed his lips, thinking. "I guess we're going to have to continue on." He started putting the packages back in the bag.

"Dasher, we can do this," he said, turning his head to the lines of reindeer. "We'll just be a little late for the first time ever."

The reindeer called Rudolph buried his head on the seat in an act of submission.

"It's okay, boy," the man said. "We've all grown a little older and more fragile over the years. Maybe it's time for you to retire."

Rudolph emitted a high-pitched whine.

The old, jolly man cocked his head to the side, taking note of Peetie. "What do we have here?" He approached Peetie. Peetie squawked and transformed into a bearded vulture.

"Whoa, boy. It's okay. I'm Santa Claus. I don't cause harm. Where did you come from?"

Peetie flapped his wings in a slow, methodical fashion, trying to be eerie and intimidating, but not ready to attack. The guy was saying that he wasn't a threat, after all. Peetie wasn't so sure. The guy did have a sleigh filled with reindeer on top of Trib and Liv's house. Oh, and a bag that holds more than its size. This was definitely sus.

"Hmm. I bet you could help. You seem like a big strong bird. Do you think you can help me deliver presents around the world? Are you a good bird?"

Good bird? Peetie was a good bird. Peetie could do anything. He wasn't sure what presents were, but if someone needed help, a good bird could help, right?

"Peetie good bird. Peetie help Santa."

"That's the Christmas spirit." Santa pointed to the rows of reindeer. "Just grab Rudolph's reins, but first..."

He sprinkled some vapor around himself and he shrunk along with his bag, then hopped into the chimney. This put Peetie on alarm mode. He flew over to the chimney and peeked down, but had to pull back when Santa popped back up and resumed his normal form.

"Well, that's done. They're going to have a magical Christmas." He laughed, and his belly shook. "Shall we get to flying, good bird? Just follow Dasher's lead." He pointed at the reindeer in the front, then hopped into the sleigh next to Rudolph.

Peetie flew over and gripped the reins in his claws, then lifted up, and the other reindeer started forward. The sleigh lifted up off the roof, and they landed on the next house. From house to house, Santa went down chimneys and popped back up a few seconds later, presents delivered. On and on they went until they were out of the city and into the Naturites' camps. There were no chimneys here, which made the process go faster. Soon, they were out of Myeinth altogether.

"Peetie! She's going into labor," Trib yelled through his connection to Peetie. "Come quick."

It was just past midnight, and Liv was going to have a baby. Peetie squawked. He couldn't do both things at once. Or could he? Peetie released some red Mæssium vapor with the pattern for replication, and a clone of himself spawned into existence as the vapor edited mass. Peetie left his clone behind to help Santa, then headed back to Myeinth. He flew as fast as he could and debated changing into his much bigger size, but he was almost there, so he just kept up his quick pace.

Back at home, he transformed back to a budgie and flew down the chimney. Trib was there and a mess was on the bed with Liv, but the baby was in her arms, suckling her breasts.

"Peetie! There you are!" Trib beamed with excitement. "Meet Andrea, our baby."

"Andrea, baby," Peetie repeated.

"That's right. You're such a good bird."

"Peetie good bird."

"Where were you?"

Peetie chirped. "Santa sleigh. Presents."

Trib laughed. "You're a funny bird. You don't have to tell me if you don't want to. We did say you could take a vacation."

Peetie blinked. He had told Trib where he'd been.

The night was chaotic, including a trip to the hospital where Andrea was cleared as a healthy baby, then they came home.

"What's this?" Trib's eyes were wide as he stared at the presents.

"Santa presents," Peetie chirped.

"They must be from my mom," Trib countered, disregarding Peetie.

They sat down and opened the presents, surprised to see children's clothing in the presents. "How did she know?" Trib said.

Peetie was done trying to explain, so he eyed the ball on his cage, opened his beak, ran forward, and attacked it full on. He was going to get that bell!

4

A Family Christmas Vacation

Ada S. Blunt

A romantic dinner, only the two of them—private service and fine dining—marked CJ's and Ava's anniversary. A year since they had been legally married. A year full of events, they miraculously survived.

"What would you say about going away for Christmas? For the one-year anniversary of our wedding?" CJ asked, gazing into Ava's eyes after sipping from the glass of champagne he had ordered. "By then, Pearl will be seven months, and we could take Marissa with us."

Still breastfeeding Pearl, Ava only took a sip from her glass, placed it on the table, and pushed it away from her. "And where would it be? I take it you have something in mind."

"I have Switzerland in mind. We could go skiing. But if you prefer somewhere else... anything you want, Baby."

With a playful smirk, Ava tipped her head back and gazed at CJ, seeming to ponder. "I don't know... Sounds tempting, but we promised your parents we'll go to Glasgow for Christmas. Basically, this would be our first real Christmas as a family. With your family. Last year doesn't count as everybody was there for our wedding. And it's Pearl's first Christmas. Could we go after?" Ava came up with an alternate plan.

"How about we take everybody with us? We could have a big party. And I know the perfect place that could fit all of us," CJ came up with another option.

"And here I thought I'm the one who always has a plan B up my sleeve. I think I like this idea better."

"Do you mind if I invite Ian? I know he's not technically family, but since he's going to be alone in London..." CJ suggested.

"Oh, I thought Ian and Ellie were together."

His forehead creased. "Not that I know of. Who told you?"

"Nobody." She shrugged, flicking a hand. "I just assumed. They seemed pretty close after what happened to Ellie. He looked after her and paid for her to move. I thought... Never mind. He doesn't like her anymore, does he? Because of the scars?" Ava's eyes glistened with tears as she sulked in disappointment.

Frowning, CJ shook his head. "No, Ian is not that shallow. He's... still trying. More like still hoping. But Ellie considers him just a friend. Ian said she actually mentioned to him, as a friend, that she's no longer interested in dating. She said she wants to be with the right person for the right reason. Which is exactly what I said when I broke up with her." His lips pressed into a thin line, and he shrugged under the weight of a troubled conscience.

Without a word, Ava stared at CJ, lips puckered, appearing to ponder. "Well... that's wise of her, I should say. Doesn't sound familiar to you, though? Didn't I think we were just friends? Didn't I confess I wasn't interested in dating?"

"You did, actually. When I took you out for my birthday dinner. Well... a week after my birthday." He cast a playful smile. "Which was actually on your birthday. But you didn't mention it."

"You knew it was my birthday?" Ava reacted, mystified.

"Not at the time. I found out months later... Which brings the question... why didn't you say anything?"

"And steal your light? You were enjoying the moment. I didn't want to spoil it." She paused, with that look she usually had when her mind cooked up something. "Anyway... if you invite Ian, I'll invite Ellie. But he better not be dumb around her. Maybe Ian needs some tutoring from his best friend," Ava implied with a smirk.

"Me?"

"Well, you could bring it up with him. He probably has to try harder and focus on the 'right person, right reason' part. And if you ask me, he's more than halfway there. He already proved he's the *right person*. And what he did for her... that's some *right reason right there*." She leaned her head, displaying an expressive grin.

CJ blinked, returning a similar grin. "Who's now Ian's advocate?" he teased.

"Well... I had time to get to know Ian better, and I think they'd make a cute couple together." A mysterious smile bloomed on Ava's lips. "And I believe she's ready. Just waiting for the *right someone* to shed the *right light* on her to shine."

Absorbed, he gazed in Ava's eyes, CJ's lips arched slightly, "Sometimes I wonder if you know what your superpower is." When Ava looked at him, eyes asking and eyebrows arched, he continued, "You make me fall in love with you every day. And you're not even trying."

She gently bit her lower lip and smiled, completely smitten. "Let's go home now. I suspect you asked Marissa not to call, no matter what. I hope the kids are okay," Ava said, checking her cellphone.

"Only asked Marissa not to call *you*. She texted me about twenty minutes ago. I wanted your undivided attention. Only you and me. Nothing to worry about, Baby. Everything's fine. Ayden and Pearl are fine. Both sleeping."

She smiled, relaxed. "Thank you... You really know how to make it special, Babe," and she began getting ready to leave.

When Ava and CJ finally arrived at the airport, everybody was already gathered, waiting.

"Sorry, we're late. We had a bit of an accident before leaving," Ava apologized. "Everyone here?" She looked around, trying to register the assembly, until Pearl began fussing, and her attention derailed.

Before Ava could realize what was happening, the party began swarming.

Luggage check and all the airport procedures, crying babies, clingy toddlers, goofy adults acting like teenagers, grumpy teenagers, and their fed up parents... the group stuck out like a sore thumb.

A private jet, waiting for them, quickly filled up. Pearl calmed once inside. Ava handed her to Marissa and turned.

"Okay... headcount." She began counting but fell short, stopped, and started again. "Who are we missing?" She scanned the airplane. "Ellie. Where is Ellie?" Ava craned her neck, trying to spot Ellie.

"Is Ellie coming?" Ian asked, his voice carrying both surprise and keen interest.

Ava suppressed a smirk. "She's supposed to. I'll call her. Maybe she's got delayed in traffic." She moved toward the quieter area at the front of the airplane so she could talk, and dialled Ellie's number.

Ellie didn't pick up. After leaving a voice message, Ava began strolling back to her seat. As she passed by the still-open door, she glanced outside and halted, lips stretching into a face-splitting grin. Ellie was running on the tarmac.

"Here comes Ellie," Ian called after he looked out the window and saw what Ava was smiling at.

She glanced briefly at Ian, only to catch his expression shining.

As she began walking back, Ava poked Ian in the shoulder, swishing into his ear, "You better be smart and don't waste a perfectly good occasion. And don't talk work." She paused and turned toward Ellie, who had just gotten on the plane, all dishevelled and out of breath. "Ellie, you can sit by Ian. Unless you want to sit on the wheel... at the back," she chuckled.

Ian rushed to get Ellie's carry-on and tucked it in one of the compartments above, pitching Ava a knowing smile.

"Well... this is going to be some vacation. I guess I'll have to behave. My boss will be there." Ellie's comment amused Ava.

"I don't see any bosses. We're only friends and family here." Ava mocked and continued swaying back to her seat.

Ian's gaze followed her with a subtle knowing smile before his eyes met CJ's, who cocked his head with a wink and a crooked grin.

The first evening began quietly. After dinner, everybody sat around the fireplace with a hot chocolate or tea, chatting away.

The chalet had enough rooms for all of the adults and older kids. Marissa and the youngest kids shared the guests' cabin. This way, the babies wouldn't disrupt anyone's sleep. And the din in the main lodge wouldn't keep the little ones awake. At least, this was the plan Ava carefully drafted, so they all could have a good time.

The following morning, after coffee and breakfast, the party began getting ready to hit the slopes. After preparing the kids for the day, Ava returned to the main lodge.

She rubbed her arms, shivering in just a skinny top. "Brrr... Oh, you're here. Where is everybody?" she asked Ellie, still sipping her coffee, by herself.

"They are all upstairs, getting ready, I guess."

"Why aren't you getting ready?"

"I'm staying here, with you. I... don't ski. I mean... I never learned," Ellie replied, raising a hesitant shoulder.

"Hmm... Well, someone's going to show you the ropes. I'm not staying here. We're all going. So, you better get ready because we don't leave anyone behind," Ava described her plan.

"I... I don't have any ski gear... I mean... I have no clue what I'd need or where to start," Ellie replied with a small smile.

Ava turned, staring stupefied at Ellie. It never occurred to her to ask. Ellie and CJ have been together for over two years. Plenty of opportunities to go skiing. Yet she says she doesn't know? *CJ loves skiing*—Ava couldn't fathom why Ellie didn't learn how to ski.

"Well, I packed more than I need. Let's get you into something. There must be stuff to rent around here or a store where we can buy whatever else you need. Come on," Ava urged Ellie upstairs.

She quickly gathered the extra stuff she had in her luggage and gave it to Ellie. A couple of missing items miraculously appeared from other family members, completing the outfit. Ava's hand, of course.

When the two returned, an ad-hoc snowball fight was in full swing outside. As soon as Ellie stepped out, a cold, lightly packed snowball projectile crashed on her forehead. Aimed at CJ, but he ducked, and the snowball flew over, disintegrating and melting on Ellie's face.

Remorse breathing through all his pores, Ian hurried up the stairs. "I'm sorry. I... I aimed for CJ."

"That's okay." Swiftly squeezing by, Ellie headed back inside.

Still standing in the doorframe, Ava just watched. Speechless.

Ian moved to follow Ellie, but with a quick stance shift, Ava stepped in front of him. One intense, meaningful glare and a slight poke of her right index at Ian's chest were enough to stop him from taking another step. Instead, she pivoted on her heels and followed Ellie.

"Baby-Girl, are you okay?" Ava almost whispered after knocking.

Ellie opened the door with a smile. "Yes, I'm fine. I had to check my makeup. I didn't want everyone to stare at my scars."

Narrowing her eyes and biting her lower lip, Ava took a deep breath. "I know time was scarce, and we didn't have the opportunity to catch up on a lot since... all that happened. Would you let me pay for you to have those scars removed?"

"Nope... They're mine. They are my daily reminder not to make poor decisions anymore."

"Come here, Baby-Girl." Ava held Ellie in a maternal hug. "Are you sure you want to come? I could stay with you."

"I'm fine... I'm coming. We don't leave anyone behind, remember?" Ellie's voice fell firm and steady.

"Okay..." Ava nodded, wrapping her arm around Ellie. "Let's go then. It'll be fun. Patti and Don will probably come with us to the beginner slopes. We need to coach Ayden, and I'm out of practice. I haven't gone skiing in five years. You're coming with us. Let's see how we split."

Once outside, they quickly figured out the teams were already formed and the rides planned.

"Ellie will have to come with us to the beginners' slopes. We'll have to find a ski coach for her," Ava said loud enough so Ian would hear.

"I could coach Ellie," he volunteered promptly, to Ellie's dismay.

"Of course, it had to be my boss offering to coach me."

"I thought I mentioned already. There are no bosses here," Ava scorned and turned toward CJ. "How are the high slopes?"

"Well, it's the Alps... They are pretty much like the Canadian Rockies," CJ chimed in with an example familiar to Ava. "Definitely not safe for beginners."

"I'll come with you," Ian snatched the opportunity.

"Okay, come with us," Ava and CJ said in unison before they looked at each other and broke into laughter.

This odd synchronicity between them, where they would utter the exact same words simultaneously, finish each other's sentences, or even reply to unspoken thoughts, was ridiculously frequent. And it always climaxed in bursts of laughter.

Ellie's expression changed for a split second. The gold speckles in her brown eyes darkened, shadowed by a cloud passing over her forehead. Ian glanced at her and caught the slight shift. She managed to chase it away, replacing it with a tentative, warped smile.

Just a quick reorganization of the drivers and passengers, and the two parties were on their way. Luckily, the beginners' slope wasn't too busy yet.

Patti and Don leisurely made their way down the undulating slopes, following the natural rhythm of the terrain. Ava kept an eye on them. A bit further up, under CJ's caring guidance, Ayden moved at a slower pace. Ava stopped from time to time and took glimpses behind, at the two.

Ellie lost her footing, erratically sliding down a steeper portion of the slope, arms flailing, sky sticks almost turning into threatening weapons. She left a high-pitched squeak as panic set in when she picked up speed. With prompt reflexes and a swift 'french fry' turn, Ian came to an abrupt stop right in front of her. The sudden halt ended in a collision, and both tumbled into a tangled heap in the snow.

Ava couldn't help but giggle as her eye caught the funny scene. "You two okay over there?" she shouted.

Ian finally managed to get up and lent Ellie a hand. "Are you okay?"

She nodded, flustered. "Yeah. If you don't count my bruised ego."

Ian turned and gave Ava a thumbs-up. "All good!" He pushed the goggles up on his head and began demonstrating the slowing and stopping techniques once more. "Don't panic if it feels like you start sliding too fast. Bend your knees slightly, keep your skis parallel, and balance your weight.

If you catch speed, either slow down or stop, then start again. How to slow down and how to stop are the only things you need to remember. Think 'food' all the time: 'pizza'—slightly turn the tips of your skis inward and the tails outward, like this, and you slow down. Or 'french fry'—your skis parallel, like this, and you'll come to a stop. And remember, I'm here."

Ellie watched, trying to copy the moves. Her eyes briefly shifted toward where Ava and CJ were, hunched over, adjusting Ayden's gear. Ian peeked in the same direction, then he turned his gaze over his right shoulder.

"Let's move over there, to the side. The slope looks gentler, and there are fewer distractions," he said, a bit too rushed, pulling his goggles back.

"Yeah, sounds good." Ellie began to slowly move to the side.

"You're still in love with him," the remark slipped off Ian's lips before he could bite his tongue.

"What'd you say?" Ellie asked, appalled.

"You say you did, but you didn't fully get over CJ. The way you looked at them this morning... Now too..."

"No, it's not it. I just can't help but think CJ and I would've never had that kind of connection. I keep wondering why I didn't see it. Probably because I'd never been around anyone in a perfect relationship, like theirs. My parents' marriage was rocky for a few years before Dad left for good. I was very young. Then, I ended up with douchebags... I didn't know what to look for in a relationship." She shrugged, suppressing a sigh. "I probably still don't. I thought what we had was perfect. It turns out it was just... okay. Sadly, I was ready to settle for *just okay*."

"If it helps, you need to know you deserve better than *just okay*," Ian muttered under his breath.

Ellie snapped her head toward him. Surprise and something else radiated from her, and the ski goggles failed to fully hide it.

"I'm not sure about it. I seem to attract and hold onto exactly the opposite," she shot back, lips arching into a bitter smirk.

"Well... good things happen when you least expect," he said and quickly changed the topic: "So... let's try this again. Bend your knees and remember 'pizza' or 'french fry'. I'll be right behind you."

Lunchtime found the entire party gathered in a private room at a local restaurant. In a secluded corner, Ava and Emily were chatting while feeding the babies.

Ian and Ellie arrived fashionably late. As her ear partly caught on their conversation, Ava turned a cocked brow. Her gaze synced briefly with CJ's before flashing Ian an intrigued look.

The telling glare stopped on Ian, and he halted mid-sentence. "Okay… okay… No work talking."

Ava's lips arched into a subtle, appreciative smile, dipping her head slightly before returning to her conversation with Emily and her attention back to Pearl.

A cozy and pretty quiet luxury resort in the Alps, the town offered the much sought-after privacy to the elite visitors. The past year was more than just eventful.

Trading the hustle and bustle of London city for the quietness of the Alps and the crisp, fresh mountain air seemed like the perfect idea. A week away, skiing and relaxing, was more than just a well-deserved break for all.

After the morning on the slopes, they voted. A quiet afternoon won. Doing nothing or not too much. Once lunch was over, some of the party strolled toward the Christmas Market, only a few blocks from the restaurant.

Choosing and buying a Christmas tree, their first Christmas as a family, wasn't just another milestone. It was important. One of those unforgettable family moments that brought people closer together. And the extended family was here, making the moment extra meaningful.

The more, the merrier. And the more joy they could bring, the better.

Even the teenagers weren't grumpy anymore. It was probably from exhaustion after the morning on the slopes. Or maybe the high oxygen levels waved its wand over moods and spirits.

Well… no reason to complain, Ava mused.

Even better, the teenagers wanted to go back to the cottage with the grandparents, Patti and Don. Dipping in the pool? A much more appealing idea than wandering around the Christmas Market.

Marissa, in charge of the youngest kids, also returned to the cottage for the afternoon nap. Just a preventative measure so the babies and toddlers wouldn't become little wicked terrorists with the magical ability to ruin everyone's vacation before it even started.

Taking Ava's hand, CJ hauled her to the side of the Christmas market, where he spotted the pine trees.

"Let's pick a Christmas tree," he said, his eyes shining with the excitement of a little kid.

"Now?" Ava's eyes widened, although she was more than ready.

"Why not? We're here, the trees are here, and we need one," CJ replied with a small shrug.

"But we are on foot..."

"Let's ask if they deliver it."

After making all the arrangements for delivery, they continued around the Christmas Market.

With curious eyes, Ava screened the stands displaying all kinds of neatly packaged mouth-watering traditional Christmas cookies.

"How many do you think we'd need?" She tried to do the math. "Or let's buy some and see how everyone likes them?" She paused, casting CJ her signature look as if an idea had come to mind. "What if we make them?"

The thought of organizing a baking party and filling the entire chalet with Christmas flavours more than appealed to Ava.

"Are you sure? I mean... we came here to relax, not to cook."

"Bake." She was quick to correct him. "Baking is fun. Why not add some fun while immersing in some local Christmas traditions?" She bounced on her toes, her eyes beaming with enthusiasm.

"I'm not sure... Mum wouldn't mind, but the others... I don't know."

"I guess you're right." She pouted. "I mean... I don't want to drag everyone into my madness... How about we ask?"

With the idea nestled in her mind, Ava looked around, hoping she'd spot someone from their party close by. But she failed to see anyone nearby.

Earlier, when CJ pulled Ava to check out the pine trees, they split into smaller groups, each wandering around the Christmas market.

About to give up scanning the place, Ava's eye caught Ellie and Ian talking to someone not far from there. She winced.

After hugging Ian, the other woman flicked her hair, leaning on Ian's arm and touching his jacket's collar. The woman's extravagant laughter resounded throughout the busy market. And the sense of superiority when she looked at Ellie? Ian and Ellie's body language? Ava's gut immediately told her all she needed to know. They appeared uneasy.

Ava didn't like the vibe of what her eye spotted. Her brows drew together. Wasting no time, she released CJ's hand and quickly made her way toward the small group.

"Hi," she began, measuring the woman from her head to the tip of her high-heeled designer boots. "If you don't mind, can I steal Ellie for a minute?" Ava took Ellie's hand, towing her back to the cookie stand.

Whomever she was, the other woman didn't recognize Ava behind the oversized sunglasses. Or she probably wouldn't have recognized her anyway. Helpless, Ian watched the two walk away.

"Mel, it was nice bumping into you. We really didn't expect to meet you here," he said, ready to leave.

"I didn't expect to see you here, either. Not with Ellie, anyway," Mel replied, rolling a lock of hair between her fingers, almost flirting. Though her tone fell brash and affected.

"Ellie and I are part of the same circle of friends. We're all here, spending the Holidays together." Unwavering starkness lined Ian's tone, in perfect sync with his telling stare.

"Oh, that explains it, then. I knew you must have better taste. I mean… I'm sure you wouldn't settle for CJ Hamilton's leftovers," brash again.

Ian's entire body stiffened as his gaze locked sharply onto Mel's. "I'm sorry. I have to go now. Nice seeing you here. Merry Christmas, Mel." He took a quick glance toward Ellie and Ava at a stand only a few yards away.

Mel disregarded all the vibes. Or, as ignorant as she appeared, maybe she didn't catch any. A spoiled brat from old money, no one could tell she ever cared about other people's feelings. And 'no'? It wasn't an answer she'd willingly accept when implied. In fact, she very seldom got a 'no' to any of her wishes.

Once she set her mind to it, Mel always went for it. It never mattered if the ladder she climbed to get what she wanted was made of human bodies, and she cared even less if others' feelings were trashed in the process.

Mel wanted Ian, and she didn't make it a secret. Smoothness? Not one of her traits. And Ellie being so close to Ian, working together, and now vacationing together—which was news to her—Mel found it... *utterly outrageous*. Her determination only ballooned.

Mel twirled on her heels and gripped Ian's forearm as he crossed in front of her, leaving. "Ian! My family is hosting a party on Christmas Eve. Why don't you come over? You could meet and connect with some important people. And, of course, there will be lots of good food and drinks." Her honeyed gaze lingered over his mouth.

"Thank you, Mel, but I'll have to pass. We have group activities scheduled for almost every evening up to and after Christmas," he lied.

"Really? You pass on the opportunity to be in good company just to be with that freak?" Mel retorted, clearly annoyed.

Entertaining Mel's fantasies longer than necessary wasn't on his plans. Not today. One by one, Ian patiently uncurled Mel's fingers from around his arm, unshackling himself from her grip.

"I'll pretend I don't understand your comment, Mel. See you in the office in the new year."

"Oh, I'm sure you understood." Before letting go, Mel's fingers clung once more around his, tight and almost desperate.

Ian leaned over her, hissing between his teeth: "She. is. not. a freak! Now, if you'll excuse me... I must go. Before anything I may regret comes out of my mouth."

As he left, Ian heard Mel's subdued scoff, "So, you are settling for leftovers."

He just bit his tongue, refraining from looking back and reacting to Mel's provocation. A muscle in his jaw flexed, and he kept going. A malicious sneer on display, she turned on her high heels and stomped in the opposite direction.

As he approached Ava and Ellie, Ian overheard the conversation between the two. "They are so good… just as I remember yours were," Ellie said through a mouthful, clearly enjoying the cookie she was chewing. "Do you remember you had to hide the cookies from us so we wouldn't eat all of them in one sitting?"

Ellie's giggle faded. A shadow moved across her expression, her miserable gaze locking into Ava's.

Ava sighed with a soft, half-smile. "And hiding them on the top of the wardrobe didn't help. Andy, my little monkey, would climb anything." Her whole being shuddered, trying to shake off and push back the dreadful memory creeping up and invading her thoughts.

"Your scars are not on the outside, Ava. I miss Andy… and all the silly things we did together when we were young." Ellie wrapped her arms around her.

Over twenty years have passed since Ava lost her firstborn to cancer. Though she now had two wonderful little humans to fill the gap left in her heart, Ayden and Pearl were never meant to replace the loss of her first child. They had their own place in her life. Somehow, they mended her heart, made her feel alive again, and gave her a new purpose. But there's no healing after losing a child, and that scar will remain forever. Buried but present.

The faint smile was still there as she looked over Ellie's shoulder, her gaze meeting CJ's, who mouthed, "Are you okay?"

She nodded and quickly craned her neck to look past him. With a puzzled expression, Ian stood behind CJ. He didn't know Ava's past and couldn't make much of what he overheard.

"Hey, Ian. Would you like to try a cookie? I thought we could add a dash of Swiss traditions to our Christmas. I used to make these cookies. If you approve, we could have a fun evening baking some."

"Yum... they're good," Ian gabbled, through a whole cookie that made its way into his mouth.

"I'd like to learn how to make them," Ellie chirped.

Ian's eyes widened as he gave a thumbs-up with both hands. "I'm... not sure how much help I'd be with baking... However, I assume there will be some dishes resulting from the process. I could help with that."

"You know how to make snowballs, you know how to make cookies," Ava smirked, alluding to the near-accident that morning. "But yeah, someone has to do dishes."

With the kids already tucked into their beds, Ava and Emily returned from the guests' house and joined the group clustered around a bonfire in the back of the luxurious cabin. Although the night was chilly, the atmosphere was warm and relaxed, spiced with chatter and mulled wine.

CJ grasped Ava's hand. "Come here, Baby. Would you like a hot drink? I guess you'll turn down the mulled wine, but there is hot chocolate. Mum made it for the kids."

Ava scoffed. "I'll take a sip from your mulled wine if you don't mind sharing."

"I don't mind at all." Tidying the blanket, CJ made room for her to sit by him.

She took a small sip from the mug he passed over, holding it a bit longer between her palms, inhaling the aroma. It smelled like cinnamon and orange zest. It smelled like Christmas.

Just a little more perfection added to the scenery before their eyes.

Mountain peaks aligned majestically along the horizon. The snowy tops sparkled in the gentle light cast by the moon as it crossed the alcove of the crisp, dark, and clear sky covered in blinking stars.

Exhilarated, Ava pointed at the sky. "A shooting star! Everybody, make a wish!"

5

Perilous Love for Christmas

Madam Crystal Butterfly

Trigger Warnings
Discussion of Murder, Alcoholism, and Illegal Substances

Julius stood stone-faced as he stood in the elevator. *The elders should not arrive until late. Mother will probably run Nubia ragged with unnecessary demands. I'm not happy about that, but I might enjoy the party this year. The company is nothing to jump for joy about. Still, it will be fun to enjoy a party with Nubia instead of having to rush her out of the room. That is as long as we do it before the party.*

After arriving in the subbasement, he noticed his father had reorganized the meeting room. The golden throne had been moved to the center back of the room. The chairs were lined up horizontally and facing the throne. It was also much brighter in the room than it usually was. Julius was surprised that Zane was already seated in the room. Julius walked over and sat in the seat next to his brother.

Zane was a muscular man with dark brown skin. His hazelnut eyes glittered in the light while a large crop of thick, curly, short black hair sat on his head. The bottom of Zane's face was home to a goatee. He wore a green dress shirt, black pants, and black leather shoes. Julius looked at his brother and said, "I should have expected you to be here."

Zane replied, "I'm shocked you didn't think I'd show."

Julius asked, "Did you come to see your dear family and meet your new sister-in-law?"

Zane, smiling, said, "Of course I did."

"Is that statement you just made a load of shit?"

Zane said, "You know it was. I'm actually here because I'm worried about Gray Eye. In all of our discussions, Father seems to want to go with Simon's idea. If we do that, it will be worse than the incident with Bliss."

Julius shared with his brother, "I know. I've come up with a more strategic method to use Grey Eye; however, I'll need the backup of both of the elders to convince father."

Zane agreed, "I'll help as best I can. I don't understand what's wrong with father. He's been giving me the vibe that he wants to take the more secretive parts of the company and make them public."

"I feel the same way. There is no benefit to bringing all of the Goodwin syndicate into the public eye."

They suddenly heard someone say, "Do what? Has that brother of mine lost his damn mind?"

Julius and Zane looked behind them and saw their uncle Gregg. Gregg Goodwin had thinning gray hair on his head. His dark mocha skin was rattled with wrinkles, while his brown eyes reminded people of a hawk. He wore a black three-piece suit with a gold chain around his neck.

Gregg said, "And what the fuck is up with that throne? Everyone, even the leader is supposed to be sitting in a circle."

Julius said, "Good to see you uncle."

"You little fool. I heard all about what you did. What the hell is wrong with you?"

"Uncle Gregg, please elaborate why you're throwing venom at me."

Gregg shared his thoughts and said, "You picked that woman over Zara. Zara can bring so much wealth to this family. Instead, you pick some broke bitch whose only job was to die in your place."

With anger in his voice, Julius said, "You may be my uncle, but if you talk about my wife like that again, I'll rip your teeth out."

Mockingly, Gregg said, "Oh, I'm so scared. I'll deal with you later. Right now, I need to handle my fool of a brother."

Gregg sat down next to Zane. He continued, "I've been hearing rumors about some new product more powerful than Bliss."

Zane said, "It's more powerful, but it's not the same as Bliss. The drug is more useful for making our agents more powerful, but it seems to drive its users insane. Unfortunately, Simon has got father considering that we should use it on the beast warriors."

Gregg said, "The fuck you say? The beast warriors are for defending the family only. Using them for more is too risky."

Julius said, "I agree, and I have a better plan for the new product. We just need to get father to hear me out."

Gregg asked, "Why won't he?"

Julius answered, "I called him a coward."

Gregg snapped, "Why the fuck would you do that to that sensitive prick?"

Julius said, "Only way I could stall him until the meeting of the elders. You know he stalls making a decision if you call him a coward. Father can do whatever he wants. If you and the other two elders agree with my plan, then he will consider my idea. Right now, Simon has him thinking about using the new product to make himself king."

Gregg said, "Ha, why the fuck would anyone want that? It's better to live in the shadows."

Julius replied, "I know, but Father is eyeing the crown for some reason."

Gregg asked his nephews, "What is this drug? How does it work?"

Four hours later, Julius sat at his desk. Julius's office had red walls and gold curtains around the arch window against the back wall. His dark wooden desk sat a few feet away from the window. The left wall was home to a portrait depicting the ocean. There were two couches facing each other on opposite sides of the center of the room. In between them lay a snow tiger rug with a glass coffee table sitting in its center.

Julius stared at his laptop, trying to fix a miscalculation. Okay, *I forgot to carry the two. Now that makes sense. Hopefully at tomorrow's meeting father will listen to reason. That so-called meeting was pointless. We sat there for two hours only for Father to reschedule. If he refuses to cooperate with me, then putting my plan in place will not be easy. I was able to get* Uncle *and* Zane *to think my plan was for the good of the syndicate. Little do they know that's not my full plan.*

Just then, his phone rang. He answered to hear Clover say, "I put a hit out on Zara."

Julius leaped up as he said, "Why did you do that?"

In a calm, even tone, Clover said, "She violated the most important rule. Never betray the syndicate."

"How did she betray us?"

"She discovered you had no interest in making her your second wife."

Julius asked, "When did that happen?"

"I suspect a month ago. That doesn't matter. She found out about Grey Eye. She's leaked the information and took off."

Julius shouted, "FUCK!"

Clover, giving her brother more details, continued, "I've sent some of our assassins and beast warriors after her. That was two hours ago, and they still haven't found her."

"Zara is not smart enough to come up with an escape plan. Someone must be working with her."

Clover said, "I would say Simon, but we always think it was him."

Julius said, "I'll inform father about the situation. He'll probably change his mind about not letting us kill Zara. Keep looking for her. I'll send out a burn notice. If our people don't find her, someone else will for the reward."

Clover said, "Alright, I'll keep you posted."

When he hung up, Nubia ran into his office with a huge smile on her face. Julius said, "Nubia, I'm sorry, but what you want to tell me has to wait."

Nubia replied, "It will only take half a second."

Julius thought, "I need to talk with father and the other men immediately. She seems so excited, and it's the first time she's ever celebrated the holidays. I should play along with whatever she's excited about for a minute, and afterwards I will send the burn notice.

"Nubia, take a seat. I have to send a message really quick. When I'm done, I'll look at what you want me to see."

Nubia said in a giggly voice, "Okay."

She plopped down on the couch as Julius wrote the burn notice. *I'll offer two million. That should be a nice enough incentive.* After sending the notice he made a call. Mitch picked up the phone and asked, "What do you need boss?"

"Go to the locate Percival Crest. Bring his brother and his sons here."

Mitch replied, "Okay, boss."

Julius hung up as he said, "What did you want to show me?"

Nubia rushed over to him and grabbed his arm. She led him out of the room, down a few halls and they walked into the new banquet hall. The new banquet hall got its name because Glades had completely refurbished it a few years earlier. When they entered the space, Julius stood in amazement at the sight of the room.

There was a giant Christmas tree decorated with blue and white ornaments. The tree sat in front of a massive window which showed the raging blizzard outside. There were blue ribbons connected by silver tinsel decorating the upper half of the window. All of the round tables had white tablecloths with blue flower centerpieces. There was a rectangular table placed horizontally with a white tablecloth and the same blue flower centerpieces.

A light snow rained down from the ceiling. The tiny snowflakes disappeared before they touched the ground. Julius smiled as he looked at the room. Nubia hugged him as she said, "It's a winter wonderland."

Julius, smiling, said, "I agree. I'm happy you showed it to me. I needed something happy. I've had a frustrating day."

"What happened?"

"I had to put out a burn notice on Zara."

"What's that?"

Julius explained, "It's an announcement of the dismissal of an agent whom the agency finds to be unreliable. She's revealed one of the syndicate's secrets and disappeared, so I also had to put a bounty on her."

Nubia said, "I wonder why she did something that dumb."

"Good question. She's lost the protection my father afforded her by doing this. I hope it was worth it. It probably won't be."

Changing the subject, Nubia asked, "Yeah, um, how much do you like the decor?"

"I like it a lot."

"Yes, I win."

"Win what?"

Nubia said, "I made a bet with your mom. If you like the design she can't drink until after Christmas."

All the blood drained from Julius's face as he said, "What?"

"Julius, your mom's problem makes her too hard to deal with."

"I agree, but I'm banking on that old bitch getting cirrhosis of the liver."

Nubia chastising Julius, said, "Julius that is your mother. You're lucky to have a mom."

Julius countered, "No, you're lucky to have a mother. I would have been better off if I had been raised by jackals. As he said it, Julius continued, "Very sad, but true."

"Julius, I have no hope of you and your dad getting along. It's been obvious for a long time that's impossible thanks to the whole Georgina thing."

"It's more than the dead wife photo thing."

Nubia, attempting to reason with Julius, said, "I know. I'm just saying, your mother may be a bitch, but you shouldn't rush her to the grave."

Julius thought, "Nubia, you are too good for this family. There are so many secrets I'll have to tell you, but not now. My birthday is tomorrow, and Christmas is in fifteen days. This is the first time I've ever looked forward to a holiday. We should enjoy this time together before I rain fire on all of this, to keep the family I want to have with you out of hell.

Julius said, "Alright, you win. Just don't get too upset when my mother throws venom at you nonstop."

"Trust me, I'm prepared."

"Babe, trust me, you're not. I'm going to have Mandy stick to you like glue now."

"Why?"

"Just don't stay in any room alone with my mother when she's sober."

The two of them looked at the room for a few minutes. Then Julius kissed Nubia before telling her he had to go. As soon as he walked out of the room Julius heard his father shout, "WHAT HAVE YOU DONE!"

"Handled a traitor the way we always do."

"Dammit, Zara's father will be a problem."

"I already had Mitch head out to get him and the rest of the men of that family."

Charles said, "Send someone to collect the women as well."

"There is no point."

"Why?"

Julius said, "Father, you are off your game. Other than a few mistresses, Zara is the only female in that family. Her mother died giving birth to her. It's the main reason why her father spoils her."

Charles announced, "I guess problem solved."

Julius agreed, "Problem solved. Father, do you not want to ask me why I put a burn notice on Zara?"

"I don't care. In the time she's been gone, things seem to be running more efficiently."

Julius said, "Whatever you say, Father. At least one problem is solved, but we still have to worry about the leak."

"Why? We will meet with all of the elders tomorrow. None of the Gray Eye has been stolen."

Julius explained, "Are you sure, and how is a leak not a problem? We don't know who told Zara about Grey Eye. Sure, I would like to say it was Simon, but it's not his style."

Charles said, "You would be correct, and I know who told her."

Julius asked, "Who, and is that person protecting her?"

Charles, not wanting to share information with Julius, said, "I'm not going to tell you, and no, they aren't. I think the only person who would give her a way out is her father. Zara is not smart, but she's not usually this stupid."

"You know who told her, well did that person influence her to tell people?"

"Who knows, son? Anyway, let's go. We need to handle the Crest family."

Julius thought, *"He's hiding something. Is he responsible for the leak? Why would he do that? If it wasn't him, then who could it be?"*

It was extremely early in the morning as a bitter Julius stood in the garage next to Mitch. *Damn my fucking parents. Do they want me to die? Nubia was exhausted when I finally got to the room last night. I thought it was a good idea to let her sleep. I should have just woken her up and begged her to fuck me. Then they wouldn't have gotten in the way.*

Julius remembered *with anger, "When she woke me up wearing that* Christmas-themed *red underwear looking like the hottest piece of ass I have ever seen. She knows red is my weakness. Dammit, I was ready to fuck her over and over again till her pussy was sore and red as a beet. She got me all revved up, and before I could get a condom mom and dad bust in. Mom makes Nubia put her clothes on then practically drags her out of the room, bitching about how they have so much work to do. Then dad tells me to take a cold shower. We have a meeting in thirty minutes.*

Take a cold shower. If I hadn't gotten a call with good news otherwise that meeting would have turned into a bloodbath. Calm down, the curse hasn't affected me in days. It's my birthday, and I'll find time to explore Nubia later.

Mitch asked, "Something wrong, boss?"

"No, has everything been handled?"

"Yes, Sir. We have the Crest family in the holding area. Percival admitted to helping his daughter escape. He made a point to not know where she went."

Julius said, "Smart man. We will find her eventually. Dammit, I wish Luke would hurry up. I wanted to have all of Nubia's gifts ready."

Mitch suggested, "Sir, if you don't mind me saying, you need to relax. You've already bought her a massive number of presents."

"I know, but this is just the most important one. Not even the house I'm building is going to be as special to her as this."

"Does your dad know you plan to move out?"

"Maybe. I'm not hiding it, so he might have figured it out."

Feeling free to share his thoughts, Mitch said, "I'm glad you're making this move. You and Mrs. Goodwin need a fresh start."

Julius asked, "When did you and your wife decide to have kids?"

Mitch shared, "Whoa, that's a story. We were married, I think, for three years. Pregnancy is dangerous, but the laws make it even more dangerous."

Julius was surprised by Mitch's response. Of course, he had never given much thought to pregnancy before now. He asked Mitch, "They do?"

"Yeah, there is always the risk of a miscarriage. With the abortion being illegal with no exceptions, it increases the danger. Worse, a lot of prenatal vitamins are illegal, and the ones the government allows are dangerous, so that's a problem all on its own. Before we even started thinking about kids, we searched for a while to find a good black-market doctor."

Julius admitted, "I've never thought about that before. I guess I need to put some more thought into kids."

Mitch asked, "You want a kid?"

"Yeah, things with Nubia have been going great. Lately, the idea of having babies with her is turning into something I want a lot."

Laughing, Mitch warned, "Kids are a pain in the ass, but most of the time they are fun. I would advise you to hold off on them at least until your house is done."

"I'll search for a doctor and then ask Nubia about kids again."

Mitch shared, "Sir, a lot of changes have happened to her pretty quickly. She's still adjusting to being a Goodwin. Maybe you should give her more time than that. She may not even want kids."

"So, I should pay a woman to carry our child invitro. It is illegal, but hardly anything I do is legal."

"Sir, that is not what I'm talking about."

A red SUV pulled up next to them. Luke got out of the driver's seat and opened the back door. An older woman with a salt and pepper afro and dark brown skin got out of the car. Her bone skinny body made her brown eyes look larger than they were. She wore a dirty yellow T-shirt and jeans.

Julius frowned as he said, "Why hasn't my mother-in-law been given warmer clothes?"

Luke replied, "There was a miscommunication. Don't worry, the person responsible has been handled."

The woman said, "Mother-in-law? What are you talking about, young man?"

Julius smiled as he said, "I'm Julius Goodwin. I, I'm married to your daughter."

The woman's eyes welled up as she cried, "Nubia, you know where Nubia is?"

She rushed over to Julius as she said, "Where is she? Where is my baby girl?"

"Mrs. Agatha, please calm down. You will see your daughter in a few days."

Agatha screamed, "I WANT TO SEE HER NOW! TAKE ME TO NUBIA!"

In a calm voice, Julius said, "Let's go for a ride. I need to take you to the house you'll be living in for now. You can get a warm bath, new clothes, hot food, and we can talk about you seeing Nubia."

Agatha thought for a moment and then said, "Fine."

They got into the back of the car, and Lucas got into the driver's seat. As the car moved, Agatha asked, "Are you really married to my daughter?"

Julius said, "We got married seven months ago. No one told you this?"

"Buddy, one day some men busted into the apartment my husband and I were living in. They threatened my husband at gunpoint to burn my red card in some blue fire. After they did, I fainted. When I woke up, I was in the back of a van wrapped in a blanket, and some woman was begging me to eat chicken broth. They didn't answer any of my questions. Just kept insisting I eat broth as they took me from place to place."

Luke said, "Like I said, boss. There was a miscommunication."

Julius said, "Okay, Mrs. Agatha, you are my Christmas present to your daughter."

"What?"

Julius attempted to explain. "Nubia understandably misses you. So, I had my younger brother get you for me. I know Christmas is fifteen days away and that's a long time to ask you to wait; however, I want you to be in better health before you see her."

Agatha Legend insisted, "I want to see my daughter now. Some men just showed up and my husband sold my baby to them. How do I know you're actually her husband?"

"I understand your suspicion, but after you have a warm meal and some new clothes, I think you'll like me a bit better."

They arrived at a small two-story house made of red brick and had a blue snow-covered roof. The garden and lights in front of the house was covered in snow. Julius raced with Agatha into the house where an army of maids were waiting for them. The foyer had white marble floors, blue walls, and a large staircase against the right wall. The left wall had a door that led to another room and a large crystal chandelier hung overhead lighting the room.

Julius said, "Great, everything is in order. After you have a few days to adjust to the place, I'll have a decorator come to help you style everything however you like. I'll stop by to make sure you're comfortable."

Agatha asked, "Will Nubia be with you?"

Julius responded, "I will bring her on Christmas. Then the two of you will see each other practically every day."

Agatha's eyes started to tear up as she said, "I know you want me to be some kind of gift. Nubia is my child. I haven't seen her in Lord knows how long. Please, please let me see my girl."

Julius took a breath and lead Agatha into the next room. It was a small living area with a large roaring fireplace on the front wall. There were no windows and only a red recliner and a black folding chair in the center of the room. Julius had Agatha sit in the recliner while he sat on the folding chair.

Julius said, "Mrs. Agatha, I am sorry about the lack of furniture in the room. I had most of the furniture taken out so you could decorate."

"I don't care about that."

"I know. Mrs. Agatha, I am planning to move Nubia and I to a new estate. Don't worry, you will have your own house on the property. Right now, I am hiding this from my mother."

"Why?"

Julius said, "She doesn't like Nubia. That's going to only last so long. Sooner or later, she's going to want to get rid of her. She can't touch her right now, but I wouldn't put it past the sad drunk to find a way."

Agatha said, "Just move Nubia out of the house. She can stay here with me."

"I can't move her out of the house until after a holiday. My family is having a very important event and until it is over it will be problematic for Nubia to leave our home. You see, my mother is an alcoholic, and Nubia is forcing my mother to be sober for a few weeks."

"Isn't that a good thing?"

"No, my mother is someone who it's better if she's not fully aware of her actions."

Agatha questioned, "You're not putting my child in danger, are you?"

"No, I would never. I care about her deeply."

Agatha raised an eyebrow as she said, "You're not in love with her."

Julius answered honestly, "To be honest, I don't know. Sometimes I think I am, but I'm not completely sure."

Agatha, taken aback, said, "Why?"

"I don't feel like I deserve her, and if I love her shouldn't I want her to be with someone who does?"

"You're a confused little man, and personally I don't know if I give a shit or not. I want to see Nubia, so I'll play along."

"Thank you. That's all I ask."

Agatha stated, "Don't thank me. I'm not doing this for you."

6

The Night of the Magi
Elizabeth Rodriguez

Maripaz sat by her window staring outside as the snow blew around the street. She wasn't used to this. The bone-chilling cold, the white powdery substance that fell from the sky, covering everything in a bright blanket. She missed the heat, the salty smell of the ocean as a sweet breeze kissed her skin. Her mind wandered to her home, still missing the small island in the Caribbean.

It called her like a soft siren song, stirring up memories that played in her mind. She sighed as she moved languidly from her chair and walked to the kitchen. She knew that she had to wrap presents for her family. Staring at the clock, she saw that it was 10 pm. Sighing, she set her mug down and headed to the pantry. Opening the door, she stepped inside, collecting the presents she had bought. She smiled at herself, knowing that her siblings wouldn't find them here. As she placed the presents on the table, her mother walked in. She stopped, her eyes widening in surprise as she told her parents to stay upstairs.

"Ay Mami, get out!" Maripaz exclaimed because she didn't want her mother to see what she had gotten her.

"*No, me hablas así!*" Mrs. Pagan retorted, her eyes narrowing at her daughter.

"But Mami, I told you I needed the kitchen," Maripaz said coolly.

"I know, I know, but your Papi wanted some *coquito*, and you told me you'd be done by 9." Mrs. Pagan said.

Maripaz looked down, knowing her mother was right. She had told her she would be done before 9. Her eyes met her mother's as she spoke, "I know, Mami, I'm sorry the storm outside caught my attention."

Her mother smiled as she walked towards her. She placed a hand on her shoulder. "It's okay, *Mija*. I'm going to go to the living room. Can you pour a glass for your Papi and bring it to me?" She asked for warmth radiating from her auburn eyes.

Maripaz nodded, and Mrs. Pagan headed to the living room. Once her mother was gone, she went to the cabinet, grabbed a glass, and placed it on the counter. She crossed the kitchen to the imposing fridge, opened it, and held a glass bottle containing the festive drink. She walked over to the cup and poured a hearty glass. She grabbed the glass and bottle and headed back to the fridge, putting the rest of the coquito away. Maripaz then headed to the living room and handed her mom the drink. Mrs. Pagan hugged her daughter and headed back up the stairs. As Mrs. Pagan ascended the stairs, she heard her brothers playing video games and her mother wishing them a good night.

Maripaz turned and headed back to the kitchen to start wrapping when she noticed her sister staring at the pile of presents on the table. Mari froze as she saw Sol staring at the presents. She walked towards her.

"What are you doing here! I said the kitchen was off limits!" she exclaimed, exasperated.

Sol stared at her, and her brows furrowed in annoyance. "This is a free country, *hermanita*, and I can go where I want. Plus, I'm hungry and wanted some more *arroz con gandules*," she stated matter-a-factly.

Mari's eyes twitched in annoyance. "Well, get your food and get out!" The words came out sharper than she intended.

Sol's eyes narrowed in a huff. She went to heat up her food. "You know, if you weren't such a procrastinator, this wouldn't be a problem." She retorted.

"I... I.... can wrap the presents when I want to!" Mari said, her annoyance was growing. "Plus, you should have texted saying you were coming up.

"*Y yo no tengo que hacer nada de eso. Esto es mi casa también.*" Sol said her words cutting as she grabbed her plate from the microwave. "If you didn't keep daydreaming all the time, maybe you'd get something done." She said as she exited the kitchen, steaming plate in hand.

Maripaz rolled her eyes, and she went back to the table where she grabbed her father's present, a beautiful cigar box she had made in her woodshop class. She smiled at the intricate carvings on the lid. She ran her fingers over the native symbols representing her Taino heritage. She went into the coat closet in the mudroom, grabbed the wrapping supplies, and came back. She then sat and started wrapping her father's gift. After she grabbed a controller and a game, she wrapped them for her little brother, Ariel. She then grabbed the vinyls and placed them in a bag for her eldest sibling, Salamon. She finished wrapping her mother and Sol's presents, which were a candle set and a beautiful book set of Tolkien's popular novels. She went to the living room and placed them under the tree. The smell of pine fills her nostrils. Her nose scrunched as she was not yet used to the strong scent.

Her mother insisted on getting a real tree. She went on and on that if she were living in Massachusetts, a real tree was a necessity. For 16 years, she was used to the fake ones. Her family had had the same tree since she was a baby. Her father also put it up the day after Thanksgiving, as her mother then decorated, putting Ms. Stewart to shame.

Maripaz walked back to the armchair by the window and watched as the winter storm continued. She sighed as she picked up her phone and stared at the time, reading 11:45pm. Tomorrow would be Three Kings Day. She should be out with her friends and family walking from home to home, having a *parranda*, their songs and merriment filling the night air. But the house was quiet; only the sounds she could hear were her brothers' games. She sighed softly to herself, and she settled more onto the chair, wrapping a large red throw around her.

Her hazel eyes moved to the basin of water and straw in the left corner of the tree. She smiled at herself, finding it silly that her parents still did that. She was too old to believe that the Three Kings would come on their camels to give her presents. As she settled on the chair, her eyes began to close as sleep overtook her.

She woke up to the sounds of shuffling around her. A strong, pungent smell filled her nostrils. As she opened her eyes, she stared at the three men dressed in ornate robes, placing small gifts under the tree. She peened to see three large camels standing patiently by the other side of the tree, snacking on the hay and water. Her mouth agape as she took in the scene. As she was about to scream, one of the Magi turned to see her stunned expression. He smiled and walked over to her.

"Please do not scream, Maripaz, we aren't intruders," Balthasar spoke, his voice calming her senses.

"Who. Who are you?" She asked, still shocked.

Caspar, the other Magi, smiled, "We are the three wise men, of course, dear child."

She blinked in disbelief. "You're real!" she exclaimed softly.

The three wise men smiled, each nodding at her response.

"Yes, we are very real," Melchior responded. "We sense that you miss home. As we have yet to place your present under the tree, I would like to offer you a different one instead."

Maripaz looked at Melchior, his kind eyes staring back at her. As she nodded, unable to speak. "I would like to grant you a night back on the island, but you must meet us at dawn, where we drop you off. Can you do that?" he asked.

Maripaz agreed fervently, feeling safe with the three kings. Caspar held out his hand, and she rose from her seat and took it. She followed them to the camels, and Caspar lifted her onto one of the camels before hopping on himself. While the other two mounted their respective camels, they all nodded. A warm glow swirled around them, and as she sat speechless, petting the camel in front of her. In a whoosh, she blinked, and she was looking at the beautiful ocean in front of her. She looked around and noticed she was at the *Balneario del Escambrón*, a beautiful beach in *Viejo San Juan*. Balthasar dismounted his camel and helped her down from Casapar's. She thanked him and looked at them.

"So, I will meet you back here at dawn?" She asked them.

They nodded, and with a blink of her eyes, they were gone. She stood on the beach, taking in the salty night air, and she smiled. She couldn't believe she was back home. She reached down to feel cool sand on her fingertips, marveling at it all. She grabbed her phone from her pocket, opened it, checked her location via her weather app, and saw that it said

San Juan, Puerto Rico. She looked around her and smiled. She felt tears prickling at the corner of her eyes, and she felt at peace for the first time in months. She put her phone away and headed out to the beach toward the city center.

Music filled the air as she moved closer; she saw people in beautiful outfits dancing along the streets. She noticed her best friend in the crowd and walked towards her. Her bestie noticed her, paused, widened her eyes, and she ran towards her.

"Mari, how are you here!" she exclaimed, hugging her tightly.

Mari hugged her back, tears falling from her eyes. She had been friends with Angela since she was in Head Start, and the move hurt her more than she realized. They both cried for a while. After a time, they pulled themselves apart and laughed, happiness filling their hearts.

"I... It's a long story, but I'm only here until dawn. I'm happy that I was able to find you. Even if I wasn't looking." Mari said, laughing softly.

"Well, if you only have until dawn, let's go back to my place and get you dressed. You can't wear what you are wearing now." Angela said, looking at Mari's pajamas.

Mari blushed and nodded her head as they headed towards Angela's home. "Mami is out with Titi Wilda, so you won't have to sit and explain to her how you are here," Angela said.

They both walked in tandem, their footsteps echoing off the cobblestone streets. As they head toward San Agustin Street, where Angela's house is. "So, tell me how you got here?" asked.

"Well, I was wrapping presents in the kitchen, and when I was done, I set them under the tree and sat on one of the chairs Papi bought recently. I stared out the window and fell asleep. I woke up to rustling and a strong scent. I looked and it was the *los Tres Reyes*." Mari paused, looking at her friend.

Angela looked at her, mirroring the same face she made when she was the three Magi.

"Seriously!" Angela asked, bewildered by her friends' tale.

"Seriously," Mari responded.

"Well, what happened next!" Angela asked, wanting to learn more.

Mari told her everything, and they continued to walk down the streets of *Viejo San Juan*. They reached her friend's home, and Angela paused. "So, you have to meet them back on the beach at dawn, right?" Angela asked.

"Yeah, I'm kind of sad about it, to be honest. But I'm happy that I get to spend time with you." Mari said, her eyes were glimmering with joy.

"Well, we only have about 5 hours, so let's make the most of it!" Angela opened the door to her teal-colored home. The girls stepped inside the beautiful foyer filled with *Vejigante* masks hung along the walls in vibrant colors. Mari smiled, memories filling her head of the countless times she spent in Angela's home. She remembered their joint fifth birthday, where the house was filled with both of their friends and families. She also remembered the beautiful "My Little Pony" decorations that filled the home that day.

Angela gestured for her to follow her up the stairs to her room. As they ascended the stairs, Mari's memories kept flowing into her mind like little vignettes of all the times that she spent in this home. As they reached her friend's room, Angela opened the door and began searching her closet for an outfit for Mari to wear. She picked out a few dresses and placed them on the bed.

"Pick something fast; we only have so much time to waste," exclaimed Angela.

Mari looked down at the beautiful gowns before her, one a gorgeous lavender color, another a vibrant fuchsia, and the last a striking sky blue, like their flag. She looked back at her friend, noticing the crimson gown that she wore. She smiled, picked up the sky-blue dress, and headed towards the bathroom to change. Once she emerged, her friend had a pair of white sandals out for her.

"Sit down, we are going to do your hair quickly," Angela said.

Sitting down on the bed, Angela began to work on Mari's long curly brown hair. Grabbing a white ribbon, Angela fashioned her hair in a beautiful yet messy bun. Pulling out a few strands of hair to frame Mari's face. Maripaz stood putting on the white sandals. She noticed her reflection in the mirror and took in her appearance. A soft thank you escaped her lips.

Her friend smiled in return, grabbed her hand, and rushed her downstairs and out to the streets of *Viejo San Juan*.

She and Angela join up with a group of neighbors, their joyous singing filling the air. An older gentleman with a salt and pepper beard, wearing a white *guayabera*, had a *güiro* and was smiling as he played. A tall, curvaceous woman in a white gown played the *pandereta* as she swayed her hips in time with the music. While a younger girl in a pink dress shook *maracas*, she accompanied them in childish enthusiasm. Finally, she noticed two men, both matching in festive regalia: one playing the trumpet and the other playing the *cuatro Puertorriqueño*.

A kind elderly lady dressed in lavender handed both Maripaz and Angela *palitos* as they joined the group. They went from house to house collecting more members to the *parranda*, creating a lovely symphony of sound that filled Maripaz's heart.

As she sang, she noticed that they were heading to the city center, where hundreds of people all danced, played, and sang, ushering in the marvelous holiday. Her soul felt connected to everyone in attendance, as *Viejo San Juan* filled the air with wondrous joy. She saw the governor come on stage, thanking everyone in the crowd for attending the night's festivities. The governor guided the Three Kings onto the stage to pass out the presents to the waiting crowd of children in front. She gasped as she noticed that they were the same men who had whisked her away back home. Their eyes met, and the Magi gave her a warm, knowing smile. She looked toward her friend, letting her know that these were the Three Kings who led her back home.

Angela looked at Mari in astonishment as they both gazed back at the Three Kings as they gave out presents to the eagerly waiting children. The night passed quickly, Mari checking her phone to see that dawn was soon approaching. Her heart felt heavy as she knew she would have to return to her new home. The two friends walked back to the beach as the first rays of the sun hit the water, causing it to shine like diamonds. The girls bid their farewells, hugging and tearing up as they parted. Mari saw Angela's form retreating to the city.

Mari sat on the cool sand waiting for the Magi to return. She stared out into the ocean as she etched the night in her memory, not wanting to forget. The Magi returned, taking her home. She petted the camels as farewell and thanked the Three Kings for an unforgettable evening, letting them know it was the best present she had ever received. The three men smiled, bowing their heads as warm light filled her living room, and in the blink of an eye, they were gone.

Mari smiled as she headed up the stairs to change, knowing that Three King's Day activities with her family would soon commence.

7

Under Fallen Snow
Valhalla Erikson

The Eternal Night approaches as snow drifts quietly over Ravenwood, settling in thin sheets along the rooftops and the curve of the cobblestone streets. The city carried its own kind of beauty, old bones dressed in iron and brick, the remnants of a Victorian age that refused to fade. Steam hissed from grates along the sidewalks as hover-cycles drifted past in low hums beside polished roadsters from another era, their chrome catching the faint light.

The atmosphere of coal, rain, and winter spice. Streetlamps flickered awake by tiny sprites as they darted between them, wings leaving brief streaks of color in the dusk. Above, the towers leaned close together, stained glass and gargoyles watching as the solstice night began its long stretch across the city.

By the time the first hour of night arrived, the streets had gone still. A single glow shone at the corner of the Old Quarter, Nirvana, its windows glowing with the warmth of firelight and muted laughter.

James sat at his usual spot, a virgin margarita resting in front of him. He never touched alcohol. At least not anymore. Old habits from the watch years clung to him. He preferred his senses sharp, his reflexes unassessed. Even off-duty, even as a knight now, he couldn't quite shake the need to stay alert.

So he nursed the drink in silence, the tang of lime cutting through the background hum of the bar.

It had been a while since he let himself come here. The warm atmosphere, the glow of solstice decorations, even the familiar drinks weren't what pulled him back tonight.

No, the real reason stood behind the counter, moving with quiet grace as she polished a line of glasses.

Leia.

Her name alone stirred something in him. A warmth that had nothing to do with the lights or the season, and everything to do with the memories he carried.

James let his gaze linger a moment longer, watching the way the soft lamplight caught in her hair. It was strange how she still felt like home after everything.

They'd grown up together in Shepard, a mountain town too small and too quiet for what lived inside them. James Holiday had always been the restless one, a Huntsman before he was ever a soldier, chasing the shadows that most pretended didn't exist. He'd spent his youth tracking things that snarled in the dark, returning home with blood on his coat and exhaustion in his eyes. There had been others, brief faces, fleeting interests, but none had ever seen him the way Leia did.

Leia never flinched at the stories. She never called him reckless or cursed his need to protect people who would never know his name. She simply listened, concerned soft in her voice, understanding in her silence. She knew why he hunted. The grief that drove him. The need to make sense of a world that had taken too much, too soon.

When he told her he was leaving Shepard to join the Watch, the United Republic's proud and disciplined force, she hadn't tried to stop him. The surprise in her eyes had faded into something gentler, recognition. She understood what it meant to go searching for yourself in the ashes of what came before.

He'd left with her voice still echoing in his mind, a quiet promise that she'd be there when the road brought him home again. And though the years had turned him into something harder, quieter, and far less certain, the memory of her understanding had never left him.

And yet, she had stayed. Leia had built something here. A bar that was more than a business.

Nirvana wasn't just a place to drink, it was a refuge, a corner of warmth carved out in a city that often had none.

He wondered, not for the first time, if she realized how much she had become that anchor for him too.

Suddenly James felt a sharp nudge against his shoulder, snapping him out of his thoughts. He blinked, realizing he'd been staring across the room a little too long.

"Don't you think you're burning holes in her back by now?" Sam murmured with a grin, balancing a tray of half-empty glasses.

James's jaw tightened. "...Wasn't staring."

"Uh-huh. And I'm not working a double shift," she shot back, lowering her voice just enough to keep it between them. "Come on, Holiday. I've seen snipers with less focus."

He exhaled slowly through his nose, eyes flicking back to his untouched drink. "Drop it, Sammy..."

The fae only smirked, bumping him once more with her elbow before heading toward the bar. "Sure, sure. Keep telling yourself that. But one of these nights, you're gonna have to use actual words instead of just brooding into your margarita."

James muttered something under his breath, but didn't look up. He wasn't sure if it was her laughter that followed him, or the quiet sound of Leia humming as she worked behind the counter, that set his chest tighter.

James's hand tightened around the glass, condensation beading against his skin. He could just... Stand up. Walk across the room. Say something simple, like *how have you been?* But the words lodged in his throat before they ever formed.

She's built a life here, he thought, watching as Leia laughed softly with a customer before turning back to the counter. *A good one. Without me. What if I don't belong in it anymore?*

"Y'know," Sam's voice cut in, light and knowing, "She'd actually like it if you talked to her instead of staring from this corner like some kind of undercover assignment."

James's head turned just enough to give her a look. Sam smirked, unfazed.

"I'm serious," she pressed, leaning her tray against her hip. "You're not as invisible as you think, Holiday. And believe me, she notices more than you give her credit for."

James glanced back toward the bar, toward Leia... Then away again, a frown tugging at his mouth. The thought of walking over there felt heavier than any mission he'd ever taken.

Sam sighed, shaking her head with an exasperated smile before heading off somewhere. James remained, caught between the urge to move and the weight of his doubts.

He was staring into the rim of his glass, lost in thought, when he felt another gentle nudge at his arm.

"Cut it out, Sammy. I said leave me alone." James muttered, not bothering to look up. Silence answered him.

When he finally lifted his head, his chest nearly lurched out of him. It wasn't Sam.

Leia stood at his table, a soft smile playing at her lips, the kind that always seemed to reach her eyes. For a second, James forgot how to breathe.

He damn near tipped off his seat, straightening too quickly. "L-Leia."

Her smile widened just a fraction, amused but kind. "You looked like you could use a refill." she said gently, tilting her head toward his half-empty glass.

James swallowed, the heat rising under his collar a sharp contrast to the cool bite of winter still clinging to his clothes. All he could do was nod, because words... The right ones... Had never come easy around her.

Later, James realized Sam must have had a hand in it. The way she'd whispered something to Leia on her way past, the way Leia glanced toward him before handing the bar off to another staff member, it was too deliberate to be chanced. Sam had always been annoyingly perceptive.

"Come with me for a second?" Leia asked, her voice soft but sure.

Before he could think to question it, she was already leading him upstairs, toward the narrow door that opened onto the rooftop.

The air hit colder up there, sharp against his skin. Snow fell in delicate flakes, clinging to their hair, their shoulders. The city below glowed in festive lights, muffled by the quiet blanket of winter.

James noticed almost immediately, Leia wasn't wearing a jacket. She stood there in her usual work clothes, arms folded loosely against the chill, as if the cold didn't bother her.

Without thinking, his hands moved. Old instincts and reflexes from another lifetime kicked in. He slipped out of his own jacket and draped it gently across her shoulders.

"You'll freeze…" he muttered, avoiding her eyes.

Leia looked up at him, startled at first, then softened, her smile tinged with something warmer than gratitude. She pulled the fabric closer, inhaling faintly as if the weight of it meant more than she'd expected.

For James, the cold didn't matter. Not when she was standing this close.

Leia's fingers brushed the fabric of his jacket, lingering as though she was memorizing the weight of it. Her voice came quiet, carried on a James of white breath.

"You never change."

The words struck something in him. A hollow ache. Because he knew they weren't true. Not completely. He had changed too much. The battles, the years, the scars that didn't always show. The person she remembered wasn't the same man standing here now.

"No…" His voice caught, and for once he didn't look away. "Leia… I've changed more than you can see."

It was clumsy, too heavy, but it was the closest he'd come to baring the truth in years.

Her dark eyes lifted to meet his, steady and unflinching. And in them, warmth. The same quiet, constant warmth she'd carried since they were kids, the kind that made the cold air feel less biting.

"You're the same James I've always known," she said softly.

For a moment, the snow kept falling and the world around them stilled, leaving only her words lingering in the space between.

They talked.

At first, it was about simple things: the town they'd left behind, the festivals under the stars, the years that had carved different paths for them both. But slowly, without either of them realizing, the words began to stretch further. To the present. To the uncertain shape of the future.

It was the first time in years James felt like he could be honest. Not just with her, but with himself. Sitting there in the cold, with snow catching in her hair and his jacket wrapped snugly around her shoulders, the weight he always carried seemed... lighter.

Eventually, Leia glanced back toward the door, duty tugging her back to the bar below. James rose when she did, hesitant to end the moment.

"Keep it," he said, when she tried to shrug out of his jacket. His tone was gruffer than he intended. "At least for tonight."

Her lips curved in that small smile again, the one that reached her eyes. She didn't argue.

James left not long after, walking home through streets muffled in snow. His chest felt strangely heavy and light all at once, filled with emotions he couldn't untangle. But one thing he knew with certainty, sharper than the cold air in his lungs.

He was damn glad he'd talked to her tonight.

That night, the thought came to him with startling clarity.

He couldn't keep doing this. Couldn't keep circling the edges of what he wanted, hiding behind excuses and silence.

He wanted—no, he needed—to stop being a coward. To stop letting the weight of the past hold him back. Leia deserved more than hesitation, and maybe Sam was right. Time had a way of running out.

He was going to ask her out.

Maybe it was the talk they'd shared on the rooftop, the quiet honesty that had left him feeling lighter than he had in years. Maybe it was the simple act of placing his jacket on her shoulders, proof that he could still protect, still care. Whatever it was, it had sparked something steady in his chest.

The next morning, James stood in front of the mirror far longer than he'd ever admit. Picking out a shirt that didn't look like he'd just come back from a job, fussing with his hair until it refused to sit wrong, even scowling at his reflection when nerves threatened to undo him.

On his way to Nirvana, he stopped at a corner shop, eyeing the meager display of winter arrangements. Real flowers were scarce this time of year, but he picked up a small bundle of artificial white blossoms anyway. They weren't perfect, but they were something.

As he walked through the snow-dusted streets, bouquet in hand, James told himself he was ready. Or as ready as a man could be when he was about to bare his heart to the only person who had ever truly felt like home.

Nonetheless, James pressed forward, the bouquet clutched awkwardly in one gloved hand. Every step through the snow felt heavier, but he kept moving, rehearsing half-formed words in his head. He had faced war, monsters, the weight of entire missions. This shouldn't have been harder than any of that. And yet his pulse thundered like he was heading into battle.

The soft glow of Nirvana came into view, its windows fogged slightly from the warmth inside. He slowed, breath curling in the cold air, and for a moment he let himself imagine how it might go. He'd walk in, find her, maybe stumble through his confession, but finally, finally... Say what he'd buried all these years.

But then his gaze slipped through the snow-streaked glass.

Leia was leaning over the counter, her hair falling loose around her shoulders as she spoke to a man on the other side. Her smile bloomed easily, her laughter carrying even through the pane. And then, gods help him... she blushed.

James froze. The world narrowed, the cold biting sharper than before. All the courage he'd painstakingly built overnight cracked and fell away, scattering like the snow at his boots.

His chest clenched, breath stuttering. *Of course. She doesn't need me. She never did. I was too late.*

Before his mind could fully register it, his body had already moved. One step back, then another, until the glow of the bar blurred into the winter night. The flowers in his hand felt suddenly foolish, cheap in the face of the scene he thought he'd witnessed.

He turned away, shoulders hunched against the wind, each step retreating faster than the last. The words he'd meant to say burned in his throat, bitter and unsaid.

James's apartment was colder than usual that night, though he wasn't sure if it was the draft slipping through the cracked window or just him. He set the flowers down on the table, the cheap plastic stems looking pitiful against the dim, lonely glow of his lamp. He slumped into the chair, elbows on his knees, dragging both hands down his face.

What was I thinking?

The question repeated like a broken record. He had built up all that courage, only to watch it shatter the second he saw her smile at someone else. The weight in his chest pressed heavier, sharper, until he thought maybe it'd crush him completely.

Restless, he pushed himself up and wandered to the shelves lining the wall. Old books, mission reports, scraps of a life lived half in duty and half in memory. His fingers brushed along worn spines until they landed on a small box wedged between them. He hadn't touched it in years.

When he opened it, a strip of crimson cloth slipped out and fluttered into his hand. Leia's ribbon.

The sight of it hit him harder than a blade to the chest.

Memories flooded in unbidden. Her laughter as a child, sunlight catching on her hair, the way she'd tie it back before running ahead of him, always faster, always brighter. He remembered the promise he made under that starry sky so long ago. To be there for her. To protect her.

His throat tightened, vision blurring just slightly.

He could sit here. Let the ribbon collect dust like the rest of his regrets. Or he could stand up, now, and face the one person who had always been there, even when he wasn't.

He clutched the ribbon tighter in his fist. *Screw it. Either I tell her tonight, or I regret it for the rest of my damn life.*

Leaving the fake flowers abandoned on the table, James grabbed his jacket and shoved it back on. The ribbon stayed in his pocket, close to him, like a lifeline.

Without another thought, he stormed back out into the winter night. This time, he wasn't going to let fear drag him away.

Snow crunched beneath his boots as James ran, breath clouding the frozen air. The streets of Ravenwood's sector felt endless tonight, strung with holiday lights that blurred past him in streaks of color. The ribbon in his pocket weighed heavier than any weapon he once carried, heavier than every mission and burden before this.

By the time he reached Nirvana, his chest was burning, heart hammering so hard it drowned out the quiet of the night.

And there she was.

Leia stood outside the bar, keys in hand, the door clicking shut behind her. The last of the lights inside flickered out as she turned the lock, hair falling loose around her face, snow gathering on her shoulders.

James stopped dead, breath caught in his throat. He should say something, anything, call her name, ask if she needed help. But instead, something inside him snapped loose.

Before his mind could stop him, his feet were moving again. He crossed the street in a blur, the snow swallowing the sound of his approach, until he was right there in front of her.

"Leia!"

The word cracked as he reached for her, arms pulling her in before he even realized what he was doing. He pulled her close, wrapping his arms around her as if protecting her from an unknown threat.

The scent of her hair, the warmth of her body against the cold night. It hit him all at once, overwhelming and terrifying.

"I'm sorry," he muttered, voice raw, almost desperate, as though apologizing for every second of hesitation, every cowardly retreat. His arms tightened around her before he forced himself to loosen the grip, pulling back slightly like he'd overstepped some invisible line. "I... shouldn't... I just-"

But Leia didn't push him away. She stood there in his arms, still and quiet, snow falling gently around them both.

"James..."

Her voice was soft, barely louder than the snow falling around them. When he finally dared to look at her, her face was flushed deep red, eyes wide in surprise. He'd thought she was beautiful when she laughed behind the bar, when she smiled at some passing jokes. But this... this was something else entirely.

Leia opened her mouth, but the words didn't come.

And James knew if he hesitated even for a breath longer, he'd lose his chance forever.

"I can't-" His voice cracked, too rough, too raw. He swallowed hard, forcing the words out before fear could strangle them. "Leia, I can't keep this to myself anymore. I've tried... by the Saints, I've tried. But every time I walk into this bar, every time I see you-" His hands fisted at his sides, trembling. "I feel like I'm back to being that stupid kid in Shepard, standing under the stars and making promises I didn't know how to keep."

Her eyes softened, but he pushed on, terrified of silence, terrified of losing the moment.

"I thought if I stayed away, if I kept my distance, I'd spare you from... From me. From everything broken in me. But all it's done is make me realize I can't imagine a life where you're not in it. I don't want to." His chest ached, breath fogging between them in quick, uneven bursts. "You're the only one I've ever wanted, Leia. Then, now... Always."

The words hung between them, raw and heavy in the winter air. He felt exposed, stripped bare in a way no battlefield had ever managed. For a second he almost wished she'd laugh, shake her head, tell him he was being ridiculous. Anything would hurt less than this silence.

James's voice broke again, softer this time, almost a plea.

"So... If there's even a part of you that feels the same, just tell me. Please. Because I can't walk away again. Not tonight."

For a heartbeat, the world seemed to hold its breath. Snow drifted lazily between them, the silence so thick James swore he could hear his own pulse thundering in his ears.

Then, suddenly, Leia's eyes shimmered. Her lips trembled as she tried to hold steady, but a tear slipped free, carving a glistening path down her cheek.

James's stomach dropped. *Gods, did I—*

But before panic could consume him, she smiled through the tears. A shaky, radiant smile that broke him all over again.

"I thought you'd never ask..." She whispered.

James froze, the words striking harder than any blade. Then the tension shattered at once, a half-laugh bubbling out of him, unsteady and disbelieving. Leia laughed too, soft and watery, as though they'd both been holding in years of fear and longing only to let it spill out here, in the snow.

They reached for each other at the same time, arms pulling tight, clinging like they were afraid to let go. James buried his face in her hair, exhaling a shaky breath that felt like the first real one in years.

Snow continued to fall, quiet and steady, wrapping the two of them in their own small world. The laughter faded, leaving only the sound of their breaths mingling in the cold night air.

Their embrace loosened just enough for James to see her face again, cheeks flushed, eyes

glistening like the snowflakes caught in her lashes.

"Leia..." His voice was low, almost reverent, as if speaking her name might break the fragile magic of the moment. His hand trembled as it rose, brushing away the tear still clinging to her cheek. "I... I love you."

The words felt terrifying and liberating all at once, like stepping off a cliff and finally learning he had wings.

Her smile broke into something soft, luminous. "I love you too, James. I always have."

The world seemed to tilt, the weight of everything... Past regrets, lost time, silent longing finally lifting from his shoulders. All that remained was her, here, now.

He leaned in, hesitant for only a fraction of a second before her hand rose to cradle his cheek, guiding him the rest of the way.

Their lips met, gentle at first, then deepening as years of unsaid feelings poured into the kiss. It was warmth in the winter, fire against the cold, a promise renewed under falling snow.

When they finally pulled apart, foreheads resting together, James closed his eyes and let the moment etch itself into memory.

The streets around them were silent, the night sky heavy with snow, as though the entire city paused to witness.

And in that stillness, one truth rang clear...

Sometimes love isn't found in grand battles or heroic victories. Sometimes it's found in the quiet, in the courage to finally speak, in the arms of the one person who has always been waiting in an endless Solstice night.

8

The Storm That Broke Her

Alanna Percival

The setting sun casts a soft, purple hue over the pewter sky. Awestruck, I stared in wonder as the snowflakes drifted down, soft and slow, fluttering in every direction, blanketing the world in shimmering white. Reaching out, I pressed my fingertips against the thin windowpane, sending shocks of frigid electricity up my arm. The edges of the large bay window were lined with frost, the glass cold as a sheet of ice. I jerked my hand away—staring at my pink fingertips briefly—I pressed my palm against the frozen glass once more.

Back home, we never experienced anything like this. Our winters were grey and bleak. Filled with heavy rain and thunderstorms. They were cold, yes, sometimes the rain would freeze, and the wind would blow so hard the shards of ice would slice your skin like glass falling from the sky.

But never was it cold enough to freeze the air itself, causing it to crystallize against the bark of a tree, transforming the once-thick aspen forest in the distance into a crystalline, mystical wood.

Never had I thought winter could be so marvelous. I thought I had experienced all winter had to offer, but never did I expect anything like what I was experiencing here in my new home of Galdheim.

A shiver ran through my body from the palm of my hand, which was still pressed against the frozen glass. The shiver made its way up my arm and down my spine, causing my chest to tighten and my heart to ache from the cold. I pulled my blanket in tighter around me, letting the shiver take over and escape out of my toes.

The crackling of the hearth was a welcome comfort. I moved towards the warmth—my thick fleece blanket draped behind me like a warrior's cloak—my gaze transfixed on the large bay window, still watching the snow fall as I pulled my blanket around my body. I slid into the pile of furs strewn haphazardly on the hardwood floor.

My new husband, Thorne, insisted the hardwood would be too cold to sit on without them, and though I protested the hideous heap, I must admit to myself that they do serve a purpose when it comes to comfort, though I would never admit it to him.

Chuckling at myself, I looked around the festive room, my gaze falling upon a tree I had acquired a couple of days ago and spent hours finding the perfect pot and stabilizing it correctly; now it was ready to be dressed for Yule.

With a flick of my wrist and a murmur of an enchantment, I watched with satisfaction as a threaded needle hovered above the small table in the middle of the living room floor. Next to the threaded needle and spool of thread sat a bowl of bright red cranberries. In a lazy, slow figure eight motion, I conducted the arcane with precision. I was the maestro of my melody as I twirled my fingers watching a cranberry hover in the air, while the needle followed the motion of my fingers skewering the small red berry straight through, leaving a trail of fragrant juices on the thread as it slid down to join the others to create my cranberry garland.

I hummed, impressed with my newfound abilities, and watched the dance between the cranberries and the threaded needle, becoming lost in a trance with the rise and fall of each berry onto the thread until my aromatic garland had been spun. I stilled my hand, the needle halting its assault on the berries. Swiftly, I moved to sever the thread and tie off the last berry and admiring my creation.

I had often made these garlands by hand as a little girl; now, as an arcanist's student, I am practicing my needlework on them once more.

The mysteries of the arcane had become a new and exciting piece of my life since moving to Galdheim. As a princess, I never had much use for the it other than theory. I had servants for everything I needed; it was done quickly and without question. But now in my newfound life in Galdheim, where I am both the lady of the house and the housemaid, I have come to love spell work in an all-new way. I have become quite adept at menial tasks, such as cooking, cleaning, and sewing. Due to my own gluttony, I have become a near master at making tea and starting the hearth with it. However, spending the full day using my power as an arcanist to decorate the little cottage left me spent!

I was learning quickly, so it seemed. During our visit to the city, one of the clerics remarked on how impressed he was with the breadth of my knowledge, especially considering it had been only a few short months since my marriage. I couldn't help but smirk as I replied, "I'd hardly dare be anything less, with my husband driving me harder than a general on campaign."

The man truly was a thorn in my side.

Not only did he upstage me at my own betrothal, winning the hearts of the common folk with his silly binding ritual, but I didn't care that it was a part of his culture; however, the people sure loved it. He then dared to insist we live in this feeble shack that he calls a home, being nothing more than a measly lord with a few hundred acres of land within one of the most remote countries in the world. Galdheim, and then from the first day of our marriage, he was insistent that I become an arcanist and master of the art—always nagging me to practice. Then, to top it off, he made me work ... for a wage!

Me! A princess of Vosenia, one of the greatest heiresses on the continent, and now he has me working on a farm as if I were a common wench!

A deep sigh escaped my lips, and I plucked a cranberry from the bowl and skewered it with the long needle by hand. I felt my anger and resentment fade slightly as my garland grew longer. Looking up, my gaze returned to the large bay window. Thanks to him, not only was I poor, but now I also sat on the floor, wrapped in a blanket, in a pile of furs...alone.

The snow had grown much deeper by now, and a wind had picked up outside, causing a draft to make its way into the small wooden shack my husband called a cottage.

The fire crackled as a wind blew down the chimney, and I scrambled to my feet to close the flue. The fire returned to life, and I counted the seconds until the wind died.

One Riverstone

Two Riverstone.

Three Riverstone.

I pushed open the flue, ever so slightly, releasing the build-up of smoke that had accumulated around the fire, and then pushed the lever up further, opening the flue all the way as the wind died down.

I inhaled deeply, smelling the charcoal air fill my nose, and pushed my hands together and upward, struggling to use my mystical abilities to guide the tainted air up the chimney and out of the house.

"We really need to fix this chimney." The words escaped my lips no louder than a whisper, though the sound of my own voice startled me. It had been so long since I had had anyone to talk to since Thorne had left for the capital.

He should be arriving home within a fortnight; perhaps that was why I was standing by the window, watching the weather... could I perhaps be?

No, I couldn't.

It was a mistaken thought. There is no way I would wait for that man.

That thorn in my side, after all he has put me through!

I paced around the furs in a huff, brushing out my creased skirts and letting my fleece blanket cape fall into the pile with a silent thud.

I used to be a princess, a woman of meaning and status, and unparalleled beauty. Now I am nothing more than a commoner's wife, a wench covered in soot and ash and forgotten grandeur.

And whose fault is that? It was his.

Thorne's.

The man who asked for my hand as soon as my father's idiotic declaration. Then he dragged me away from my father's castle and set me in this crumbling cottage as though I were some milkmaid plucked from the fields.

I hate him for it.

He even refused my dowery, and now I must live in this hovel, in these ... these slums!

Uuhhg!

I hate him!

I spun around and pounded my fists against my knees in a fit of anger, rage, and vengeance; it filled my very being. I pressed my eyes together tightly and took a shaky breath, calming myself.

Flattening my palms against my skirts, I attempted to smooth the creases that never seemed to leave, my reflection flashing back at me from the darkened glass of the window. I was no longer the jeweled princess I once was. Now, I was a pale, tired girl who waited—waited for him.

I examined my reflection; it was the first time I had gotten a good look at myself in a long time, since there were no mirrors in my new home. My appearance had shifted since leaving the castle. My chest, hips, and thighs had become more robust from the hearty food and the manual labor that had become a new normal in my life. My face had also become more than it once was. My cheeks were no longer sunken at the cheekbones; instead, they were full and plump, they rouged slightly under my eye, and they even dimpled when I smiled in a girlish way.

My auburn hair was healthy and full; the thick, loose curls draped against my defined shoulders. My green eyes shone in a way they never had before, and I smiled at the new me I had never expected to see. I was beautiful in a common sort of way, similar to the farmer's daughter I used to admire in the city square back home in Vosenia. The one all the boys swooned over.

My reflection was illuminated by the tiny mage lights that I had put up around the house in alternating colours of white, red, and green flames. Each intricately designed copper sconce reflected the light in unique patterns on the walls.

Over the last few weeks since his absence, I have been practicing my arcana for the holidays. I don't know why it had become so important to me, but I wanted to celebrate the holidays the way we did back home. With lights and decorations and a big old Yule Tide tree in the corner of the house. The tree was up, but I had yet to decorate it.

Since I was still stringing the decorations together. Now, by hand, since I was too exhausted to continue summoning from the aether.

Back home, our tree would be decorated with ornate glass bulbs and glistening tinsel. But here in this lonely shack, I was left to create my own decorations. So far, I had painted walnuts in varying shades of gold and silver, attaching a brass hook and some red ribbon. Strung aromatic cranberry garlands to drape across its branches, backed gingerbread men and drilled holes through their heads, much to my own content, and strung the same red ribbon through those holes to hang them from the branches. I had even spent the time collecting fallen pinecones to paint and fasten ribbons, too, as a replacement for the bulbs I had become so accustomed to.

I had even woven a wreath from fallen evergreen branches and fastened pinecones, painted nuts, and cranberries to it; It was stunning. Although it was quite feral in its appearance. Just as my tree would be.

I loved it.

Because I had made it.

I hung my wreath above the hearth. Now, in my reflection in the window, it seemed to encircle my head, reminiscent of a woodland crown.

I sighed ...

I missed my home.

I missed Vosenia.

I missed my crown.

Perhaps that's why I waited. I waited for news from home, for something to break this silence, for the world beyond this dreary hearth. That is all. I wait for myself, not for—*him*.

The wind blew once more outside, blowing loose snowflakes into a frenzy of a dance, and I remember the way he looked at me that first time I tried to use my abilities to light the fire and nearly caught the curtains instead.

His eyes had been so warm, his laugh was so inviting, and his smile was intoxicating.

I chuckled to myself at the memory.

Why does my heart still race when I recall his hand closing over mine, steady, certain, unshaken by my temper?

He treated me like an equal.

No courtier, no lord, not even my father ever dared treat me as an equal.

They called me beautiful, untouchable, spoiled, even.

But Thorne called me *capable*. And worse—he meant it.

I bit the inside of my cheek and turned away from the beautiful woman in the green dress who stared back at me from the window.

My mind raced. It is nothing. It is gratitude, nothing more. I am grateful he did not laugh when I failed, grateful he taught me how to hold my power without fear of it. Grateful he listened when I spoke.

Gratitude is not love.

Is it?

Love is soft and foolish, and I am neither.

I am proud. I am still a princess, no matter how stained my gowns or how crooked this chimney. I will not fall in love with this Thorne of Galdheim, not with the man who has stolen my crown and shackled me to this half-life.

And yet ... I turned back to the window, finding myself staring at the road, and wondering if he misses me too. Reaching out, I clutched the sill with cold fingers. Outside, the storm was rising, a thousand white flakes whipped into a frenzy by the wind. They danced and scattered, only to be hurled back together again, swirling in patterns too wild to tame.

So, this was winter. My first true winter. Not the painted scenes from palace tapestries or the dainty snowfall glimpsed through a jeweled carriage window.

No.

This was raw, merciless, alive. The wind howled as if the mountains themselves had a voice, the snow drifting sideways, piling against the crooked chimney I so despised.

And yet I could not look away. It was chaotic, reckless ... and beautiful. Much like *him*.

I squeezed my eyes shut, forcing the thought down, burying it as deep as I could. No. I will not compare Thorne to snow. He is not some marvel of nature; he is a man—stubborn, infuriating, aggravating in every possible way. A man who should be nothing more than my jailer.

And yet ...

My throat tightened. The storm raged on, filling the horizon with white, and I bellowed at the storm.

"I do not *love* him."

The gale shrieked, the flakes danced harder, but my heart pounded with a treacherous rhythm, betraying me even as I clung to the lie.

I ran back to the hearth to pull the lever to close the flue once more as the wind picked up, and I hastened to suffocate the flames before they filled the house with smoke.

I was surrounded by darkness. Save for the tiny flickering mage lights I had fastened to the walls with enchantments.

My eyes adjusted to the selenium tones of winter twilight, the snow reflecting the dim moonlight through the large bay window into my home. The glass itself seemed to shiver with the weight of the storm pressing against it, yet inside, all was silent save for the faint crackle of the dying embers. I rose slowly, clutching the fleece blanket once more around my shoulders, though it gave little warmth in the growing cold.

I stared at the silent storm unfolding before me, a world remade in silver and pewter. The only solitary object in that endless expanse was the old oak tree standing in the center of our field, its bare branches like blackened veins clawing at the sky. The wind whipped the snow around it akin to a furious ribbon dancer, wild and relentless, each movement deliberate, each flourish brimming with a meaning I could not decipher.

Every twirl was a battle, every dip and dive a struggle for power over the unseen hand of the wind. It was not mere weather—it was an opera, fierce and haunting, playing itself out upon the stage of our land. A performance witnessed by no one but me, as though nature itself had chosen me as its lone audience.

And I—once a princess, once adorned in jewels and silks, wearing a crown of gold—now stood in rags of wool and soot, humbled and captive, given this spectacle. A gift from the storm. A cruel gift.

I pressed my forehead to the cold glass, unable to look away—my breath fogging the window. The storm raged with abandon, but there was a haunting beauty in it, an untamed defiance.

I loathed the way it stirred me, how it reminded me of him.

Of Thorne.

He was the storm: unyielding, infuriating, refusing to bend even when I commanded it.

That's when I saw it—movement, beyond the old oak tree. Blurred by the storm. The shadow, the form growing as the storm rose and fell.

At first, I thought it was a trick of the snow, some wayward drift twisting itself into shape, only to be torn apart by the gale again. But no—the figure remained. It staggered forward, wavering against the white abyss, its outline sharpening with each faltering step.

My pulse quickened. It could not be—he was not due yet. And still, my traitorous heart leapt to the thought of him, of Thorne pushing his way back to me through the storm, as though the storm itself could not deny *him* passage.

No. It is not him. It cannot be him.

I will not *wish* for it to be him.

I clutched the blanket tighter, drawing it close beneath my chin as if it might shield me from the truth I did not want to face. The figure grew clearer, broad-shouldered against the whirling snow, relentless in its advance. The wind tore at him, tried to swallow him whole, but still he came on.

Why would he fight the storm so? Why come back to me?

"Because you want him to," the storm whispered.

I shook my head violently, the words echoing as though they belonged to someone else, whispered from the very marrow of the storm. My breath grew shallow, my forehead pressed harder to the glass, fogging the windowpane until I could barely see.

And yet, through the haze, the figure loomed larger, undeniable now, drawing closer with every heartbeat. The oak tree bowed before the storm, but he did not; the figure was defiant.

My breath caught. His stride was uneven, his body bowing against the gale as though every step cost him dearly. The storm swallowed him whole, then spat him back into my sight, each lurch forward more desperate than the last.

"No ..." The word scraped from my dry throat.

I wanted to deny it, to turn away, to cling to the comfort of loathing him. But his form buckled in the distance, his knees striking the whitened ground, and in that instant, my denial shattered.

The blanket fell from my shoulders as I ran to the door, throwing on my boots and heaving it open against the vacuum of the storm. My bare arms burned as the cold bit into my bare skin, the wind clawing at my hair, at my skirts, at my very breath. I guarded my vision with my arm.

Snow blinded me, cheeks raw from the cold, yet still I pressed on, boots sinking deep into drifts that reached past my ankles. My heart thundered in my ears, louder than the storm itself.

"Thorne!" I shouted, though the wind devoured his name. His head lifted faintly, a shadow of recognition, then he sagged forward again.

When I reached him, my hands found him burning beneath the frost, his skin fevered even through the snow was clinging to his clothes. Blood, dark and half-frozen, stained the wool at his side. My chest seized. He had fought something—someone—that was when I noticed his horse was gone, he was completely alone.

"Fool," I gasped, half in anger, half in panic. "What fight did you start this time?" I accused.

His eyes cracked open enough to find mine. Even through the haze, his mouth turned up at the corners into a small smile. "Thought coming home like this might make you happy, for once," he jests, keeling over once more in pain. He lifted his head once more, the smile gone, and he looked at me as though he trusted me, utterly, without hesitation. As though I were his salvation.

I hated the way it broke me.

With a strength I did not know I possessed, I pulled his arm over my shoulders, my body buckling beneath his weight and the cold as I dragged him step by stumbling step back toward the house.

The storm fought me for him, tugged at his cloak, shoving against my chest, howling in my ears, biting at my bare skin, and whipping my hair across my face, but I refused to yield.

At last, the door slammed shut behind us, the sudden silence of the cottage deafening compared to the tempest outside. The fire was nearly silent now. The smoldering light of the embers remained, casting a dim golden hue across the evergreen garlands I had strung along the mantel, the mage lights I had summoned danced within their copper sconces, illuminating the wreath I had foolishly woven to remind myself of better days, speckling the mantle with pinpricks of starlight in the selenium darkness.

I lowered him onto the bed of furs in front of the hearth, breathless, cold, and trembling. The scent of pine and spice filled the room, mocking me with warmth and festivity while I knelt beside my bleeding husband, my hands shaking as I reached for him.

I should not care. I *cannot* care.

And yet, I did.

Quickly, I stoked the embers and infused them with what little arcana I could muster until a small fire crackled to life, filling the area next to the hearth with warmth as I opened the flue slightly, the firelight flickering across his pallid face. His breath came shallow, ragged, misting faintly in the cold air that still clung to us. My eyes darted to the blood soaking his tunic, darker now, seeping into the furs like ink into parchment.

"By the gods, what happened?" My voice broke, the words choking me as I pressed my hands to the wound.

"Bandits," he replied, his voice low, like velvet being dragged over gravel. "They took my horse and all my belongings. Left me for dead in the woods," he coughed, and he bled more with each ragged gasp.

My fingers came away slick from the wound as I pulled my hands away, trembling. "You cannot do this to me, Thorne. You cannot die here, you owe me—"

The garlands I had strung over the mantel swayed gently in the draft, pine needles spilling down like funeral offerings. The wreath above the hearth hung mockingly, a crown for a widow.

Was this to be the holidays, my pitiful attempt at cheer, twisted into a cruel parody: what joy is there in winter if he dies?

"I don't love you," I whispered fiercely, the words spilling out as though they might shield me from the truth. "I don't. I *hate* you. You're arrogant, stubborn, impossible—"

His lips parted, as though he tried to laugh, but only a rasp escaped. His head turned slightly toward me, his eyes glassy yet steady, and that look—gods, that look—was worse than any dagger. Trust. Faith. Love.

Tears blurred my vision. "Stop looking at me like that! I don't love you, but I can't let you die!" My hands returned to the wound with a towel and pressed harder, desperate to staunch the bleeding, my body betraying every word.

"I won't let you," I sobbed, "I —"

The storm outside howled, rattling the shutters, as if the world itself mocked my denial. My chest collapsed under the weight of it, the words tumbling free before I could stop them.

"*I love you.*"

It was raw, cracked, jagged as glass, but once loose, it could not be unsaid. I pressed my forehead against his, my tears falling hot against his fevered skin. "I love you, and if you leave me now, I will never forgive you."

My magic flared without me calling upon it. Heat rushed through my veins, golden light emanated from my palms, and spilled from my fingertips into his wound.

I gasped; I should not be able to summon, let alone have spellwork so powerful it could be seen. The light shimmered faintly against the crimson blood, illuminating the wound. The arcane thread that flowed through me felt clumsy, and frantic, and wild, almost unnatural—but it was working.

"Aether, do as you will, save him," I sobbed no louder than a prayer.

My breath was frantic as the bleeding slowed beneath my hands; his breathing became more even, more steady. My eyes shot from the wound to find his face, his strong jaw speckled with the shadow of a beard, his full lips twisted into a grimace—his eyes closed, color slowly returning by the barest degree to his cheeks.

I had practically depleted my arcana decorating the little cottage today. I shouldn't have any left, and yet, deep within my veins, it stirred. I scraped for everything I could find within me, and I poured every ounce of will and fury and hate and love and desperation I had denied into my veins. The wind continued to howl its opera outside until I thought the storm would tear the roof from the cottage with the sheer force of it.

And when at last the glow dimmed and I collapsed against his chest, I felt his heart still beating beneath my cheek. Weak, but steady.

Alive.

The garlands above the hearth swayed again, this time not like mourning—but like a blessing.

His chest rose beneath my cheek, steady now, blessedly steady. I dared not move, afraid it was some cruel dream conjured by my desperation. But then his hand—trembling and heavy as stone—lifted to rest weakly against my shoulder.

My breath caught.

"Thorne?" My voice cracked, raw from tears. I pulled back enough to see his eyes flutter open, faint but focused, his mismatched gaze finding me. One blue eye and one green eye staring at me as though the storm and the blood and the darkness beyond us didn't exist.

"You're a stubborn fool," I whispered, brushing damp hair from his forehead. "You weren't due to arrive home for weeks. Why did you battle this storm?"

He tried to smile, but it twisted into a grimace. "Takes ... more than a storm... to be rid of me."

Relief broke over me in a sob that nearly undid me again, but I swallowed it, clinging to the fragments of composure I still possessed. I guided him gently against the furs, tucking the blanket around him, my arcana still thrumming faintly in my veins like an ember refusing to die.

His gaze drifted past me then, toward the hearth. The firelight flickered over the garlands I had so carefully woven, the wreath above them, the small bundle of candles I had set upon the sill. The tree was sitting bare in the corner, and the pile of pinecones, nuts, and cranberries that were waiting to be dressed.

His lips curved faintly, this time without pain. "You decorated," he murmured, wonder threading through his voice.

Heat rushed to my cheeks. "It's nothing," I stammered, fumbling with the blanket as though it needed adjusting. "I only thought the cottage should feel less... bleak."

His hand found mine, rough fingers closing over my trembling ones. My limbs are still vibrating from over exhaustion. He held me there, his eyes locked on mine, no storm, no shadow, no crown between us.

He lifted his hand and rustled through his coat pocket, pulling out a small package and handing it to me. My brow knitted between my eyes as I took it, carefully unwrapping the brown paper and ribbon made of twine. Inside the wrapping was a small, flat glass diamond with an intricately designed glass angel attached to it, threaded with ivory. It was beautiful, my first bauble to celebrate my new life.

"I love you too, Elaine," he whispered.

"I would risk everything to make you happy on the holidays."

And at that moment, even as the storm howled outside, I felt as though the world itself had stilled.

9

Bound By Yule

G.P. Engdahl

Chapter 1

24th of December 1810

The annual Christmas Eve Ball at the Danton Estate was the jewel of the winter season, drawing London's wealthiest families and most influential elite. The town buzzed with anticipation for the Prime Minister's grand event, while his only daughter lingered in bed long after dawn.

A sharp knock echoed through the room. "Come in," Kat called.

Daisy, her maid, entered, carrying Kat's evening gown. "Still in bed, Miss Danton?" she chided, tugging open the curtains. Sunlight spilled across the room, and Kat shrank under the covers. Duty, after all, could not be delayed—not on the morning of her first season.

She slipped into a simple morning gown with Daisy's help, fastening the corset with a sharp tug that made her gasp. "Sorry, Miss, but your mother insisted it be the latest London fashion," Daisy murmured. Kat laughed softly, letting out a breath she hadn't realized she was holding. Her golden-red hair, catching the morning light, was braided down her back.

Downstairs, the dining room was quiet except for the crackle of the fire. Her father sat reading the morning paper, brows furrowed.

"Anything new today, Papa?" Kat asked, as a servant poured her tea.

"Just the usual," John Danton replied, setting the paper aside. "And the excitement of tonight's ball."

Kat arched an eyebrow, glancing at her mother. Something felt ... off.

"Go on," her mother murmured, eyes flicking toward her father. "Tell her."

"There was … an unusual jailbreak in France," John said at last. "Scotland Yard and the French authorities are on it, so no cause for alarm. The ball will proceed as planned, and our estate is secure."

Kat felt a flicker of unease but said nothing. "Only a few prisoners?" she pressed.

"Yes, dear," her father said, offering a reassuring smile. "Nothing more."

Breakfast continued with light chatter, though Kat's mind lingered on the thought of French escapees loose in London. Her father's attention soon returned to the paper until a footman entered bowing low.

"Apologies, sir," he said quietly. "Her Royal Highness requests your presence. She says it is urgent."

Kat exchanged a glance with her mother. Both women pretended indifference, though curiosity pricked at her.

"Thank you," John said, rising to his feet. "Bring the carriage around front." He kissed his wife and daughter lightly on the cheek before departing.

Kat sipped her tea in silence. Her mother's eyes lingered on her thoughtfully. "Since it's Christmas Eve, you have a few hours free," Mary said. "Enjoy them before preparations begin."

Kat nodded, rising from the table, a knot of curiosity twisting in her stomach.

An hour later, Prime Minister Danton stood in the drawing room of Buckingham Palace, where a footman announced the arrival of Queen Charlotte. She entered with quiet authority, gesturing to the cushioned chairs.

"Please, Prime Minister Danton, have a seat," she said.

He complied, eyes steady on hers. "If you were curious, the King is unwell and will miss your ball tonight," Charlotte began. "But there is the matter of your bloodline. I assume you are aware of the jailbreak mentioned in this morning's paper?"

"Yes," Danton replied. "The Danton's back in history have taken care of these occults."

"Yet I feel a disturbance," the Queen said, her gaze sharp. "Does Katrina know about her bloodline?"

Danton shook his head. "No. I should tell her, but tonight is her first season. I do not wish to overshadow it."

Charlotte inclined her head. "Very well. I trust you, Minister. I look forward to seeing you and your family this evening."

Chapter 2

Later that evening, the Danton estate had transformed into a winter's dream. Greenery draped the main banister and wrapped around the support pillars, while a red-and-gold carpet ran from the grand staircase into the ballroom. Candlelight glittered off silver tinsel and golden ornaments, casting the room in a warm, festive glow.

Kat, dressed in an emerald-green gown, stood amidst the crowd. Young suitors glanced her way, their admiration polite but obvious. Unlike her friends, this was her very first season. She felt a flutter of nerves but kept her composure—all except for Dimitri, who noticed every small hesitation.

Dimitri and his mother approached. "Good evening, Kat, Mary," his mother said, kissing Mary Danton on the cheek. Mary returned the greeting.

"Kat, you know my son, the Viscount Ashford?" she added.

Kat curtsied. "Yes, we are acquainted," she replied, her voice steady as Dimitri took her gloved hand.

"May I say, you look stunning this evening, Miss Danton," he murmured, brushing her knuckles with a small kiss.

She blushed. Their mothers exchanged knowing nods. "Mary, shall we leave them be?" Dimitri's mother suggested. Mary gave a quick nod and a pointed glance at her daughter: keep it brief—other suitors await.

He whispered, "A little nervous, are we?"

"Isn't it obvious?" she replied.

He gave a reassuring nod. "It's alright. I can tell."

She nodded, taking a steadying breath. She opened her mouth to comment on the morning's news, but a sharp throat-clearing froze her words. A tall, dark-haired man stood before them, at least a foot taller than Dimitri. His brown eyes bore into Kat as if measuring her, hair swept neatly to the side, dressed in black with gold cuff links.

"The next dance, perhaps?" the man said, his French accent smooth. "I am Lord Delacroix, at your service."

Kat curtseyed. "Katrina Danton, pleased to meet you." She caught Dimitri staring and subtly warned him with her eyes, then pulled him aside.

"What is your problem?" she hissed.

"I saw him this morning in the news, one of the escaped prisoners," he whispered, eyes flicking to Delacroix. "I only want to ensure your safety."

Kat exhaled, steadying herself. "I can handle a few suitors, including you, Dimitri. Now, if you'll excuse me." She turned back toward Delacroix.

He met her halfway. "May I have this dance, Miss Danton?"

"Yes, good sir." She took his hand. Dimitri lingered at the edge of the dance floor, drink in hand, uneasy.

As they danced, Delacroix's smile never wavered. "What brings you to London for Christmas?"

"You," he said simply, spinning her back to him.

"Oh?" she asked, innocently.

"I heard about you," he continued, voice low, "and had to come."

Kat noticed a shadow cross his face when she asked about family. She quickly softened her tone. "I apologize if I overstepped."

He shook his head. "No, you did not."

The music swirled around them, but for Kat, it seemed distant, reduced to the sound of their steps on the polished floor. Delacroix leaned closer, his voice low and smooth. "Come, I have a surprise."

Before she could respond, he grasped her hand and led her toward a dim corridor at the edge of the ballroom. The laughter and music faded behind them, replaced by the echo of their footsteps and the shadowed silence of the hall. Kat's heart raced, and a scream escaped her lips as she tried to pull away.

His men were quick. They bound her and dragged her into the waiting carriage, hidden in the gloom just outside the estate. Delacroix leapt in, commanding, "Go!" The horses surged forward, snow spraying in their wake as the carriage plunged into the storm.

Dimitri, sensing something was wrong, raced to the corridor—but it was empty. "Kat?" he whispered, his voice swallowed by the howl of wind outside. The snowstorm whipped across the grounds, leaving him desperate and alone.

Chapter 3

The carriage rumbled down the road, rocking Kat from side to side. Bound tight, she couldn't steady herself. Delacroix sat on one side of her, one of his men on the other, while two more faced her across the bench. The last, the driver, urged the horses forward with reckless speed through the storm. In Kat's opinion, he was a madman.

The carriage was pitch-dark, even the windows covered. Somewhere inside, glass and metal clinked together with each jolt. She realized it was a lantern, left unlit. The faint smell of oil teased her nose, stirring a desperate wish for light.

"Where are you taking me?" she asked, squirming. The ropes dug deep into her arms, pinning them to her sides. Her thoughts drifted back to the ballroom. Dimitri had warned her about Delacroix, but she hadn't wanted to believe him. Now she wished she had listened. He was one of the escaped prisoners.

"Shut up," one of the men snapped, raising a hand as if to strike her.

Delacroix caught his wrist. "No one lays a hand on her," he hissed. The man grunted and lowered his hand.

Fear pressed in on her, sharp and heavy. She had never felt so helpless, and the need to escape burned inside her. "Let me go!" she cried, the sound muffled when Delacroix clamped his hand over her mouth.

"Only us on the road, sir!" the driver shouted from above.

Delacroix nodded and motioned for a lantern. "Light it now."

One of the men obeyed, and the carriage filled with a dim glow. Kat glanced at Delacroix, his hand still firm over her mouth. For a wild moment, she thought of biting him—but stopped. His faint smile told her he noticed.

"If I take my hand away, will you stop screaming?" he asked, gaze fixed on hers.

She blinked once, nodding. Slowly, he pulled his hand back. She released a shaky breath.

"You are a small part of my master's plan," Delacroix said, cupping her chin. "And to answer your first question—you'll find out soon. But no, we are not letting you go." He chuckled, his men joining in.

Kat's chest tightened. Dimitri ... I'm sorry for not listening. Please help me. She was certain God had heard her prayer, but did her family, or Dimitri` even know she was gone? Or were they still inside, caught up in laughter and pleasantries, while she was carried away into the storm?

Meanwhile, back at the ball, no one had noticed Kat's disappearance—at least not right away. However, after an hour had passed most of the young suitors in the room, started murmuring to their mothers and their pals of Kat's whereabouts. Dimitri, who had gone out searching for her, came back with no luck. Some of the young men asked where she was. "She needed some fresh air, I assume," he said, assuring them she was alright. His chest tightened knowing who was responsible. But why her? Was it because she was the Prime Minister's daughter? No, he thought, there had to be more. A motive perhaps? He shook his head as he walked. Seeing her mother, she noticed too by the way he looked and the looks the mothers in the room gave her.

Mrs. Danton, upon seeing Dimitri, pulled him aside. "We need to talk in private," she whispered. He nodded and followed her down a corridor and into a drawing room located south of the ballroom. There she shut the doors and turned to face him. "Kat's missing, isn't she?" she asked.

He nodded. He hated himself for allowing [SS1] Kat to dance with that man. He had warned her but hadn't heeded it. Why? He thought. She always did that. Plunged ahead before thinking.

"I believe so. But I think I know who," he replied.

"Tell me everything you know," she said in a low voice.

"Delacroix, one of the French prisoners, I believe," he said.

She drew in a breath, knowing some of them had gone unnoticed by the authorities. "And you're sure it was him?" she pressed.

"Positive," he replied. "I am certain-his words cut short with the doors bursting open and John Danton standing there looking alarmed.

"What is this I hear? My daughter is missing?" he asked, fear creeping into his voice, his hands shaking.

"Dimitri, here was about to tell me everything he knew," she said. "He was with her, weren't you?"

He nodded. Dimitri then told them both of what happened up until she had slipped out the door with him. "He made it look like they were stepping outside for fresh air but, I didn't think so," Dimitri said, finishing.

John was pacing and glanced at the clock. Only a few hours left of the ball. "We will wait until morning," he finally said, bringing his attention back to his wife, Mary, and Dimitri. "If she is not home by then, we will act." He then left without another word. He bade Mary Denton good-night.

Chapter 4

Christmas Eve, after midnight.

After what felt like hours, the darkened carriage came to a halt. Delacroix cut Kat's bindings, and his men exchanged questioning glances. "I know what I'm doing," he muttered. Kat, relieved to be free but still fearful, hesitated to move. The storm raged on, and she shivered, her winter cloak left behind.

Delacroix grabbed her arm, guiding her with unflinching eyes. "Follow me," he said, voice commanding. "Do not run. Do not think of running." She blinked, nodded, and he loosened his grip just slightly. Together, they trudged through the snow, his men trailing behind in silence. Her breaths came shallow and ragged, chilled by the biting wind.

They approached an old, abandoned castle. Its once-grand stone walls were crumbling, moss and ivy clinging to every surface. Delacroix led her to a stone archway beneath the castle, green ivy brushing past her shoulders as he pulled it aside. Inside, the passage was dim, lit only by a lantern carried by one of his men, casting flickering shadows along the stone walls.

At last, they reached a heavy iron door. One of Delacroix's men yanked it open, and he pushed Kat inside. She fell onto the cold floor with a shriek. Turning to his men, Delacroix said, "Leave us." The men hesitated, then obeyed.

Kat sat on the stone floor, her heart racing. Delacroix stepped in, his gaze cold and piercing. He stooped slightly, measuring her like prey. She backed away, pressing herself against the wall.

"What do you want from me?" she whispered, voice hoarse.

"Do you understand what your family has done?" he asked, tone low and dangerous.

"My family has done nothing—it's you," she hissed.

Delacroix smiled, eyes glinting. "A smart mouth, I see." He raised a hand, and the smack landed sharply across her cheek. She gasped, clutching her face.

"Do not ever speak to me like that! Get up!" he barked. She rose slowly, shaking. He stepped closer, and she instinctively backed into the cold wall.

"Your bloodline is responsible for every occult disappearance. My boss—the head of the occult—will revive all the hidden groups that have ever existed," he said, letting his gaze linger on her neck.

Kat's mind raced. My family ... my bloodline did that? Is this what my father does? Or has done? Her confusion must have shown.

"I will take that as a no," he chuckled.

"So ... my family?" she stuttered, trying to piece it together.

He nodded, then grabbed shackles lying nearby and secured her to the wall, the iron clinking sharply. "Be still," he commanded, cupping her chin. His gaze held her, compelling her to obey. She blinked, nodding slowly.

Delacroix leaned closer, just enough to brush her neck. She trembled under the touch. "Shh, it's alright," he murmured. A subtle prick startled her—he had drawn only a tiny trace of blood, enough to mark her without harm. He handed her a handkerchief to press against the small puncture.

Wiping his mouth, he straightened and left, slamming the heavy iron door behind him.

Minutes passed. Her neck ached; her pulse quickened. What just happened? Is he ... a vampire? Before she could dwell on it further, voices echoed outside—Delacroix and another, foreign and unfamiliar.

"Did you bring her?" the stranger asked, thick accent cutting through the darkness.

"Yes, she's in the cell," Delacroix replied.

"Excellent. The occult groups are ready to rise again. But first ... " The stranger leaned close, whispering words Kat could barely catch. Ransom. They want my father. Panic surged. She needed a plan. Escape seemed impossible—but maybe, just maybe, she could outsmart them.

25th of December, 1810–Christmas Day

The next morning, all of England, London and its surroundings alike, lay under a thick blanket of snow. The frost glistened in the pale winter sun as the deep toll of Westminster Abbey's bells rolled across the city, marking Christmas. But in the Danton household, there was no joy. Kat hadn't come home.

John and Mary rose with heavy hearts. John alerted his most trusted advisers and messengers and instructed the staff to keep a careful lookout. No word would leave the house; no one outside would know until they had answers.

"John, what are we going to do? How could that escaped prisoner take her?" Mary asked, her voice trembling as they sat for breakfast in the dining room. The fire crackled, but the room felt unnervingly quiet.

"She will be found" he said, holding her gaze. "My agents are on it."

She nodded, a tear slipping down her cheek. "I have no idea why Delacroix would target our daughter. But they will catch him, and he will pay," he added firmly, squeezing her hand.

Dimitri sat quietly with his mother, barely touching his breakfast. His father had passed when he was a boy, leaving only the two of them.

"Can't eat, dear?" she asked, noticing his distraction.

He shook his head. From his pocket, he drew a small ring box and opened it briefly. Inside lay his grandmother's ring—his father's mother—a double band of white gold set with blue and white princess-cut diamonds. He shut it quickly, shoving it back into his pocket.

His mother caught the motion. "You were going to propose this morning, weren't you?"

He nodded, cheeks flushing. Then he spoke of contacting the Dantons for updates on Kat. "Go," she said, placing a hand on his shoulder. "And keep me informed." He kissed her cheek and left.

A few minutes later, Dimitri rode to the Danton estate. A footman took his horse to the family stables, and he was led into the drawing room. John and Mary rose as the footman announced, "A certain Lord Ashford is here to see you both."

Dimitri bowed politely. After greetings, he asked, "Any news?"

John shook his head. "I alerted secret, trusted messengers to the city and countryside. They are on the hunt, so no need for concern, son."

Lord Ashford squared his shoulders. "Allow me to help find her—"

"No," John interrupted sharply. "Absolutely not. I will not have you get yourself killed."

"I can help," Dimitri said firmly. "I am not fully human."

Mary and John's jaws dropped in astonishment.

John blinked, then regained his composure. "What? Not fully human? If not, then what are you?" he asked, still stunned and slightly concerned.

"I see your concern," Dimitri said calmly. "But I am not who you think I am. I am ... a demigod."

Mary sank into the cushioned sofa, stunned. John took a seat beside her, staring across the room at Dimitri.

"Is there anything I need to know about why Kat was targeted?" Dimitri asked, looking from one to the other. They exchanged knowing looks, hesitant to speak.

Before they could answer, a footman entered the room. "Excuse me, sir, but this note was nailed to the front door," he said, handing over an envelope of crème paper.

"Thank you," John said, holding it carefully, as if it were fragile. The footman nodded and left. Mary urged him to open it. John nodded, flipped it over, and broke the unusual wax seal. It was neither English nor

French. He recognized the symbol—one used by a former occult group. He shrugged, trying to hide his unease, and unfolded the letter:

Dear Prime Minister,

We have your daughter, Katrina. Release the occult groups at once, or we will be forced to turn her into a vampire and bind her to one of our sects. Fail to comply, and you shall never see your daughter again.

Signed,

Lord Delacroix

"Is this what you've been doing, John?" Mary demanded.

"Yes," he replied. "Alongside politics and the duties of the Crown, I worked to put these occult groups away. Since Kat's birth, the Royal family asked me and my agents to remove them. The country had been stable ... until now."

Dimitri rose, determination in his eyes. John mirrored him.

"Go," John said, his voice firm but weighed with concern. "Find my daughter and bring her home. I don't know what you are, but if anyone can save her, it's you. Just ... be careful."

Dimitri nodded. "Yes, sir," he replied, bowing slightly.

He called for his horse and rode to the divine shrine temples just outside Westminster. The old stone walls were dark, dimly lit by flickering torches. He fell to his knees and prayed to the gods, seeking guidance.

A note appeared on the wall beside him: We will help you. But by rescuing a mortal, you must be willing to give up your mortality. Are you willing to do so?

"I ... yes," he whispered. Love for Kat surged through him. He would sacrifice anything.

In response, a sword appeared, its blade ordinary at first, but at the slightest motion, it ignited with fire. Dimitri grasped it, heart pounding, and ran into the cold streets, determined to bring his beloved home.

Chapter 5

30th of December 1810

Christmas Day came and went. Kat sat in cold, damp silence, waiting for the scrape of a tray sliding into her cell. The chains weren't tight—just enough to keep her tethered to the wall, enough to remind her she was a prisoner. They brought water daily, food sometimes, even a blanket she couldn't wrap around herself. Why keep me alive? What are they planning? Her own plan simmered, fragile but not yet lost.

She pressed her head back against the stone when voices drifted near. The occult leader's tone was sharp.

"It's been days and still no word from Danton." He paused. "Wait—she might hear us."

Delacroix's footsteps came closer. Kat stilled, closing her eyes, letting her breath fall in an even rhythm. He peered through the bars, exhaled, and whispered, "She's asleep."

Satisfied, the leader continued. "No reply from Danton means we proceed. The others will be pleased. And the girl?"

Delacroix asked carefully, "What about her?"

A low chuckle. "She'll make an excellent vampire. She's pretty enough. Consider her yours." The voice faded into silence.

Kat's eyes flew open. Her chest tightened. Turn her into a vampire? No. Never. She tugged at the chains, wrists aching, but nothing gave.

Delacroix's key scraped against the lock, the shackles falling away from her wrists. Kat rubbed at the raw skin, backing against the wall, her breath quickening.

"It's all right," he murmured. His eyes caught hers, dark and unyielding. "You are mine, Katrina. No one else will have you."

She shook her head, pressing harder into the stone. "Never."

His voice slid through her like smoke, soft but commanding. "Yes. Mine." Her defiance faltered as his will pressed into her mind, twisting around her thoughts. She tried to look away but couldn't.

Delacroix drew a dagger across his palm. Crimson welled. He caught her chin and forced her mouth open. "Drink," he ordered, the word carrying the weight of compulsion. Hot, metallic blood filled her tongue, searing down her throat. Her stomach turned, but she couldn't stop.

"That's it," he whispered, almost tender. "Now you'll never leave me."

Before his lips could meet hers, a thunder of hooves shattered the air. Shouts cut through the cold silence. Delacroix's head snapped up. The pounding grew louder—dozens of horses.

The cavalry.

And at their head, sword drawn and cloak flying, was Dimitri Ashford.

Delacroix dragged her close and carried her through another passageway. One of his men had brought the horse that had been with the carriage. "Hop on," he commanded. Kat obeyed, trembling as he helped her mount. He climbed up behind her, and together they rode away.

As they rounded a corner, Dimitri appeared, blocking their path. He pulled on the reins, and Delacroix did the same. Behind him, the cavalry formed a tight line. "Let her go, Delacroix!" Dimitri shouted.

Delacroix chuckled, leaning close. "She's mine now. She's marked—and soon will turn."

"No," Dimitri whispered through clenched teeth. He glanced at Kat. She mouthed, I will never be his. He understood too late.

Delacroix reared his horse and fled. Dimitri ordered the cavalry to hold back and infiltrate the castle. He spurred his horse, chasing Delacroix. Soon, he caught up, forcing his horse in front of Delacroix's. Startled, the vampire lost control, and Kat was thrown off.

"No, Kat!" Dimitri screamed. He slid from his horse and ran to her. She had hit her head, lying still on the snow. Delacroix laughed, but Dimitri checked her pulse. She was alive, though barely.

"If she dies ... she turns," Delacroix growled, before Dimitri struck, sending fire streaking across the snow. The flames consumed Delacroix and his horse.

Dimitri scooped Kat up, careful not to jostle her. Together, they rode back toward the Danton estate. The doors burst open as staff and the doctor rushed out. They carried her inside and laid her in her room. Dimitri stayed in the corridor all night, finally falling asleep on a chair.

Morning came. A maid opened the door. "She's asking for you," she said.

Dimitri's heart caught. He stepped inside. Kat lay propped against her pillows, her neck and wrists still marked but healing. "Oh, Kat," he whispered, sinking into the chair beside her.

She stirred, eyes fluttering open. "Why are you crying?" she asked softly.

"I thought I might lose you," he said, taking her hand gently. "Are you okay?"

She nodded, breath catching. "I heard you … I love you too."

Dimitri smiled, rising to one knee. He held up a ring. "Katrina Danton, will you marry me and become Viscountess Ashford?"

Tears welled in her eyes. "Yes," she whispered. He slid the ring onto her finger and leaned in for a tender kiss.

Before she could speak, he added, "Yes, I did get your parents' permission."

Kat stayed in bed, her fingers clutching the ring, a smile spreading across her face.

Outside, the staff pressed forward, straining to hear, and her parents quietly cracked the door open. Mary Danton smiled warmly, and John nodded, pride shining in his eyes. Relief and delight filled the room as they shared the moment, knowing Kat was safe and that a new beginning awaited her and Dimitri.

10

Sins of Christmas Past

Molly Jones

Trigger Warnings
Violence
Gore

The snowflakes slowly floated down, the clock on the wall reading 12:25a.m. It was officially Christmas, but the blood soaking into the sparkling white snow emphasized that the body frozen in place in front of me would never see another Christmas. The limbs lay feet from the body, splayed out in all different directions. Controlled chaos is immediately what comes to mind as I look around the scene.

"Detective Rockland, you might want to see this!"

A deep sigh escapes as I head towards the voices of the other officers on the scene. I let my mind catalog every detail that I pass, it starts to create a complete picture in my mind. The snow, the covered pool, the house that is too perfect compared to the blemish the body has created. The Christmas decorations around the house only emphasizing the brutality of the murder that took place here.

"What do you have?" I ask, stopping next to Officer Nicholes. I feel my blood freeze in my veins as I take in the scene in front of me. "Is this a joke?"

"No sir. We found it this way and made sure no one disturbed the scene," he shifts uncomfortably. "That's why you got called to the scene."

I shift, agitated, looking around once more at everyone around, now suspicious of every person on scene and the civilians looking on from behind the crime scene tape. I look again reading the words carved into the side of the house.

> *Detective Rockland*
>> *One for you, four more for me*
>> *By end of Christmas, all will see*
>> *The blood left on white*
>> *What a beautiful sight*

I read the words over-and-over again. The crude poem addressed to me, with no clues to the psychopath that left these words behind. I clench my fists, rage coursing through me at the idea that someone innocent died for this person's game. A game that apparently is going to have many more victims if I can't solve this puzzle.

"Officer Nicholes!" I bark, straightening up. "Tell me that CSU has found something, anything, that can help us find this bastard."

"There was something else left on the body..." Nicholes hesitates, clearly uncomfortable at having to be the one that deals with me. He shifts as if he is wanting to turn and leave.

"I am waiting," I say impatiently, looking over Nicholes. I notice a bead of sweat rolling down his temple, and it makes me feel nervous for the first time in years. Officer Nicholes is by no means someone who sweats at a crime scene. He's been on the job for over 20 years. Whatever this next news is, won't be good.

"Listen, I just want to point out that I was against bringing you in on this," Officer Nicholes says, shoving his phone into my hands. "I'll be back over by the body."

I wait for him to walk away before looking down at the phone. I take a deep breath, making sure to steal myself for whatever I am about to look at on this phone. After a few more moments, I finally look down, and the world immediately starts to spin.

There on the screen is a picture of another picture. One I am intimately familiar with, that I have memorized. The picture is of me from 10 years ago with my best friends from college. The five of us look so carefree and happy in the picture. These are people that I thought would be a part of my life forever, until one moment tore us all apart, or more accurately, made me walk away from them. I freeze, looking back towards the body, the very headless body.

"Does anyone know who the victim is?" I say, my voice strangled with fear. The confidence I've carried throughout my career gone in an instant. Dread taking over every part of my body, unwilling to accept what I know the answer is going to be.

"The ID found on the body says that the victim is one Culver Rivers," a uniformed officer spouts off. To that officer, this is just another crime scene, just another day on the job, just another body. But for me, everything changes in that moment. Culver Rivers' face stares up at me from the screen on the phone, still clutched in my hand.

"Detective Rockland, did you hear me?" Nicholes asks, grabbing my shoulder.

"Fuck," I mutter. "I know who did this," I say a little louder.

"What do you mean you know who did this?" Captain Johns says, coming up from behind me.

I hand him the phone, still staring at the body, the red now turning a weird off-red color from it melting into the snow. I think back to the night that changed my life, one moment in time that changed the course of all of our lives.

"We need to find Victory Bergs," I say, finally turning to look at my captain. "She is the one who responsible for this."

"You got all of that from a carved in poem, a photo, and the victim's name?" he questions me warily.

"I didn't need the poem," I try to deflect for a moment, unsuccessfully.

"Start talking," he huffs, crossing his arms over his chest.

"She holds every person in the photograph responsible for the death of her twin sister," I admit. "And if I am being candid, she has every reason to feel that way. It's why I cut myself off from every person in that photograph." I turn away from Officer Nicholes and Captain Johns. I shiver as the snow starts to come down harder, blurring the world in front of me. "Her sister died 10 years ago today."

"So, how do we find her?" Nicholes asks probably the most important question so far. "Because let's be honest, whatever happened 10 years ago led up to this but isn't going to be helpful with stopping this person. She wants revenge. Is she going to succeed beyond Mr. Rivers over there is what we need to be focusing on?"

"I know where she is going to be, because I know where they are all going to be today. They go to the same place every year on this day. The only difference is that now they bring their families," I rush. "I'll tell you where to go on one condition."

"Let me guess, you want to come with," Captain Johns grunts. A man of few words, like always.

"That's the deal. Take it or leave it," I offer, standing my ground as the chill seeps through my clothes.

"Well, let's get going then. We don't have time to waste," he orders, motioning for me to follow him. "We will call backup on the way to wherever you tell us we need to go."

We pull up outside the Bendict Country Club. A perfect picture scene between the snow and the quaint cabin feel of the country club. The pine trees around the cabin covered with a dusting of snow just helps to complete the scene. The Christmas lights lining the cabin, making the shimmer of the snow light up the ground around it.

"This is small for a country club," Nicholes says, having pulled up behind us and gotten out of his cruiser.

"It's not open to the public any longer, but it is owned by Leon Gauger. He is the one in the picture on the very left. It was owned by his parents and left to him when they passed. He shut it down a few years after but kept the cabin. They have been using it since for these events," I explain. "This is also where Charity died."

"So, how do you want to do this?" Captain Johns cuts in. "Should we just raid the place?"

"No, I'll go in first. I don't want anyone getting hurt if she is already here, and the calvary just goes in guns blazing, that is exactly what will happen," I state.

"You know that isn't how things work," he snaps.

"Sir, respectfully, it is Christmas. I just want everyone to walk away from this alive," I say simply. "I'm going in, whether you like it or not."

"Fine, we will do it your way for now. But the moment I don't like the way it is going, we are going to come in after you," he advises. I nod my head in agreement, happy that he is at least giving me this much.

I grab the vest out of the back of the shop and strap it on. Just another layer of pointless protection, because after today, no matter how this ends, I'll never be able to come back to this job. I've been running from my demons for 10 years. I may not have helped end a life, but I didn't step up to do anything about it after it happened. I could make excuses about how we were kids, how we didn't know any better, but none of that matters.

After making sure my vest, gun, and radio are in place, I turn towards the cabin. Just looking at the snow covering the cabin and the trees around it, I can almost pretend none of this is happening. It all looks so picturesque, like a scene stuck in time. I slowly start to walk towards the front door, the sound of fresh snow compacting beneath each step. It takes me forty-seven steps to reach the door. From outside, I can hear the music and laughter of a life that has forgotten about me.

I hesitate, looking back towards the officer that are waiting for my signal. I don't know what is going to happen on the other side of this door. I don't know how many people are in there, or how many innocent people might get caught in the crosshairs of a woman who lost the most important thing because of a select few. I raise my hand and knock hard against the door, hoping it is heard over the sounds inside.

It feels like time slows down as I wait for the door to open. Thoughts and memories keep filtering through until finally the door is pulled open. I know the person on the other side, Owen Fitzgerald. Another intended victim on this Christmas. He is talking to someone behind him when he opens the door, not even looking to see who is waiting for him on the other side. The irony of what an easy target he just made himself isn't lost on me in this moment.

"Owen," I clear my voice, catching his attention. "I need to come inside. It's a matter of importance. I am assuming that Dylan and Leon are here too?"

"Will, what are you doing here?" he asks, a sneer sliding across his face. "I thought you were too good to hang out with us these days. How long as it been anyways?"

"Owen, I don't have time for your bullshit. Let me inside and get the guys. We all have a problem a whole lot bigger than me forgetting to send you cards on your birthday," I snap.

Before he could reply, a blood-curdling scream echoed throughout the cabin. I grabbed my gun off my hip and shoved past Owen to go into the main lounge area. But I knew I was too late. The game had already started back at that house, the evidence bleeding into the snow.

"Well, look who made it just in time," Victory cackles, a 9mm pistol hanging loosely in one hand while her other hand is wrapped around a child that can't be older than five. "I was hoping my little clues were going to be enough to get you here in time."

"Victory, let the kid go. You have us here. You don't need the children," I try to negotiate with her. "Owen, Dylan, Leon, Culver, and I are the ones to blame. Just let everyone else go."

"Did you enjoy how I left Culver for you? The red sure did look pretty against all of that sparkling white, don't you think?" she laughs.

I watch as the child in her arms hiccups on another sob, a dark patch appearing on his pants. I try to look around to see if there is any way to deescalate the situation. I notice that everyone has slowly started to leave the room except me, Owen, Dylan, Matthew, and the woman that must be the child's mother. The absolute fear on her face makes every muscle in my body spasm with the need to get the child away from Victory.

"Victory, we can talk about all of this. Just let the boy go," whispers softly leaving my mouth as I take another step towards her.

"Why?! My sister didn't have that choice, did she? When she cried and begged for you guys to take her home after what Culver did, you just ignored her. She wouldn't have been behind the wheel of that vehicle that night, drugged out of her mind, with drugs he gave her, if one of you had stepped up and said something! Done something! And you, you are the worst out of them all! A police detective! You could have said something all these years! You could have looked for her killer!" sobs moving through her body, spit flying out of her mouth from her yelling.

I take another step forward, my gun staying steady, aimed directly at her. I try not to let my focus get stuck on the child in her arms. I take a moment to really study her. Victory's eyes are unfocused, the pupils blown wide, the green of her eyes a mere ring around the outside. Her light blond hair is in disarray, as if she hasn't brushed it in months. Everything from her head to her toes looks out of control.

"Victory, no matter what you do now, this isn't going to end how you want it to. The kid is innocent. Please, please just let him go," I beg.

"I don't need this kid to make my point! Culver has already paid for his part! I couldn't leave anything to fate with him! He had to pay, and he paid in blood!" She continues to laugh, the laugh starting to take on a manic sound. The child in her arms cries become louder the longer she laughs. Finally, she pushes the child to the side. The force of the push makes the child hit the ground with a loud thud. The moment he hits the ground, his mother is already there, scooping him up and running out the side door without hesitation. "Merry Christmas!" she screams after them.

I let out a loud breath of relief knowing that those two are safe. I can live with any fall out past this point. I know, just like the guys behind me do, that the sins of our past are finally catching up to us. Victory's laugh cuts off abruptly, as if all the wind has been knocked out of her. Her eyes focus on me, sending a shiver down my body.

"Victory, you need to put the gun down. This has to stop here. No one else needs to get hurt. Your sister wouldn't have wanted this," I press. "Please. Just put it down and let me take you in."

An ugly sneer starts to take over her face, taking over any ounce of beauty it once held. I watch as she lifts her gun, her hand now as steady as a rock. Unmoving, unflinching, uncaring, pointed directly at me. The world comes to a stop, and every sound around me sounds muffled.

A loud gunshot rings out from inside the cabin, making me start immediately running towards the door.

"I shouldn't have let him go in," the thoughts coming relentlessly, every possible scenario running through my head.

"Captain! Wait for backup!" I hear officer Nicholes call from behind me. But I can't stop. I can't let someone else pay for the biggest mistake I've ever made. Because it's my fault we are all here, and my fault that Charity Bergs never saw another Christmas.

11
Trapped Inn
Moxie G.

Trigger Warnings
Stalking
Blackmail

While the spaghetti was boiling on the stove, Desdemona fumed over the argument she had with Bailey earlier. He frowned at his phone, heavily breathing. Silence lingered in the air like smoke. The audacity he possessed to say what he said made her ass itch.

"Being wrong is the worst thing you could be."

Honestly, she couldn't believe he said that. There were worse things than being wrong. Like hating people who drink lattes.

On their first night in the cabin, she couldn't even enjoy the matching plaid pajamas they were wearing. The steam coming from the pots made her sweat a little bit. Then, she could feel the inside of her pajamas.

The beeping of the timer made her flinch. She drained the pasta before mixing it with the tomato sauce. Its homey smell made her feel cozy. Until Robin came in with a bottle of red wine.

"Why's it so tense in here?"

"Des thinks it's okay to be wrong, as if it's not the most humiliating thing you can do," Bailey said, pushing his black hair back.

"It sounds like you're exaggerating a bit."

"Are you siding with her?"

"Yes. I'm sorry that you can't handle being wrong."

Desdemona put the spaghetti on three white ceramic plates, screaming internally. She sat down with them and started eating. The dramatic way he twisted her words was infuriating. She picked up her phone and typed out a truthful answer.

"What the drama king meant to say was that I don't believe being wrong is the end of the world. Just admit to being wrong and move on."

Robin's brow furrowed after he read her response. He opened the bottle and poured red wine halfway in two empty glasses. For a minute, she felt vindicated. The past four hours have been absolute hell.

Snow piled up outside the cabin, so she couldn't leave. Unfortunately, she was stuck with the petty aftermath of a small argument. It was three days away from Christmas, and they were supposed to be snuggling by the fireplace. Holiday cheer couldn't flourish in these conditions.

The sound of a fork clanking against a plate grated on her nerves. There was no way she could let this shit go on for the next three days. She stopped eating and tapped Bailey on the shoulder. That was when he finally looked at her.

"Can you fucking relax?" Desdemona signed, giving him a dirty look.

Bailey let out a heavy sigh. "It's hard to do that when I'm upset."

"Try harder."

"Fine. This isn't over."

She rolled her eyes before she continued eating. It tasted just like the spaghetti her mom used to make. Warmth and comfort from the meal reminded her of last Christmas, minus the passive aggression. This sulking needed to end before Christmas.

The first sip of the wine made her feel more relaxed. When she ate the last bite of the spaghetti, the glass was empty. Robin downed his wine with one sip and looked at her with a concerned expression. He leaned closer to her before he spoke.

"How do you like the place?"

"I love it. It's cozy and familiar," she signed. "I'd watch the snow outside, if it wasn't piling up three feet."

"We could watch the snow on TV if you want."

"I'd love that."

"Alright. I'll get everything set up."

Robin turned around and whispered to Bailey. He left the kitchen excitedly. As Desdemona got up, her boyfriend picked up the dishes. They locked eyes while he washed them. Her heart fluttered from getting lost in those haunting forest green eyes.

Damn. I'm supposed to be mad at him! she thought.

She pushed a stray copper-red curl behind her ear and walked into the living room. The fireplace was crackling with flames, and the TV was turned on. Once she sat on the black velvet couch, a movie scene of a couple playing the snow captured her attention. The thought of playing in the snow put a wistful smile on her face.

The tapping of her nails on the back of her phone was just as satisfying as the winter wonderland before her eyes. A rich smell of cocoa filled her nostrils as she watched that same couple ski down a slope. She was caught by surprise when the spot next to her dipped. During a commercial break, she turned her head and ended up locking eyes with Bailey again.

He was sitting right there, holding two mugs of hot chocolate. When he handed her one of them, she took a sip. Warmth in her body and heart betrayed her mind. The silence between them was awkward.

The movie started again, and they watched the couple wrap presents. Robin didn't come in here like he promised. Did he get lost in the cabin?

Five minutes passed, and she started getting worried. She flipped her phone over and sent him a quick text. It was left on read, with no reply.

She let out a frustrated sigh. Then, she put her mug down and searched the kitchen. Robin wasn't there. Footsteps followed behind her as she searched every room upstairs for her friend. Honestly, she was too focused on finding him to care.

Of course, Desdemona felt a tinge of disappointment when she didn't see him in any of them. The minute she turned around, she bumped into Bailey. He stared down at her with an expression of concern.

"What's wrong?"

"Robin completely disappeared. He never skips out on watching movies with us," she signed.

"He said he was getting some extra blankets from the basement. He'll come back soon."

"I hope so."

They went back downstairs to the living room. The lights were turned off and an animated movie was playing on the tv. Desdemona searched for the remote and let out a frustrated sigh when she didn't find it.

The sun started to set, leaving the room in darkness. A shiver went down her spine. While the movie continued, they both finished their hot chocolate. Bailey hadn't answered their ten phone calls.

Suddenly, Bailey's phone rang and an unknown number flashed on the screen. He looked down at the screen with a furrowed brow. Desdemona watched him closely, at the edge of her seat.

Bailey answered the call. "What is it?"

"Christmas spirit is in the air. Too bad it's being ruined by a petty fight," the caller said, in a gruff voice.

"What the hell would you know about our relationship?"

"I know you have five minutes to hide, or I'll take one of you as my gift."

"Is that a threat?"

"No. It's a fucking promise. Start running."

The call ended. Bailey and Desdemona looked at the screen in horror. They held hands as they rushed upstairs to a guest room. Being trapped in the cabin with a sick stalker wasn't a part of their plans.

Right after they locked the door, the lights were turned off. Desdemona sat on the full sized bed, with her knees to her chest. Her heart was beating in her ears as she watched her boyfriend turn pale. Footsteps creaked against the floor downstairs.

What kind of twisted game was this? The brochure never mentioned the possibility of a mysterious creep living here. Otherwise, both of them would've stayed at home. At least, no one would've threatened them in Fayville.

Those footsteps padded up the stairs, causing Desdemona's heart to drop. Bailey picked her up, and carried her into the candlelit bathroom. As the footsteps drifted closer to the bedroom, he closed and locked the door. With one glance at the mirror, Desdemona noticed her honey brown complexion had been flushed pink. She held onto him for dear life.

"I'm sorry, Des," Bailey whispered.

His words melted her heart in a way she couldn't help. Tears filled her eyes. In the daunting silence, they both hid in the bathtub behind the black curtain. Her face was soaked with tears as she tried to keep her breathing steady.

She let go of her boyfriend and typed up a response on her phone. This moment had her feeling more raw than she expected. Bailey stared at her with a curious expression. His features softened when he read her response.

"You're forgiven, babe. I couldn't stay mad at you."

The soft kiss they shared eased the tension between them. She broke the kiss and moved closer to Bailey when the door jiggled violently. Both of their phones lit up in the dark.

Thank God *he can't see us.* she thought.

The shaking of the doorknob stopped, only granting her temporary relief. A message from an unknown number popped up on her screen. Her heart dropped when she read it.

Come out. I have a special surprise for you.

This had to be a trick. Desdemona didn't know what the surprise was, but she had a bad feeling about it. There was no way she would let herself and her boyfriend get harmed. When something got shoved in the lock, she trembled with terror. Then, the door slowly creaked open.

She peeked from behind the curtains, and noticed the door was wide open. Silence filled the room, yet it felt like a trap. When her and Bailey left the bathroom, there were candles scattered around the bedroom. Rose petals covered the bed.

What the hell? she thought.

Desdemona glanced at Bailey with a raised brow. Strangely, they couldn't find the stalker in any of the other rooms. Just in case the intruder was lurking, they rushed back into the guest bedroom. Paranoia twisted her stomach in knots as she put a chair under the doorknob. No more sneaky surprises.

They sat on the bed, snuggling closely together for warmth. This wasn't how Desdemona wanted to spend her night with Bailey, but at least they were safe. For now.

She could feel her boyfriend's heartbeat under her hand. The throbbing between her thighs had her cheeks flushing with heat. Now wasn't the time for her to be aroused.

The way Bailey held her, with his hand almost touching her ass turned her on. And his thigh being right on her pussy didn't help. Her mind was focused on using him to get herself off. The thought got her wetter.

The lustful gaze they shared sent a shiver through Desdemona.

"What's wrong, baby?" Bailey asked.

She signed. "I want to fuck you without taking my clothes off."

"Go ahead. Rub your wet pussy against me."

She started bucking her hips, and grinding on his thigh. A needy moan slipped past her lips as pleasure took over her body. Her hands held onto Bailey's muscular arms tightly.

Slow saxophone music played in the next room, despite the fact that neither of them touched their phones. Desdemona didn't mind the music, because she was focused on how good she was feeling. Her panties were soaked, and she was pretty sure Bailey could feel it too. He held onto her hips while she fucked herself on him.

Intense waves of pleasure washed over her as her moans got louder. She was so close to climax, she could almost taste it. Her eyes rolled to the back of her head.

"Come for me, baby," Bailey said in a husky tone.

Desdemona's body trembled as an orgasm rocked through her. While she caught her breath, she leaned on him. The music stopped when she opened her eyes.

The creaking of the floorboards in the next room alarmed her. She shared a confused glance with Bailey. The footsteps came to a sudden stop, stirring up suspicion.

Desdemona and Bailey left the guest roomand walked right into their bedroom. The door was wide open and a pair of gray hiking boots lay at the foot of the bed. A sliver of hope cut through the spine-chilling terror that had been overwhelming her. This meant that Robin wasn't lost, since he left his boots here. Bailey took out his phone and called him.

"Robin, what the hell happened to you?" he demanded.

Robin hesitated. "I was just...looking for blankets. What's up?"

"Some sick bastard is stalking and taunting us."

"Damn, that's crazy."

"That's all you have to say?"

The call dropped. Bailey stared at the screen in disbelief. Robin's voice echoed while they were talking on the phone. It sounded closer than she expected.

Because of this realization, she rushed to the closet and opened the door. Behind the clothes she pushed aside, Robin was standing against the wall. He stared back at Desdemona with wide eyes.

She snatched the phone from his hand. Her heart dropped when she read the message that was sent to her phone. The one telling her and Bailey to get out of the room. But seeing outgoing calls to her boyfriend's phone infuriated her.

"I can explain. This isn't what it looks like," Robin said in a defensive tone.

12

Starship Dominatrix: Have Yourself A Deadly Little Crisis

Dustin J. Craig

> **Trigger Warnings**
> Child endangerment to violence exposure
> War trauma with PTSD themes
> Graphic Violence
> Religious Imagery Used Satirically
> Excessive use of pumpkin spice seasonal flavors may cause flashbacks
> to holiday marketing trauma.

Jack sat staring at his zwanzig decaf double-shot pumpkin spice extra mocha cappuccino with whipped cream and cinnamon sprinkles. The big bold words of 'We Won the War on Christmas' plastered on his BlackHoleBucks Café coffee cup taunted him. It featured Baby Jesus in a Santa hat riding a missile, gold glitter garland around the rim, and Santa and his elves firing candy-cane rifles at nondescript protesters.

Jack rolled his one good eye at the absurdity of the label while his cybernetic ocular implant in his other eye socket glowed red. He reluctantly sipped his coffee from the tacky cup, harboring a profound hatred of Christmas. For him, Christmas wasn't hope. It was a brutal reminder of trauma.

Talonor was Jack's massively muscular minotaur-like alien husband. He decked the Galley aboard the Dominatrix II with improvised decorations. Broken plasma coils as garlands, jury-rigged emergency glow sticks as lights, and a broken antenna array as a tree with plasma grenades for ornaments decorated the room.

"Nothing says 'peace on earth' like explosives on a dead antenna. You're really pushing the limit with that one, Cowboy," Jack muttered before taking another begrudging sip. He smirked bitterly. "One spark and your Christmas tree turns this whole galley into roasted chestnuts."

Talonor placed a crystalized Aetherium core on top of the 'tree' as he swished his tail. "It's about the holiday spirit, Jack. Family. The light in the darkness. Doesn't any of that matter to you?"

Jack snorted. "Last time I had Christmas spirit, it came in a bottle labeled one hundred five proof, and I can't even have that anymore."

"C'mon, Jack. Where's your holiday cheer?"

"There is no holiday cheer in a galaxy this fucked. You can sing carols, stuff stockings, and wish each other a merry fucking Christmas, but leave me out of it."

A raider encampment that once housed an old mining facility on the moon of Eisgait was covered in snow and ice in the cold dark dead of night. Frosnik 'Krampus' Volzen trudged through the snow through the encampment. He earned that nickname because of his relentlessness and cruelty. It didn't help that his alien features were goatlike. He could never play that down—so he owned it.

He opened the door to his cabin, where a fire was waiting for him. He took in the usual comforts of home, glad to be back...and alive.

"Branel? Bran, I'm home!" he called out.

A boy the same species as Frosnik came barging out of his room. "Dad!" the kid said enthusiastically, running up to Frosnik with his arms outstretched.

Frosnik dropped his sack and opened his arms wide. He crouched and hugged his son, then kissed his forehead. "Ah, it's good to see you, my boy! Just in time for Christmas."

"Where did you go, Dad?"

"I went to go get you a Christmas present."

Branel cocked his head. "For three days?"

Frosnik laughed. "It's a very"—he booped Branel's nose—"special present." He opened his sack and fished out a Holographic Entertainment Arts Device and handed it to his son.

Branel's eyes lit up. "Whoa! For me, Dad?"

Frosnik chuckled. "It's the latest model. I thought you'd like it."

Branel brushed his fingers reverently across the polished device. He slid it over his head, and holographic displays flickered on. The device booted up with a cheerful chime, and a dialog box appeared.

"It...it's asking for a password," Branel said. "Dad? What's the password?"

Frosnik winced. "Uh...it's...complicated. I'll figure it out later."

Branel pulled off the device. "Dad, did you...steal this?"

The fur on Frosnik's neck bristled. "Don't talk like that, son. It's for you. That's all that matters."

Branel stood perplexed as he stared at the device. "I...I don't want it."

"C'mon, son. It's your Christmas present—"

Branel shoved it back into his father's hands, his eyes welling with tears. "I said I don't want it!" He bolted from the room, leaving Frosnik alone with the toy as useless as his lies, torn between his raiding lifestyle and fatherhood.

Jack entered the bridge, and the AI Auxiliary crew were busy at their stations. He carried a DataPad with him to do some late-night crew evaluations for the end of the year.

Alistair, the AI acting captain, sat in the captain's chair.

Jack approached the chair. "You're dismissed, Lieutenant."

Alistair immediately yielded the captain's chair and walked a few steps as Jack sat down. Alistair glanced back at Jack and gave a small smile and a nod. "Merry Christmas, Captain."

Jack scoffed with a quick exhale through his nose and a soft grunt. He turned on his DataPad.

Jack's sister and first officer, Yvonne, walked onto the Bridge. She crossed the room and sat down in her chair as she addressed Jack. "Merry Christmas, bro."

"Yeah, whatever," Jack said.

"It's about time we spend at least one Christmas together."

Jack rolled his eye upward as he plunked his DataPad on his lap with a sharp huff. "Number Two, I don't want to hear it." He sighed. "Everyone's been wishing me a 'Merry Christmas' all day. I don't celebrate it, I don't exchange gifts, and I certainly ain't gonna wish them great tidings of comfort and motherfucking joy."

"Why do you hate Christmas so much?"

"I don't want to talk about it."

"Is it because of what happened when we were kids?"

Jack tapped his DataPad screen, trying to distract himself from his sister's comment.

"Jack, you have to let that go. Yes, it was horrible, but things have changed for the better, haven't they?"

Jack continued his work in silence.

"Haven't they?"

Jack ignored Yvonne's desperate attempts to reach her brother's heart. It was as cold as the vacuum of space.

"Captain," an AI officer called out from the comm station. "We're getting a distress call from the moon of Eisgait. Raiders have ransacked their colony, stolen all their BioGel and supplies. The colonists are requesting immediate intervention."

"Not our jurisdiction," Jack said as he continued to evaluate crew members.

"Jack!" Yvonne snapped. "How can you be so heartless?"

"Look, if we ran out and saved every single person from their problems, we wouldn't be able to do our jobs."

"And our job is to protect people, Jack. People are starving without their BioGel. They're probably cold and helpless without their supplies. I mean, what else are we doing other than just cruising around in space?"

"Patrolling The Sphere."

"And that includes taking care of any distress call. Give the order to investigate."

Jack felt a migraine coming on. It was harder to ignore than his sister. "Fine, fine. You win." He called out to the pilot. "Lieutenant, open a wormhole to Eisgait. Low orbit."

Frosnik sat in front of the bonfire outside in the middle of the encampment. He pulled his fur cloak around him to stave off the cold from creeping up his back. He turned the H.E.A.D. around in his hands, trying to figure out how to bypass the password. He ignored the roughhousing and shouting around the encampment from the drunk, rowdy raiders wearing Santa hats. His mind turned over with the sight of his son breaking into tears over something he thought would bring Branel a bit of the magic of Christmas in his eyes.

A big, burly man on crutches hobbled over to the log Frosnik was sitting on. He had lost a foot that still bore the cauterization from a stray plasma bolt from many years prior. The man had a bald head and a black beard, wearing the orange pelt of a jasger dire wolf.

"Hey, Krampus," the man said, standing over him. "Mind if I sit here?"

The interruption broke Frosnik from his thoughts. He glanced up and recognized the man. "Oh. Hey, Cookie." He scooted over and dusted some snow off the log.

Cookie lumbered next to Frosnik, sat down, and leaned his crutches against the log next to him. He held his hands out in front of the bonfire to warm them up, then glanced to the H.E.A.D. in Frosnik's hands. "What's that?"

"It's a gift I gave my son."

"Didn't Bran like it?"

Frosnik's fur bristled. "He said he didn't want it." He relaxed and sighed. "I risk my neck with every raid to provide for him, and this is the thanks I get."

Cookie snorted. "Bah. Kids don't get it. They don't care if you bled for it, so long as it ain't theirs. You drag back shinies, food, liquor—whatever—and they just see another thing stolen. That's what they'll always see."

Frosnik turned the H.E.A.D. over in his hands. The holographic interface caught the firelight. *Another thing stolen,* he thought.

Cookie went on. "Truth is, Bran will come around. The boy will learn the same as we all did—nobody gives you anything in this galaxy. You take it, and keep what you can carry. That's the only way any of us live past winter."

Frosnik's jaw tightened as he stared at the dancing flames. He remembered the look on his son's face—the tears and the disappointment. It didn't look like a boy learning a lesson. It looked like a boy losing faith in his father.

"Yeah," Frosnik muttered. "That's what I'm afraid of."

Jack zoomed his ocular implant in on the entrance to the encampment. The two guards were oblivious to him, Talonor, and the AI crew members who were lying prone in the snow.

"What do you see, Jack?" Talonor asked.

"Well, from the heat signatures through the walls, I gather about twenty, maybe twenty-two humanoids," Jack said. "Can't tell you their gender, or how old they are."

Talonor thought for a moment with a quizzical look on his face. "So, what's the plan?"

"I say we gun it. Since there's little cover between here and the entrance, the element of surprise is not on our side."

Talonor continued to think. "We could dress up as carolers..."

Jack shot Talonor a look.

"What? Maybe they'll be more willing to talk if we show mercy. Otherwise, we'll become the monsters we fight."

"I highly doubt that raiders will care if we're humanitarian or not. We are only marks to them." Jack continued to scope out the encampment with his implant.

"Well, what's our goal?" Talonor asked. "Just kill them all? There's got to be a better solution. It is Christmas after—"

"I don't care if it's Christmas, Easter, or losing a goddamn tooth. Our job is to eliminate the threat to the colonists so we don't have to do this again."

Talonor rubbed his broken horn. His thoughts raced for any possible solution, and then he nodded. "Alright Jack. I'm behind you all the way."

*   *   *

"Bran?" Frosnik said as he rapped on his son's door.

"Go away!" Branel called out from the other side.

"Bran, I need to talk to you. Can you please open the door?"

Silence met his plea.

"Bran, I...I get why you're upset with me. I fucked up. I want to make it right. Can you please open the door so that we can talk?"

Frosnik stood by the door, hoping to get an answer. The door opened, and Branel sighed. He trudged to his bed, then sat cross-legged at its head.

Frosnik was trepidatious as he slowly entered his son's room. He inched closer. "Bran. What I did...it was wrong. I betrayed your trust, and for that, I owe you an apology."

"Dad, you shouldn't apologize to me. You should apologize to the colonists you stole from."

Frosnik sat at the foot of Branel's bed. "It isn't that easy, son. You don't understand."

"I don't like it when you raid, Dad."

"Bran..."

"I want to hear it from you. That you won't raid again."

Frosnik was at a loss for words. He had to tell his son what he wanted to hear, but he couldn't lie to his flesh and blood.

"Dad? Are you going to raid again?"

Frosnik opened his mouth, but no words came out. He didn't want to fail him.

Before he could answer, plasma bolt fire rang through the encampment from outside. Raiders scrambled for their weapons and barked orders, and they heard the screams of agony in the throes of death.

"What is it, Dad?"

"Hide under the bed. Don't come out until I tell you it's safe."

"But Dad—"

"Go. Now." Frosnik hurried out the door, but before he left, he stopped, turned around, and said, "I love you, Bran." He locked the door from the inside. He left the room then closed the door behind him.

Jack and Talonor led the charge with the AI crew close behind. They had stormed the gates and laid waste to a dozen raiders. The duo hid behind sandbags and barrels for cover. Talonor alone had gunned down eight by himself, while Jack had taken out only four.

The AI crew had all but taken out the rest, and Jack inched through the encampment, searching for any sign of life.

"Do you see any more, Jack?" Talonor asked.

"Damn. I can't see anything out of my implant. They must have activated an EM field around here to block its signals.

Out of the corner of his good eye, he saw movement inside a cabin. He raised his plasma bolt rifle and slowly crept toward the structure.

Frosnik was prepared to fight back. He raised his plasma bolt rifle at the door, waiting for death to come knocking. He looked through the sight of his barrel, but his gaze turned inward and saw the same man, still a raider. He looked toward the door to his son's room, but teetered toward holding the barrel tighter. He glanced out the window and saw all his friends had been slaughtered. Cookie's body was lying in full view, charred from plasma bolt fire. It seemed like he was the last one standing. If he had died, Bran would be without a father.

Tears welled in his eyes, and he pointed the barrel downward. He threw it on the floor, got on his knees, and raised his hands behind his head, waiting for the end.

The door burst open, and Jack had his rifle pointed directly at Frosnik's head. Jack was about to pull the trigger.

"Dad!" Bran yelled as he ran out of his room.

"Get back in your room, Bran!"

Jack's breath caught. A child on the premises was the last thing he expected.

Bran ran between Jack and his father, shielding Frosnik as best as he could.

Frosnik grabbed Bran and held him tight. He stared at Jack, not wanting to go in front of his son. He looked up at Jack with pleading eyes, begging for mercy.

Jack's aim wavered, and a tear fell from his cheek. He saw himself in the eyes of Bran. The same scared little boy he once was. Jack lowered his rifle and walked toward Frosnik and Bran, staring at them. He stood above them for a moment, and the father and son winced, waiting for the end.

Jack reached out his hand, offering to help Frosnik to his feet.

Frosnik looked into Jack's eye and saw something he had never seen before. Compassion. He looked at Jack's hand, then back at Jack's unwavering gaze. He reached up, took Jack's hand, and Jack helped him stand up.

Jack swallowed his pride as he shook Frosnik's hand.

"Merry Chrismas," Jack said.

Jack turned and walked out the door with his rifle at his side, rubbing his temple.

Frosnik and Bran were perplexed by the strange interaction, and Frosnik held Bran close to his side.

Outside, a random raider charged Jack, and Jack lazily shot the raider, blowing his head clean off. The body fell with a sickening thud, and Jack motioned for the crew to make their exit.

Jack sat at his desk, writing a report of the incident in his Captain's Command Chamber on the Dominatrix II. He got to the point where it came to recounting his altercation with Frosnik.

Yvonne entered the room. "So, how did raiding the raiders go?"

Jack placed his elbow on his desk and rubbed his hands. "I finally found something worth saving in this shitstorm."

"And what's that?"

"Christmas. It's not about giving cards or exchanging gifts. It's about giving a damn to the people we love. It's about protecting each other even while death is staring you in the face. It's about hope when all hope is lost, and about courage to stand up against those who have wronged us."

"Wow," Yvonne said, leaning back with wide eyes.

"What? What is it?"

"Oh, I'm just shocked you actually learned a lesson...for once."

Jack grunted and rolled his eye.

Yvonne smiled. "Merry Chrismas, Jack."

Jack looked into his sister's big, beautiful blue eyes. "Merry Christmas, Number Two."

Yvonne left the room, and the door hissed shut behind her. Jack sat back in his chair, placing his arms across his chest.

He shook his head, selected the entire bit about the father and son. He deleted it and then hit submit.

A sleigh carrying months' worth of ransacked BioGel and supplies sat in front of the colony's door. People opened the gates and were shocked to see all their belongings back in their possession. People passed out supplies and BioGel, including a few H.E.A.D.s.

Frosnik and Branel watched from a distance behind the trees to see their excitement.

Branel tugged at Frosnik's cloak and looked up to his father. Frosnik could see the joy and pride it had given his son, and to Frosnik, that was the greatest gift of all.

13

Silent Night, Deadly Night
Sandra Lynn Williamson

Chapter One

*C**old Cabin, Hot Coffee*

Snow slammed against the windshield, thick and blinding, the kind of storm that swallowed whole cars. Noelle Winters tightened her grip on the wheel and leaned forward, every muscle taut. She hated this stretch of mountain highway even on a good day, and tonight it was Christmas Eve, black ice under her tires, no one around for miles.

She should've stayed at the ranger station. Should've admitted the storm was too much. But she'd promised her mom she'd be there for Christmas morning, and Noelle didn't break promises.

Headlights caught movement. An elk lunged out of the treeline, eyes glowing in the beam of the headlights.

"Shit–" She jerked the wheel. Tires skidded, the SUV fishtailed hard. The world spun, metal screamed, and then the vehicle plowed nose-first into a snowbank. The airbag never deployed. Silence dropped heavy, broken only by the tick-tick of the engine as it died.

"Great." Noelle sat there, heart hammering. Cold crept in fast. She checked her cell. Nothing. Of course. She cursed under her breath, pulled her ranger jacket tighter around her, and grabbed her flashlight.

She pushed out into the storm. Wind clawed at her face, snow swallowing her boots. Panic whispered that she'd freeze before sunrise. Then, a light. A single warm square glowing through the trees. A cabin. About a fifty yards back. Smoke in the chimney. "Thank God."

Noelle forced herself toward it, lungs burning, legs numb. She banged on the door, the sound almost lost in the roar of the wind.

It opened to a burly chest and a shotgun.

Noelle froze, breath fogging white. She lifted her badge with a shaking hand. "Park ranger. Vehicle's in a ditch. I need shelter."

The man filling the doorway was broad, bearded, scar slashing through his brow. Eyes flat, assessing. Not the kind of guy who trusted easy. He didn't move. Didn't invite her in.

Noelle's teeth chattered. "Look, you can shoot me or let me in, but I'm not freezing to death out here."

A beat of silence, then he stepped aside.

She stumbled in past him, into heat, wood-smoke, and the kind of silence that felt like it belonged to someone who hadn't celebrated Christmas in a long damn time.

Chapter Two

Close Quarters, Hot Trouble

Inside, the cabin was small. One bedroom, a kitchen, a bath, and a stone fireplace throwing shadows across rough log walls, which absorbed the heat. Table and chairs by the window, gear stacked in neat piles. Everything about it screamed temporary, functional. No tree, no decorations.

The man set the shotgun against the doorframe. "Elias Ward."

"Noelle Winters." She peeled off her soaked gloves, flexing fingers that burned as the blood returned. "Thanks for the warm welcome."

He grunted, not quite a laugh. "Storm like this, I don't open my door to just anyone."

"Good thing I'm not just anyone." She dropped her badge on the table and rubbed her hands in front of the fire. The warmth hit hard, sweet, like life crawling back under her skin.

He poured coffee into a chipped mug and set it in front of her. Strong, black, no questions asked. She took it, met his gaze, and held it. He didn't look away.

Noelle wasn't used to being stared at like that...like he was measuring her weight, her worth, her threat level. Most men looked at her badge and saw authority. Elias looked at her and apparently saw a problem.

She sipped. "You live up here year-round?"

"Sometimes."

"That's a non-answer."

He leaned back against the counter, arms folded, muscles shifting under the worn flannel. "You ask a lot of questions for someone who almost froze to death."

"Occupational hazard," she shot back. "I'm a ranger. Asking questions keeps people alive."

For the first time, the corner of his mouth ticked, the closest thing she'd seen to a smile.

Noelle sat at the little scarred wooden table, the fire snapping between long silences. She wrapped her hands around the mug like it was the only thing keeping her alive. Elias didn't touch his coffee, just watched her with that steady, unblinking gaze.

"You always this cheerful with company?" she asked, interrupting the quiet.

"Company's not something I get much of."

"Shocker," she muttered, taking another sip.

One brow lifted. "You always this mouthy with the man who has a shotgun?"

She leaned back in the chair. "You didn't shoot me. Which tells me either you're not a complete asshole, or you wanted to see what kind of trouble just landed on your porch."

That almost-smile tugged at his mouth again. "Maybe both."

The silence stretched, the storm hammering the walls. For the first time since the crash, Noelle felt something loosen in her chest. A laugh threatened, surprising her. She bit it back, shaking her head.

"What?" Elias asked, voice low.

"Nothing." She smirked. "Just never thought I'd end up on Christmas Eve drinking coffee with a mountain hermit who thinks sarcasm counts as conversation."

His gaze held hers a second too long, and she felt the heat crawl up her throat.

Then the storm slammed against the cabin harder, rattling the shutters. She turned her head toward the window just as the motion sensor light popped on, laughter dying on her lips. Her breath caught. "Elias. You expecting company?"

"Hardly." He followed her gaze.

Fresh boot prints, her tracks having been covered, leading straight to the cabin door.

Chapter Three

Tracks in the Snow, Heat in the Veins

The wind cut like knives when Noelle followed Elias out onto the porch. Her boots sank deep. Her ranger flashlight sliced through white haze, beams bouncing off a million glittering flakes.

The tracks were obvious. Heavy boots, deliberate, circling the cabin.

"Not random," she said, crouching low. "Whoever it was... they were watching."

Elias gripped the shotgun tight, following the beam of light as she scanned the tree line with that soldier's stillness she recognized instantly. Nothing about him said panic, but every line of his body was wired, ready.

They moved together, quiet, following the trail. Around the corner of the cabin, the prints stopped at a window. Snow piled on the sill where someone had leaned close to look inside.

Noelle's stomach turned. "They were checking the rooms. One by one."

He didn't answer, just kept moving. They found the same story at the next window. All the way around. Every window marked with boots, a silent orbit closing in on them.

By the time they reached the shed at the far edge of the property, her pulse hammered against her throat. The door hung open, latch broken.

Inside, tools were scattered like someone had rummaged through in a hurry.

"Supplies," Elias said flatly. "That's what they're after."

Noelle scanned the prints again, forcing her breathing to even out. "No. If all they wanted was supplies, they wouldn't have walked the whole house. They were casing it." The truth hit her cold. "They were looking to see if anyone was inside."

Elias's jaw locked, eyes narrowing at the dark woods. "Then we just told them they're wrong."

The wind howled harder, whipping snow through the broken shed door. For the first time since she'd left her SUV, Noelle felt something worse than the storm creeping in. Whoever had walked this property wanted more than firewood. And they weren't finished yet.

Chapter Four

One Bed, No Rules

The wind rattled the cabin like it wanted in. Noelle's boots were wet, her fingers stiff, her body humming from the cold and the adrenaline of tracing those tracks, which had disappeared thanks to the weather.

Elias moved beside her, quiet and deliberate. He didn't look at her, but she felt him, warm, steady, solid, like a shield she didn't know she needed until tonight.

"You should sleep," he said, voice low, almost gentle.

"Nope. Not until we know whoever that was is gone," she muttered, shrugging out of her wet jacket and hanging it over the chair. "Besides, I'm fine."

"You'll get frostbite if you stay like this," he countered, and she caught the edge of a smile in his eyes. He was serious, but there was something else there—a thread of humor, or maybe concern. "Come with me."

She followed Elias into the tiny bedroom; a small mattress shoved against the wall. He left the door open, set the shotgun by the bed, and moved to the window. Dim firelight from the living room allowed them to see. He stepped to the side, moved the curtain back, and glanced outside. He stood there a long moment, then stepped back as if satisfied they were alone. For now.

He tugged a second blanket over the mattress, tossing it across the center.

"Both of us," he said simply.

Her stomach jumped. "Both of us?"

"You think I'm giving up my only chance at body heat?" The corners of his mouth betrayed him with a smile.

She rolled her eyes, but her pulse betrayed her. "Fine. But no funny business." She stripped off a long tee shirt and pants but left on her thermals.

"Funny business?" His voice was low, teasing. "High school humor again?"

She chuckled, climbing in, sliding under the thick blanket. He followed, settling close, their shoulders brushing first, then arms, then the rest of the warmth from his body leaking into hers.

The fire cast shadows that danced across the walls, and for a long moment, they just listened: snow thrumming against the cabin, the faint creak of logs settling, and each other's steady breathing.

"You always live this way?" she asked softly, staring at the ceiling.

"Alone?" His voice was rough, thoughtful. "Yeah. Feels like peace most of the time."

"Doesn't it get lonely?"

He didn't answer at first. "It didn't... until now."

Heat crept along her spine. She turned just a little to look at him, daring to meet the vulnerability he'd offered. The intensity in his brown eyes made her stomach tumble with butterflies, and she felt a rush, fear, want, desire, all tangled together.

She reached for his hand, sliding hers under the blankets. His fingers found hers, rough and warm, and held on. Not just comfort, but intent.

The first kiss came slow, testing, feather-light, just enough to ignite a spark. Then it deepened, urgent, a friction of mouths and whispered breaths. Her hands slid up to his chest, feeling the strength under his flannel, the heat radiating off him, matching her own.

The world outside, the storm, the footprints, the threat, all faded into a blur. All that mattered was him, her, the tight press of bodies under blankets.

Noelle gasped softly, his lips trailing along her neck, her hands tangled in his thick hair. Every brush of his fingers, every press of his chest, was a promise of heat and safety, danger and desire all rolled into one.

Finally, they paused, breathless, foreheads pressed together, the warmth of the bed and their bodies mingling, a tentative comfort settling in the storm.

"You're already trouble, I can tell," she whispered, half-laughing, half-breathless.

"And you're crazy enough to stay," he murmured, brushing her lips again.

Outside, the wind raged. Inside, the fire and their bodies burned brighter.

Chapter Five

Heat in the Storm

The fire popped softly, the last of the embers painting his features in gold and shadow. Noelle tucked herself closer, her cheek against his shoulder, listening to the steady rise and fall of his breath.

"Elias?" she whispered.

"Mm?"

"Don't you ever get tired of being out here alone?"

For a long moment he didn't answer. She thought maybe he'd drifted to sleep...until he shifted, his hand tightening over hers under the blanket.

"I told myself I liked it. The quiet. The space. No one to answer to, no one to lose." His voice was low, rough, as though the words had splintered on their way out. "But... it wasn't peace. It was just empty."

Her chest ached. "And now?"

He turned his head, just enough that their eyes met in the faint light. There was no smile this time, no teasing, only truth. "Now I can't remember why I ever thought I wanted that."

Heat prickled along her spine, not from the fire, but from the way he said it, like she was the shift, the reason. She swallowed, her throat tight.

"I know empty," she admitted, voice barely a breath. "It's worse than danger. At least danger makes you feel alive."

He brushed his thumb over her knuckles, slow and steady. "You don't feel empty now, do you?"

"Not now." She shook her head, pressing her forehead against his chest, whispering into the quiet. "Not with you."

The silence that followed wasn't hollow. It was full.... of warmth, of firelight, of possibility neither of them dared name.

She felt his hand still tangled with hers, rough and solid, his thumb stroking over her skin like he couldn't stop himself. The silence between them burned hotter than words.

Then he turned, just slightly, closing the distance until his breath ghosted across her lips. That tiny shift snapped something inside her. She surged forward, catching his mouth with hers.

This time, there was no hesitation.

The kiss deepened, teeth bumping softly, lips moving with a hunger that surprised them both. He slid his arm around her waist, hauling her flush against him, and the solid heat of his chest pressed into her curves. The storm outside faded into nothing. There was only the press of him, the taste of him, the way every kiss seemed to say *I want more.*

She threaded her fingers into his hair, tugging, desperate to feel him closer. He groaned low in his throat, the sound vibrating against her lips, and rolled, pulling her beneath him.

The blanket slipped down, baring them to the cool air, but their bodies burned hotter than the firelight. His flannel rasped against her thin thermal, and the friction sent a rush of heat spiraling through her.

She gasped against his mouth as his hands skimmed down her sides, firm but careful, like he was memorizing the shape of her. She tugged at his shirt, needing to feel skin, needing him. He broke the kiss just long enough to strip it off, the firelight catching the hard lines of muscle across his chest.

For a moment she just looked, breath shallow, before she pressed her palms flat against his bare skin. He was hot to the touch, the steady beat of his heart under her hands as frantic as her own.

Their mouths found each other again, hungrier now, lips bruising, tongues sliding in a rhythm that was as wild as the storm. The blanket twisted around their legs as they tangled, rolling together, her laughter breaking on a gasp as his mouth trailed along her jaw, down her neck.

She arched into him, her own clothes becoming unbearable. He removed her thermal top with a messy pull, tossed aside with no care, followed by the cling of her thermal bottoms. Skin against skin at last, every inch of contact sparking, searing, impossible to ignore.

They kissed like they'd been starving for years, like the night had forced them together just to remind them what it was to feel alive. He mapped her body, reverent and demanding all at once, while she clung to him, digging her nails into his shoulders as if to anchor herself.

Time blurred. There was only the slick slide of mouths, the press of chests, the desperate need that rose and crashed over them like a wave. Every kiss rocked them deeper, every gasp tangled them tighter, until the outside world, storm, tracks, danger, ceased to exist.

Breathless and tangled in heat and sweat, they broke apart just enough to rest forehead to forehead. The fire crackled, the storm clawed at the cabin, and they lay there, hearts racing, lips swollen, bodies humming with a connection that felt as dangerous as it did undeniable.

"You sure about this?" Elias asked, voice came rough, almost ragged.

Noelle's laugh came out shaky, tracing the line of his jaw. She smiled slyly. "I've never been more sure of anything."

And with that, he kissed her again, and the storm inside the cabin raged hotter than the one outside.

Chapter Six

At Last

The fire had burned low, a faint amber glow licking at the edges of the hearth. Shadows moved across the cabin walls, long and fluid, wrapping them in their own secret world.

Elias's moved his lips over hers with a hunger that had lost all patience. The teasing was gone. What remained was need, raw and undeniable. Noelle clung to him, tugging at him, desperate for more, for all of him.

"Elias..." his name escaped her lips as he skimmed her ribs, settling at her hip, anchoring her.

"Tell me you want this," he murmured, pressing his forehead against hers, voice hoarse with restraint.

Her immediate answer came in the form of her body arching into his, and her mouth finding his with an urgency that left no question. "I do. I want you."

The last of the barriers between them came away in a rush, his pants lost in the tangle of blankets, his boxer briefs and her panties and bra flung into the air, their laughter caught in messy kisses. Then there was nothing left but skin, heat against heat.

For a moment, they stilled, just looking, breathless, stunned, as if they'd both stepped off a cliff together. His eyes searched hers, a storm of need and something softer. She touched his cheek, thumb brushing the stubble there, and whispered, "Don't stop."

He kissed her again, slower now, reverent, before turning her over and easing down on top of her. His body covered hers, solid and sure, every line of him fitting against her as if this had always been waiting. The press of him stole her breath, not from weight, but from the intimacy of it, the closeness.

When he finally slid into her, it was careful, controlled, his breath shaking against her skin. She gasped, clutching at him, digging her nails into his shoulders. The storm outside could have risen again and torn the cabin apart...she wouldn't have noticed. There was only this: the deep, consuming rhythm of them moving together.

Their kisses turned frantic, lips bruising, then softer, lingering, like they couldn't decide if they were devouring or cherishing. Every brush of his mouth against hers was a promise, every whisper of her name a tether holding her to him.

The heat built and built, their bodies chasing a crest they couldn't slow. Noelle tipped her head back against the pillow, her cry muffled by his kiss as the world shattered around them. He followed with a groan, clutching her as though he could sink into her entirely, as though letting go would be unthinkable.

They collapsed together, tangled in sweat and breathless laughter, the blanket half on the floor. For a long moment, neither spoke, the only sound the slowing thud of their hearts, still pressed chest to chest.

Elias covered them and kissed her hair, a simple, unguarded gesture.

Noelle smiled into his shoulder, too sated to tease, too undone to deny it. She just curled closer, her hand splayed against his heart and let the warmth of him lull her toward sleep.

Outside, the storm was gone but the cold consumed. Inside, its fire lingered, burning in the quiet space they had finally claimed together.

Chapter Seven

Danger on the Doorstep

The storm had eased overnight. Snow drifted against the cabin walls like it wanted to bury them alive. Noelle woke to the faint scrape of boots against the porch. Her stomach dropped.

"Elias," she whispered, sliding from the bed.

He was already awake, standing near the door, shotgun at the ready. "I hear it too," he whispered, voice low. "Stay back."

"Hardly." She moved with him to the window. Footprints...someone had circled back. Someone was testing the doors now.

"Counted every window again." Noelle murmured, tension tightening her chest.

"Good," Elias said. "Means they're bold...or stupid."

The cabin door rattled. A shadow slipped under the porch roof, trying the handle.

Elias waited, shotgun raised.

Noelle drew her knife, stepping beside him.

The door opened, and the intruder froze, axe in hand.

"Drop the axe. Come in. Close the door behind you." Elias held the shotgun steady. With coordinated precision, Elias drove him back toward the corner while Noelle pressed forward, knife at the ready. Every motion was sharp, controlled, full of adrenaline.

Finally, the intruder went down, hands pinned against the rough cabin floor. Noelle pressed her knife closer. "Why? Why come here?" she demanded. "This place obviously isn't empty."

The man spat, defiant. "Supplies. Food, fuel... whatever we can find. Easy pickings. You got a problem with that, bitch?"

"That's ranger bitch to you. Now, who else is with you?" she pressed, keeping her voice steady despite the adrenaline.

"Friends," he sneered.

Elias's jaw tightened. "Looks like you hit the wrong cabin." He handed her a length of rope he had near the door. Noelle tied him up while Elias stood by with the shotgun. Her pulse still pounded, a mix of fear and adrenaline.

"You shouldn't have come back," Elias said flatly. "Next time, you might not be so lucky."

The man glared, but it was over. Neutralized. For now. Noelle would have to keep an eye out for the rest of his team.

She let out a shaky breath, backing away. Her heart was still racing, her hands trembling from the fight and the storm and the rush of working side by side with Elias.

"You okay?" He glanced at her, voice low, rough but lighter than it had been.

"Yeah," she whispered, still flushed. "Thanks... for having my back."

He gave a small, almost-grin. "Ditto."

Outside, the storm settled.

Noelle heard an engine, and the snowplow rumbled past the driveway. "How about you give me a ride to town to drop this guy off at the sheriff's department... and then come with me to my mom's for Christmas?"

He blinked. Then smirked. "You're full of dangerous ideas, you know that?"

"No," she said, grinning. "I'm full of brilliant ones."

He laughed, running a hand over his beard. "Brilliant... I can work with that." He grabbed his coat and keys, glancing at the bound burglar. "You've got him handled?"

She smiled, hiding her fluttering heart. "Absolutely. Now let's go before the snow buries us again."

Chapter Eight

Home for Christmas, Hot for Trouble

After they dropped the burglar off at jail, they drove to her mother's cabin.

They climbed out of his truck and headed for the door, Elias following close behind, jacket zipped, hands stuffed in his pockets. He wasn't saying much, but his presence was warm, steady, grounding. Noelle liked that more than she cared to admit.

Her mom opened the door before they could knock. "Noelle! And... you brought company?"

"Mom, meet Elias," she said, nudging him forward. "He... helped me out last night."

Elias offered a small, polite nod. "Good morning, ma'am."

Her mother's eyes softened. "Well, you certainly picked a strong one."

Noelle snorted. "Understatement."

Inside the cabin was cozy and smelled like pine and cinnamon. It was the kind of scent that wraps around you like a hug. Snow clung to the roof, frost glittering on the windows. A fire crackled in the stone fireplace, a gorgeous tree twinkling with soft lights, and the smell of roasting ham making her stomach growl.

Elias hung his coat and scarf, scanning the room, then glanced at Noelle. "Nice place," he said quietly.

"It's home. I grew up in this cabin," she said, leaning back against the doorway, watching him. Something about seeing him here, away from danger, made her chest tighten in a different way. Warm, easy, and a little dangerous in the best possible way.

Mom called from the kitchen, "Dinner's almost ready! You two better wash up."

Noelle grabbed Elias's hand, tugging him gently. "Come on. Don't make me drag you to Christmas dinner too."

He let out a laugh, low and amused. "I'm already hooked. Let's see what you've got."

Noelle grinned, letting herself relax for the first time all day. Snowstorm, intruder, adrenaline... gone. For now. Here, it was just her, her family, and him.

And maybe the best Christmas she'd ever had.

Chapter Nine

Silent Night, Wicked Heat

The cabin was quiet for a moment, the fire crackling in the hearth as Noelle's mother bustled out the door to deliver the neighbor's plate of Christmas goodies.

Noelle leaned against the counter, sipping her hot cocoa. Elias stood nearby, watching her, body relaxed but taut, like a predator in repose.

"You know," she said softly, letting her voice linger in the warm air, "I didn't think I'd ever have a Christmas like this. I've spent most alone at the ranger station."

Elias nodded, and stepped closer, heat radiating off him. He studied her.

"Life has a way of keeping you on your toes," she said, voice trailing off. Then she laughed, light and nervous. "But somehow, this... feels right."

"I couldn't agree more." His hand brushed hers as if by accident, and the spark of contact made her stomach clench. He leaned in, slow, patient, giving her time to pull away. She didn't.

When his lips met hers, it was gentle at first, testing, tasting, letting the tension dissolve into heat. Her hands rose to his chest, feeling the solid weight beneath flannel, tracing the curve of his shoulders, the strength in his arms.

The kiss deepened, slow, deliberate, a delicious friction that left them both breathless. She tangled her fingers in the back of his hair as he pressed closer, letting the world outside...the snowstorm, the intruder, even Christmas chaos fade into nothing.

When they broke apart, noses brushing, foreheads touching, Noelle's chest heaved. "This... this is perfect," she whispered.

Elias's lips twitched at the corner, that small, almost-smile that made her heart stutter. "You think so?"

She nodded, eyes sparkling, voice soft but sure. "I think this... is my best Christmas ever."

He caught her hand, giving it a gentle squeeze. "I'm glad I'm here for it."

And for the first time all season, Noelle let herself sink fully into warmth, snowstorm and danger forgotten, just the fire, him, and the quiet magic of the moment.

14

A Christmas Vacation in a Winter Paradise (Romance)

Athena Lightwood

Prologue

It's a beautiful autumn day with leaves turning brown and trees nearly bare.

'I am, Iris Anderson: married to my husband for five and a half years.

'I am Leo Anderson; a father and husband, and together, we have a five-year-old daughter named Freya.'

"Where should we go on vacation?"

"I don't mind where we go."

"I think you should choose the destination."

"May I suggest somewhere like Paris?"

"Yes, I would love to spend Christmas in Paris."

"I want to play with you, please."

Yes, of course, darling. I'd love to play with you. What should we play?"

"I want to play with my dolls with you."

I spent the rest of the afternoon with my daughter. Later that evening, I looked over the city of Amores and the distant mountains, which seemed to pulse with life.

Chapter one

It's nearly the end of November, and I'm genuinely concerned about how our daughter will cope with the flight.

But there's nothing to stress over — you'll be with her. Iris, you're a wonderful mum to our daughter, he told me.

I thanked him, saying I would try my best. where are we going on vacation? Paris. I'd like you and Freya to travel separately from me, just in case anything happens.

'I, get your point, but I wish we didn't have to do all that. I'm worried she's still a bit too young to go abroad. Iris, that's why we're not flying together — to protect you from any potential danger. The next day, we head to the private airport, we arrived about twenty minutes later, all three of us in the same car.

I was the first to get out, and I immediately saw someone step out of the other car — it was Bella, my best friend. I was like, "What the hell are you doing here?" she said, she'd always dreamed about going to Paris and so, she decided to hijack my private jet.

I rolled my eyes sarcastically, teasing her about wanting to have a date night with Leonardo and me without Freya. She was happy to babysit, saying she loved taking care of our girl, and Leo and I deserved some alone time.

I've heard Paris called the city of romance, especially around Christmas when snowflakes start falling. No two snowflakes are alike, just like people.

I think we're all unique in our own way; if we weren't, the world would be pretty boring. But life's chaos means nothing stays the same.

When the plane is landing, I hope this trip turns out amazing. As the jet doors open, I notice it's pretty chilly and snowing heavily — we're the last flight to land before a big snowstorm. After a few days in France, we settled into our hotel penthouse. Freya's playing with Bella, or as she calls her, "auntie" which is absolutely adorable.

I decide to spend some time with Leonardo and go out exploring Paris during the snowstorm. We make sure we're dressed warmly, and Bella and Freya stay cosy at the hotel. Iris, what should we do? I suggest we go to the Eiffel Tower and see the light show every night. We agree and choose to walk through the snow instead of taking a taxi.

It really is so beautiful…Now it's mid-December, and two weeks have flown by. For our last night, we're having dinner at a restaurant in the Eiffel Tower. The view looks like a snow globe; the smell of cinnamon fills the air, making everything feel even more festive.

When the waiter asks if we're ready to order, I say yes, I hadn't realised he was there. I said, like second-nature, I want a slice of pineapple on my pizza, a medium-rare steak, and a glass of white wine."

Leonardo orders the same, but instead of wine, he decides to have a glass of Irish whiskey. I ask if whiskey is what he's been dreaming of for our date. Suddenly, an announcement over the speaker interrupts us — something about snowstorms.

The waiter says the Eiffel Tower is closed because of the heavy snow outside, and it's unsafe. Weirdly, we're the only ones in the whole restaurant. I'm constantly worried about Freya. He reassures me that she's safe and well with Bella.

I call Bella, as the thought of not knowing Freya knew where we were, haunted me, telling her we're stuck at the Eiffel Tower.

I step away from Leo; sometimes he just doesn't understand why I worry so much. Bella promises that she'll explain the situation to Freya and reassures me that it will be okay…honestly I wonder where I'd be without her. I ask how our little girl is doing and Bella replies, saying

"She's playing with her Barbies in the penthouse living room, as per usual." She chuckles as I tell her to say goodnight for me and remind Freya how much we love her, even when we're away. I know Leo would just say that I was being theatrical, and maybe I am but I just can't stop that doom-filled feeling that overtakes me.

Chapter two

As I sat on the phone with Iris, I asked her, "Do you want to talk to Freya?" She replied shakily "Yeah, I want to talk to Freya, please."

Freya, smart as always, figures I'm speaking to her mum and asks "Why aren't my mummy and daddy back home? What do you think the mummy might be saying?

I explained, "Sweetie, your dad and mummy are stuck in the middle of a heavy snowstorm, Mummy was just telling me, she would like to speak to you."

Freya suddenly reaches for the phone in my hand, eagerly saying, "I want to talk to Mummy right now!"

I responded quickly, chuckling a little. Okay, give me a minute…Your little girl is eager to talk to you."

Iris quickly says, "Yes, please just put her on immediately."

Freya took the phone and said excitedly, "Hi, mummy! Why aren't you and Daddy home yet? Auntie Bella and you, said that you would be home soon. It's soon now, why aren't you back? Barbies are boring without you…"

Iris, with a calming tone, said, "Sweetie, there was a snowstorm earlier, and we are now stuck here. But you don't have to worry about me or daddy; it's getting pretty late for your bedtime already.

I love you, Freya, to the universe and back.

Before Freya could hang up, Iris asked, "Can you please put Auntie Bella back on the phone?" Freya responded, "Okay."

'Iris then said, "Goodnight, my love." Now, back on the phone, Iris said, "Please keep her safe, and happy." I could tell she was worked up, she never handles being away from Freya unexpectedly well.

She thanked me profusely, whilst still reminding me to keep Freya safe.

"Iris, listen to me, I have got Freya, she is safe and I promise, nothing will happen… Okay?"

Iris replied, "I know… I worry, I should go now, Leo is probably looking for me. Thank you, Bella, seriously."

Chapter three

After Bella hung up, I went back to Leo. He was waiting in the corridor, "Hey, I take it Freya is okay." He smiled and I smiled back, I wish I wasn't so worried but I can't help it. "Yeah, she's good… I know you just think it's me being crazy but like, I just can't help it, He took my hand and brought me closer into a hug.

"You don't need to explain yourself, I get that I go on about your worrying but I do admire how much you care, about her.

I looked up at him and smiled, a genuine smile, "Thank you, Leo, that truly means a lot."

He then started moving us together, he drew his hand away from me and opened a bathroom door that I hadn't even noticed was there, "Shall we? A distraction to pass the time, like old times.

'I, nodded, despite my overwhelming concern for Freya, Leo never seemed able to fail at making something good out of a situation. As we moved into the small bathroom, he started kissing me, his lips soft and his cologne filling the air, I nudged my face into his suit.

The door shut behind us, clicking as it was locked, was the start of a brilliant night.

I gently placed my arm around his shoulder, and as he looked into my green eyes, he softly said, "I know, having sex in the bathroom isn't the most romantic place."

I understand that this room is the only place where we can truly be alone. I want you to feel special, as if you are the only one who knows all my secrets. I care about you deeply and wish I could give you everything in this world.

Early the next morning, we finally managed to leave the Eiffel Tower.

I was relieved to finally put that experience behind me, although I couldn't lie, the night wasn't bad.

It felt more like something out of a Hallmark Christmas movie rather than a romantic dinner with my husband. Now I can finally see our daughter, Freya.

I never want to go on a date in a snowstorm again! We walked back to the hotel, grateful that I had a coat to keep me warm. When we entered the penthouse, Freya hurried over to me excitedly, "Mummy, you're home!" I opened my arms to embrace her, and she hugged me so tightly that she didn't even look at her daddy.

Leo gently said, "Hey, my darling Freya. I'm sorry it took all night to come back home.

"It's fine Daddy, I knew you and Mummy would always be back."

I turned to Bella and said, "Thank you for taking such good care of my little girl." She smiled warmly and replied, "Anytime you need, I could see on her face that she was hesitating, wanting to say something but she didn't. I suppose even she noticed my concern last night. She then mentioned to me, "It's been a long and eventful night, for everyone. I gotta head out now, I have to be at work in a few hours."

I spent the rest of the evening playing games with Freya—first UNO, then playing with her dolls. As bedtime approached, I gently said, "Freya, it's almost time for bed, I'll come read you a story." She looked up at me curiously and asked, "Why do I have to go to bed now?" I softly replied, "Honey, you need your sleep to grow into a beautiful young girl someday."

I told her I would go brush my teeth, and while she was doing that, I picked out her favourite bedtime story—The Princess and the Pea.

After reading her the story and tucking her into bed, I kissed her cheek and whispered, "Goodnight, I love you, sweetie."

Then Leo, in a low, almost whispering voice, asked, "Do you want to watch a Christmas movie?" I nodded happily and asked, "Can we have some chocolate popcorn and Bailey's, hot chocolate, please?"

He smiled and said, "Anything else?" I said no that's all. We ordered room service, which arrived after about twenty minutes. I cuddled under the covers with Leo, he asked, "What movie do you want to watch?" I paused for a moment, then replied, "Love Actually—the perfect choice for tonight."

As I wrapped my arms around Leo, he whispered, "I could stay in this room as long as I have you by my side because, Iris, you are my whole universe...the stars dance when I'm with you."

After the movie, I fell asleep peacefully in his arms, feeling safe and loved. The next morning, I woke up beside Leo, how incredibly fortunate I am to be married to my wonderful husband and mother to our beautiful daughter.

Later, I heard a knock on the hotel door. I opened it to find Derek Whitehouse, a dear friend, whom I had invited. Freya was there, curious as ever, "Who is this, mummy?" she asked curiously. I reassured her, "Oh honey, he's one of mummy and daddy's friends—like your Auntie Bella, who's your mommy's best friend."

I then called Bella, asking if she could take Freya out for a little while. Bella replied saying it was alright and was over within the next 20 minutes. I appreciated Bella's help and support, especially because Freya never left my side unless it was with her, and sometimes even I need privacy.

Chapter four: Derek and Iris

After Iris' friend, Bella, had been and left with Freya, I tenderly said, "I don't know what to say, Iris but I am getting divorced from the woman I truly love and care about with my whole heart." I sighed, although it felt so wrong, I knew talking to someone was ultimately my best choice.

Iris says simply in her gentle voice."Sometimes the best way to love is to let her go." Hearing this, I started to cry; tears welling up in my eyes were streaming down my face as I tried to cover it with my trembling hands. It feels as if my whole world is falling apart, and the tears seem endless. I am deeply heartbroken, and as much as I wanted to run, I knew losing her would kill me if I didn't get help.

The lawyer called me to inform me that my wife wanted a divorce, after hearing nothing for ages and has already signed the divorce papers via email, which she forwarded to me. I find myself unable to look at the email right away; my mind is overwhelmed.

My heart feels like it's being physically torn apart. I have been married to my wife for two years, a time filled with ups and downs, shared hopes, and dreams for the future until she disappeared, left with no word and it hurt because she chose to file for divorce just before Christmas, a time traditionally associated with joy and togetherness, but more so because of the promises of a long-lasting life spent together that we were going to have.

I sat there, the world spiralling around me. I knew when I eventually signed the documents, I'd be a free man with a whole new chapter; a chapter filled with finding myself again, and getting over Harley, whilst also focusing on my work.

A while later, with the support of Iris and Leonardo, I'd signed the paperwork and was officially sent to the lawyer. The signing was just the beginning, there was so, so much more to unpack from here, and I had to manage it all while trying to stay afloat and not lose myself. Sometimes I wish I couldn't feel, I loved Harley, more than life and I had nothing else going for me but her, without her I have no purpose and no hope.

Chapter Five

'I watched discreetly as Derek signed the paperwork, I'd never seen him so distraught. Harley was his life and almost everything he did was for her, his heart beat for her and honestly, losing her might be the one thing that truly breaks that man.

I've known him for a while, nothing stopped his stride, he was as strong as iron and wasn't known for breaking, however the man I see before me is not derek, it's the empty shell of the man he was before losing that woman.

'I said to him, "You should stay with us over Christmas, it's the least we can do and honestly, you shouldn't be by yourself during this...We know you haven't really got anywhere else to go.

Derek slight with smile and I politely refused, Leo moved from my side and sat by him, saying, "Please, stay. It's honestly not a problem, you need people, people you need people. Especially at Christmas, it's no time for someone to be alone; especially not alone and broken."

Chapter Six

By 5pm, Bella and Freya had returned from playing outside in the snow. I asked, smiling as they took off their coats, "Did you two have fun?"

"Yes," Freya says sarcastically, with a playful smirk, as if she's trying to hide her feelings.

I wondered why she's always so full of sarcasm.

Before I could ponder a response, Bella said, "That kid is very clever... She was asking about divorce, and why Derek was going through one. She really doesn't miss a beat, does she?" Bella chuckled it off, then said a brief goodbye before leaving.

Freya came up to me and asked, "What is a divorce? Auntie Bella said you knew."

I sat her on my lap and started to explain, "So, you know how and Daddy I are married, and have been since before you were even born."

"Yeah... Because you guys were in love,"

I carried on, jokingly raising an eyebrow at her comment, "Yes, well, sometimes a Mummy and Daddy realise they don't like each other, and so living together becomes really hard because if you don't like someone, it's hard to share and be around each other."

"So, like when you don't like a classmate and like, you stay away from them to stop being annoyed." She said inquisitively, probably thinking of some arch-nemesis in her pre-school class.

"Yeah, exactly like that, when you're married, there's a piece of paper that says you're married and therefore should live together, to stop being together all the time, you have to sign more paper that says you're not married. That's a divorce. Does that make sense?"

She sat for a moment, then asked, "What will we do, together... not divorced, for Christmas?"

I giggled at her comment, then said, "Well, Derek is staying so perhaps we could all play a game or go for a walk after presents, then obviously have our amazing Christmas dinner. That sound good enough for you?"

"Yeah, I think so." She replied. I started tickling her and she fell into a fit of laughter, not much beats hearing her sweet little laugh.

Chapter Seven

Three days later

It's finally Christmas Eve and Freya is super excited about our holiday traditions. I always watch 'Home Alone' on Christmas Eve with my favourite hot chocolate.

I'm so excited to pass down the Christmas spirit to my daughter on her fifth Christmas Eve.

I remember when I was her age, waking up early on Christmas morning and waking everyone up My mum wasn't thrilled about that. Anyway, Iris, stop reminiscing! Freya walks into our hotel room, climbs onto the bed, and snuggles between us.

I announced to everyone. 'Let's watch Home Alone first.' The movie starts, and I love spending time with Leo and Freya — it's honestly my favourite part of Christmas.

Chapter Eight

Iris said that I should try and connect with people, so she said that I should go out for coffee with her friend, Bella. I then started planning to ask Bella out for coffee — just as friends.

It's only been a few days since the divorce. I casually approach Bella and say, 'I know it's Christmas Eve, but it's not too late for a quick coffee?' She agrees, 'Yeah, I'd love that.' I grab my coat and boots quickly.

I opened the door and, like a gentleman, says, 'Ladies first.' Bella thank me, and we leave the hotel, walking through a beautiful, snow-covered Paris, lights everywhere, like something out of a holiday story. I watch her as we exit the building, she is rather beautiful.

Then I kissed her...

That stupid kiss I gave her? Totally out of the blue. I apologised, telling her I couldn't help it because I desire her so much.

Bella looks surprised and walks away, saying, 'Seriously, Derek? No kissing your friends, I get your all screwed up in your Divorce and life, but get some actual help instead of throwing yourself at people."

I realise I messed up, especially on Christmas Eve.

I ask if I can walk her back to her hotel, and she agrees. I say good night, wishing her Merry Christmas, and finally breathe after that chaos. I don't understand why I kissed her — I'm freshly divorced, she's amazing, but I should really take some time to find myself again.

Chapter nine: The ending

The next day, Freya wakes me up shouting, 'It's Christmas, I want my presents!' I tell her she can wait until I make my coffee.

Once I do, she happily opens her gifts, then Leo walks in, turns on the fireplace, and takes his seat next to me. I watch Freya's face light up, and I look into her deep blue eyes — same as Leo's, she does have my hair and my smile, I think she's beautiful.

Leo surprises me with a gold heart necklace, and I gave him a special diamond watch. Lunch rolls around, and we agree to eat in the hotel room, a proper roast dinner.

Bella joins us, and we chat about Christmas memories. Freya asks if she can go play with her toys, and I tell her yes.

Then I notice Bella and Derek acting kinda weird — she says Derek kissed her, which isn't like him, and I just walk off. I told him I already apologised and asked him to drop it, but I'm not in the mood to argue, especially not on Christmas.

Later, we all head to the rooftop to watch the fireworks over Paris, snow falling, stars shining, and the city glowing. It's honestly one of the most perfect Christmas nights. I kiss my husband, feeling so grateful for this trip.

I tell Bella and Iris that maybe one day she'll find her own love story.

 I'm not sure what's next, I leave that up to the universe. Bella, maybe someday you'll get your fairy tale too. Whatever happens, I believe in the magic of the season.

Friends, family, loved ones — just like snowflakes, we're all different and a little weird. Even in difficult times, remember that there's always a glimmer of hope and light at the end of the tunnel to help you through.

15
Snowflakes and Second Chances
Simone Sumner

Chapter One

Maplewood smelled like cinnamon, pine, and fresh snow. Twinkle lights wrapped every storefront, the lampposts wore little red bows, and the scent of roasting chestnuts mingled with the warm steam of cocoa carts. The town square was alive with laughter, music, and the crunch of boots on freshly shoveled sidewalks. Winterfest had arrived, and I was determined to survive it without losing my sanity—or my dignity.

"Cookies, everyone! Fresh gingerbread and chocolate-chip chaos!" I called, hustling trays toward the event booth. My scarf was slightly crooked, my cheeks flushed pink, and my boots dusted with snow. Controlled chaos was kind of my brand.

"Piper, careful!" Marcy shouted as I sidestepped a toddler in a snowman onesie. "You're going to topple the whole tower!"

"I thrive under pressure," I said, rolling my eyes. I stacked the last tray, thinking I was finally in the clear—until I saw him.

Ethan Blake.

He was leaning against the railing by the fountain, casually inspecting a string of lights, hands shoved in the pockets of a leather jacket that somehow still looked rugged after ten years. That same crooked smile. That same mischievous gleam in his eyes. My stomach did a very undignified flip.

I froze. Gingerbread tray poised in midair. My mouth opened, and nothing came out.

"Need a hand?" he asked, his deep voice beside me. I jumped, nearly dropping the cookies, as he caught the wobbling tower with one hand.

"Uh—thanks," I stammered, snapping out of it. "I didn't mean to—"

"Relax. I've got you," he said, setting the tray down safely. "Just here for the holidays," he added casually, like that explained everything.

I arched an eyebrow, lips twitching into a smirk I didn't mean to. "Right. A decade-long disappearance, a failed music career, and now—'just for the holidays.' Very subtle, Ethan."

"Still got that sharp tongue," he said, grinning. "Some things don't change."

My heart thudded painfully, but I squared my shoulders. "Neither does mine," I said, brushing imaginary crumbs off my apron. "Now, if you'll excuse me, I have cookies to manage, and you have...whatever it is you're doing."

"Watching the mayhem," he said with a mock bow. "It's a talent, really."

I rolled my eyes and moved toward the front of the booth, determined to avoid the flutters of old feelings and the warmth creeping back into my chest. I'd survived ten years without him. Surely I could survive a few hours of Winterfest.

That was until the mayor—bless her meddling heart—stepped onto the stage, microphone in hand.

"And now, folks!" she boomed, eyes twinkling like a Christmas tree herself. "This year's Winterfest scavenger hunt will be hosted by none other than...Maplewood's own Piper Lane and Ethan Blake!"

My jaw dropped. Ethan's eyebrows shot up, and the corners of his mouth twitched with a grin that suggested he already knew how I felt.

"Oh, perfect," I muttered under my breath. "Holiday chaos, cookie crumbs, and my ex...all in one festive package. This is going to be fun."

Ethan leaned closer, voice low. "See? I'm not completely useless."

I swatted his arm, trying not to smile. "Try harder."

And just like that, the Winterfest magic—and trouble—had officially begun.

Chapter Two

The hardware store was quieter than usual after hours, the fluorescent lights humming softly above us. I shivered despite my coat, wishing I'd worn something warmer than this thin sweater. Ethan, of course, looked entirely too comfortable, propped against a shelf with his hands in his pockets like he owned the place—which, technically, he didn't.

"Okay," I said, spreading the scavenger hunt clues across the counter. "We need to make these challenging but not impossible. Last year, people spent twenty minutes trying to find the giant candy cane. It was—I glanced at him, "Ridiculous."

"Challenging but not impossible," he repeated, glancing over to inspect the papers. "Got it. You know, you've always been a little bossy."

I shot him a look. "And you've always been annoyingly smug."

He grinned. "So, nothing's changed. I like consistency."

I rolled my eyes. "Yeah, well, I prefer people who don't run when things get hard."

His grin faltered. "That's—" he paused, running a hand through his hair. "That's unfair."

I raised an eyebrow. "Oh? Or maybe it's just accurate."

He sighed, shoulders stiff. "Look, I didn't just...vanish for no reason."

I stared at him, all the old hurt rising like bitter steam. "Then what reason? You left without a word. Ten years. Just—gone."

He hesitated, glancing at the floor, then back at me. "I left to chase a music production dream. It...it crashed. Badly. And I didn't know how to tell you without making things worse."

I bit my lip, trying to hold back the mix of anger and residual longing. "Making things worse? You think ghosting someone you supposedly cared about counts as 'making things worse'?"

He winced. "Yeah. I messed up. Big time."

The silence stretched, heavy with unsaid words. I wanted to shove him out the door, but a part of me still remembered why I fell for him in the first place.

Then came the unmistakable creak of the hardware store door, and I groaned.

"Mrs. Harper," I muttered under my breath.

She stepped inside, eyes sparkling like she knew all the town's secrets—and had the intention of revealing every single one. "Oh, look at you two!" she chirped, pointing above our heads. "Mistletoe! How festive!"

I glanced up. Sure enough, a sprig of greenery dangled from the rafters, perfectly centered above the counter. My stomach flipped.

Ethan's mouth twitched. "Well...this is awkward."

"Yeah, no kidding," I said, stepping back slightly.

Mrs. Harper clapped her hands. "A little holiday cheer! Don't make me leave without seeing a kiss!"

I groaned again, wishing she'd just disappear. Ethan shifted, pretending to examine a random shelf while I tried to focus on the scavenger hunt clues.

Neither of us moved toward the other, yet the tension in the small space was electric. A beat too long, a breath too close. And then Mrs. Harper finally wandered off, satisfied she'd stirred enough trouble for one night.

I exhaled shakily, keeping my eyes on the counter. "We—uh—we should probably...keep working."

"Yeah," he said softly, his voice lower now. "Keep working."

We bent over the clues together, close but not touching, each of us pretending the mistletoe—or the history between us—didn't exist. But I could feel it.

And I hated that I could feel it.

Chapter Three

The next few days were a whirlwind of holiday chaos. Ethan and I were everywhere at once—at least, it felt that way.

Decorating the massive town Christmas tree was our first "official" task. He insisted on stringing the lights himself, claiming he had "an eye for symmetry." I rolled my eyes, tucking my hands into my coat pockets as he climbed the ladder like he owned the place. "You're going to electrocute yourself," I warned.

"I've survived ten years in L.A., Piper. I think I can handle a few strings of lights," he replied without looking down.

Later, a spontaneous snowball fight erupted when I was delivering hot cocoa to the kids on the square. It started small—just a soft toss from him, which I returned with a perfect underhanded fling. By the time Marcy and half the town joined in, we were slipping in snow, laughing so hard my cheeks hurt, and ignoring every adult decency rule I'd ever had.

Even judging the ugly sweater contest couldn't dampen the playful tension. Ethan wiggled his eyebrows at the particularly garish tree-sweater combination of a participant, and I elbowed him. "Seriously, you're too old for this," I said.

"Never too old for Christmas mischief," he shot back.

That night, after the square had emptied and the lights were twinkling against the dark sky, I locked up the bakery and found Ethan crouched outside, adjusting a string of malfunctioning lights above the door.

"Can't let my favorite bakery look sad on the main street," he said, standing and brushing snow off his jacket.

I leaned against the doorframe, pretending to be casual. "You're like some sort of holiday superhero, aren't you?"

"Maybe," he said, tilting his head. "Or maybe I just like being around things—and people—that feel like home."

I blinked, caught off guard by the vulnerability in his voice. "Maplewood doesn't exactly need me to remind it it's home," I said softly, trying to keep my guard up.

"No, not the town," he said, taking a slow step closer. "You."

I shook my head, forcing my focus elsewhere. "Ethan...don't."

He chuckled, low and knowing, but didn't move closer. "I didn't say anything. Just stating facts."

The old pull—the one I'd tried to bury for ten years—twisted in my chest. I wanted to lean into him, to let him prove that maybe he had changed. But I remembered the voicemail, the sudden disappearance, the heartbreak I'd nursed quietly for a decade.

So I hugged my coat tighter, smiled a little too stiffly, and said, "Well...the bakery looks great. Lights are perfect. You did good."

"Thanks," he murmured, his eyes holding mine a second too long before he finally walked down the sidewalk, leaving me with the soft glow of Christmas lights and a heart that refused to stay put.

Maplewood was magic, all right. But it wasn't just the town. It was him.

Chapter Four

I was halfway down Main Street, carrying a tray of peppermint bark to the Winterfest stage, when I heard his voice.

"...Yeah, I'll be back in L.A. by New Year's," Ethan said, low and casual over the phone.

I froze, my stomach dropping into the snow-dusted sidewalk. Back to L.A.? Already? Just when I'd started letting him back in, just when Maplewood—maybe even I—had started to feel like home again.

I didn't hear the part about him declining the job, about him staying in town for the sugar mill. My ears only heard the betrayal. The heartbreak. The old wound ripped open again, raw and furious.

I slammed the tray onto a nearby counter inside a coffee cart, fuming. "Figures," I muttered to myself. "You never change."

Ethan rounded the corner moments later, his phone still pressed to his ear. He saw me, and his face fell. "Piper—wait. I can explain—"

"Don't," I snapped, brushing past him. My hands were shaking—not from the cold, but from anger, disappointment, and that familiar ache I'd tried to bury for ten years. "I just...I can't. Not tonight."

He tried to reach for my arm, but I jerked away. "Piper, listen—"

"No," I said, sharper than I intended. "I heard what I needed to hear. You're leaving. Again. Have fun with your New Year's in L.A., Ethan."

He froze, confusion and panic crossing his face. "Piper, that's not—"

I turned and walked away, the festive lights and laughter of Winterfest blurring into a haze. My heart felt heavier than it had in years.

All the while, I knew he didn't deserve my fury—but right now, I couldn't bring myself to care. I couldn't watch him walk away again.

Later that night, I watched the Winterfest stage from a distance, choosing the shadows over the crowd. The town cheered, music swelled, and I stayed silent, pretending I was fine.

Ethan lingered near the stage, phone pressed to his ear again, jaw tight. I saw him glance at me once, his expression breaking in a way that made my chest ache even more. He realized I'd misunderstood, but he couldn't exactly run over and fix it—not without spoiling the surprise he'd been planning.

So we stood there—two people who should have been together—separated by a single phone call, stubbornness, and a history that refused to stay buried.

I bit my lip, shivering in the cold, and told myself I was protecting my heart. But deep down, I knew I'd never be able to fully protect it from him.

Chapter Five

I stood at the edge of the town square, hands stuffed deep into my coat pockets, scarf pulled tight around my neck. Snow fell in soft, steady flurries, dusting the twinkling lights on the massive Christmas tree at the center of the square. The crowd buzzed with excitement—children tugging at parents' hands, couples leaning close over steaming mugs of cocoa, friends swapping laughter and holiday gossip.

Me? I was trying very hard to stay invisible. I wanted to hide in the shadows, ignore the fluttering in my chest, and pretend like Ethan Blake didn't exist. But then I heard the familiar scrape of boots against snow and the low, unmistakable hum of his voice.

"Maplewood," Ethan said into the microphone, his tone firm yet warm. "There's nothing like coming home. This town...it's magic. And I've realized something. I don't just want to visit—I want to stay."

I froze. My breath caught in my chest. Stay?

"I've bought the old maple sugar mill," he continued, eyes sweeping the crowd until they landed on me. My pulse spiked, my heart skipping a beat. "It's going to be my home...and if you'll let me, I'd like to make it ours."

A hush fell over the square, broken only by the soft crunch of snow beneath boots and the distant jingle of holiday music. My cheeks burned, hot and cold at the same time, as disbelief collided with hope.

"And to Piper Lane," he said, lowering his voice so only I could hear, "I'm sorry. I'm sorry for leaving, for hurting you, for all the years of silence. I never stopped thinking about you, and I hope you can forgive me."

The ache of old pain, the sting of heartbreak I'd carried for ten years, and the warmth of something new swirled together in my chest. I wanted to run into his arms, but first...I had to get a little revenge.

I scooped up a handful of snow and hurled it at him.

"Hey!" he laughed, dodging just in time as the crowd erupted in delighted cheers.

"Oh, it's on!" I shouted, racing him around the square, dodging between cocoa carts and laughter-filled children. We slipped, slid, and collapsed into heaps of snow, laughing so hard that our cheeks hurt. The townspeople clapped, whistled, and cheered. For a moment, it was just us, all the tension of years melting away in the cold night air.

Finally, out of breath and grinning like idiots, we stumbled under the mistletoe hanging above the fountain. His eyes softened, searching mine. My chest tightened, and I knew I couldn't fight it any longer.

I tipped onto my toes and kissed him—softly at first, savoring the familiarity, then deeper, letting everything I'd held back for a decade spill out in that one moment. His hands found my waist, pulling me close, and I melted against him as the snow swirled around us.

When we finally pulled apart, faces flushed and breaths misting in the cold, he rested his forehead against mine. "Maplewood, the lights, the snow... it's all better with you," he murmured.

I smirked, brushing snowflakes from his jacket. "You really are impossible, you know that?"

"Yeah," he grinned, pressing a quick kiss to my temple. "But worth it."

We lingered there for a moment, letting the festive chaos swirl around us—the glow of the tree, the smell of cocoa, the laughter and cheers of neighbors and friends. Then I took his hand, letting him pull me through the square, warm against the winter chill.

At the edge of the fountain, he paused, pulling me close once more. "So...second chance?" he asked, his voice teasing, but there was something tender underneath.

I laughed softly, shaking my head. "Only if you promise not to disappear again."

"I promise," he said, his grin turning mischievous again. "But if I ever try to run, you have full rights to pelt me with snowballs—year-round."

I laughed, the sound echoing through the sparkling square. "Deal."

Hand in hand, we walked through the glowing streets of Maplewood. The lights reflected in his eyes, making him look ten feet taller, a little magical. And for the first time in years, I felt at home—not just in the town I loved, but with the person I never stopped wanting beside me.

Maplewood shimmered around us, alive with warmth, laughter, and holiday magic. And so did we.

16

Miss Tilly Rae Excerpt

KF Thérèse

Boone shivered miserably. Finally, the train station appeared in sight but it felt like the horse was trotting at a snail's pace.

"A ... almost there ... So ... sorry, it's a bit mi ... miserable" Dale forced a grin, both shivering, sitting side by side.

"Th ... the sh ... shit we d-do for love I g ... guess," Boone muttered, shoving his head down into the neck of his jacket.

"I re ... reckon that's the first I've heard you swear in t ... two weeks," Dale laughed, though he immediately regretted the sharp intake of cold air.

The horse finally broke into a full gallop when the lights of the station came into view. Dale figured the horse must be just as desperate for a warm stall as they were for a warm train car.

"Y ... yeah, well ... Tilly ma ... maybe mentioned my f ... foul mouth once or twice," Boone grinned to himself as he squeezed farther into his jacket.

"*Of course* she did," Dale barked out another laugh.

"Tell me more about th ... that Mark fella. Tilly sh ... sure went on how he saved the day," Boone huffed.

"Aw, a ... aint much to say. Just a wallflower. Always been keen on Delilah and a real silent type. When you and Delilah were together there, boy he were one sad sack. Saw him a f ... few times in town, moping like a kicked pup."

"Who could be fond of Delilah?" Boone wondered out loud.

"You certainly were," Dale tutted.

"Yeah, because she was easy," Boone shrugged, which gained him a swift smack upside the head.

"Hey!" Boone retorted, too cold to take his hands out from under the blankets and rub his sore head.

"You know better than to talk about a woman like that. Didn't yer daddy ever teach you nothin'?" Dale grumped.

"My daddy were a worthless sack of shit ... he taught me how to be just like him," Boone grumbled bitterly.

Regretting his words immediately, Dale frowned deeply, struggling to find a way to apologize, but it never came. They carried on the ride in strained silence, both equally eager to leap down and get their horse stabled for the next two nights before rushing into the warm train station.

It felt like the heat might never return to Boone's body. Curled up right beside one of the several blazing wood stoves in the station, they waited for the midnight train. One of the station attendants took pity on the frozen pair, bringing two cups of coffee over to where Dale sat, looking at Boone curled up with his head tucked into the jacket and arms wrapped around his knees.

"You two were fools to ride after the sun went down, on a wagon no less!" the attendant chuckled.

"*Fools* is certainly a word for us. Much obliged," Dale said, sipping the coffee gratefully before getting up to pass Boone his.

Dale knelt down, giving Boone a little nudge.

"Here, this should help," he hummed quietly.

"Thanks," Boone muttered, taking the cup and holding it tight in both hands.

"About before ..."

"Don't mention it. I shouldn't have snapped like I did," Boone sighed.

"Naw, lemme talk, Boone. I want you to know you ain't nothin' like your daddy. You are workin' hard to change, and that's somethin' that man ain't ever gonna do if he is still out there. You're a good man, Boone. I wouldn't keep you 'round my boy if I thought otherwise."

"Thanks, Dale," Boone said in a small voice, looking a little shocked.

"I mean it, Boone … Aw, hell!" Dale sighed, sitting down next to him with a groan and smirking.

"Gettin' too old for these floor chats, even with Jackson. Listen, you've been with me through the worst days of my life. You've taken on mindin' Jackson with me without even so much as me askin' …"

"I love that kid like he were my own. You ain't ever gotta ask me."

"I *know that*, believe me. I see it in how you fuss over him, how riled up you get over them boys pickin' on him. I *appreciate* it more than I could ever say. It ain't easy doin' this alone. I ain't got his momma to help me, to be kind and patient with him in ways I just … " he sighed, rubbing his eyes to hide the tears in them. "I ain't ever gonna be enough to replace her. He misses her every day, but it makes this a little easier knowin' I got you keepin' an eye out for him. And I ain't ever seen you act so mature as you have since you met Matilda. You've changed. You've *grown up*. Jackson and I are all alone in this world now. I'm sure he appreciates havin' an *Uncle* … I know I sure appreciate havin' a *brother* now."

Boone quickly looked away, concealing the tears in his eyes as he cleared his throat and elbowed Dale.

"Would you quit it? You're gonna make me get all sentimental," he croaked, sniffing loudly.

Dale half laughed, leaning back against the wall. "Too late for that, I'm afraid."

The pair appreciated the three-hour train ride. Within minutes, they were out like a light, snoring away. If there were ever a pair of brothers, those two certainly acted like it. Both were equally disappointed when the attendant came by and jostled them, and their train nap came to a halt.

"This is your stop, fellas. Up you get!"

Groggy and a little disoriented, the two lazily yawned, rubbing their eyes, and stepped off the train onto the bustling platform. Piles of beast-men crowded to board the train, and they ended up on the main line. Obviously, a pair of country bumpkins to this jostling crowd suddenly awoken and grimacing back at the crowded station, they fled the dizzying platform.

"Why do we do this every year again?" Dale complained, rubbing his stiff neck as he scanned over the map posted outside the station.

Boone sighed, smiling roguishly as he nudged Dale. "Because our town ain't got much of anything for Jackson or ladies who deserve nice things." Glancing up, he followed Boone's nod toward a group of frocked-out women in silk skirts and fur coats. "Sure don't make 'em like that back home," Boone chuckled, hooking his fingers in his mouth and letting out a shrill whistle.

"Would you grow up?" Dale forced a frown, chuckling to himself inside.

"What? I can admire beauty. Ain't that what fancy city folk call it?" Boone laughed, giving a wave to the women now whispering and giggling.

"Usually, people admire beauty in art galleries or out in fancy city gardens, not a group of blushing girls hardly old enough to even look at. C'mon, you old dog," Dale mused, grabbing Boone's ear and tugging him along behind him.

"Yowch! Okay, okay! Don't tear my dang ear off!" Boone lamented, following obediently.

Matilda and Jackson were awake for a while. Jackson was playing with his wooden soldiers while Matilda made pancakes. Humming to herself, she smiled over her shoulder at Jackson who was mumbling to himself in his game.

"Blueberries or brown sugar in your pancakes, Jackie?"

"Blueberries, please, Miss Matilda," Jackson chanted, trying to stack two toy soldiers on top of his little wooden horse.

"What would you like to do today?" she asked, sprinkling blueberries onto the pancake in her skillet.

"Can we build a snow fort? This time, no one will jump on top of it," Jackson asserted.

"We could do that. Maybe I can make some drinking chocolate for us, too."

"Really?! Daddy never makes drinkin' chocolate anymore!"

"Oh? Why doesn't he make it anymore?" Matilda asked, glancing over her shoulder.

Jackson's face fell, his ears drooping as he fiddled with his little wooden soldiers.

"It was my Momma's favourite."

Matilda quickly plated up their breakfast, setting a mound of pancakes in before him and pushing a smile as she sat across from him.

"It sounds like you both miss her very much, but you know something? Sometimes little reminders like drinking chocolate or blue ribbons can make us feel peaceful in their memories."

Jackson tilted his head. "Blue ribbons?"

Touching her throat, she traced her fingers along the blue ribbon choker that never seemed to leave her neck.

"This belonged to my mother. She and my father are both in heaven now." Matilda said with misty eyes and a lump obstructing her throat.

"I wonder if they met my Momma," Jackson whimpered, poking at his pancakes.

Suddenly, Matilda stood up and walked over to the cupboard, where she found a few bits of baking supplies. Her eyes fell on a large bottle of maple syrup, a sigh of relief escaping her. Before pouring some on her serving, a generous amount of delicious sweetness found its way over Jackson's pancakes. His face lit up, eyes wide at the pool of syrup oozing on his plate.

"I can *really* have this much?" he giggled.

"Just don't tell on me," Matilda giggled back, bringing a finger to her lips.

Syrup-dripped chin and nightshirt, Jackson was. Matilda made a mental note to wash the evidence of mischief before Dale returned, but the delight on little Jack's face was worth the trouble.

"Daddy said I might get an Auntie soon," Jackson said offhand, not realizing the absolute magnitude of what he had just revealed.

"Pa-pardon me?" Matilda nearly choked on her coffee.

"He said him and Uncle Boone are going into town for somethin' special, somethin' that might get me an Auntie soon. I didn't know my Daddy had a sister," Jackson chattered innocently, as his poor teacher's heart felt as if it might break out of her chest.

Was Boone going to propose?

Satisfied with the toys he had picked out for Jackson, Dale's eyes lit up thinking about the little one's reaction to the collection of tin cars and tractors, a jack-in-the-box, a new bag of marbles and a hobby horse with a wheel on the end so he could run around with it. Boone had even gotten him a new set of jacks and a deck of brightly coloured playing cards. His 'big' plan was to teach Jackson how to be the best card player in town by the time he was eight. Dale wasn't sure if to laugh or scold Boone, but he couldn't bring himself to rain on his parade. It was mid-afternoon, and the two men were still picking their teeth from lunch as they ambled down one of the bustling streets.

"What's next?" Boone asked, glancing over at Dale's list.

Dale grinned down at the note as he skimmed it. "Gotta pick up this list of books for Matilda. She said it should be easy enough to find them at any bookstore. Also, she asked me to pick up some picture books for Jackson. Guess she wants to give him somethin' for Christmas, too."

"Real good woman you managed to snag."

"She sure is. Now, I just gotta find the right ring," Boone sighed. They had already passed several jewelry shops, but nothing caught his eye. In reality, what his eyes fell onto was far too expensive. Boone began to worry he'd find anything at all. Anything to meet his budget and pretty at the same time, Matilda-worthy.

"How about we go check out some secondhand shops? I bet they got all kinds of nice stuff," Dale suggested.

"Secondhand?" Boone frowned.

"Aw, don't act like you're so highfalutin. Ain't a thing wrong with secondhand. The ring I got Jackson's Momma were secondhand. Got a gorgeous ring for half what they want in them jeweller's shops."

"Really?!"

"A'course! C'mon. I recall there were a few on the side streets. Let's go. It's on the way to the bookshops, anyway."

Rubbing her hands together and blowing on them, Matilda laughed as Jackson dug out further into a snowdrift. They had been working on the snow fort for a good hour now, and the cold was beginning to set in.

"Jackson, why don't we get the sled and head into town?" Matilda presented an enticing offer, rubbing her arms.

Curiosity shining in his eyes, Jackson poked his head out from the fort. "What's in town?"

"Chocolate, of course." Matilda chuckled.

Jackson was quick as a whip, crawling out and running around the back of the house.

"I'll get the kick sled!" he howled.

Matilda hardly had time to fetch her reticule before Jackson appeared in the doorway. After triple-checking that all the windows and doors were secured, Matilda tried the key in the door before finally locking the house and then unlocking it to make sure it actually worked. Jackson watched her with a tilted head, his brows drawn together.

"Why'd you do that?" he asked.

"Do what, sweetheart?"

"Lock and unlock, and lock the door again?"

Matilda squirmed, her ears tipping back as she gingerly looked down at the key in her hand.

"I ... I suppose I don't know why. I simply always have."

"Don't that make things take longer?" Jackson asked.

"It does ... but it makes me feel better. Shall we be off then?" She pushed a chipper tone once more, tucking the key into her reticule as they walked out to the sled. While Jackson settled himself on the seat,

Matilda checked twice more to make sure the key was actually in her little bag before putting the whole thing in her inner coat pocket. She tugged on her gloves and patted over the spot of her pocket one last time for good measure before setting off.

Jackson giggled, kicking his feet and cheerleading for Matilda to go faster. Now that a handsome amount of snow was on the ground, the kick sled sped down the main road like a dream. What normally took a half-hour walk was cut down to a mere fifteen minutes thanks to the lovely little sled. *I'm gonna get one of these for myself*– Matilda made a mental note. In the spur of the excitement for a new adventure, Jackson forgot to put the sled cushion on or bring a blanket, and, at the end of the ride, crimson cheeks on display, he admittedly felt a little cold.

"You can have my scarf on the way back," Matilda offered as they lifted the sled up off the road and onto the little boardwalk in front of the general store. Jackson greeted the shopkeep eagerly, his tail wagging wildly behind him.

"Guess what we are making?!" he giggled, peeking over the edge of the counter at the older man.

"Oh my! Well now, let's see ... Maybe a cake?" Mr. McNiel chuckled.

"Nuh-uh!" Jackson giggled.

"Hmm ... Perhaps some cookies, then?"

Jackson's eyes went wide, and he looked up at Matilda.

"Could we make cookies?"

"Well, I suppose I don't see why not. Perhaps we can make some sugar cookies for when your father and Boone come back," Matilda hummed, her own tail wagging at the idea.

"Sounds like a fine thing to come home to. Where are those two off to?" Mr. McNiel asked, turning to look at his baking supplies behind the counter.

"They have gone to the city. Caught the midnight train last night. We have plenty of flour, but I suppose we'll need some butter and sugar. Could I also get several bars of chocolate? We were planning to make some drinking chocolate originally, but I suppose sugar cookies would make an excellent addition"

Mr. McNiel laughed, pulling down the ingredients for her from his shelves. "Mercy me! Sounds like quite a lot of treats for young Jackson. You'll spoil the boy."

"You wait here a moment. I keep the butter in our cold cellar, in the back. Won't be long."

Jackson eyed the wax-paper-wrapped chocolate bars, his tail wagging as he stood on tiptoes to spy over the counter, captivated.

"You mind those hands, Jackson. You'll get prints all over poor Mr. McNiel's counter," Matilda reminded him as she casually glanced at a paper. The front door bell rang, which wouldn't have been much to consider for Matilda had she not felt someone staring at her while she skimmed the paper. Glancing up, she was met with a rather sour-faced Delilah.

"Why are *you* with that boy all alone?" Delilah snipped, rather accusingly, as she pointed a finger at Jackson.

"Goodness! Well, *hello* to you as well. I am watching Jackson for Mr. Criley while he and Boone have gone to the city if you *must* know," Matilda said, moving to stand protectively in front of Jackson.

"Don't you think its a little *inappropriate?*" Delilah sneered.

"I beg your pardon? What on earth is inappropriate about me minding a child to whom I teach? I am simply doing a favour for a member of my community."

"Well, someone might get the wrong idea. We wouldn't want *that,* would we?" Delilah hissed.

"What *exactly* are you implying?" Matilda seethed, her eyes narrowing.

"Well, minding Dale's boy for him? Gettin' all friendly with his farmhand? Someone might think you're gettin' fresh with the *pair of them.*"

Matilda's jaw dropped, and her eyes rounded wide with dread. She turned an eternally grateful small smile when Mr. McNiel emerged into the storefront, his ears pinned back his mien displaying a fierce scowl. "Delilah, that's *enough!* The man's boy is *right here!* Your order is around back. Just go get it and *get out!*"

"All by myself? But Theodor ..."

"You seem plenty capable of much *nastier* work than pickin' up your own order. I've asked you once. Don't make me ask you again. Out!"

Huffing, Delilah seethed, spinning on her toe as she marched out of the store in a rage. Mr. McNiel looked apologetically at Matilda, who was still shocked beyond words.

"Please pay her no mind, Miss Matilda. Delilah is a sour woman."

"Th ... thank you, Mr. McNiel ... I believe we should get going," Matilda stammered, her face crestfallen as she scrambled to count out her coins. It seemed every time she neared the end, she miscounted. Crumbling, her nerves frayed, she covered her face, letting out a little sob. Mr. McNiel gave her arm a pat, counting the coins and putting the rest back in her coin purse.

"Please don't fret, Miss Matilda. Delilah is a foul woman when she wants to be. I give you my word. Not a soul in this town would think evil of you."

Matilda nodded, pushing her best smile and sniffling.

"Thank you, Mr. McNiel. Let's be off, Jackson."

"I'll carry the bag!" Jackson insisted, eagerly reaching up as far as he could to take the bag from Mr. McNiel before following behind Matilda.

Jackson's felt muddled the whole ride back. He didn't understand what Miss Delilah had said to Miss Matilda, but he knew it was vile. The warm smile plastered on Miss Matilda's face said she was happy, but from her eyes, he could guess she was really sad. It was the same troubled feeling he had whenever he asked Daddy about Momma. Daddy always smiled when talking about Momma, but his eyes looked like he wanted to cry. He didn't like it. He didn't like this feeling one bit, but he knew he couldn't do anything to change it now. Jackson was clever enough to know Miss Matilda would never explain to him. The first thing she asked of him was to keep from his Daddy what he heard Miss Delilah say. If he couldn't ask his Daddy ... then he'd have to turn and ask Uncle Boone when he got back.

Sitting on the train, Boone kept peeking inside the little velvet box in his hands, with each glance, the grin splitting his face growing wider. After four second-hand shops, the perfect ring finally presented itself. A shimmering pink garnet twinkled back in the low light of the train car. Set on a rich gold band with a twin set of little diamonds hugging either side, the ring was absolutely perfect for Matilda. Boone could hardly wait to bend the knee and ask Matilda to marry him. He had it all planned out, looping in his mind. Christmas Eve, when they cuddled around the fire at the farm. Dale teased him on and off the whole day about asking her on Christmas Eve. He eventually relented and admitted that Christmas was the perfect occasion. Matilda had fussed and fawned about Christmas as soon as Thanksgiving ended. And while it was still some weeks away, Boone's heart raced with anticipation.

Matilda was perfect. She was everything he could have asked for and more. She was better than he could ever deserve, and somehow, she loved him back. And that was more than he hoped for.

While Dale dozed away in the seat next to him, Boone couldn't help but dream about what life would look like once they got married. He knew that part would take a while. He wanted to save up and buy Matilda a proper dress for their wedding day. He wanted to get a house in order, or at least properly planned, before getting hitched. Squeezing the ring box in his hand, he leaned against the window and stared out into the glittering winter night whizzing past them.

I promise I'll do right by you, Tilly ... I'll make you the happiest woman alive.

Drinking chocolate and cookie dough seemed to lift any spirit. Even the most defeated beast-man. Matilda giggled delightedly at the sight of Jackson's entire face light up after taking the first sip from the warm cup in his hands, chocolate smeared on his cheeks, up to his ears.

"It's so good, Miss Matilda!" he squealed, squirming and giggling as he kicked his feet and gulped back a huge sip that almost hurt going down.

"I'm very glad to hear it," she continued giggling, turning back to her own cup and sipping it gratefully. After a long day in the cold outside, a cheery fire in the woodstove and warm drinks was the perfect end of the day, and the two felt as snug as a bug in a rug.

Jackson served as an excellent helper in the kitchen and passed her everything she asked for, fetching anything she needed. When finally the two sat down, and Matilda pulled out a book to read a story to Jackson, anxiety crept back into her weary mind.

"When can we cut out the cookies, Miss Matilda?" Jackson asked, his little tail wagging as he sipped his drinking chocolate.

"Soon, dear. The dough needs to chill outside first."

Jackson was babbling away to her while she anxiously chewed her nail. He stopped the blabber, cocking his head. "Miss Matilda?"

"Yes, Jackson?" She muttered anxiously, her gaze still fixated on nothing specific, as she weathered her nail down further.

"What's the matter?" he asked in a small voice.

Matilda looked at her hand and shook her head, batting her lashes a few times, realizing what she was doing.

"Oh dear! I'm sorry, Jackie ... I just ... I suppose I got lost in my mind with worries," she confessed.

"About what happened earlier?" he whimpered.

"I'm afraid so," Matilda sighed.

"Miss Delilah seems like a meanie. Uncle Boone never brought her around or talked much about her. Only when Daddy asked if he was still seeing her. I think she is just mad that Uncle Boone likes you more."

It warmed her some to know that Boone seemed so adamant about their relationship that even little Jackson knew how much they cared for each other. Still, her mind wandered into dark places. Did anyone actually believe she was romantically or, God forbid, *sexually* involved with Dale as well? She shuddered at the thought. She cared about Dale, of course, but her heart belonged to Boone. She wanted only him to touch her, and she planned to give him her first *time*.

"Let's read this story then. I'm sure by the time we are done, the dough will be ready for cutting and baking," Matilda forced a smile, opening the book as Jackson snuggled in beside her.

The rest of the evening went by with blissful distraction. By the time the cookies had finished baking, Jackson was dozy, nodding off by the time the cookies had finished baking. With a warm cookie in hand and a glass of water, it was rather easy to coax Jackson into bed. Before Matilda finished one more page in the book, he was asleep. The half-eaten cookie was taken from his limp hand and was set next to his glass on the bedside table.

Without Jackson as a distraction, she grew more antsy and she found herself pacing and chewing her nails once again. Eventually, the pacing and fretting wore her down, though it was well into the early morning hours. As soon as she sat down on the sofa, her eyes drooped, and sleep finally silenced her mind.

Before seven the following morning, Boone and Dale crawled quietly into the house, figuring Jackson and Matilda would be still sleeping. They were half right. As Dale poked his head into Jackson's bedroom, he found his son finishing his cookie from the night before.

"Hey buddy," Dale whispered, grinning as his son leapt from his bed and threw his arms around his father.

"Shh, Miss Matilda is still sleepin' on the sofa. How was your weekend?" Dale hummed, kneeling down as Jackson regaled him with all the fun they had the day before. Dale couldn't deny how good the house smelt. He perked an ear and heard Boone and Matilda sharing a quiet conversation in the main room. Jackson started squirming in a telling way.

Dale's eyes narrowed slightly assessing his son. "Somethin' you ain't tellin' me, Jackson?"

"N ... no sir ..." Jackson hummed.

"Jackson," Dale insisted, his tone unwavering.

"W ... well, I uhm ... I need to talk to Uncle Boone about something," Jackson mumbled.

"Boone?" Dale arched a brow.

"Please, Daddy? I just ... I *need* to ask him somethin'," Jackson squirmed some more.

"You can ask me anythin', buddy. I'm sure I can help," Dale offered.

His ears tipping back, Jackson whispered, "I can't ask you, Daddy. I promised Miss Matilda."

Dale hummed, none the wiser to the chaos that was about to come crashing down. Shrugging, he rose and stuck his head out the door. "Boone?"

"Yeah?" Boone responded, lifting his head from behind his hat. Laying on the couch, Matilda looked terribly insecure. Dale snorted, stepping out and arching a brow at the two.

"I sure hope you were keepin' your lips to yourself, young man," Dale mock scolded.

Boone laughed. "Absolutely, sir. Wouldn't dream of it."

"Jackson needs you," Dale mused, stepping into the kitchen and plucking a cookie off the plate on the table.

"It's been a long time since we had cookies on the table. These are delicious, Matilda!" Dale called, childishly stuffing the cookie into his mouth and plucking another. He settled down in his chair across from Matilda, idly chatting as Boone went into Jackson's room. Neither were aware of the bombshell poor little Jackson was dropping on Boone's jaded and frayed temper. While Dale discussed the books he had found for Matilda, their heads jerked simultaneously when Boone roared from Jackson's room.

"She said *what?!*"

"Uncle Boone, wait!" Jackson cried as Boone stormed out of his room, heading straight for the door.

"What in God's name are you yelling about?" Dale called, his eyes going wide when a frantic little Jackson ran after Boone.

"Whoa! Jackson, wait!" Dale cried, leaping to his feet to catch Jackson, with Matilda hot on his heels.

"Boone!" Matilda called, her heart racing once more. She raced through the door, and out into the snow, barefoot.

Dale managed to scoop Jackson into his arms. The little one was in tears as he clung to his father.

"Dammit, Boone! Stop!" Dale snapped, his ears splayed back as he snarled his words.

Boone finally stopped, his body shaking with rage as he stood with his fists at his sides and ears spread back. Matilda gingerly approached him, putting a timid hand on his arm.

"Why didn't you tell me?" Boone seethed.

"I didn't want to upset you ..." Matilda whimpered.

"What the hell do you think I am now?!" Boone snapped, turning to glare hard at her.

Matilda was taken aback, not only by his anger but also by the tears running down his face.

"Will someone tell me what the *hell* is going on?" Dale ground out.

"M ... Miss Delilah s-said m-mean things t ... to Miss Matilda and ... and I d-didn't tell you because I promised to keep it secret b ... but ... sh ... she was so sad an ... and I didn't know why!" Jackson wailed, fisting his eyes and rubbing his runny nose across his arm.

"Oh Jackie ... I didn't know you were so upset," Matilda whimpered, tears pricking her eyes.

"What on Earth did she say that has caused so much upset?" Dale huffed.

"Somethin' fuckin' *foul*," Boone spat viciously, pinching his eyes closed.

"Boone!" Dale snapped.

"I don't give a *fuck,* Dale! She crossed a line. Damn her! She crossed a line and I ain't puttin' up with it!" Boone snarled, turning back towards the road and taking off in a run. Matilda tried to go after him, but Dale was quick to catch her by the Elbow.

"Shoes and coat, I'll go get the sled, and if you could help Jackson into his coat, I'd appreciate it. We gotta get to him before he blows his top," Dale spoke with the assured urgency only a father had ...

17
Snowbound Strangers
Torry Weatherspoon

Denver International Airport, Christmas Eve

"Attention passengers, all flights have been grounded due to inclement weather conditions," announced an airline worker over the intercom system. "We are sorry for the delays, and Merry Christmas."

The announcement was met with moans, groans, and upset passengers. People scrambled towards ticket counters, phone pressed to their ears, voices sharp with panic and frustration. Suitcases rolled fast, children cried, and curses slipped out louder than intended.

Nick Boyd stood still in the middle of the terminal waiting area, jaw tight beneath the scarf looped at his neck. He wasn't surprised—he could feel the storm in his bones hours before the announcement, but the finality of it still hit like a gut punch. He was supposed to be in Chicago by now, sitting at his grandmother's side instead of staring at snow hitting against the glass.

He exhaled through his nose, muttered something under his breath, and adjusted his carry-on bag. No use in calling the airline. No flights meant no flights. What he needed was food and a nice, stiff drink. He needed to head somewhere to wait this storm out before he lost his patience completely.

That's how he found himself under the blue glow of the *Blue Sky Bar,* sliding onto the last open stool at the far end.

Beside him, a woman shifted her gift bag to make space. Long, wavy hair framed her face, and a gold cross necklace glinted against her sweater. A vodka cranberry drink sat untouched in front of her, condensation dripping down the glass. She glanced his way, eyes sharp and warm all at once.

"Rough night?" she asked.

Nick smirked without humor, nodding toward the windows where snow swallowed the runway whole. "Flights are grounded. We're all here for the night on Christmas Eve."

The bartender, with his Santa hat slouched to one side,, shuffled over. "What'll it be?"

"Whiskey. Neat."

The woman tapped the menu. "Cheeseburger and fries, if you still have any left." She caught Nick's look and grinned. "Don't judge me. A burger and fries beat pretzels from a vending machine anytime."

He shook his head, a quiet laugh slipping out despite the storm inside his chest.

"I'll have the same thing she's having, but with a Coke."

And just like that, the weight of the night shifted—just slightly—as *Let It Snow* by Boyz II Men rolled smooth through the speakers above the bar. The smooth harmonies rising over the clatter of glasses and the dull roar of stranded passengers. Jasmine's lips curved as she tilted her glass, the ice clinking softly.

"Guess the universe is trying to lighten the mood," she said, swaying just enough on her barstool to catch the rhythm.

Nick's mouth tugged into something close to a smile. "Boyz II Men makes everything sound easier than it is."

She turned to him then, extending her hand across the narrow space between their stools, "Jasmine. Jasmine Harrison."

He took her hand, warm against his, and held it for a second longer than necessary. "Nicholas Boyd. But my friends call me Nick."

Her brows lifted playfully. "So...am I supposed to stick with Nicholas until I ear the upgrade?"

He smirked, leaning an elbow on the bar. "Depends. Are you planning on being around long enough to qualify?"

Jasmine laughed, a soft sound that cut through the chaos of the bar. She tucked a loose curl behind her ear as she smiled at him, and Nick found himself watching the movement more closely than he meant to.

Her gaze dropped to the scarf around his neck. "That scarf must have some miles on it. Looks like it's been through a few winters."

Nick tugged at the frayed edge, thumb brushing the yarn. "Graduation gift. My grandmother made it when I finished vet school. I've kept it ever since."

Her smile softened, her tone shifting. "She must be proud of you."

Before he could answer, his phone buzzed against the counter. He flipped it over, and the screen lit up with his wallpaper—him in a cap and gown, arm wrapped around an older woman who was grinning like she'd won the lottery. Jasmine caught it before he could dim the screen.

"That's her?" she asked gently.

Nick's throat tightened. He nodded. "Yeah, that's Grams. She raised me. Made sure I had everything I needed, even when she didn't. She's the reason I made it through school." His voice dropped, rough around the edges. "She's sick now, never really recovered from getting Covid. This might be her last Christmas."

Jasmine stirred her drink, watching the ice spin in the red liquid. The weight of his words hung between them, heavier than the storm outside.

"I'm headed back to Chicago too," she said finally, her voice quiet but steady. "My sister just had a baby, so I wasn't gonna miss meeting my niece. But..." She trailed off, pressing her lips together before finishing. "It means seeing my mother. Haven't really talked to or seen her since she kicked me out at eighteen."

Nick turned toward her, studying the way her eyes held steady even as her fingers toyed with the rim of her glass. He didn't speak right away. When he did, his voice was low and deliberate. "You walked away and built something anyway. That should count for something."

For the first time since she sat down, Jasmine's smile wasn't just polite—it was real, soft at the edges. And when she brushed her hair behind her ear again, Nick couldn't pretend he wasn't drawn to the simple grace of it.

She broke the silence first, lifting her glass and taking a slow sip before setting it back down. "So, a veterinarian, huh?"

Nick's eyes locked onto hers. "Is that a good thing or a bad thing?"

Her lips curved. "Depends. Are you any good at it?"

He took a sip of his drink, letting the whiskey burn before answering. "I keep things alive that can't speak for themselves. Dogs, cats, rabbits, horses...you name it. They don't tell you where it hurts, so you learn to see what most people miss." His gaze lingered on her for a beat. "Guess I've gotten pretty good at reading the quiet."

Jasmine blinked, caught off guard by the weight in his voice. She let out a soft laugh, twirling her hair with her finger. "So, you're saying you can read me already?"

A faint smirk pulled at his mouth. "Better than you think, Ms. Jasmine Harrison."

She burst out laughing, loud enough that a few stranded travelers glanced over. She shook her head, her hair bouncing as she grinned at him. "Not you calling me by my complete government name."

Nick smirked, leaning back in his stool. "What can I say? It just rolls easily off the tongue."

Before Jasmine could fire back, the bartender came over, setting a fresh vodka cranberry in front of her and another whiskey neat for Nick. His Santa hat was still crooked, but his smile was tired and practiced. "Another round on the house. Merry Christmas, folks."

"Thanks," Jasmine said, lifting her glass slightly.

She swirled the drink, watching the ice tumble around before glancing at Nick. "So, since you're reading people tonight...I'll save you the trouble." She took a sip, then set the glass down. "I'm a sports medicine therapist. Rehabilitation, recovery, and ensuring people get back on their feet after injuries. It's what I moved to Denver for."

Nick intriguingly tilted his head. "Explains the confidence."

Her smile faltered just slightly, softening at the edges. "Maybe, but confidence doesn't always cover everything." She hesitated, her fingers tapping the side of the glass. "Going home means facing my mom again.

She kicked me out when I was eighteen. Said I could either live by her rules or not at all. I chose not at all."

She exhaled slowly, the music from the speakers wrapping around the moment. "I built a life here. I have a career, and I'm proud of it. But walking away back into that house after all these years...feels like stepping into the same storm I've been running from."

Nick studied her, silent for a while. Then he lifted his glass. "Storms don't last forever." His eyes caught hers, and he saw a glimmer of hope there. "Sometimes facing 'em is the only way out."

Jasmine tilted her head, a grin tugging at her lips. "So, what else do you think you can read about me, Dr. Boyd?"

Nick leaned closer, his voice low enough to make it feel like a secret. "That you talk with your hands when you're passionate. You tuck your hair when you get nervous. And you laugh harder when you're trying to keep from saying something real."

Her laugh burst out again, bright and warm, and she swatted at him. "Now you're just showing off."

The bartender slid their food across the counter—two plates of burgers and fries, steam rising into the air. Jasmine pulled her plate closer, inhaling like it was fine dining. "Now *this* is Christmas dinner."

Nick shook his head but couldn't fight his smirk. "You're really gonna try to romanticize an airport burger?"

"Romanticize?" She popped a fry into her mouth. "Don't knock it. Comfort food is love, and if you disagree, then you're eating it wrong."

They fell into an easy rhythm after that, trading bites of fries and teasing each other about condiments—her drowning them in ketchup, him dipping his in the pile he made on the side. The storm outside faded into the background, replaced by the warmth between them that neither had expected when they sat down.

When the check came, Jasmine reached for her bag, but Nick was faster, He slipped his card onto the tray before she could even protest.

"Nick..."

He cut her off with a look that was steadier than stern. "I've got it."

Her smile softened. "You don't even know me."

He met her eyes, holding them. "I know enough."

The word lingered between them, heavier than the music overhead. Jasmine tucked her hair behind her ear again, trying to mask the way she blushed.

By then, the bar had started to empty. Families sprawled across gate chairs, travelers dozing in uncomfortable positions. The TVs buzzed low, but the storm still raged, snow hitting the wide airport windows.

Nick glanced around, then back at her. "Come on, let's find somewhere quieter."

She hesitated only for a second before sliding off her stool. He carried both their drinks as they walked out of the bar and towards a quieter corner of the terminal—an empty row of seats tucked against the glass where the only view was the snow-filled runway.

They sat side by side, their bags at their feet, the silence settling softly between them. Jasmine sipped her drink, her shoulder brushing his. "Well, Dr. Boyd," she said with a small smile, "what do your powers of observation tell you now?"

Nick glanced at her, really taking her in, the storm reflected in the glass behind her. His voice was quiet and steady. "That I'm exactly where I'm supposed to be."

Jasmine rubbed her hands together for warmth, glancing sideways at him. "So, what now? Are we just gonna stare at the snow until we lose our minds?"

Nick smirked, pulling his phone from his coat pocket. "I've got a better idea." He tapped the screen, and a soft R&B beat spilled into the quiet air. *"Honest"* by William Singe began playing.

Jasmine tilted her head, recognizing it immediately. "You listen to William Singe?"

"Lately?" Nick said, leaning back in his seat. "Nonstop. This song has been on repeat in my head all week. Something about it just...sticks. I've been a fan of his for years, though."

She smiled, the corners of her mouth curling as she tucked a loose curl behind her ear. "Okay, Dr. Boyd, I see you. Didn't peg you for the soulful type."

"Don't let the scarf fool you," he grinned, "I've got layers."

She burst out laughing, shaking her head. "Not you trying to make 'scarf guy' sound deep."

"Hey," he said, mock-offended, "this scarf is legendary."

"Yeah, ok. Sure it is." Her voice softened as she looked at him again. "But the song...it's nice. Kind of perfect, actually."

They let the music fill the space while they talked—about his grandmother's stubborn way of pretending she wasn't sick, about Jasmine's sister calling her five times a day with baby updates, about how neither of them ever expected to be stuck here, and about finding a total stranger that they vibe with.

Somewhere between laughter and silence, Jasmine leaned closer, her head resting against his shoulder. Nick shifted just enough to let her fit there comfortably, then pulled his scarf loose and draped it across them both.

The song played through once, then again. By the third time, their words had slowed, their breathing syncing, and the storm outside blurred into nothing.

Together, they drifted into sleep—warm, close, comfortable, and no longer strangers.

Jasmine stirred first, blinking against the soft gray light bleeding through the giant windows. The storm had finally calmed, leaving the runway buried under fresh snow. She shifted, realizing her head was still on Nick's shoulder, his scarf tucked around both of them.

Nick opened his eyes a moment later, groggy but aware. He gave her a small smile. "Merry Christmas."

Her laugh was quiet, still heavy with sleep. "Merry Christmas."

He stretched, standing slowly. "I'm gonna hit the restroom. I'll be right back."

She nodded, pulling his scarf tighter around her shoulders as he walked off.

But Nick didn't head for the restroom. Instead, he ducked into one of the airport shops just as the gate was opening. Shelves of snow globes, keychains, and mugs lined the wall. He scanned until his hand landed on a single shot glass, clear with bold block letters: *Denver International Airport.*

It was cheesy, but it was perfect.

By the time he returned, Jasmine was sitting up straighter, smoothing out her curls, trying to shake off the weight of sleep. He held out a small paper bag.

She frowned, taking it. "What's this?"

"Christmas present," he said.

She pulled the shot glass from the bag, reading the words with a slow smile. "You got me...a Denver Airport shot glass?"

He smirked, sliding back next to her. "Our origin story. I figured you shouldn't forget where it all started."

Her laugh was soft and genuine, but there was something else behind it—something warmer. She shook her head, clutching the glass. "Nicholas Boyd, you're ridiculous."

"Yeah," he said, leaning back with a grin. "But now you've got proof that I was here."

She tucked her hair behind her ear, biting back a smile that threatened to give her away. For the first time, she thought maybe the storm had done them a favor.

By afternoon, sunlight finally broke through the clouds. The snow-plows had done their work, leaving the runways clear, gleaming against the white drifts piled to the side. The intercom crackled with the words everyone had been waiting for: "*Attention passengers, flights to Chicago are now boarding.*"

A cheer rippled through the terminal. People stretched, gathered their things, and shook off the long night.

Jasmine glanced at Nick, hugging her gift bag close. "Looks like this is it."

"Yeah," he said, trying not to let the weight in his chest show. "Back to reality."

She smiled, small but sincere. "Thanks for...last night. For the burger and fries. For the music. For the scarf, even though you didn't actually give it to me."

He chuckled. "And don't forget the legendary Denver Airport shot glass."

Her laugh came out softer than before, touched with something unspoken. "That too."

They lingered in silence a moment longer, then finally moved toward the gate with the rest of the crowd. The goodbye felt heavier than either expected, like they were leaving something unfinished in that corner of the airport.

Boarding was slow; families shuffled with bags, and announcements echoed overhead. Jasmine found her row, slid into the window seat, and tucked the shot glass safely into her bag.

When she looked up, Nick was standing in the aisle, glancing at his boarding pass with raised eyebrows. "Guess you're stuck with me a little longer," he joked, sliding into the seat beside her.

Her jaw dropped, then she burst out laughing, shaking her head. "Ain't no way."

"Fate," he said with a smirk, buckling his belt. "Or maybe the airline just has a sense of humor."

She tucked her hair behind her ear, smiling so wide it hurt. "Looks like Chicago's gonna get real interesting."

Nick leaned back in his seat, their shoulders brushing again as the plane rumbled to life. "Yeah, real interesting."

Nick stepped out of the Uber and stood for a moment on the icy sidewalk, his bag slung over his shoulder. The small brick house looked the same as always, the roof lined with lights that leaned a little to the left, a faded wreath hanging on the door. For a second, he just breathed in the cold Chicago air, letting it sting his lungs, before he finally walked up the steps and knocked.

The door creaked open, and the smell hit him before anything else. Turkey, ham, and mac and cheese bubbled in the oven. Collard greens simmered low on the stove, filling the whole house with the kind of warmth no storm could touch.

"Baby," his grandmother said, her voice breaking into a smile as wide as her arms. She was smaller than he remembered, her frame more fragile, but her hug was just as strong. "You made it."

Nick buried his face against her shoulder for a moment, scarf pressed between them. "Wouldn't miss it for the world."

She pulled back, swatting his arm lightly. "Don't lie to me. You almost did. I heard about them airports."

He laughed, shaking his head as he stepped inside. The living room was dressed up for the holiday—tree glowing in the corner, stockings hanging by the mantle, family photos crowding the shelves. For the first time since the storm, he let the tension leave his body.

"Sit down," she said, already shuffling toward the kitchen. "There's food waiting, and I know you didn't eat nothing decent all day."

Nick sat, his scarf still looped around his neck, watching her move slower than she used to. It made something twist in his chest. The scarf suddenly felt heavier. He pulled it loose, holding it out. "You remember this?"

She paused, looking down at the worn yarn. Her smile softened. "Of course I do. Took me three weeks and half a box of Band-Aids. You wore it that whole winter like it was made of gold."

"Still do," Nick said quietly.

She reached out and touched the edge of it, her hand trembling just slightly. "Don't you go looking so serious," she said, narrowing her eyes. "You got a whole life to live. Don't spend it worrying about me."

Nick swallowed hard, nodding, but said nothing.

He sat at the kitchen table; the smell of the food wrapped around him like a blanket. His grandmother moved between the counter and the stove, humming a carol under her breath as she stirred a pot.

He watched her closely, noticing the way she leaned heavily on the counter than she used to, as well as the pauses she took between steps. The woman who had once carried him on her back through snow drifts now seemed to carry her own body with effort."

"Grandma," he said quietly, "you should sit down. I can get that."

She waved him off, shaking her head. "Don't you start. I've been cooking Christmas dinner since before your mama was born. I can handle a pot of greens."

Nick frowned, his fingers drumming against the table. "I can see you slowing down."

She stopped then, resting her hand on the counter, her shoulders dipping for just a moment before she straightened again. When she turned, her eyes were soft but steady. "Baby, that's what happens when you live long enough. Bodies slow down, but my heart?" She touched her chest. "That's still strong. Please don't waste your time worrying about when I'm gonna leave you. Use it to live."

The words hit him hard. He dropped his gaze to the scarf lying across the table. "You know I don't want to lose you."

"And you won't," she said firmly, crossing the room to press her hand against his cheek. "Not the parts that matter." She smiled, but then her eyes narrowed in that way only grandmothers could. "Now tell me, when are you finally gonna settle down? You think I don't notice all these years you've been married to your work?"

Nick let out a short laugh, rubbing the back of his neck. "I...met someone, actually."

Her brows lifted. "Oh really?"

"It was nothing," he said quickly. "Just...a spark. One of those things you don't plan on. I doubt I'll ever see her again."

His grandmother studied him, lips curving into a knowing smile. "Mmhmm. You'd be surprised what life brings back around when it's meant to be."

Nick tried to smile, but the memory of Jasmine laughing in that airport bar pulled at him harder than he wanted to admit.

By the time the plane touched down in Chicago, the storm had finally given up. The city below was still dusted in white, the kind of Christmas morning that would've felt magical if her stomach wasn't in knots.

Her sister's house sat on the edge of Bronzeville, every window glowing gold against the snow. The second she stepped inside, the smell hit her—turkey, cornbread dressing, candied yams, and ham glazed just right. It was the smell of home. The one she hadn't walked into in nearly ten years.

"Jas!" her sister Keisha squealed, wiping her hands on a dish towel before pulling her in. "Girl, look at you! You got that Denver glow or something."

Jasmine laughed, hugging her back. "I missed you, too."

Keisha grinned, guiding her into the kitchen where the table overflowed with food. "Mommas in the living room with the baby. She said she didn't think you'd show."

Jasmine's smile faltered. "Yeah, well...she was almost right."

Before Keisha could respond, their mother's voice floated in from the next room. "Keisha, who's that at the door?"

Jasmine's pulse quickened. She stepped into the living room, the same furniture she remembered from her childhood—same couch, same floral curtains. Her mother sat in her recliner, holding the baby. When she looked up, her eyes went wide.

"Jasmine?"

"Hey, Momma," Jasmine said softly.

For a moment, it seemed like it might be okay. Her mother's lips twitched, almost smiling—until she set the baby down in the bassinet. "You look tired. Denver not treating you right?"

Jasmine forced a laugh. "Denver's fine. It's been good to me."

"Good enough that you couldn't come home sooner?

The room tensed. Keisha looked between them, ready to jump in, but Jasmine raised a hand. "I came now, didn't I? That's what matters."

Her mother folded her arms. "You left without a word. Didn't call. Didn't visit. And now

You show up like nothing happened."

"I didn't just leave, Momma. You told me to go."

Silence. Heavy and sharp. The only sound was the baby's soft cooing.

Her mother's voice was low when she spoke again. "You were reckless—hard-headed. I did what I had to do."

Jasmine's throat tightened. "You kicked me out because I wanted to live my own life. Because I wouldn't let you decide who I was supposed to be."

Keisha stepped forward. "Alright, y'all, it's Christmas…"

But Jasmine shook her head, eyes burning. "No. I'm not doing this again. I came to meet my niece, not to beg for peace." She turned toward the door, voice trembling but firm. "Merry Christmas, Momma."

Keisha called after her, but Jasmine was already grabbing her coat. The cold slapped her face the second she stepped outside, the wind sharp but freeing.

She walked down the block, pulling her scarf tighter. Her chest ached, but there was relief in it too—like letting go of a weight she'd carried too long.

She rounded the corner toward the small convenience store on the corner.

The bell over the door gave a tired little jingle when she stepped in. Heat rolled over her face. The aisles smelled like coffee, salt, and winter on rubber mats.

He was there. Plaid coat, scarf, and that easy, crooked smile like he already knew she would show up.

"Jasmine Harrison," Nick said, like her name tasted good. "Merry Christmas."

She exhaled a laugh she didn't know she was holding. "You've gotta be kidding me."

"Chicago likes a reunion," he said. "You okay?"

Jasmine glanced at the glass door. Snow started to fall lightly. "I met my niece, and she's so beautiful and perfect." Her mouth tightened. "My mother, not so much."

Nick nodded like he'd expected that answer and didn't need the details to respect the weight. "Walk with me?"

They paid for coffees and stepped back into the cold. The block was quiet. Wreaths drooped on porches, and a plastic reindeer leaned against a fence like it had given up.

"So," he said, handing her a cup, steam lifting into the air. "How honest do you want me right now?"

She smiled despite herself. "Playlist honest or doctor honest?"

"Playlist honest," he said. "I'm proud of you for going."

"I walked out."

"You walked out for your peace. That counts."

They turned the corner. Voices carried from the open door of a two-flat half a block down. A man jogged onto the sidewalk, scanning the street like he was searching for someone.

"Yo! Jas!" he called. "Keisha's blowing up my phone. You good?"

Jasmine held up her coffee. "Taking a walk. Trying to cool off."

The guy slowed, relief dropping his shoulders. He was tall, caramel-skinned, and bundled in a gray beanie and coat. He looked from Jasmine to Nick and did a double-take.

"No way," he said, a grin breaking. "Nick Boyd?"

Nick blinked. "Marcus?"

Marcus pointed. "University of Illinois. Freshman year. You had the busted laptop and that cheap pair of headphones you swore were 'studio quality.'"

Jasmine's head snapped between them. "Hold on, you two know each other?"

Marcus stuck out a hand, and they dapped each other up, laughing. "Small world," Marcus said. He turned to Jasmine. "Jas, this man pulled me through Chem 101with notecards and gas-station pizza."

Jasmine stared at Nick. "You know my sister's husband?"

Nick ran a hand over his beard, smiling like fate had just walked up and introduced itself. "Guess I do."

From the doorway upstairs, Keisha leaned over the railing. "Jas, you okay?"

"I'm fine," she called back. "I just needed air."

Keisha spotted Nick and waved, curious and grinning already. "Hi, I'm nosy. I'll ask questions later."

"Later," Jasmine said, laughing.

Marcus shoved his hands into his pockets. "Mom went to lie down. I think she's embarrassed that she started it. She'll calm down though, you know how she is."

Jasmine's chest ached in that old, familiar place. "Yeah."

Marcus nodded toward Nick. "You coming by, bro? We got enough food to feed the block."

Nick hesitated, his eyes flicking to Jasmine first. She felt it too, that careful, new thread between them tugging.

"Rain check," Nick said. "I'm headed back to my grandmother's. It's been a minute since I made it home for Christmas."

Marcus clapped his shoulder. "Do that, and tell her Merry Christmas from the Greens. Definitely swing by later if you can. The door's always open."

He jogged back towards the stoop. Keisha blew Jasmine a kiss and disappeared back inside. The block went quiet again.

Jasmine tucked her hair behind her ear. The wind tugged the ends of her curls. "Marcus Green. Wow."

"The world is smaller than we think," Nick said. "Some threads were already there; we just didn't see them yet."

They walked without talking for a full minute. The calm felt earned. Jasmine finally stopped, turned to him, and held his gaze.

"Thank you," she said.

"For what?"

"For not trying to fix it. For just...being here."

He looked at her like he did at the airport right before sleep took hold of them. "I like being here."

She laughed softly, shook her head, then reached into her coat pocket and pulled out the shot glass. She turned it in her palm, Denver's airport letters catching the thin winter sun.

"Our origin story," she said.

"Evidence," he said. "In case you try to pretend it was a dream."

"It already feels like one."

He glanced down the street, then back at her. "I want you to meet my grandmother. Not today if that's too much, but soon. She'd like you. She has a way of seeing people clearly."

Jasmine swallowed. Fear and something sweeter collided in her chest. "I'd like that."

He took his phone from his pocket and held it out. "So I don't have to trust the airline to seat us together again."

She put her number in and sent herself a text. Her phone buzzed in her hand. She saved his name as Nick Boyd (Scarf Guy). He glanced over at her phone and smirked.

"Scarf guy, huh?"

"It's iconic now, so don't fight it."

A car rolled past, tires whispering over packed snow. Somewhere a radio played an old R&B Christmas cut, muffled and warm. The world felt like it had finally unclenched.

"You going back in?" he asked.

"I should," she said. "I owe Keisha more time with her, and I want another look at my niece's cheeks before they change tomorrow."

He smiled. "Text me after."

"You text me after you kiss your grandmother and make a plate," she said. "Mac and cheese, ham, turkey, and all the sides. I'm not playing with you, Dr. Boyd."

He laughed and playfully responded, "Yes, ma'am."

They stood there a second too long, both of them aware of it, but neither of them moved. She stepped in first, hands sliding up his coat, the air between them fogging in the cold. He bent into her, soft and sure. No rush. No panic. A kiss that said last night wasn't a layover; it was a takeoff.

When they broke, she was smiling. "Go," she said. "Before I keep you here and your grandma reads you for filth."

"She would," he said, grinning. "And I'd deserve it."

He walked backward a few steps, then turned and started toward the corner. She watched him until he looked back and lifted his hand. She lifted the shot glass in return. He laughed, shook his head, and kept going.

Jasmine stood there with snow squeaking under her boots and a warmth in her chest that didn't come from the coffee. She tucked the glad into her pocket and headed for the steps, lighter than when she'd left.

Across town, Nick took the stairs to his grandmother's door two at a time. He paused on the stoop and pulled the worn scarf tight around his neck. He smiled and knocked.

His phone buzzed. A message from an unsaved number flashed on the screen.

It's Jasmine. *I'm staying.*

He saved it, then opened the door.

What started as a snowstorm hadn't ended. It had turned into something that was just beginning.

18

The Nutcracker

V.A. Vance

Trigger Warnings
Consensual Non-Consent
BDSM

The Gold Coast was alive with the unusual blend of Christmas cheer and summer heat. The city was decked out in tinsel and twinkling lights, while the sun blazed down on the beachgoers below. Silas, lounging in his penthouse, took in the festive view, his mind already spinning with ideas for his next performance. He grabbed his mobile phone from beside him and logged into his OnlyFans account. Checking his private messages, he saw one from Lily indicating that she was confirming their meetup and would arrive at their scheduled timeslot, which was in 15 minutes. Silas readied himself mentally, then propped his phone on the floor stand and started a livestream, his third for the day. Within seconds of going live, the viewer numbers climbed from the 20s to the 50s to the hundreds. The camera was aimed at torso height, showing his perfectly defined abs, which he was currently rubbing moisturiser into. The comments on the screen read with all the familiar and usual remarks like 'Oh, daddy', 'mmm baby', and the occasional smirk-worthy comment like 'Oh, I wanna slip and slide off those abs please'. Silas spoke to his audience; his deep, husky voice, thick with an Australian accent, was a drawcard for so many of his international viewers.

His latest 'victim' was Lily, a petite blonde with a fiery spirit and a penchant for pushing boundaries. She had reached out to him, eager to explore her fantasies of consensual non-consent, and Silas was more than willing to oblige. The anticipation alone had him on edge, ready to deliver a show that would leave his fans begging for more. When Lily finally arrived, dressed in a seductive red dress that hugged her curves perfectly, Silas felt a thrill of excitement. She stepped into the penthouse, her eyes wide with a mix of exhilaration and nervousness.

"Welcome, little flower," he said, his voice a low growl. "Ready to make some holiday magic?" Lily nodded, her breath coming in short gasps as she took in the lavish surroundings.

"I'm ready," she replied, though her heart raced with the weight of the moment. What if the reality of this encounter fell short of her expectations? Silas didn't waste time with small talk - he saw no point in it. Taking her by the hand, he led her to the centre of the room, where a large, luxurious Christmas tree stood, adorned with glittering ornaments and lights. The ornate fireplace, decorated with an assortment of festive ornaments, also held tools that hinted at the pleasures and pains that awaited her. The juxtaposition of holiday cheer with the rawness of her desires made her pulse quicken.

"Before we begin, let's establish our safe words," he reminded her, his voice firm but steady. "Red for stop, yellow for slow down. Understood?"

"Understood," she replied, her eyes sparkling with a mix of trust and uncertainty.

As Silas' demeanour shifted, taking on a more dominant air, Lily felt a flutter of excitement and trepidation.

"You're mine now," he growled, pulling her close, his grip firm yet gentle. "And I'm going to use you for my pleasure."

Lily's breath hitched, a mix of fear and thrill coursing through her veins.

"Please, don't—"

"Shh," he interrupted, his grip tightening, and she felt a rush of surrender wash over her.

"You don't have a say in this. You're here for my enjoyment, and I'm going to take what I want."

With a swift motion, he pulled out a length of red velvet ribbon, binding her wrists together and securing her to one of the metal rings on either side of the fireplace. A shiver of vulnerability coursed through her as she struggled against the bindings, her heart racing with both fear and exhilaration. Lily struggled slightly, her breath coming in quick gasps, but her eyes betrayed her excitement. Now bound to the fireplace, he removed his singlet, revealing his washboard chest. With one decisive movement, he tore his singlet in two, placing one as a blindfold over Lily's eyes and the other on the fireplace - for later.

"Please, loosen the bindings, or at least let me see," she begged, her voice wavering with uncertainty. "Not a chance, sweetheart. You're mine to play with."

As he began to explore her curves, his hands roaming over her skin, a mix of desire and fear bubbled within her. The anticipation was electric, and yet a voice in her head whispered doubts. Would she truly enjoy this?

"Look at you, all tied up and helpless," he murmured, his voice thick with desire. "You're so fucking beautiful like this."

Lily whimpered, her body responding to his touch despite her protests. Silas relished the contrast—the push and pull of her desire and resistance.

"You want this, don't you?" he whispered, leaning close, his breath hot against her ear.

The question sent a jolt of conflict through her. She did want this, but the reality of being at his mercy was terrifying.

"Yes," she whispered, her voice barely audible, more a shudder.

"Good girl. Now, let's give them a show they'll never forget."

With that, Silas adjusted the camera mounted on a stand to capture their performance. The thought of the audience watching sent a thrill down her spine, layering the experience with an exhilarating pressure. Lily was securely bound to the fireplace. Silas took a moment to admire his handiwork. The red velvet ribbon contrasted beautifully against her pale skin, and the twinkling light of the fairy lights cast a soft, ethereal glow over her body. He could see the rise and fall of her chest, her breath coming in quick, excited gasps. He walked to the phone mounted on a stand and adjusted its position to get a better view of the depravity that was about to ensue.

"Please," she whispered, her voice trembling with a mix of fear and anticipation. "Don't do this, not like this."

Silas' smile was wicked, his eyes gleaming with dark intent.

"Oh, but I am," he growled, his voice a low rumble that sent shivers down her spine. "And you my little flower, are going to love every second of it." With that, he balled up the remainder of his torn singlet and shoved it into her mouth. She was going to be silent; she was going to take everything he gave her; she was not going to complain; and she was going to be his in every way possible.

He stepped closer, his hands roaming over her body, exploring every curve and contour. He could feel the heat radiating from her, the tension in her muscles as she struggled against her bonds. His touch was firm, possessive, leaving no doubt about who was in control. "Look at you, all helpless and at my mercy," he murmured, his voice thick with desire. "You're so fucking beautiful like this."

Lily whimpered, her body responding to his touch despite her protests. Silas loved the contrast, the way her breath hitched and her eyes fluttered closed as he teased her, his fingers skimming over her sensitive spots. He leaned in, his breath hot against her ear.

"You want this, don't you?" he whispered, his voice a seductive purr. "You want me to take control, to use you for my pleasure."

Lily's breath hitched, and she nodded slightly, her eyes meeting his with a mix of defiance and surrender. "Yes," she admitted, her voice barely a whisper, more a muffled cry.

The first gasp fell from Lily's lips with the innocent hush of surprise, but the next arrived shattered and desperate, pulsing with the raw, bright edge of surrender. Every muscle in her body tensed, then melted, the violence of her own desire written in the arch of her back and the clutch of her thighs around Silas' waist. He held her with one hand splayed across her sternum, pinning her against the cool marble of the fireplace as if she might try to bolt, even now. His other hand, fingers long and brutal, moved without hesitation beneath the hem of her dress.

She'd imagined this moment, but fantasy couldn't prepare her for the uncaring hunger in his touch. With neither warning nor mercy, he drove two fingers inside her, the blunt force of the invasion knocking the air from her lungs. The jolt was electric: pain laced with involuntary pleasure, the boundaries between them dissolving into a single, searing point of contact. The bindings at her wrists creaked as she strained, her entire body a map of exposed nerve endings. Silas' thumb found her clit and circled it with methodical cruelty, evoking a fresh shudder that rippled through her. She squeezed her eyes shut, the world reduced to the bright, jangled rhythm of his hand moving inside her. There was no room for thought, no coherent sense of time—only the escalating demand of her own body, and the certainty that his was the only will that could soothe it.

As if in a trance, Silas' free hand traced the line of her jaw, then gripped her throat, applying the lightest pressure until Lily's breathing stuttered. He watched her face with a predator's fascination, his eyes unblinking as a solitary tear broke free and rolled down her cheek. The tear glimmered in the twinkle of fairy lights, briefly catching the gold and red before vanishing into the hollow of her neck.

"You're so fucking perfect like this," he growled, his voice thick with need. "Ruined and trembling, and nobody's but mine."

His words wormed their way through the haze and landed somewhere deep in her chest, combusting into heat. He shifted his stance, forcing her legs wider, and the movement sent another quiver through her. The fingers working inside her never slowed, maintaining the same relentless cadence, while his thumb tormented the engorged nub above with ever-tightening circles. Lily's hips bucked in response, helpless and reflexive. Her mind warred with itself: a part of her wanted to beg him to stop, to retreat from the brink, while another part wanted nothing more than to be shattered and remade under his hands. She moaned behind the gag of his torn singlet, the sound guttural and barely human. Silas responded with a pulse of laughter, half-amused, half-maddened by her helpless need.

"That's it, flower," he whispered, lips grazing the shell of her ear. "Give it up. Let go for me."

He increased the pressure on her clit, thumb flicking and swirling in a cadence cruelly attuned to the trembling in her thighs. She felt herself unravelling, each stroke intensifying the frantic beat of her heart, each twist of his fingers inside her wringing a sharper whimper from her throat. The humiliation of crying in front of him was matched only by the thrill it sent through her; her shame had never been so alive, nor so sweet. He withdrew his hand from around her throat, leaving her gasping and empty, every nerve in her body shrieking for more. He leaned in, licking the tear from her cheek with deliberate slowness, letting her taste her own desperation on his tongue.

Silas' stare never left her face as he dropped to his knees with the casual arrogance of a conquering soldier. The movement was so abrupt—so predatory—that for a heartbeat Lily's mind blanked, flipped end over end in a vertigo of anticipation. He knelt between her thighs, the bone of his jaw brutal against the soft flesh of her inner leg, anchoring her in time and space. For a long, trembling moment, he simply breathed her in, letting the humid warmth from his mouth drift over her, teasing her through sensation and the promise of sensation.

Then his hands were on her knees, legs thrown over his shoulders, spreading her further, until the stretch in her hips bordered on pain. He leaned forward, and the first touch of his tongue was a hot, obliterating shock that ricocheted through her body and left her vision swimming. He lapped at her with the confidence of a man who had never known defeat, carving methodical circles around her clit, refusing to grant her the direct, searing pressure she already ached for. Every pass of his tongue coaxed out a new, involuntary tremor in her thighs; every calculated delay built a bonfire of frustration that threatened to consume her.

Above the blur of her own need, she heard the low rasp of his voice, dark and thick: "You like that, don't you?" It wasn't a question. It was a measured statement of fact, issued with the cruel expertise of a man who saw her as a set of weaknesses to be tested and broken. The words vibrated against her, sinking in deeper than any physical touch, and she found herself nodding, her chin working helplessly against the blindfold. He took the signal as license to escalate. His thumbs pinned her thighs down hard, keeping her open and exposed, and now his tongue moved with intent, flattening against her clit and dragging slow, wet lines up and down its length. Lily writhed in the velvet ribbons binding her to the fireplace, the fabric cutting deeper into her skin as she fought to buck against him. The lights from the Christmas tree refracted through her tears, painting the world in fractured halos of gold and red. Part of her registered the small, choked noises escaping her own throat, the embarrassment of them rebounding against the stone and glass of the penthouse, but humiliation was just another spice in the cocktail now flooding her veins.

He shifted his angle, his nose pressing hard against her pubic bone, and began to suckle in earnest. The sensation was so sharp, so overwhelming, that Lily lost track of her limbs; she was nothing but an arch of raw nerve and need, a creature remade by his mouth. She tried to beg, but the wadded singlet in her mouth turned every plea to nonsense. The only language left to her was the spasm of her legs and the convulsion of her hips, all of which he handled with relentless, unhurried strength.

He leaned in, his tongue returning with doubled fury, and this time gave her no quarter. He ground the flat of his tongue against her clit, lips sealing around it, and sucked with a force that sent a white, blinding shock through her. Her body convulsed, every cell alight with the violence of release, and she screamed into the gag, shaking so hard she nearly dislocated her shoulder against the ribbon. He drank in her sounds, her helplessness, with animal satisfaction, and did not let up, pushing her through climax into aftershocks so intense they bordered on pain. Only when Lily was reduced to limp, twitching incoherence did he soften his grip, letting her collapse against the fireplace in a puddle of her own sweat and tears. For a while, there was only the numb relief of collapse. The world refocused around the pounding of Lily's heart and the icy press of the marble at her back. Her limbs hung boneless, slack in the grip of their velvet bindings. Her whole body, from the raw skin at her wrists to the shuddering aftershocks in her core, radiated with a fatigue so deep it doubled as a kind of warmth. Beside her, the Christmas tree pulsed with its hypnotic lights—gold, red, gold—each bulb a small, silent observer to her ruin.

Silas let her dangle, limp and gaping, while he took in the aftermath of his handiwork. She could sense him looming above her, the air displaced by his breath and the shadow of his arm as he reached up to untie the ribbon that lashed her to the fireplace. The release was as sudden as the initial restraint: Lily's arms dropped, blood surging back into her hands, pins and needles burning up her forearms. She barely had time to gasp before he had her flipped over, her cheek pressed against the cool granite hearth, his hands quick and businesslike as they gathered up her wrists and re-bound them together with a new twist of scarlet cloth. She whimpered—a reflex, not even a protest—helpless to do anything but yield to his efficiency. This time, he cut the length of ribbon with his teeth, the thread parting with a soft snap that felt perversely ceremonial. He didn't bother with words, not even the low, taunting commands she'd come to expect. Instead, he scooped her up, one arm beneath her knees and one bracing her shoulders, and carried her to the bed as if she were nothing more than a prize to be moved from one display to another.

The bed was huge, circled by a headboard of wrought iron branches that snagged her eye even through the blur of tears. She landed on her back, wrists pinned above her head, legs splayed and useless beneath the hem of the ruined dress. Silas wasted no time; he lashed her arms to the highest rungs of the headboard, binding her so that every muscle in her upper body was forced into a perpetual, vulnerable stretch. The mattress gave beneath her, a subtle cradle compared to the cold hardness of the marble hearth, but Lily could not draw comfort from it. She was as exposed here as she'd ever been, every inch of her skin flushed and hypersensitive, every joint and tendon stretched to its limit by the velvet ropes biting into her wrists. Her muscles twitched with the exhausted aftershocks of orgasm, but her mind floated somewhere above her body, untethered and wild, unable to find purchase on anything so mundane as relief. The air above the bed shimmered with heat and the scent of sex—her own, pungent and narcotic, layered over the salt-spice of sweat, the faint resin of pine needles crushed into the carpet by frantic knees, and a dark, bitter note that could only be the man himself.

The Christmas lights, reflected in the high penthouse windows, haloed every movement in surreal colours: the blue-white shimmer of a distant galaxy, the blood-red of a warning flare, the gold of a fallen halo. She blinked, slow and heavy-lidded, and felt the sticky gloss of tears still painting her cheeks. She was helpless, bound, and on display, but in the sick, humming chamber of her chest, anticipation still sizzled—a low, electric dread that she was not yet finished, that he was not yet satisfied. "You ready?" he asked. All she could do was nod - yes, as she braced herself for what was to come. For a moment, Silas simply knelt beside her, elbows braced on the mattress, hands stroking the backs of her knees as if reacquainting himself with her shape. The slowness of his touch was almost more devastating than his earlier violence; it was clinical, appraising, the way a collector might study the curves and veins of a rare orchid before uprooting it. Lily felt each brush of his thumb as a spark beneath her skin. She found herself straining against the velvet binding, desperate for movement, for agency, for anything other than the suffocating stillness of his attention. He gave her none. Instead, he took hold of her right ankle, pulled it straight, and began winding a length of crimson velvet around it. The rope was soft, but the intent behind it was not; he cinched it tight, then tied it off to the cold iron of the bedframe, spreading her leg toward the far corner with a final, savage tug. She yelped, but the noise died in her throat, stifled by the memory of his hand on her neck. He repeated the process with her left ankle, leaving her splayed and utterly defenceless, every limb held fast and useless above or below her.

The sensation was almost too much to process: the ache in her shoulders, the burn at her wrists, the humiliating throb blossoming between her legs as the open air cooled the slickness he'd left behind. Her body was a study in contradictions, shot through with equal parts pain and want, and for one wild, disorienting moment, Lily had the sense that she was split into two selves: one that watched from the ceiling, bemused and faintly horrified, and another that was a raw nerve, writhing at the center of the bed, hungry for whatever came next. He straddled her waist, pinning her hips down with the weight of his body, and leaned in close, his breath hot and damp in her ear.

"You look like a fucking angel," he murmured, voice thick with something that might have been reverence or derision; with Silas, it was always both. "Shattered and shining. I could keep you like this forever."

She tried to shake her head, tried to deny the truth of what he said, but her limbs would not obey. He traced a line down her sternum with the back of one knuckle, slow as a bead of water on glass. The touch was feather-light, but it left a trail of fire in its wake, igniting goosebumps on her arms, her chest, the soft quivering plane of her stomach. When he reached her waist, he paused again, as if savouring the momentary anticipation, then bent to press his mouth against the strip of skin just above her navel. Lily gasped. The sensation—heat, suction, tongue—was almost unbearably intimate. He worked his way down her body with a series of slow, deliberate kisses, each one planting a fresh seed of humiliation-pleasure in her gut. She wanted to curl in on herself, to hide her face from the relentless scrutiny of his gaze, but the blindfold was still in place, leaving her in darkness save for the constellations of Christmas lights mapped on the inside of her lids. He reached her thighs and paused there, lips hovering just above the pulsing, aching ache of her folds. She could feel the tremor in his breath; she could hear the faintest growl of hunger, animal and unfiltered, leaking from the back of his throat. Then, with no warning, he buried his face between her legs.

The first touch of his tongue was a jolt, almost painful in its intensity. He licked her from base to clit in one long, slow drag, savouring the taste as though it were the first and last thing he'd ever eat. His hands locked around her thighs, holding her open, steadying her as she bucked against him. He lapped at her mercilessly, flicking the tip of his tongue over her swollen clit with ruthless precision, then plunging lower, tongue-fucking her with the same relentless rhythm his fingers had owned minutes before. She screamed behind the gag—a hoarse, wordless shriek that sounded more animal than human. Her hips strained against his grip, fighting for escape, but he pinned her down easily, never breaking the cadence of his assault. She lost all sense of time, of self, of anything but the white-hot, needlepoint pressure building inexorably inside her. The world shrank to the narrow, burning corridor between her legs, to the greedy, consuming mouth at its centre, to the knowledge that she was helpless to do anything but give in. He didn't let up. He kept her perched on the edge of climax, alternating between cruel, feather-light flicks and punishing, full-tongued laps, never allowing her the satisfaction of falling over. The frustration—the denial—was a torture all its own, and Lily felt herself slipping into a kind of delirium, her senses scrambled, her thoughts reduced to a single, desperate plea: please.

Whether he sensed it or simply decided he'd had enough, Silas redoubled his efforts. He sucked her clit into his mouth and bit down, just shy of pain, and the shock of it sent her spiralling into a second, shattering orgasm. She convulsed, nearly tearing the bedframe from the wall, every muscle in her body clenching and unclenching in rhythm to his tongue. Tears streamed from beneath the blindfold; her throat ached from the force of her screams. When she finally collapsed, spent and sobbing, he licked her clean with the slow, reverent tongue of a man worshipping at the altar of his own destruction. Only when she was limp and silent did he release her legs, untying the velvet cords from her ankles with a gentleness that felt almost obscene in its contrast to everything that had come before.

Silas stood up, a smug grin on his face. He removed the cover from Lily's eyes. As her eyes found focus, her gaze travelled down his muscular torso to the bulge in his Aussie rules football shorts, straining against the fabric. Her breath caught in her throat as he slowly lowered his shorts, revealing his massive, throbbing cock. She had seen it before, but mentally jerking him off was a far cry from what she was about to face now—literally. Silas was in no hurry. Even as his cock jutted violently, glistening wet at the head, he took a moment to map the tableau before him: Lily splayed naked and helpless beneath the fractured constellation of fairy lights, wrists cinched so high the tendons stood out on her forearms and mouth slack with exhaustion. His own breathing had turned ragged, every inhale thick with the dual musk of sex and pine, but he wielded his hunger with the precision of a craftsman—deliberate, almost tender in its cruelty. He pressed his palm flat to her lower belly, holding her pinned, and with the other hand guided his cock along the slick, swollen seam of her labia. He moved slowly, savouring the friction, the way her whole body jerked in involuntary response to each teasing pass. He could have plunged into her in a single savage thrust; God knew he wanted to. But he preferred the dance, the gradual escalation from denial to surrender. The head of his cock nudged her entrance, slipped, retreated, and traced slow circles just above her clit, smearing pre-cum over her as if marking territory. Lily writhed under his hand, the muscles in her thighs flexing against their velvet restraints. Each glide up and down her slit left her wetter, slicker, the lips of her pussy glistening and pouting, begging for what he refused to give. When he finally allowed the tip to breach her, just barely, she gasped—a primitive, guttural sound that vibrated through the length of his cock. He felt her clench around him, desperate for fullness, and almost laughed at the shudder that ran through her. He pulled back, drawing another groan from her throat.

"Patience," he murmured, brushing the side of her face with the back of his knuckles.

"Say please."

There was a long, ragged silence, punctuated only by Lily's uneven breath. She opened her mouth, tried to form the word, but it got stuck behind what remained of her pride. He waited. The moment stretched. He pressed the head of his cock back to her entrance, not entering, just threatening, just enough to drive her mad.

"Please," she finally whispered, barely audible. "Please, Silas, I—"

He plunged into her in one motion, bottoming out with a single, brutal thrust. The shock of it knocked the air from her lungs; she arched so hard the ropes strained at the bedframe. He groaned in concert, savouring the clench and flutter of her cunt as it tried to accommodate him, as if he were too much, as if he might split her open. He buried himself to the hilt and then held there, savouring the exquisite, overwrought grip of her body around him.

For a moment, neither of them moved. The only sound was the high, animal keen of Lily's breath, the wet pulse of her heartbeat telegraphing itself into his cock. Then, slowly, he began to fuck her—not fast, not yet, but with a measured, punishing rhythm, each stroke designed to probe and torment, to force her to feel every possible inch. He watched her face as he did it, watched the way her mouth twisted and her brow furrowed behind the blindfold, watched the tears that began to slip from beneath the velvet band. He angled his hips, changing his thrusts, dragging the broad head of his cock against the soft, swollen bundle of nerves at her front wall. Lily's whimpers grew louder, more urgent, her hips rising to meet every downward drive. He leaned over, bracing one arm on the mattress beside her head, lowering himself so the sweat of his chest mingled with her tears. His other hand slipped down to her clit, pinching and rolling it between thumb and forefinger with the same merciless discipline he'd shown before.

"Look how greedy you are now," he hissed, each word a hot thread in her ear. "Wasn't enough to come on my tongue, was it? You want me to ruin you."

Lily didn't answer—not with words. Her whole body was answering, shivering and writhing, the velvet rope creaking against the headboard as she fought for the leverage she'd long since lost. All she could muster was a nod. Her cunt gripped him, milked him, the fluttering contractions making it impossible to hold back his own climax for long. He felt himself circling the edge, the tidal pull growing stronger, and he slowed his hand on her clit, denying her, torturing her, until her head thrashed side to side and she was howling against the gag. Her guttural moans told him she was close - dangerously close.

"Not yet," Silas said, almost conversational, as if this were a business negotiation. He pulled out nearly all the way, leaving just the tip inside, and slapped her clit with the thick shaft of his cock once, twice, three times, each time drawing a fresh shudder from Lily's contorted body. Then he slammed back into her, all the way, and the sound of flesh striking flesh echoed off the high glass windows like a thunderclap. It was too much. Her body went rigid, toes curling, back arched so high he thought she might snap in half. She seized around him, a wet, convulsive spasm that very nearly milked his cock. The near-orgasm almost wracked him, blurred the edges of everything, and for a second, he thought he might pass out from the violence of it. He collapsed forward, catching himself just before he crushed her, and buried his face in the sweat-damp tangle of her hair. He stayed there for a long moment, listening to the twin thunder of their heartbeats, the slow ebb of desperate breath. Lily was limp beneath him, boneless and spent. Her wrists still straining against the headboard as if even now she refused to believe she'd been reduced so completely. When he drew out his cock it left her with a faint, sticky pop, and her fluids smeared across her thighs like paint.

Lily's head lolled to the side. Her lips parted, desperate for air, but she said nothing. There was nothing left to say. Silas slowly withdrew, his body still trembling with the aftershocks of their encounter. He stepped back, his gaze roaming over Lily's bound form, a satisfied smile spreading across his face.

"Well done, little flower," he murmured, his voice a low, content rumble. "You pleased me greatly." Lily's breath came in slow, steady gasps, her body still trembling with the aftermath of their intense encounter. Silas stepped forward, gently untying her wrists and helping her to stand.

"Thank you, master," she whispered, her voice soft and grateful. Silas' smile was genuine, his eyes warm with appreciation.

"The pleasure was all mine," he said, his voice a low, satisfied growl. "But I have a feeling our audience isn't quite satisfied."

As Lily caught her breath, still trembling from their intense encounter, Silas watched her with a dark, hungry gaze. He could see the mix of satisfaction and curiosity in her eyes. He saw how she bit her lip and how much she wanted him, how much she wanted more, all while feeling conflicted—and he knew she was ready for more. He smirked, his mind already racing with ideas to push her boundaries even further.

"You think that was intense, little flower?" he murmured, his voice a low growl. "We're just getting started."

Lily's eyes widened, but there was a spark of excitement in them. "What do you have in mind?" she asked, her voice barely above a whisper.

Silas' grin was wicked as he stepped closer, his hand cupping her chin, forcing her to meet his gaze. "I want to push you, Lily. I want to see how much you can take." He led her to the large floor-to-ceiling windows, the city lights twinkling below like a sea of stars. He pressed her against the cool glass, her breath hitching as the chill contrasted with the heat of her body. "Stay there," he commanded, his voice firm and unyielding. Lily complied, her body trembling with anticipation. Silas stepped back, his eyes roaming over her form, taking in every curve and contour. He reached into a nearby drawer and pulled out a set of leather cuffs, a blindfold, and a riding crop. Lily's eyes widened at the sight, but she didn't protest. He walked towards the phone, still live-streaming every moment shared between Lily and himself. His chest shiny with sweat, he asked his audience, "Will these do kittens?" The comments scrolled up the screen all in agreement, some even self-nominating to be his next victim. Silas smirked with pride and power as he made his way back to Lily, his audience blessed with the sight of his tanned, tight buttocks.

"Safe words still apply," he reminded her, his voice stern. "Use them if you need to."

Lily nodded, her breath coming in quick, excited gasps. "I understand."

With swift, practised movements, Silas secured the cuffs around her wrists and ankles, binding her to the window frame. He then placed the blindfold over her eyes, plunging her into darkness. Lily's breath hitched, the sensation of being completely vulnerable sending a rush of adrenaline through her. Silas stepped back, admiring his handiwork. The sight of her bound and blindfolded, completely at his mercy, sent a surge of power through him. He could feel his cock hardening again, the anticipation building within him like a storm. He grabbed the phone, the stand and all and panned across Lily's form. He zoomed in close to her covered face, showing the blush on her cheeks and the redness of her lips. With the phone in one hand, he picked up the riding crop with the other, the leather cool and firm in his hand. He trailed it lightly over her body, the sensation sending shivers down her spine. Lily's breath came in quick, ragged gasps, her body tensing with each touch. Her body responded with nipples hardening with the pleasure of his touch.

"Please," she whispered, her voice trembling with a mix of fear and excitement. "Be gentle."

Silas chuckled, a dark and dangerous sound. "Gentle isn't in my vocabulary, sweetheart. You wanted to be pushed, and I'm going to give you exactly what you asked for."

With that, he brought the crop down on her thigh, the sharp sting making her cry out. The sound of her pain mixed with pleasure sent a rush of excitement through him. He could see the red welt forming on her skin, a mark of his dominance. "Fuck," she gasped, her body trembling. "That hurts."

"Good," he growled, his voice thick with lust. "Pain and pleasure are two sides of the same coin, Lily. Embrace it."

He continued to strike her, each blow precise and measured, leaving a trail of red welts across her skin. Lily's cries filled the air, a mix of pain and ecstasy that sent shivers down his spine. He could see her body responding to him, the way her breath hitched and her muscles tensed with each strike.

"Please," she begged, her voice a desperate plea. "I can't take much more."

Silas stepped closer, his breath hot against her ear. "You can, and you will," he murmured, his voice a low, commanding growl. "You're stronger than you think, Lily. Embrace the pain. Let it fuel your pleasure." He struck her again, the crop landing on her ass with a sharp crack. Lily cried out, her body arching against the glass. Silas could feel his cock throbbing, the sight of her bound and at his mercy driving him wild with desire. He dropped the crop, his hands roaming over her body, exploring every inch of her heated, marked skin. He could feel her trembling beneath his touch, her body responding to him despite the pain.

"You're so fucking beautiful like this," he growled, his voice thick with lust. "Completely at my mercy, completely mine."

He positioned himself behind her, his cock pressing against her entrance. With a single, powerful thrust, he entered her, the sensation of her tight, warm pussy enveloping him, sending shockwaves of pleasure through his body. The comments were racing, his audience hitting over 650 now. Lily cried out, the sound a mix of pain and ecstasy as he began to move, each thrust driving deeper, harder. He could feel her body responding to him, her moans growing louder, more desperate with each movement.

"Fuck, yes," he groaned, his voice a mix of pleasure and dominance. "Take it, Lily. Take every inch of me." He increased his pace, each thrust sending waves of pleasure coursing through him. He could feel the tension building within him, the coil of ecstasy winding tighter with each movement. Lily's body trembled, her moans growing louder, more urgent as she neared the brink.

"Come for me, baby," he urged, his voice a low growl. "Let me feel you come undone."

With a final, powerful thrust, he sent her tumbling over the edge, her cries of pleasure echoing through the penthouse as she came undone around him. The sensation of her body clenching around him, the waves of her orgasm pulsing through her, sent him spiralling into his own release.

"Oh fuck!" he roared, his body shaking with the force of his climax. The rush of pleasure coursed through him, intense and overwhelming, leaving him breathless and spent. As the waves of their shared orgasm subsided, Silas slowly withdrew, his body still trembling with the aftershocks of their encounter. He gently removed the blindfold and uncuffed Lily, helping her to stand.

"You did so well, little flower," he murmured, his voice a low, content rumble. "You took everything I gave you and more." Lily's breath came in slow, steady gasps, her body still trembling with the aftermath of their intense encounter. She looked up at him, her eyes filled with a mix of gratitude and awe.

"Thank you," she whispered, her voice soft and genuine. "That was... incredible." Silas' smile was not warm; his eyes filled with intent. "The pleasure was all mine, Lily. And I have a feeling our audience enjoyed it just as much."

Silas turned and walked towards the device to address his audience. He watched as Lily grabbed her belongings, got dressed and walked towards the door. Silas stood facing full frontal to the device that recorded the whole interaction. He placed a hand over his cock, strategically covering it from full view. He moved closer to the camera, grabbed the disposable wipes and cleaned himself off before asking his viewers to rate the experience. As the comments came racing in, Silas chuckled to himself as he looked around, amused by the contrast of festive cheer and raw, primal desire, but he did not stay there long. He scanned the comments as they came in thick and fast. "Merry Christmas, my little fuckers", he spoke into the camera. The 486 viewers wanted more; they were begging for it - and he loved it.

19

Silent Night, Shattered Truths

D.J. Sumpter

Trigger Warnings
Infidelity/Moral Ambiguity
Exploration of Repressed Sexuality
Marital Conflict and Emotional Distress
Automobile Accident and Injury
Blood and Medical Trauma

Snow tapped against the windshield in hurried flakes, a thousand tiny white sparks spinning down out of the black sky. The heater hummed too hot, the dashboard lights too bright, the car radio crooning faintly from the party playlist they'd forgotten to shut off.

She sat in the passenger seat, stiff as porcelain, the faint scent of her perfume—ginger, clove, and vanilla—clashing with the smell of wet wool and his aftershave. In her lap, folded papers glared like a wound.

"You used to hold my hand when we drove at night," she said, voice low and tight, not looking at him. "Do you remember that?"

His fingers tightened on the wheel. The road ahead stretched endless and silver, salt scattered like sugar across the blacktop. "I remember."

"You don't touch me anymore."

The words hung between them, heavy, undeniable.

He kept his eyes on the road. "That's not true."

She laughed then—sharp, bitter, not her laugh at all. "When was the last time you kissed me without thinking about it? When was the last time you even—God, when was the last time you wanted me?"

He swallowed hard. The wipers thumped back and forth, hypnotic, his silence louder than her accusation.

Her nails scraped the edge of the papers in her lap, and she finally turned to him. "I want a child. I want a family. I want a life that feels like it's moving forward. And all you do is... retreat. Into work. Into silence. Away from me."

His grip bit the steering wheel. "It's not the right time."

"It's never the right time with you." She snapped the papers up and slapped them against the dash, the sound like a gunshot. "So I made a decision. These are divorce papers."

The word cracked something open in the car. Divorce. It had the sound of finality, the tolling of a bell.

He almost swerved right then—not from ice, not from speed, but from the weight of that word.

Her eyes gleamed wet in the glow of passing headlights. "I won't keep begging you to want me. I won't keep living in a house where I feel like a stranger. I don't want just a nursery. I want a home that *wants me back.* Last December you strung lights at midnight because I said the living room felt sad—remember that?"

He did remember. Not just the lights, but the year before, when she'd fallen asleep on the couch with half a ribbon still in her hand and he'd covered her with the red throw that shed fibers like holly berries. He remembered the way she used to tuck her feet under his thigh when the roads were clear and the night was theirs, the small squeeze she'd give his knee at yellow lights as if to bless their luck.

"We used to..." She groped for a word, then let out a wrecked laugh. "We used to be silly. You'd balance a star on your head like a crown and refuse to take it off until midnight. You called me Firefly. Do you even remember that?"

The name struck him in the sternum. Firefly. A soft, private light. He remembered pressing his mouth to her wrist in the kitchen, the flour on her knuckles, how easily his body had answered hers before the hardness set in—before he taught himself not to look too long, not to feel too much. Before he learned the choreography of distance.

"I remember," he said, and it sounded like a confession.

"Then why did it stop?" She faced him fully now, the papers trembling in her hands, voice low, aching. "I kept thinking it was a phase. Your long hours. The promotion. The market. Something to get through. But you weren't going *through* anything—you were going *away*. Every year I've put up the same box of ornaments and felt you move an inch farther. There's a space even the tree can't fill."

He felt something buckle. He could have told her that he tried to touch her sometimes in the dark, and his hand stalled midair, as if hitting glass. He could have told her he had started counting reasons not to try. Instead, he looked back at the road like it might absolve him.

He glanced at her, quick, sharp, his heart hammering. "You think a child will fix us?"

"I think a child would have given us something to build on. To fight for. To love together. But you've refused me, year after year. And I—" Her voice broke, then hardened. "I don't believe you ever wanted me at all."

The car seemed smaller suddenly, the air thinning, his chest tightening under the press of her words. His jaw clenched. He wanted to protest, to deny, to tell her she was wrong—but the lie was so heavy it stuck in his throat.

Instead, he muttered, "You don't understand."

"Then explain it to me!" she burst out, her voice shrill, cracking. "Explain why you pull away from me in bed. Explain why you look right through me. Explain why every Christmas, every birthday, every moment that should feel full just feels empty. Explain it, damn you!"

The snow fell harder, thickening, the road vanishing under white. His hands trembled on the wheel, the tires humming too fast against the slick surface. He could feel her eyes burning into him, demanding the words he could never say.

Because the truth wasn't about money.

Or timing.

Or even her.

The truth was sitting in his chest like a stone: he couldn't give her what she wanted, because he didn't want her. Not that way. Not anymore. Maybe not ever.

But the words were poison, so he kept them inside, teeth gritted, his body rigid.

"You can't even look at me," she whispered. "You can't even say it."

His head snapped toward her, anger boiling where fear had sat. "And what would I say? That I'm not enough? That I don't want a child to fix a marriage that's already broken? That I—"

The car jerked violently. In that single instant, his eyes were on her, not the road, not the patch of black ice glistening ahead like glass. The wheel slid beneath his grip, useless, as the tires lost purchase.

The world hinged. Headlights slid across a skin of black water, thin and gleaming. For one lucid slice of time, the hood was a mirror, and he saw them both inside it—her mouth open to shout, his teeth bared around a word that would never finish. The tires found nothing. The sky tipped.

Her hand shot across the console and caught only air. The coffee cup in the holder leaped, flung a dark arc that hung in the air like ink, then broke across the ceiling. The car pirouetted gracelessly, a toy in a careless palm. Sound arrived late: the rasp of rubber, a low metal howl, the soft, cruel thud of snow receiving them.

Gravity chose a direction. His seatbelt cut into him; his head snapped; stars crowded his vision. The smell was hot and sweet and wrong—airbag propellant, coolant, a copper edge. Outside, the night smeared into gray ribbons.

When they stopped, the silence was obscene. Snow sifted down through the cracked seal like confetti at the end of a play no one had wanted to watch. He tasted fabric on his tongue and the metallic bloom of his own blood.

The radio, battered, kept crooning tinny holiday cheer: *All is calm, all is bright.*

Steam hissed from the crumpled hood. The windshield veined with fractures, leadwork spreading across glass. Airbags sagged like deflated lungs.

He groaned, head ringing, blood warm at his temple. Beside him, she moaned faintly, trapped against the passenger door, her arm at a sickening angle, her hair matted dark with blood. "Blue box... under sink..." she muttered, delirious, eyes rolling back.

Through the shattered glass of the driver's side window, a shape appeared—dark coat, tall frame, snow clinging to his hair and shoulders. A man.

The man's voice was urgent but deep, steady, cutting through the ringing in his ears. "Don't move. I've called 911. Stay with me."

Strong hands reached in, gripping his shoulders, steadying him as he fumbled with the seatbelt. The stranger's eyes caught his—dark, alive, burning with something that made his chest seize in an entirely different way.

It felt like being seen.

The hands were large, steady, careful as they pulled him out from the twisted frame of the driver's seat. He stumbled, knees buckling, and those same hands caught him—soft but firm, holding him up as if he weighed nothing.

"Easy," the stranger said. His voice was deep, the kind that resonated in the chest more than the ear, but gentle all the same. "You're bleeding, but you're standing. That's good."

Snow swirled around them in the beam of the ruined headlights, flakes catching in the man's dreadlocks. They were long, well-kept, dark ropes that framed a face both strong and soft, his skin glowing with the warmth of deep bronze under the cold night sky. His eyes—God, those eyes—were gentle, but when they fixed on him, it was like they looked through flesh and bone, right into whatever he'd been trying to bury all these years.

The husband shivered. From the cold, yes. But not only.

"My wife," he rasped, spinning clumsily toward the passenger side. "She's—"

"I checked." The stranger's voice steadied him. "She's alive. Breathing. But she's pinned in there. We wait for the fire crew to get her out." He lifted a gloved hand, showing the faint tremor in his fingertips. "I did EMT training—three years back. If I force it, I'll kill her."

His chest heaved. He pressed his palms to the frosted glass of her window. She moaned faintly, head lolling toward him, eyes fluttering open for a breath before slipping closed again. "Stay with me," he whispered through the crack in the shattered pane.

The stranger touched his shoulder, grounding him again. The heat of that touch burned straight through his coat. "She's holding on. Help's coming. You need to sit before you collapse yourself."

But he couldn't sit. Not yet. His whole body buzzed with adrenaline, grief, guilt, terror—an orchestra of panic playing inside him. He staggered back, nearly falling into the snow, until the stranger caught him again.

"Hey. Look at me."

He did. Against every instinct, he looked into those eyes. Brown, rich, impossibly kind. Piercing, yes, but not cruel. They softened at the edges, like embers warming instead of flames consuming.

For a suspended moment, the world narrowed to just that gaze. The hiss of the ruined car, the radio still wheezing out a warped *Silent Night,* the blood dripping warm down his temple—all of it faded under the weight of being seen.

The stranger held him there, steadying his shoulders with those strong, careful hands. "Breathe," he said. Just that. A command, gentle but impossible to disobey.

And he did. For the first time since the papers had flared between them, he actually breathed.

Snow clung to the stranger's coat, melting into dark patches. His dreadlocks brushed forward as he leaned in, closer than necessary, checking the cut on his temple with surprising tenderness. "Not too deep," he murmured, thumb grazing the skin just shy of the wound.

The husband's pulse jumped. He felt the touch far deeper than the scrape deserved.

Behind them, his wife groaned again. He spun back toward her, guilt a knife in his ribs. She was still alive, still trapped, still there.

Yet his body remembered that other touch—the stranger's warmth pressed against him, the quiet strength in his hands, the unyielding calm in his voice.

Sirens wailed faintly in the distance, growing louder.

"You should sit," the man said again, softer this time, coaxing. "Stay with me till they arrive."

The husband lowered himself into the snow because his legs no longer trusted him. The stranger crouched beside him, close enough that their shoulders brushed. Snow fell into the space between them, only to melt as fast as their heat closed it.

"You're going to be alright," the stranger murmured.

The husband turned his head, drinking in his profile against the flashing red-and-blue of the approaching emergency vehicles. A stranger. A man he'd never seen before, yet one who carried something unmatched, some impossible warmth that reached places inside him his wife's hands hadn't touched in years.

And for a dangerous, electric heartbeat, he let himself want.

[...]

The hospital was all fluorescent light and antiseptic air, the world reduced to paperwork, questions, and waiting. They rushed her into emergency surgery, words like *hemorrhage* and *stabilize* circling his ears until they lost meaning.

He collapsed into a plastic chair, hands trembling. Blood still clung to his hairline, sticky and half-dried. His coat was damp with melted snow. His body buzzed with exhaustion, yet he couldn't stop shaking.

And then the stranger was there again. Not gone. Not just a rescuer at the scene. Here. Sitting beside him, dreadlocks tied back now, presence filling the sterile space with something human, something warm.

"You should drink water," the stranger said, pressing a paper cup into his hand.

He blinked down at it, then up at those eyes again. Gentle. Piercing. Unyielding in their kindness. He took a shaky sip, the water cold, grounding.

"You didn't have to come," he said at last, voice raw.

The stranger tilted his head. "You didn't need to be alone."

The words cracked something inside him in ways the crash hadn't.

They sat in silence. Families huddled together, nurses passed by. But here, in the corner of the waiting room, it felt like its own world.

"You from here?" the stranger asked after a while, voice low enough that it didn't disturb the fluorescent hum.

"Close," he said. "Twenty minutes west. We used to come into the city for the lights."

"My grandmother used to drag us to see the Rockefeller tree," the stranger said, a warmth passing over his face at the word *grandmother*. "Jamaican winters are only on TV, so she'd make cocoa so thick the spoon stood up in it and tell us to pretend the cold was a game. She said Christmas isn't about weather; it's about whether you show up." He looked at the husband as if the line weren't a joke, as if it were a key. "I still make it that way. The cocoa."

"I burn everything," he said, surprised to hear the truth come out light. "She—my wife—she hides the smoke alarm batteries in December because I forget and it screams at us during dinner."

The stranger's mouth softened. "Sounds like you try."

"Trying is not the same as wanting," he said, and the sentence dropped between them like a tool he was suddenly strong enough to set down.

A cart rattled past. Somewhere a child laughed, the sound slippery and bright, wrong for the hour and still, somehow, right. He studied the stranger's hands on his knees—broad, relaxed, the veins like riverlines under skin—and then the careful way he didn't stare back. Not a vulture's patience... a witness's.

"What were you doing out there?" he asked. "Walking in this?"

"Closing shift two blocks over," the stranger said. "I take the long way home when it snows. Quiet makes the streetlights ring." He glanced up. "Then I heard the brakes. I always look."

He nodded as if *always look* explained everything. Perhaps it did. He felt the bench give slightly as their shoulders found the same angle, as if the seat had been made for two people to carry weight unevenly together.

"I don't know your name," he said suddenly.

"Nesta."

The husband tried the shape of it silently and felt something inside him rearrange. "Thank you," he said, and meant it for more than the call, more than the steadying hands.

"You're welcome," Nesta said, and it sounded like *I'm here.*

He passed the cup back; the stranger's thumb steadied his knuckles, and neither of them moved.

Hours blurred. He drifted at the edges of sleep, head dipping forward. At some point, the stranger shifted closer, letting his shoulder rest lightly against his. Just enough to steady him. He let himself lean.

A memory stung him awake: he'd faked the flu last Christmas; she ate cake alone at the table with unlit candles.

By the time the surgeon came, his nerves were raw threads. *She's stable now. We controlled the bleeding. She'll be in ICU through the night.*

He nodded. Thanked them. His mouth worked, but none of it felt real.

They wheeled her past, pale beneath the halo of hospital lights. His chest clenched so hard he thought it would crack. *I did this.* His silence, his denial, every holiday where he'd hidden behind excuses—he'd driven her here as surely as the skid on ice.

He couldn't stay under the hum of lights, couldn't sit in the sterile buzz of machines. He rose and walked. Past nurses. Past families. Past a Santa pin with chipped enamel grinning on a clerk's scrubs. He pushed through the doors and into the night.

Cold air hit like absolution. Snow fell heavy, blanketing the lot. He pressed his palms to his eyes, trying to hold the tears in before they froze.

Footsteps crunched behind him.

"I thought you might need air."

The stranger.

Snowflakes caught in his dreadlocks, his coat collar high against the wind. Warmth radiated from him even here, where the cold bit bone.

"She almost died," the husband rasped. "Because of me."

"You didn't put the ice on the road."

"But I wasn't watching," he said. "I was too busy fighting with her. Too busy drowning in—"

"Drowning in what?"

He wanted to lie. But those eyes pulled the truth from him.

"Drowning in myself," he whispered. "In everything I can't say. Everything I can't be."

Silence stretched. Snow gathered on their coats, their lashes. The world seemed to hold its breath.

The stranger lifted a hand, slow, deliberate, brushing a flake from his cheek. The touch lingered, thumb grazing skin, heat against the frozen night.

His lips parted. He shouldn't. His wife was upstairs. His whole life would shatter if he leaned closer.

But he did.

The stranger met him halfway. The kiss was not gentle, not patient. Hungry. Snow melted on their lips, breath burning. He clutched the man's coat, dragging him closer, as if he'd waited years for this impossible moment.

Danger. Release. Christmas lights strung too tight, finally snapping free.

When they broke apart, foreheads pressed together, his breath came ragged. "I—I can't—"

"You already did," the stranger murmured. Eyes dark. Voice low. "And you don't have to run from it."

He closed his eyes, trembling. He could still taste him—salt, cold, warmth that wasn't supposed to exist. For the first time, he felt both ruined and alive.

Snow fell harder, blanketing their footprints, erasing the path back.

And in the hush of Christmas night, he knew: nothing would ever be the same. They stood there as if the snow might bury the moment and save them from it. He let go of Nesta's coat, fingers tingling where the fabric had been, aware of every small sound—salt grinding under a distant tire, the whisper of the automatic doors, the air handling unit exhaling like a sleeping animal.

Upstairs, he could imagine the ICU corridor: the soft hydraulic hush of doors, the syrupy beep of the monitor, the slow rise of his wife's chest under a thermal blanket. *Firefly*, he thought, and the word hurt the way cold hurts—sharpest where the blood runs nearest to skin.

"This isn't a decision," he managed. "It's... it's a fracture."

Nesta's eyes didn't flinch. "Fractures still heal. They just don't heal into the same shape."

A nurse stepped outside to smoke and, seeing them, turned away with the courtesy of someone practiced at setting down what is not hers to carry. He felt the old reflex surge—deny, retreat, make a clean line back to the life that waited like a metronome. But the line wasn't clean; it was a thread sawed by guilt and need.

"I have to go back in," he said.

"I know." Nesta's voice was free of claim. "I'll be here a little longer."

He nodded and, for a beat, could not make his feet obey. Then he did the human thing, the next necessary thing: he went toward the doors, toward the lights and the beeping and the life he still owed—carrying in his mouth the taste of snow and someone else's warmth.

20
Spoiling Savannah
Ginny B. Logan

Trigger Warning
Graphic Sex

Chapter 1

Wrapped in the luxurious soft sheets, and intoxicated by his woodsy aroma, Savannah didn't want to get out of bed. But she had a morning spa date with Angie and the bridal party. It was the big day; Angie and Dave were getting married. As Angie's sorority sister, it went without question that Savannah would be one of her bride's maids. Thank God she wasn't the maid of honour. She didn't want that much responsibility, not when it was her week off from her successful psychiatry practice. Attending a destination wedding over the holidays meant she could escape other people's problems and the family drama of her brother's divorce. A messy arrangement since he and his ex owned a lucrative business together. Savannah gladly accepted the wedding invitation. Meeting up with Sebastian had been a pleasant surprise.

He tightened his arm around her waist and nestled into her neck from behind. She couldn't help but push her ass into him, feeling him stiffen against her. He groaned.

"Does this mean we have time for another go?"

She closed her eyes, wishing she could transport herself back in time. They'd gone to high school together, and college, but they never connected. They ran in different circles. That is, until Dave joined Sebastian's law firm. They'd become quick friends, and Dave invited him to the wedding. During the rehearsal dinner party, she saw Sebastian with fresh eyes. He noticed her too, and they hit it off.

"I really should go."

"Angie would understand."

She laughed and slipped out from under his arm. "You know that's not true."

"Yeah. But it made you smile. That's worth it."

"You've made me smile before."

"I'd like to make you smile more."

She turned to face him and grinned with a suggestive arc of her eyebrow. An involuntary squeal escaped her mouth as he pulled her back into bed. In his arms, she pressed her lips against his. Warmth tingled through her. Lost in his scent, she rocked her naked body against his, kissing him deeply. He flipped her over onto her back, pinning her legs with his. Lowering his weight onto her, his hard dick pressing into her low belly. She arched against him, thrusting her breasts up.

He whispered, "Ask me to make you smile."

She giggled, "Will you make me smile?"

He lifted himself off and tilted his head to the side expectantly.

"Will you make me smile...please?"

"That's my girl." He slipped lower until he held her legs apart.

Her breath caught in her throat as he kissed her inner thighs and her soft mound. Memories of last night flashed in her mind. It had been clumsier than usual. She blamed the tequila. Shots had always been her weakness. Had she known she'd end up with Sebastian, who had a cock that was perfectly straight and just right, she would have practiced more restraint. They'd both reached their climax, but she knew they could do better.

He licked her inner folds, gently opening her with his tongue. Tasting her arousal, he pressed her legs further apart and buried his face in her slick. Shockwaves of pleasure moved through her, making her moan. He flicked his tongue over her clit. His cock ached to be touched, but he kept his hands on her, squeezing her thick thighs and ass. She started panting, and her hands reached out for his hair. He focused all his energy on her.

"Oh... Yes! Yes!"

Her wetness filled his mouth. His cock straining for attention, and he groaned deeply. He resisted touching it, instead riding the waves of Savannah's pleasure until she settled, breathless. He sat up, wiping her cum from his mouth.

"Oh, Sebastian...you're really good at that." She smiled.

"And there's my smile. You're so beautiful."

She blushed and propped herself up on her elbows. "So, should I return the favour?"

His dick twitched at the suggestion.

A ringtone interrupted them. It chimed a cheerful melody, which contrasted Savannah's reaction.

"Shit! That's Angie wondering when I'll be there. I'm sorry. I'll owe you one." She kissed him quickly and scurried off the bed.

Cock in hand, Sebastian watched in mild shock as Savanna threw on fresh underwear and a bra while simultaneously texting Angie.

"After the spa, we'll meet the guys for brunch. Will you be there? Then we have to get dressed. There'll be photos. Then the ceremony at sunset. God! That'll be beautiful over the water." She sighed while she pulled up her jeans.

Sebastian let his eyes linger on how they hugged her ass, slightly jealous. His cock still straining for release.

"There'll be more photos, then the reception." She slipped on a loose-fitting white shirt, then grabbed her hairbrush. Quickly working out the knots in her shoulder-length sandy brown hair, she watched through the mirror as he got out of bed and approached her. Distracted by his toned muscles and erect cock, she put the hairbrush down.

"Sounds like you'll be free after the reception."

She nodded.

"I'll collect what you owe me, then."

She licked her lips. All she needed to do was turn around and get on her knees. It would be more fun to stay and play with Sebastian than to get her nails painted. She eyed his dick through the mirror, not wanting to wait. Before she could give in to temptation, a phone rang out.

This time it was Sebastian who cursed. "That's mine. I better answer it." He rushed over to his pants and dug out his cellphone. "Hey, Ma…Yeah…I know…I know…I know…Yes, Christmas is about family being together. I'm sorry…I know…It's a wedding… You're right. They chose a terrible time to get married. I promise to be home for New Year's." He shot Savanna a desperate look of apology. Last time his mother called, she'd kept him on the phone for almost an hour.

She bit her lip, watching him scramble to get dressed while holding the phone to his ear. A man who cared about his mother was an endearing quality. He stepped into his shoes and grabbed his jacket. Patience wasn't one of her best qualities, and she pouted, convincing herself that Angie would understand if she were late.

"Yes, Ma, I know…" He locked eyes with Savannah and it was like time stopped. He hooked one hand behind her head and leaned in close. She gazed up at him expectantly. With the phone away from his head, he whispered, "I'll come find you after the reception." His lips crashed into hers.

Tingles moved down her belly and between her thighs. She parted her lips, welcoming his tongue to dance with hers. Now, not later, she wanted him now.

He pulled back, jaw tense and eyes burning. Instead of taking her up on it, he stepped back, holding the phone to his ear again. "Mmhmm…I know, Ma…" He mouthed the words, "I'm sorry," to Savannah, and left.

Chapter 2

The vaulted ceilings of the reception hall carried the applause from the wedding guests as Angie and Dave stepped out onto the dance floor. Her white satin dress shimmered as she swayed. Standing with the rest of the bridal party, Savannah stared adoringly at them. She'd known Angie since their first day in freshman year. They lived in the same dorm and became fast friends. All of their other girlfriends had partners and were married or engaged.

Savannah softened her stance while watching the couple dance. Angie laid her head on Dave's shoulder, warming Savannah's heart. Their love permeated the room, and even Savannah's most cynical self couldn't deny the power of companionship. The problem was, Savannah could never marry, not after watching her father cheat on her mother while he travelled as a musician. To protect herself from letting that happen, she chose never to date a man for longer than a few months.

A sharp elbow poked her side. She turned to find Abigail, the maid of honour, who gestured with a subtle tilt of her head to a table near the back corner of the hall. There, Sebastian stared at her with such intensity it rooted her in place. It was as if he was staring into her soul.

"That guy's been staring at you all day. Isn't that Dave's new friend? He's sexy, but a little scary."

"Yes, he is."

The corner of his lip curled up ever so slightly, making her lady bits ached for his touch.

The song ended, and everyone clapped. Savannah tore her attention away to cheer for her friends. The DJ invited everyone to join the bride and groom on the dance floor. Abigail's husband, John spun her under his arm so her coral chiffon skirt swirled as they joined in. The musk of Maurice's cologne tickled Savannah's nose as he came up beside her.

"May I have the honour of a dance with you?"

"Um..."

"What?" Maurice smiled. "It's been wonderful seeing you again, Savannah. I know things ended weird between us. I'm sorry. I never meant to hurt you."

A tentative glance in his direction, and a rush of feelings fluttered in her stomach. Their relationship had been fiery and fast. Only he lied about being with another woman after months of being together. She blocked him and moved on. But despite that, her desire to feel his arms around her pulled at her each time she thought of him. Finding him among the groomsmen had stirred up all those old emotions.

"Give me a chance to twirl you on the floor and I promise you'll have a good time."

She fought her urge to look at Sebastian. If she did, it would just be a repeat of last night. She'd excused herself from Maurice's company to be with the bride and the rest of the girls in the bathroom. That's where Abigail started pressuring her to get back together with Maurice. After too many shots of tequila, it was sounding like a good idea. On the way back to the dance floor, she bumped into Sebastian, and their eyes met. The party fell away, and her knees weakened. The rest of the night became a blur of pleasure and play. She'd forgotten all about Maurice until she had to pose with him and the other groomsmen in the photos.

"Shall we dance?" Maurice asked.

"No, thanks."

"Come on, Savannah. Don't be like that. I know you went off with Sebastian last night. I'm not threatened by him. Let me show you how to treat a lady."

Abigail caught Savannah's attention and mouthed the words, "Dance with him."

Savannah swallowed her misgivings for the sake of Angie and Dave. She smiled politely and held out her hand. Maurice snatched it. He pulled her onto the dance floor and yanked her into his arms. His body pressed against hers with his hand firm around her back. Without missing a beat, he led her around the floor with grace. His presence consumed her as it had all those years ago. Her stomach fluttered with excitement with each twirl and spin. She beamed at him, remembering all the good times they'd shared. When the song changed, he held tight to her hand, leading her off the dance floor.

"Hey, can I show you something?" His mischievous look stirred her curiosity. She'd always loved the dates he'd taken her on. Each one offered another adventure, with surprises at every turn. Some of them ending in the naughtiest ways imaginable. The thought that Maurice could have something up his sleeve made her inner belly tingle with excitement.

Her breath caught in her throat. "Okay."

He took her hand, led her out of the reception hall, and through the resort. Christmas trees lined the corridors, decorated with twinkling lights, tinsel, and stars. The party faded into the distance, replaced by ocean waves.

"Where are we going?"

"You'll see."

They went outside into the warm tropical air. She glanced up at the night sky twinkling with millions of stars, distracted as he led her down some stairs to a row of hotel rooms overlooking the ocean. He scanned his key card and held open the door to his room.

"Maurice, why did we leave the party?" Savannah stepped across the threshold, eyeing the big bed.

"I had to have you alone, Savannah. You have every right to be mad at me, but don't deny that you've thought about us since it ended. I know you have because I can't stop thinking about you."

She turned away to hide the automatic roll of her eyes. The softness of his hand on her cheek, steering her attention back to him, made tingles run down her neck into her belly.

"I know I screwed up. Being in this wedding together gave me a chance to try to mend our relationship. What I did was stupid."

"And selfish."

"Yes, and selfish. I'll do whatever you want to have a second chance."

"I'm not interested in anything serious, Maurice."

"I know. But us being here at this wedding together... I'd be a fool to pass up this chance."

"Why did you bring me here?"

"This is crazy, what I'm about to say. Forgive me... I want to taste you again. Remember how I used to make you squirt? Would you like me to do it again?"

Her mouth hung slack.

"I won't unless you're willing. You're so sexy, Savannah. You deserve only the best. Remember how I made you cum, before? Just give me permission, and I'll take the lead like I did on the dance floor."

She couldn't deny the interest in having Maurice give her an orgasm. He was a good dancer, but he was an even better lover. A hint of mischief pulled at her lips. Not many men could live up to her expectations. Maurice was true to his word. A blush rushed over her cheeks at the thought of Sebastian looking for her at the party. Could this be her gift to herself this holiday season? A couple of men underneath the Christmas tree?

She whispered, "You know I like being naughty?"

He arched an eyebrow at her and steered her toward the bed.

Her hand on his chest stopped him. "This doesn't mean we're back together."

"I know." He smirked. "Consider this my gift to you."

A flutter danced in her low belly, and she bit her lip. He guided her to sit on the bed. She pulled up her coral skirt and slipped off her white lacey underwear. Maurice dropped to his knees between her thighs, hungry to begin. She whimpered at his gentle touch. Warm tingles moved up her legs into her belly. He leaned into her bare sex, taking a deep inhale. Sliding his hands under her ass, encouraging her knees to bend, opening herself more to him—and her own urges. She cooed as she felt the tip of his tongue just outside her sweet hole. A gasp escaped her lips as he slowly licked upwards between her labia, tasting her sweetness. She thrust her pelvis, longing for him to move his tongue, which rested right on top of her clit for what seemed like forever. Slowly, his tongue started moving back and forth. A moan of pleasure rose from her throat, and she arched back. He pursed his lips over her hardened clit and massaged it with his tongue while gently sucking.

Savannah cried out in shock, then moaned low as Maurice kept working. His hands spread her open further. She pulled her knees back, exposing herself. Her pussy pulsating and tensing. Ripples of pleasure coursed through her as deep groans filled the room, growing louder and louder as Maurice sped up. His hard cock pressed against the zipper of his grey pants, but he ignored it; there was only one thing he cared about in that moment, and he wouldn't stop until he succeeded. A single drop breached out of her and ran down between her sweet lower cheeks, spurring him on. He pressed down a little harder, the pulsating increasing. Savannah's eyes rolled back in pure bliss, unable to move or stop the building pressure tingling below. She knew what was coming as her body shook uncontrollably and her moans turned guttural, and higher pitched. Then the sweet relief of her orgasm rushed over her; so powerful that a torrent of her juices exploded like a geyser out of her.

Maurice moved his head out of the way, just in time, witnessing a soda can's worth of fluid jet passed, soaking the blanket. Savannah groaned and panted with each diminishing blast, until she was spent. He stood admiring her lying flat on her back, legs spread, panting from pleasure. Grabbing a towel, he wiped her juices from his face. A silly grin danced into his eyes at a job well done, and he passed her the towel. She wiped her legs and pussy. Not bothering to put her underwear on, she handed them to Maurice. He snatched them and brought them to his nose, sniffing hard.

"Mmm. I will cherish these."

Savannah laughed.

"I'll escort you back to your room so you can freshen up. Unless you want to use my shower?"

"I'll use yours." She turned toward the bathroom and felt Maurice follow behind her. She turned and stopped him. "You've already had a shower, Maurice," she teased, and closed the door behind her. She cleaned herself up with a washcloth, then fixed her makeup. When finished, she came out, smoothing down her dress. "Are you okay if we go back to the party separately? I don't want Angie or Abigail poking their nose in my business."

"Of course. My only ask is that when our paths cross again, you'll give me a chance to play with you again."

She wrapped her arms around his neck and brought her lips near his. "After what you've done to me today, how could I not?"

A low growl rumbled in his chest, and he pressed his lips against hers so she could taste herself on his lips.

"Until next time, sweet Savannah." He patted her on the bum as she left.

She walked back into the music of the party, finding the dance in full swing. The base reverberated through her chest. It surprised her that she couldn't find Sebastian when she scanned the room. Though her time with Maurice had been fun, she had no interest in reigniting their relationship. He was a good lover, she wanted to leave it at that. Sebastian, on the other hand, she wanted to explore again.

Chapter 3

Savannah spent the next few hours dancing, drinking, and eating, all while in the back of her mind she wondered where Sebastian had gone. She couldn't avoid Maurice when the groomsmen and bride's maids all danced in a circle around Angie and Dave. He kept trying to catch her attention, but she continued to ignore him. She wanted to be with Sebastian, not Maurice. Later, Angie threw the bouquet, and Savannah purposefully let other single ladies scramble for it while she stood with her arms crossed over her chest.

Abigail shook her head. "I don't get you. You're such a catch. Why won't you settle down with a man?"

"Not every woman needs to settle, Abigail. Besides, I haven't found a man who can handle this." She gestured to herself with a devilish smirk.

"You have Maurice wrapped around your little finger."

Savannah shrugged.

"No? Maybe Dave's new friend, then?"

"What about him?"

Abigail chuckled. "Oh, Savannah, you're trouble. Don't wait too long, or a catch like Maurice will slip you by." She squeezed Savannah's hand and walked away.

Savannah rolled her shoulders back, not wanting to admit that Abigail was right. Maurice was a catch and had given her some of the best orgasms in her life. She scanned the hall in search of him, deflating a little at the sight of a blond woman in his arms. The skin on Savannah's neck prickled; the woodsy aroma from someone behind her consumed her.

"You're not as much trouble as I am." The low growl in her ear stole her attention. His breath on her neck sent chills down her back.

Not wanting to turn around, she leaned back into Sebastian's chest. "Mmm...I like trouble."

"Is that why you snuck off with Maurice?"

Her breath caught in her throat, and she nodded.

"Hmm... troublesome girls need to be taught a lesson."

She pressed her ass back, feeling his cock stiffening inside his black pants.

"Is that a yes?"

She spun around and wrapped her arms around his neck, pulling him close. Their lips nearly touching. "Yes, please teach me a lesson, Sebastian."

A grin pulled at his lips. He took her hand and led her out of the party. A large fish tank separated them from a bar lounge; the light through the water rippled on the floor. They reached the elevators, and he punched the button. He pulled her into his arms and crushed his lips against hers. Melting in his arms, she moaned through his kiss.

"Are you going to finish what we started this morning?"

He kissed her deeply in reply.

The same ringtone from that morning interrupted them. He pulled back, cursing under his breath. Savannah bit her lip, anticipating him answering his mother's call. His dark eyes drilled into hers as he pulled out his phone. To her surprise, he tossed it into the aquarium with a plop. Savannah stared at the drowning phone in disbelief.

"What about your mother?"

"Oh, Savannah. I love my mother, but she won't cockblock me tonight."

Savannah giggled.

"There's my smile." He caressed her cheek, staring into her eyes. "All these years we've known each other, did you ever imagine this?"

She shook her head.

"Your allure is impossible to ignore. Good thing we're here together now."

"It sure is."

A smug grin pulled at his lips with the chime of the elevator. He grabbed her and stepped in. The doors hadn't closed before he had her pressed against the wall, claiming her mouth again. When the door opened, he hoisted her over his shoulder.

"Sebastian!" she squealed.

He smacked her ass in response, carried her to his room, and dumped her on the bed with a bounce. Savannah playfully crawled away, causing him to grasp one of her ankles. She looked back and their eyes met; she melted, drunk with lust. Sebastian yanked her towards him, making her giggle as she slid under him from the mighty heave. Her dress pulled up, exposing her bare bottom.

"Oh, Savannah... tsk, tsk. No undies?"

She bit her lip and shook her head.

"You're in big trouble." He rolled her on her back and spread her legs wide. "What have you been up to since I last saw you? You're so wet already." He slowly traced her pussy lips with his finger, as she whimpered and squirmed. Nipples hard, skin tingling with excitement, her breath caught in her throat.

"No, don't answer that. It's a good thing you're ready to go. I've been aching to be inside you all day."

He shifted off the bed, removing his suit jacket and unbuttoning his shirt. She propped herself up on her elbows, watching him revealing his muscular chest. As he undid his belt buckle, she licked her lips. A smirk pulled at the corner of his mouth, watching her reaction. He pulled off his pants, exposing his rigid, hard cock.

Savannah's mind whirled with the possibilities. Something was different about him, but she couldn't put her finger on it. Men in the past had been dominant, and though she melted for them, none gazed into her soul the way Sebastian did. She ran her fingers over her bare skin, aching for his touch.

He crawled back on top of her, kissing her deeply and rubbing his dick against her clit. She moaned into his lips and arched against him. The tease was too much; she squirmed, trying to angle her opening to his tip.

His lips brushed against her ear. "What do you want, Savannah?"

"You inside me!" she said breathily. He stopped moving. Pinned underneath him, she struggled to get what she wanted. "Please, Sebastian!"

"Say it."

"Please, Sebastian, I want you inside me!"

He chuckled lightly. "That's a good girl." Between gentle pecks along her neck and collarbone, he said, "Here's what'll happen, Savannah. I'll fuck you until I cum deep inside you. Then, you'll lick your lady juices off me until I'm hard again. Then, you'll suck me until I cum down your throat." She shuddered as heat covered her skin. "How's that sound?"

"Oh! Yes, please!"

With a shift of his weight, his hard cock slid into her. She moaned as ripples of pleasure washed over her; another orgasm threatening to explode. He thrust into her, over and over. He angled her legs to get deeper. Fingernails dug into his back as her orgasm ripped her apart. Cries of pleasure filled the room. Not relenting, Sebastian kept his rhythm steady, carrying Savannah through waves of her orgasms before he finally finished. He held her in his arms, until both their breathing calmed.

Without prompting, Savannah sat up, slipped out of her dress and crawled lower on the bed. Sebastian's eyes widened as Savannah started licking her juices off his semi-hard cock. With each lick, his dick twitched back to life. Soon it was stiff, and Savannah wasted no time drawing him fully into her mouth. He groaned as she masterfully twirled her tongue around his shaft and then sucked him deep. His eyes rolled back in his head. The thought of pleasuring Sebastian had been at the back of her mind all day. Now, she wanted his dick at the back of her throat.

"Oh, Savannah! I'm going to cum!"

She sucked harder until sweetness exploded down her throat, and she happily swallowed his cum. Licking her lips, she crawled up to nestle into his chest. His arm wrapped around her, fingers caressing her skin.

"That was hot."

"It sure was. Had I known, I would've stopped you from heading off with Maurice earlier."

"Oh?"

"Yeah. What did he offer you?"

"Does it matter?"

Sebastian paused to think about it.

Savannah pushed herself up. "It doesn't. Maurice and I have a past. That's where he's going to stay."

"What about us?"

Her conversation with Abigail rang in her ears. She couldn't pass up the chance to be with Sebastian, and the prospect of being with him more than casually made her chest warm and gooey. Plagued by the fear of rejection, she bit her lip with uncertainty.

"Now that I've had you, I won't let you slip away that quick."

"Sebastian, I'm not a woman who likes to be tied down." He arched an eyebrow at her, and she blushed. "I meant, I do better solo. But if you want to play from time to time..."

"Whatever you want. Just when you're with me, you're mine."

Her stomach fluttered with excitement. No point in denying herself more play with Sebastian, she opted to do it until it wasn't fun anymore. If that lasted longer than a couple of months, then so be it. She kissed him. "Yes, sir."

Sebastian gripped the back of her neck, holding her as he ravaged her lips. He pulled back, his voice gravely and deep. "That's my good girl."

She smiled at him.

"And there's my smile." He stroked her cheek, then tucked a strand of her sandy-brown hair behind her ear. "So, maybe we should do this again at New Year's."

"You're going to make me wait until New Year's?"

"Well, no..." Sebastian glanced at his stiffening cock.

Savannah followed his gaze with a devilish grin.

Thank you for reading! This is the first published story from Ginny B. Logan. She's a prolific writer who lives what she writes about, at least sometimes. It was edited by Faye Knightly, author of Breeders, and Ancients. Thanks to her friends on TikTok, this anthology came to be. As a new indie author, she's thrilled to share her erotic tales and all the naughty little bits. Would you like more? Let Ginny know by emailing: admin@nofi.ca

21
Silent Night

Rayona Lovely Wilson

It's Christmas Eve. I should be home—kneeling in a sea of wrapping paper with my nieces and nephews, laughing while they beg to open "just one" gift before midnight. That thought is the only thing keeping me going, pushing to get done in this too-quiet office. One more file to submit, one more email to send, and then I'll be free for the week.

"Jahlani," Tyler's voice cuts into the silence. He leans over my shoulder, close, his breath fanning my neck. I stiffen, shifting forward in my chair. "Please tell me it's done."

"I'm submitting it now." My voice sounds steadier than I feel. I glance at him, then back at the glowing screen. *Almost free. Just finish.*

"Good," he says, his hand settling heavy on my shoulder. It lingers longer than I want it to. My pulse jumps. I've told him before not to touch me, but the message never seems to land.

"I should get going now." I push back my chair, standing, but his grip tightens on me.

"Wait." His smile doesn't reach his eyes. "I have a gift for you since you stayed and helped me finish."

Every instinct in me screams *no*. But he's already steering me toward his office, his hand clamped like iron. I stumble, my protest thin in my throat.

"Tyler— my family's waiting. I've been here all day." They never start without everybody being there. I don't want to ruin the tradition.

The door shuts behind us with a click that echoes. My chest caves inward. The warmth of Christmas, of home, of safety feels miles away.

"Sit," he orders, shoving me toward the couch. I fall, breath knocking out of me. My mind splinters. The holiday lights flicker outside the window, blurred through sudden tears. I hear my nieces' laughter in memory, a ghost of what I should have.

"Please," I beg. "I n-need to go home." My words dissolve in the air, swallowed by the office walls and Christmas music playing throughout the building. He looms above me, a shadow blotting out every thought of escape.

"You know you want me," he says, slowly unbuttoning his suit jacket. "I see the way you look at me, and you stayed late to help me finish this."

"No." I try to stand, but he grabs my wrist. "Y-you asked me to stay. You're the boss. I need to go." I watch as his fingers trail down to his belt. "I-I'll r-report you," I stammer.

And then pain, sudden and sharp, explodes across my face as his hand cracks against my cheek. My head whips to the side, a metallic tang filling my mouth. My ears ring, drowning out even my voice.

"Who's gonna believe you?" he whispers, pinning my wrists down against the couch. "There are no cameras." He leans down, placing a kiss against my cheek, then moves down to my throat.

"Please ..." I scream as he sinks his teeth into my throat.

I don't remember when the tears start, only that it feels like Christmas is gone—ripped from me, shattered—leaving nothing but the taste of blood and the sound of my heart breaking in my chest.

The office door slams behind me as I stumble into the early morning cold. My chest heaves, lungs clawing for air that won't come. The December wind cuts across my face, stinging the fresh bruise blooming on my cheek. I wipe blood from the corner of my mouth with trembling fingers, only to smear it further across my skin.

I look down at my ripped shirt, my tie hanging loose, belt crooked. My reflection in the dark office window is a stranger. My hair wild where he yanked it terrifies me. I tug my coat around me, but it does nothing to cover the cracks inside.

Go home. Drive. Get to your family. Pretend. Smile.

My keys rattle violently in my hand, I drop them twice before getting into my car. The steering wheel is foreign under my palms, slick with sweat. The radio comes on automatically, cheerful Christmas music spilling into the silence. I slam it off as my breath fogs the windshield, shallow, uneven.

I start the engine, and the headlights cut through the empty parking lot. The road blurs. My cheek throbs where his hand struck, my lip split and burning. My wrists ache from where he pinned me down and squeezed hard. Every time I blink, the office walls close in again, and I can't breathe. Every time I move, the pain gets worse. If I could walk, I would.

"Stop," I whisper to myself as my voice cracks. "Stop thinking. Drive."

I pull onto the road, my tires crunching over thin ice. The world is so quiet. My family is probably pouring cocoa, handing out gifts, waiting for me. My sister will ask where I am. My nieces will ask if Uncle Jahlani's coming.

Tears spill hot, blurring the red and green holiday lights strung along the trees above. I swipe at my eyes with the back of my sleeve, but my vision keeps smearing. The wheel jerks under my unsteady grip.

"Focus."

The headlights of an oncoming car flare brightly, and I flinch. My tires skid over the ice, spinning me sideways. The world tilts. Screeching metal, a violent jolt, my body thrown against the seatbelt. Glass cracks, spider webbing across the windshield as the car slams into a snowbank.

Everything is silent.

I gasp, chest tight, ears ringing. Pain radiates through my shoulder where the seatbelt bit into me. My ribs where I hit the steering wheel ache. My head swims. I try to breathe, but each inhale scrapes against the sob already lodged in my throat.

Outside, snowflakes drift down, soft and indifferent. Inside, I shake, staring at my bloody reflection in the shattered glass. All I can think is: *I should be home. I should be safe. I should be with my family celebrating Christmas Eve.*

But I'm not.

Something icy and wet soaks into my clothes, seeping through every layer until my skin is ice. I try to move, but the car is on its side. My seatbelt digs into my shoulder, locking me in place. When water spills across my face, rising fast, panic shreds through me.

I thrash, clawing at the belt. It won't budge. The water creeps higher, lapping at my lips.

I'm going to die.

My family will wonder where I am. My nieces will think I forgot them. They'll never know what happened, what was taken from me.

The cold swallows my face. My lungs burn. My last thought is bitter: *I deserve this. I couldn't stop him. And now I'm going to die.*

It's okay, though. I'd rather die than face what happened.

Air explodes back into me with a violent cough. My chest heaves, every inhale like knives. I blink, dazed, but the darkness won't lift.

Above me, blurred against lights and trees, is a man with long hair falling into his face. His voice cuts through the ringing in my ears.

"Oh God—you're breathing. Keep breathing. The ambulance is coming."

Ambulance. The words drift around me. I try to answer, but nothing leaves my throat.

"Hey, stay with me. Open your eyes."

I want to, but my eyelids are too heavy. My body shifts—hands hauling me upward, cradling me—and I wonder if I'm already gone, carried off somewhere else.

"You're safe now," he whispers, so close his words warm my frozen skin.

Safe? I'll never feel safe again.

Christmas was supposed to be special, like it has been every year. Now, I hate it. I hate this day, hate what it used to mean.

"He's sleeping right now. The doctor said he's lucky. It could've been worse."

Mom's voice pulls me from the dark, soft and far away at first—as if echoing underwater. Then the pain comes. My head throbs. My chest is tight. My throat burns every time I breathe.

I open my mouth, but nothing comes out. Not even a whisper.

"Let the kids open their gifts," Mom says somewhere nearby. "I know they're being patient, but they're kids." There's a faint laugh, tired but real. "He would want them to enjoy Christmas morning. We'll get home as soon as possible."

Christmas. The word floats through the haze belonging to someone else's life.

I blink until the blur clears and find her sitting in a chair by the window, hair pulled back, glasses slipping down her nose. The sight of her makes something in my chest ache. I lift my hand—slow, trembling—until she sees me.

"Jahlani," she gasps, standing so fast the chair scrapes against the floor. "Sweetie, you're awake." She's beside me in seconds, taking my hand, pressing it to her chest. "I was so worried. I'm sorry your Christmas is starting off like this."

I shake my head. Christmas doesn't matter. Nothing does. I want to go home.

"How are you feeling?"

I try again to speak, but my voice isn't working. Panic creeps in as I reach for my throat. Why can't I say anything? What happened?

"Woah, sweetie, breathe." Her hand moves to my shoulder, but the pressure sends pain shooting up my neck. I jerk back with a hiss. "I'll get the doctor."

No. I don't want her to leave. I grab her wrist—weakly, but enough to stop her. The look on her face makes my stomach twist. I must look terrified. Maybe I am.

"Jahlani, breathe. Slow down." She rubs my head like she used to when I was little, voice breaking. "One breath at a time."

The door opens. The sound makes me jump. A man walks in, smiling politely as he steps closer. His shoes squeak against the tile. White coat. Clipboard.

My body goes cold.

"I'm Dr. Paul Lacy," he says gently. "It's good to see you're awake." He pulls out a small flashlight and leans over me. "Can you do me a favor and follow the light for me?"

He reaches toward me—and before I can stop myself, I flinch hard, heart slamming against my ribs.

"It's okay," he says quickly, freezing mid-motion. "You're safe, alright? I won't touch you."

Mom looks between us, worried. "He's having trouble breathing. I was just about to find someone."

The doctor nods and gives her a small, reassuring smile, but I can't look at him. I squeeze my eyes shut, willing myself to calm down—but behind my closed eyes, I see Tyler. His hands. His weight. The sound of my own voice begging him to stop.

"Jahlani?" the doctor says softly. "I'm going to have the nurse bring you something to help you relax, okay? Just to help with the pain and panic."

I nod, but I don't believe him. My lungs burn, every breath scrapes raw against my chest. I want to go home. I want it to be Christmas again, but before all this happened. I want to be the person I was yesterday.

The machines beep beside me—steady and slowly, everything blurs again. The doctor's voice fades. Mom's hand stays in mine, and as I sink back into the dark, all I can think ...

Why did this happen to me?

"Do you want to talk with your mom here? I wanted to go over your injuries and some inconsistencies I noticed," Dr. Lacy says. He's holding the clipboard, fingers tight around it like he's bracing for something. His eyes flick from me to Mom.

"What do you mean?" My voice comes out small. I stare at him, confused. My mind's still somewhere else, replaying headlights, tires and the sound of my own breathing breaking apart.

"Would you like your mom here while we talk?" he asks quietly. "Your privacy is important."

I glance at Mom. She's still gripping my hand, eyes glassy with worry. I don't want her to hear whatever he's about to say. It's her favorite holiday. How could I ruin that?

I also don't want to be alone with him. I can't win.

"Why don't I go grab some coffee?" she says after a moment, her thumb brushing my knuckles. "I'll come back right away."

When she leaves, everything is louder—the hum of the machines, the drip of the IV, the pulse in my throat. Dr. Lacy drags the chair closer, the scrape of its legs making me flinch. I'm sure he notices.

"You were in a car accident," he says gently, lowering himself into the chair. "And while your injuries aren't life-threatening, I'm concerned about what may have happened before that." He sets the clipboard in his lap. "Every time I'm near, you flinch or panic. And there are bruises on your wrists and throat that don't match your seatbelt pattern."

My heart stops. Does he know? Oh God, he knows. I look at the blanket, but it's just white. I can't find air. My fingers dig into the sheets.

"Jahlani," he continues, voice soft but steady, "whenever somebody comes in from an accident, they're examined head to toe for injuries. That's standard. But some of what we found… it doesn't look like something from the crash."

I shake my head, hard, trying to rattle his words loose before they stick. "I don't—please don't—"

He pauses. "You had other bruises. Different shapes. Like you were grabbed. If you're willing, I'd like to talk about—"

"N-no." It bursts out fast and sharp. My throat closes around the sound.

He leans back, eyes kind but heavy. "Okay. That's okay," he says, hands lifted slightly. "But if you were hurt by someone, you don't have to go through this alone. There are people here who can help. You're safe right now."

Safe. The word is wrong. Nothing feels safe. The lights are bright, making my head ache. I can't look at him. I can't look at anything.

His voice keeps going, but it's far away now, underwater. All I hear is the echo of my own heartbeat and that one word—assaulted—reverberating inside my skull until it's just noise.

I press my palms to my ears. I want it to stop. "I want to go home," I whisper. It barely sounds like me.

Dr. Lacy nods slowly. "We'll take care of you first. One step at a time." He stands, quiet as he can, and leaves me there with the beeping machines and the ache in my chest.

The moment the door shuts, I let the blankness take me. It's easier that way—just letting everything fade out until I don't have to be here. Until I don't have to be me.

***

The door opens again, slow and careful. I'm not sure what time it is, but I need to leave. I can't be here anymore

"Hey, sweetheart," Mom whispers, stepping back into the room with a paper cup in her hand. The smell of coffee fills the air, warm and bitter. "You okay? You look pale."

I nod quickly. My voice doesn't come. It's trapped somewhere behind the tremor in my jaw.

She sets the cup on the tray beside me and sits back in the chair Dr. Lacy was in. The warmth of her hand finds mine, but I don't squeeze back. I can't. If I do, she'll know. She'll feel everything shaking under my skin.

"What did the doctor say?" she asks softly.

My mouth opens, but nothing comes out. The words pile up behind my teeth — He knows. He saw. He asked. Instead, I mumble, "Just... checking things."

She nods, but her eyes linger too long, searching my face. "You scared me, Jahlani. When they called about the accident, I thought I was gonna lose you."

Her voice cracks and I wish I could tell her the truth — that part of me already feels gone. That I don't even know who's sitting here right now. But the thought of saying it, of watching her face shatter, makes my throat close up again.

So, I stare at the blanket instead, the same white noise I've been hiding in since it happened. I focus on a loose thread until it doubles, then triples, until my vision fuzzes out completely.

She squeezes my hand. "I'm here, baby. Whatever it is, we'll get through it. It's your favorite day of the year. Maybe we can go home soon and be with everyone."

I nod, but words don't reach me. They float somewhere above, in that safe space I've built between the world and what's left of me.

And I stay there — quiet, still, gone — while she sits beside me, not realizing I'm already somewhere she can't follow.

2.

"Jahlani, you have a visitor," Mom says gently, sitting on the side of my bed. "I told him I'd ask you first before letting him in."

I open my eyes slowly. The world's still too bright. I blink at her, not sure who would want to see me. I don't want to see anybody. I just want the room dark and quiet again. But I don't say that.

"He's the one who pulled you out of the car," she explains. "He said he wanted to make sure you're alright."

The man who pulled me from the wreckage. I remember his arms around me, his voice in my ear — steady and calm even while everything burned and screamed. For a second, I thought he was an angel.

"Are you okay with that?"

I don't know why I nod. Maybe because saying no feels wrong. She squeezes my arm and leaves, the click of the door pulling something inside me tight.

A few minutes later, the door opens. A man dressed in black steps in, his movements careful, almost hesitant. His hair's tied back loosely, strands falling across his face. One of his hands is bandaged.

"Hi," he says softly, sitting in the empty chair beside my bed.

I watch him, not able to say anything because my throat is locked.

"Glad you're alright," he murmurs after a beat. "My name's MinJae. You're Jahlani, right?"

I blink at him. He smiles — small, patient.

"Do you speak Korean? Or maybe you prefer English." he asks, his voice dipping as if he's worried about saying the wrong thing. When I shake my head, he exhales in relief.

"Okay, how are you feeling? Probably not great."

My voice still won't work, but I find myself watching him. The guy who saved me.

He hesitates, studying me with quiet eyes. "Those bruises on your neck and wrist ... are those from the accident?"

My breath catches. I pull my hands beneath the blanket, hiding the bruises even though it's too late. How did he notice?

"Did you talk to the doctor? Or your mother?"

The question lands heavily. I close my eyes and take a long, shaking breath. Tyler said he'd kill me. He said he'd kill my family. I can't. I can't tell anyone.

He leans forward slightly. "If you want, I can help you talk to your mom."

I open my eyes and look at him. Why is he trying to help? He doesn't know me. Why does he care?

"It's Christmas," he says after a moment, his voice almost a whisper. "It should be a happy day."

Christmas. The word twists in my chest. It's supposed to mean warmth, laughter and lights — but all I feel is the weight of what happened. The icy hands that took everything from me.

Tears sting my eyes. I open my mouth to say something, anything, but the words dissolve before they leave.

"You don't have to be afraid. It'll be okay. You can tell them."

It's not okay. It'll never be okay. I want to believe him, but I can't. My world isn't the same anymore. It's cracked, and I'm falling through it.

"Breathe, Jalani."

I shake my head, trembling. I'm not safe. I'll never be safe. The tears spill, hot and relentless. My body shakes uncontrollably. I want to disappear.

Then I feel his hand close over mine — steady, warm, rough. Not like the hands that hurt me. His grip is gentle, grounding, real.

"If you don't want to tell anyone," he says, voice breaking slightly, "tell me. So it's not heavy on your heart."

I want to. God, I want to. But I can't. I shake my head.

"That's okay," he says quietly. "You're not ready. But when you are — you can trust me."

The door opens. Mom's standing there, watching me, her eyes full of concern. I pull my hand back before she sees.

"The doctor says you can go home if you'd like," she tells me.

Home. My apartment feels like the only place I can disappear.

"Why don't you come with me instead?" Mom says. "Be around your family for Christmas. You've been through so much. It'll make you feel better."

It won't. Nothing will. But I can't say that. I nod, though, pushing myself up and the room tilts, spinning.

"Slow," MinJae murmurs, a hand hovering near my shoulder but not touching.

I nod again, my chest tight. I don't deserve his kindness — or hers. They should both go enjoy their Christmas and forget I exist.

But they don't.

And that's what hurts the most.

The bathroom light hums above me, echoing off my skull. The light shows everything I wish would stay hidden.

Mom packed my clothes from home. A hoodie. Sweatpants. New shoes and socks. Things that smell faintly of detergent and her. I stare at them sitting on the counter for a long time before I move.

My fingers shake as I peel away the hospital gown. My skin feels foreign — mapped with bruises that don't belong to me. I don't look closely. I just breathe. In. Out.

MinJae's voice drifts through my head, soft and steady.

Breathe. You're safe now.

I grip the edge of the sink, bow my head, and try to believe it. But the memories come — headlights, glass, the sound of my own voice begging for it to stop. And his voice. Always his voice.

A sob escapes before I can swallow it back. My reflection blurs in the mirror — eyes swollen, lips trembling. I look like someone else. Someone I don't want to be.

I slide down the wall until I'm on the cold tile, knees pulled to my chest. The hoodie slips from my lap onto the floor. I press my forehead against it, the fabric dampening beneath my tears.

If you don't want to tell anyone, tell me so it's not heavy on your heart.

He made it sound easy. Like words could lift something this heavy. But it's not just heavy — it's buried. It's inside me. It's in my bones.

I choke on another sob, gasping between breaths, and I remember the way his hand felt — warm, solid, human. The only thing that didn't hurt to touch.

And that's what undoes me. Not the fear. Not the shame.

His kindness.

It splits me open. The tears, the guilt, the silence I've been holding like a shield. I can't stop it. I don't even try.

I let myself cry. I cry until my chest aches and my throat burns. Until there's nothing left but shaking.

When I finally get up, my reflection stares back — ruined, red-eyed, and broken.

I whisper the only words I can remember.

Take a breath.

The air trembles in my lungs, but I breathe anyway.

Even if I don't believe I'm safe yet. Even if it's just for one second.

When I pull the hoodie over my head, I glimpse the bruises on my wrists and look away fast as my throat tightens.

Jahlani. Breathe. You're safe now.

MinJae's voice plays in my head like a song that doesn't belong to Christmas.

I lean against the sink, my reflection swimming in the mirror. Outside, faint holiday music drifts from whatever Mom put on the TV — soft and cheerful.

Christmas used to mean something. Lights. Laughter. Cinnamon in the air. Now it just feels like another day I have to survive.

My hands shake as I pull on the sweats. I whisper the words again — take a deep breath— and try to believe it'll be okay, just for a heartbeat.

But when I look at my reflection one last time, I know this Christmas will never feel the same.

(Take a deep breath)

22

Jingle Balls

Ginger Moonwitch

Trigger Warnings
BDSM
D/S
Impact Play
Piercings
Tail Play

Character Descriptions

Santa

Height-6'2
    Eyes-Icy blue
    Appearance- Big, muscular, dad-bod sexy santa, tattoos (reindeer, presents, naughty and nice list, infinity with ms.clause name) long white beard.
    Schlong- Jacob's ladder (one for each reindeer)

Krampus

Height-9'4
    Eyes-Red

Appearance- Huge, muscular, ripped, sexy krampus, black and grey swirled skin, grey curled horns, tail with arrow pointed tip.

Krampus

Christmas Eve, December 24, the day before the holly-jolly family bullshit. I fucking hate this time of year. The only good thing about it is causing fuckery for mister Old Saint Nicholas. Messing with that happy dipshit is the only fun I get.

I conjure my portal and step out into the North Pole. The cool chill from the snowflakes drizzling down has me cringing. Christmas is only good for scaring the bad kids.

The small cabin sits in the middle of the forest. Lights twinkle on the trees as smoke flows from the chimney. Every year I come to have a little meeting with Santa.

He disapproves of me messing with his precious holiday.

Well, fuck him and the sleigh he rode in on. I don't care what that cookie-munching, milk guzzling, Christmas bitch thinks.

I fling the door to the cabin open and step in. The warmth from the fire smacks me in the face. This cabin only holds a bed and 3 toy chests. Two chairs sit off to the side. The bed frame is made of iron and is sturdy as fuck.

As much as I pretend to hate these meetings, a shiver shoots up my spine for what I know is to come.

The sound of the door smacking into the wall draws my attention to it. Santa in all his glory steps into the threshold, his bushy brows pinched in frustration, while the rest of his face remains blank.

I can't lie; he's a handsome fucker. Although he's shorter than me by a few feet, he radiates strength and power. He ignores me and moves into the cabin with a gracefulness that I know is all an act.

His fingers unbuckle the belt around his waist before moving on to pop open the buttons to his red fur coat. The fabric slides off, showing his tattooed forearms and firm body. Pictures of his reindeer, presents, and his nice list form a sleeve of artwork over those biceps. Everyone thinks he's a fat jolly saint, but I know the truth.

Under the white muscle shirt is a toned dad bod, the slight abs visible yet cushioned. There is nothing flabby about this man. I can see the faint outline of the gold hoops that run through his nipples pressing against the shirt.

My tail flicks behind me as I run my eyes up and down his body. "Hello fat ass, has it been a year already?"

His icy, piercing gaze snaps to me as his lips press together in a thin line. "I don't understand how you seem to forget your manners every fucking year. But don't worry, we will fix that." He stalks towards me, his hand shooting out to grip my throat in a firm hold. His thumb and index finger press my artery, cutting off the blood flow to give me that dizzy sensation.

A gasp leaves me as he swipes a leg, ripping mine out from under me. My knees crack against the wooden floorboards as I lock my gaze on him.

"That's better, you know you're supposed to greet me on your knees. It's a good thing I give you an attitude check every year. I swear you'd be a bigger pain in the dick if I didn't. Now address me properly." His voice is firm and level. Though I know he's going to enjoy the pain he's planning to inflict on me tonight.

"Good evening, Saint." I grit out as my lungs burn from his grip on my throat. My eyeballs are on the verge of popping out of their sockets. He gives a last squeeze and releases my neck, his open palm slapping my cheek twice.

"Good whore. Now while you're down there, you might as well put that mouth to use." Santa rips the zipper of his pants down and reaches a hand in. The massive yule log he packs in those tight pants almost smacks me in the face. My mouth drools as I take in the carefully placed piercings that make up the Jacob's ladder on the underside of his shaft.

His fists wrap around my horns as he wrenches my head towards his cock. "Open your fucking mouth."

I'm pathetic for him. My mouth opens on command, tongue flopping out like a puppy as a line of drool drips down to the floor. Santa smirks down at me; using his hips, he slaps me with his hard rod. I know the rules. No hands.

With nothing but my tongue, I slurp his tip past my lips. His salty, sweet candy cane flavour explodes over my tastebuds. The second my lips wrap around his head, my saint snaps his hips. Every inch of his magnificent shaft fills my mouth and breaches my throat.

The smooth metal of his Jacob's ladder caresses my tongue as I gag. My eyes fly open, tears burning behind them. Santa doesn't give me a chance to adjust, using my horns to control my head. The jingle of his balls ringing in my ears with each thrust.

Spit drips out from the corners of my lips as he face fucks me. My tears leave black salty tracks down my cheeks as I sputter and choke.

My saint throws his head back, a deep gruntal groan leaving him with a hiss. "Fucking divine, I missed this fucking mouth. We might have to make our meetings a twice a year thing."

I look up with glassy eyes, my nails digging into my thighs as I focus on breathing through my nose. Each thrust has more tears pouring as I slurp and suck. My tongue laps around his shaft, toying with the veins and piercings.

My eyes roll back in my skull; Santa pushes my head down, smashing my face to his pelvis. The scent of his musk and shortbread cologne fills my nose. I thrash my head as my air is cut off by his cock. His peppermint splooge shooting down my throat. It's too much for me to swallow; ropes pour out of my mouth and nose. The minty shit burning my nostrils.

After a few seconds, he releases me and shoves me away. I gasp and cough as I suck in precious air. My tongue darts out to lick my lips, not wanting to waste a single drop of its goodness.

"Wipe your dirty face and get on the bed. Second position," Santa's deep voice orders. He spins on his heels, giving me his back, and moves to the toy chest. Using my arm, I wipe the mixture of drool, cum and tears before getting up. My legs shake, and I stumble towards the bed.

I crawl onto the silk sheets, moving to the centre on my hands and knees. Dropping my shoulders, I stretch my arms out towards the headboard. My ass up high in the air as I widen my knees, pointing my feet towards each corner of the footboard. I know what's about to happen.

Santa's steps ring loud in my ears as he approaches the bed. I keep my face tilted to the right, his fingers trailing over my ass cheeks and up the length of my tail. "Good whore. See, you just need to be reminded of your place."

He grips my tail just above the middle and maneuvers it closer to him. His free hand gripping my left cheek as he wrenches it apart. The sound of his 'hawk tua' is like a gun being fired, his spit splattering on the tip of my tail.

"I'm just gonna borrow this for a minute." He chuckles.

My arrow tip spears through my puckered hole, stretching me open as I cry out. Santa's deep belly laughs, mocking me as he pushes more of my tail inside me. "Deep breaths, Krampsy, just need to get you loose. Do NOT move!"

The bitch unceremoniously shoves my own fucking tail up my ass!

My lungs burn, still trying to recover from the facefuck as I relax my ring of muscles. Inner walls pulsating around my tail, my body stiff with my attempts to stay still.

Santa moves towards the end of the bed, the familiar sensation of garland wrapping around my ankle. He pulls it further apart and ties my hooves to the post, moving to the next; he repeats the process.

I whimper as the new angle has my tail shifting in my hole. My cock rock hard under the small strip of fabric that I wear tied around my hips for modesty. Right now, I'm sure the cloth is flapping freely, showing off my throbbing shaft. Santa strides towards the head of the bed, his hands gently encircling my wrists as he ties tree lights around my limbs.

My saint pulls the string of bulbs tight and ties the length to the headboard. I can't move, completely bound to his mercy. My eyes roam up his body. The man is naked from the waist down. He winks at me and grips the edge of the muscle shirt stretched over his torso.

He rips it off over his head, my gaze moving to the gold hoops with little snowflakes in the centre. Santa stares into my soul, his hand moving behind me. My tail thrusts in deeper, and I mewl like a kitten as he fucks my tail in and out of my hole.

My Saint's hand reaches under me, his fist wrapping around my cock as he squeezes the tip. "You know the rules. You better not cum until I tell you. Understood?"

I bob my head against the bed, and I moan. "Yes, saint."

He gives me a quick, rough stroke before releasing my dick. Moving out of my eyeline, I feel the shift on the bed as he mounts behind me. "I always look forward to your yearly attitude checks. Your tight ass is always so greedy for my cock."

My tail gets ripped out with a pop, and I groan, my shoulders pressing into the bed. Something smooth and flat skims over my right globe, while my Saint's fingers massage my left. "Like every year, you are at the top of my naughty list. Let's clear the slate, shall we?"

The object retreats for a brief moment before he brings it down across my ass. Pain radiates through my backside as the paddle heats my skin. I cry out a moan, my ass arching up into the blows.

Pain blends with pleasure, my cock throbbing as I leak from the tip. My balls are heavy and full. We've only just begun, and I already want to blow my load. The slaps have me crying out as Santa spanks my naughty ass.

He covers every inch, even aiming for the underside to get the sensitive sit spots. I'll be feeling his torment for days after. The paddle moves lower, catching my hanging baubles.

I choke as my delicate balls sway and burn from the slap. My fists grips the cord of the lights wrapped around my wrists. "I'm sorry, I'll be a good boy, I promise!" I sob out, fiery pain covering my ass and balls.

Santa lays the paddle on my back. I feel him shift and then his lips press a gentle kiss on each cheek. "Good boy, I know you don't mean it. But I look forward to punishing you for your broken promise next year."

He leans down and places a kiss on my tender chestnuts, his tongue licking up my sack as he soothes my flesh. Pleasure shoots up my spine from the gentle caress, his warm wet mouth sucking them in.

His spit coats my testicles, sucking in soft pulses as they shift deeper behind his lips. Santa strokes my snow globes as he works. He pulls off with a wet pop and straightens up.

"Now, let's get to the fun part. My dick needs some love again. And I have a perfectly good slot right in front of me to stick it."

Santa

I bring my hand to my mouth and spit into my palm. Using my personal lube to coat my shaft. I soon need to get going, and at this point I won't have time to give my slut any aftercare. Usually we make these sessions an all-day ordeal, but I had some last-minute things that needed my attention.

My fingers tweak the balls of my first ladder piercing, the sharp bite of pain fuelling my lust. I grip my base and swipe up my whore's cheeks, rubbing it up his crack. Lining my tip with his hole, I give an experimental press on the puckered rim.

"You might want to relax. Your tail did a shit job at opening you up, and I don't have the patience to wait." I give him a second, watching as he takes a deep breath and sinks his torso deeper into the bed.

His muscles ripple as my Krampsy relaxes. I hum and press against the ring of muscles again. "Good slut. That's it, relax and open that pretty hole for your saint." I rock my hips and feel my tip pop past his pucker.

My bitch's muscles clench around me, and I groan. His warm ass flutters around me. I don't want to rip him, so I slowly gyrate my hips to help. Feeding him an inch slowly.

My first barbell slides in as Krampus gasps and grunts. "Dasher." I push further to the second.

"Dancer."

Another inch, another piercings. "Prancer."

Krampsy tenses up under me as he whimpers. "Wait, I need a minute."

I gently pet his back, the paddle having fallen to the bed long ago from our movements. "Relax and be a good boy. I know you want to get to Rudolph."

My hips pause as I give a few shallow thrusts with the inches he's already taken. My slut relaxes, a breathy moan leaving him as his hole tries to suck me in. I thrust deeper. "Vixen. Almost halfway there."

I look towards his hands, his knuckles white as he grips the cord of lights. Krampsy's chest rises as he pants; I know he's on the edge. But after years of our Christmas Eve sessions, I have him trained. He will wait for my command.

"Comet."

"Cupid."

"Donner."

"And Blitzen."

I still again, Krampus twitches on the bed as he rocks his hips back on my shaft. The greedy whore is just begging for more. "And now for the most famous of them all."

I ram the last few inches in, bottoming out as my whore cries out in bliss. The slut's back arches as his screams play the best music I've ever heard.

"Rudolph."

Krampus withers and squirms on my cock as my length throbs inside him. I'm being nice and giving him a moment to adjust. His muscles relax, and he stills on the bed, chest heaving with gulps of air.

"That's a good bitch. Now fucking take it." I pull out to Dasher and slam back in. With everything I've been doing, my release is on the edge. Though I know I'll be able to go another round after this.

My thrusts are brutal and punishing as I slam in and out of his tight, warm, juicy ass. I can feel how tightly coiled he is as he holds off his release. His moans, grunts and whimpers urge me to fuck him harder. My jingle balls slap against my cum dumpster's holly berries as I plow into him.

Krampsy is a puddle of sweat, leaking cum and boneless limbs beneath me. Right now, I only care about my pleasure. My hand cracks his ass cheek, and I watch the flesh ripple. Reddening and welting up with a pretty imprint of my hand.

I grip his hips, my nails digging in, and slam deep with a roar. My peppermint cream fills his hole to the brim. Spurt after spurt leaving me as my vision whites out. My body twitches with aftershocks, my chest heaving as I catch my breath.

Bending slightly, I look at his throbbing erection. The tip leaking that beautiful spicy icing onto the bed beneath him. "What a good little slut. You didn't cum. Don't worry soon. I'll let you blow soon."

My cock is still half hard as I slip out of his hole. My white and red glittery, swirled spunk drips out, flowing down his crack and covering his upper thighs.

I grab the garland holding his ankle, snap it off the bedpost and repeat the process with the other. My hands circle his hips, and I flip him over on his back. Krampsy's wrists pull on the cord of lights as they cinch tighter, cutting off the blood flow.

His tiny loin covering flaps up his abs, the beautiful grey and black marble cock jutting up in the air. I bend low, my tongue swiping up a string of cinnamon sugar cookie cum. A groan builds in my chest as I tease the slit with my tongue.

Krampus moans like the slut he is, my lips wrap around his tip and I give him a little suck. I might be a sadist with my naughty boy, but I'm not a selfish lover. He'll be satisfied before the night is out.

I pull more of his length into my mouth, taking special care to run my tongue over the veins. His balls are drawn up to his stomach, and I know it won't take much to set him off.

My cock is rock hard again, and I pull off him after a final deep throat guck. Gripping his thighs, I make his ankles act as earrings and line my cock up with his sloppy hole. My cum eases the way as I push in with a grunt.

I shift an arm to hold both thighs up and back, as I reach between his legs. My fingers curl around the base of his shaft as I ram my Christmas tree up his chimney. Krampus's eyes bug out as I quickly fist his cock.

"I wonder how much juice is in these berries. We better milk you dry." Shifting my hips, I angle my tip at his prostate and demolish the sensitive spot.

Krampus is a babbling mess as he screams and begs me to slow down, my hips snapping faster than I would flick the reins of my sleigh. His eyes slam closed, and he opens his mouth on a soundless scream. Back arching and body twitching as he explodes.

Ropes of his spicy jizzum splatters over his abs, his hole clenching down on my cock as his climax tears through him. My fist speeds up, jerking him faster. I give him slow, long, deep strokes.

"Come on, slut, give me another. I know your balls aren't empty yet." My words set him off.

More spurts of his release shooting out in sticky globs, coating his chest and neck. The big bad asshole is a withering, whimpering mess. I can barely move from how hard his muscles are squeezing my cock.

I release his thighs; they spread and flop down onto the bed. Every inch of his body convulses. Gripping his balls, I roll them in my hand as I pump his still hard cock.

My release is tethering on the edge, my jingle ornaments tight to my body. "One more bitch."

I slam in three more times and fall over the edge. Squeezing his nuts, I angle his cock down his body and watch as Krampus cums a third time. The force powerful enough to coat his face. I pump my hips as I ooze into his hole. My load is too much for his already stuffed cavern, and my candy cane cream drips out around my dick.

Pulling out, I watch my sparkly cum drip from his abused puffy hole. The dude is an absolute wreck, his body twitching and mouth gasping like a fish. I stand up from the bed and look down at my artwork.

Checking my watch, I realize I'm out of time. I grab my pants and slip them up my thighs as I stare at Krampus.

Krampus

My brain is mush, my body spent as I watch my Saint get dressed. He stands at the foot of the bed as he buttons his pants up. "Did you enjoy the show, my love?"

I turn my head to the side as my cum drips down my cheeks. Looking to the corner, I see who he's talking to. Ms. Clause is sitting in the cuck chair, her legs spread over the armrest as she twitches with pleasure. Standing between her legs is her elf, face deep in the cookie.

The little elf has blonde braided pigtails hanging down her back. A tiny frilly short tutu around her hips. It's not long enough to cover her ass, and I see the glint of the snowflake butt plug shoved in her hole.

Ms. Clause pets the elf's head as she urges her back. "Yes, dear, that was quite the performance. Probably better than last year." She picks up a shortbread cookie off the side table and rubs it between her folds.

The elf turns to face me, her chin dripping with pussy juices. Santa smiles and holds out his arms. "There's my little Elfie. Were you a good girl for your mistress?"

Santa's wife stalks towards me as Elfie runs to my Saint. He scoops her up into his arms. At the same time, his wife scoops up cum off my chest with her cookie.

"Yes, Daddy, I was a good girl for my mistress. I made her cum four times!" Santa kisses her deeply as he holds her in the crook of his arm.

Ms. Clause's fingers swipe through my crack, collecting her husband's cum. She smears it on the cookie that is now iced with all our releases. The woman pops it in her mouth and groans.

"I fucking love Christmas Eve." She bends down and licks a line from my belly button up to my lips. "Hey Krampsy, you were such a good boy. Can't wait for next year."

Santa sent the elf down and patting her head. "Elfie? Daddy and Mistress have to go. I lost track of time. Can you be a good girl and give Krampus some aftercare?"

The pixie stick bobs her head quickly, giving them each a kiss. Santa and his wife hold hands as they leave, the faint sound of the reindeer and sleigh bells ringing before they take off.

Elfie skips over to me and jumps up on the bed. "Hey Krampus, it's been a few years since I got to give you aftercare." She carefully unties my wrists, and my arms fall to the bed.

She curls up under my arm and stretches up her head. With the small amount of muscle control I have, I bend down and capture her lips. Ms. Clause's gingerbread snatch juice coats my tongue as we share a gentle kiss.

Elfie pulls back and snuggles in close. "I'll clean you up soon; I know you like your cuddles after a hard fuck."

I chuckle and wrap my arm tighter around her. Nuzzling my chin into the top of her head. My mind is already counting down until next year.

"I fucking love Christmas."

23

Yule-Tide Glimmer

Juniper Sage Wester

Rainbow puddles are shining, all slick on the street,
Yule carols play loud in the seventy-five heat.
The palm trees stand glowing, but no, not for me.
Our holiday spirit is Grandma's decree
She claims pine is poison, so plastic it stays.
No one dares question the choices she makes.
The dinners lie perfectly, all laughter and chatter
But baking with Papa, that's all that matters.
Warm cookies in the oven, handcrafted with love,
Grim warnings of eyes, watching from above,
They speak of a stranger adorned in all red,
Hollow eyes; creepy laughter fills me with dread.
"Just believe" they all say, though I mostly just stare,
But Papa is love, at least he still cares.

Grandma wraps gifts like a battle to win,
Tape on her fingers and bows tucked in thin.
She measures each ribbon, she scolds every crease,
Her smile is a warning, not any real peace.
The lights on the rooftop stay tangled all year,
Too brittle to move, yet she calls them "good cheer."
We all learned to praise them, though ragged and dim,

For daring to question is treated as sin.
Her moods rule the household, her glare sets the stage,
A tyrant in tinsel excused by her age.
So quiet we tiptoe, so carefully near,
Obedient children kept frozen in fear.

Where is Dad, you ask? Well, in the back with a beer,
Eyes glued to the screen, the game is more dear.
Seven feet of empty, beneath a gray cap
Black curls stay hidden, his heart under wraps.
"Hey kid, tie this down!" from the boat he'd call.
Commands not connections, big feelings made small.
Cowboys stars on his most favorite tees,
As if a logo could stand in, for him or for me.
Swap meets and yard sales shape my weekend fate,
A blur of discarded treasures, lessons could wait.
Try to reach him, and you will very soon find,
It's a trap, he's a ghost, with a scoreboard mind.

Baking cookies with Papa, outdoor feasts in the sun,
Seventy-five degrees, laughter, warmth and fun.
The tree's spoils spilled wide, toys shimmer in the light,
Perfect for play, for wonder, for simple delight.
The damper arrives when Mama comes calling,
Her presence a shadow, the fun quickly stalling.
No yard to run in, no family, no cheer,
Just her dark man and his kid; empty and drear.
The wind seems to hush when we cross her door,
And the toys lose their sparkle, the magic no more.
Papa's warm smiles, far away from that gloom,
A flicker of joy trapped in a shadowed room.

Three presents for me under their fake tree,
The number doesn't matter, it never did, not to me.

The paper flies wildly from my small, eager hands,
As the dark man's girl snatches it; his rules, his demands.
Locked boxes and secrets fly with me on planes,
Everything hidden, even love lost its name.
I count the minutes until I can get away,
From Mama's dull house, so lifeless and gray.
The air feels heavy, the rooms all too still,
No laughter, no warmth, just a cold, quiet chill.
And even the gifts, meant to sparkle and shine,
Feel trapped in that house, never truly mine.

The big banks tanked, and, to be frank, it was clear,
The home Grandma built brings nothing but fear.
Wallets opened wide, only to cough up thin air,
We all trudge along to the next city's glare.
Where gambling and nightlife rule over cheer,
And no one seems to notice the loss of the year.
This certainly won't teach me what life ought to be,
No lessons, no warmth; just neon and spree.
Holiday feasts, once at family tables with kin,
Traded for card games and buffets, chasing the big win.
The laughter feels hollow, the joy bought and sold,
A mockery of stories we'd once been told.

Grandma says she's tired of the city's fast pace,
Sick of western sun burning bright on our face.
She longs for the old days, a world far away,
Where cornfields stretch endless and Amish kids play.
But first comes a detour, neon lights in the haze,
A desert that glitters, a city ablaze.
Pam trees surrender to towers of light,
The heat stills lingers from signs burning bright.
Covered bridges await, though years intervene,
Giant popcorn, misled youth, and German cuisine.

Ribbon-tied sausage, a feast she had planned,
Yet it never feels like mine; just the life *she* had manned.

Snowy covered bridges, ice dangling from each tree,
Gray skies bring a shiver, a bitter cold breeze,
Catholic school children sing, voices sweet and light,
As shoppers bustle past in the harsh winter night.
The smell of schnitzels and coffee floats the air proud,
Smiles hidden, fighting quietly, perseverance unbowed.
Tense air for dinner with no words spoken,
Hidden secrets buried until spring is awoken,
New flowers pierce the dew reaching for sun light,
Papa's brother is gone, he passed in the night.
Money grows tighter, and stress thickens the air,
All scrambled and argued for left behind wares.

Plates of chicken clatter, voices rise and squeak,
While quiet glances tell stories no one dares speak.
Papa stays steady, though wearied and worn,
A beacon of warmth in a household forlorn.
His hands work in silence, his heart quietly kind,
A soft, steady anchor for the chaos behind.
The world could collapse, yet he'd never complain,
Just hum through the noise, unmoved by the strain.
His eyes hold a patience no one can define,
Calm temper shaped by storm, his very own design
Through all the chaos his love brings joy,
Much more than fake grins and bundled-up toys.

At Grandma's I'm unheard, calling Mom is fresh air,
A small taste of freedom, no moments to spare.
Deep still in my mind, the dark man awaits,
His shadowed presence, heavy at the gates.
The new year arrives, and the secret spills out,

Grandma's curiosity sharp, her voice full of doubt.
Boxes line the hallways, artwork stripped bare,

The walls feel colder, a home with no care.
"You think it's better with your mother," Grandma sneers,
"Living here, you never had to share your fears."
I bite back a grin, quiet but proud,
Even in her wrath, my defiance avowed.

A single candle burns on a cupcake that night,
One hot July evening, no snowflake in sight.
I long to escape the turmoil that plagues,
The fighting and chaos during Grand-MAS day.
The season of cheer is forced and contrived,
With rules and expectations that barely survive.
They say someday you'll beg for forgiveness,
But I only feel trapped in their hollow bitterness.
Mama moved east where lighthouses gleam,
Atlantic waves crashing, a far away dream.
There I can breathe, let the salt fill the air,
Finally a freedom, beyond their despair.

Students speak a language that sounds like slow English,
Struggling through syllables, each word sounds unfinished.
The fast-talking new kid, always out of place,
Tossed into a family whose rhythm I can't quite pace.
Stories of family gatherings that I've never known,
Leave quiet, sharp scars that have silently grown.
Yuletide began with block parties and cheer,
Dads laughing with glee, warmth ringing so clear.
Time passed and celebrations shifted in tone,
Cold dinners replaced what once felt like home.
Fear creeps in slowly at the distressed family table,
Mother then saves me, first chance she is able.

I sit on the patio, and I listen near,
At families laughing with holiday cheer.
I wonder how many are feeling like me,
Trapped in a house where they'd rather not be.
At Grandma's I wake to presents galore,
But her love is tied to the junk from the store.
Each ribbon and trinket leaves something unsaid,
A hollow exchange where affection is dead.
At Mom's, the drum beats a much harsher refrain,
All joy is reduced to a chore-bound chain.
I swear when I have a family one day,
I'll never let holidays feel this same way.

Silver rings glint bright with a devil dogs attire,
A lease has been signed, and a test sparks the fire.
A promise of life, a small miracle blooms,
With gifts wrapped in paper that quietly looms.
The holiday hums with illusions of cheer,
A life that was promised but warped year by year.
I chose him in part for the praise they bestow,
But their voices are chains, and the weight only grows.
"He's perfect for you," they insist each day,
Then why does his silence chase me away?
Just fall into line, do your time, you will see,
The holidays shimmer with promises of glee.

What makes them so gleeful, the feasts or the wine?
Or family portraits that all mis-align?
What happens when walls are built over decay,
When cracks in the heart spread wider each day?
Most tumble headfirst to temptations that bite,
Or sink in the void of an endless night.
But me, I perform as the part they assigned,

A mask on my face and a chain on my mind.
Applause from the sidelines, yet none of it real,
Each laugh that I force is a wound I must conceal.
The season grows colder the longer I play,
A pageant of hollowness, sharp and well-staged.

The white walls seem darker, this life feels a cage,
A picture-perfect family, stripped of its glaze.
Tired boots by the door, his green shirt worn thin,
A ghost of a man with no fire left within.
Eyes locked to a screen, some war he won't fight,
While I battle alone through the cold of each night.
The photos all smile though the silence is loud,
A gallery staged for the sake of the crowd.
They said be the wife, keep the house, hold the line.
But my spirit keep screaming "This life isn't mine."
So I run with the sirens, a fire in my chest,
While he fades into nothing, a life spent depressed.

The news says a sickness sweeps through the land,
Society shuttered by its own heavy hand.
Masks on our faces, locked inside day and night,
Even getting groceries becomes a fucking fight.
Forced to comply while I run every call,
Watching people fade as the sickness takes all.
I come home to Jameson, so empty and still,
A quiet despair bends me to its will.
This holiday season brings silence and fear,
Isolation sharp, cutting close, cutting near.
Yet my little one, too young to comprehend,
Finds joy in small things, a light I defend.

Suddenly something snaps, muscles release
A breath of fresh air, though the peace will soon cease.

Divorce papers signed in a camper so small,
A home that felt mine, yet a personal thrall.
Little eyes search for gifts underneath no tree,
"Sorry, baby, some things are never free."
Months of despair creep in, slow and severe,
A shadowed existence where hope disappears.
The holidays hollow, stripped of delight,
No sparkle or warmth in the dim winter light.
I carry the weight that the grown-ups ignored,
Learning that love often comes with a sword.

Feeling defeated, little blue eyes stare,
Pushing me forward toward gifts to prepare.
Next year they will wait beneath a bright tree,
It's not the presents that count, at least not to me.
The camper feels cozy, warmth rising all 'round,
A quiet reprieve from the chaos we've found.
My partner holds me close quiet and near,
A soft sweet reminder that someone is here.
It's not about sparkle or holiday show,
But living with hope, and watching it grow
In moments like this, fragile and true,
The season survives when love carries through.

Dad sends a message not wanting a fight,
Papa's grown weary, he's losing his light.
I'm sad and I'm torn and in turmoil I ponder,
Should I go, should I stay I'll never not wonder.
Days later, he's gone, just like that, a blip,
I know there'll be anger I didn't make that trip.
I couldn't, how could I? With all that was said,
They think it's forgiven because grandpa is dead?
They built me, they broke me, yet they never cared,
Thirty-one years and the memories still glare.

No cookies, no swap meets, no laughter, no cheer,
Just ghosts at the table when Yule draws near.

I reach out to Mom, I reach out to Dad,
I feel like the accident neither one planned.
Begging for love, they fed me their pain,
My tears join the storm and fall with the rain.
I look to my daughter and instantly smile,
Ne'er would I let her feel small or exiled.
I want her to flourish, to laugh and be free,
Not burdened by weight that tried to break me
We've never known riches but still we survive,
With love as our anchor we are aching to thrive.
The cycle is broken, the wounds start to mend,
As doubt begins to fall, a new hope ascends.

"T'was the night before Christmas" is read in our house
All the creatures are sleeping, except for the mouse.
No tinsel or ribbons, Yule is different for me,
Presents wrapped neatly under a Juniper tree.
Everything feels perfect until there's a shift,
Happiness falls and quickly it drifts.
The bad man is coming, he's trying to get in,
Why oh why can I never just win.
Something wanted, peace taken, I cannot breathe.
Our only option is simply to leave.
So we pack and we panic, we've no time to stay.
To start a new life where the Saguaros sway.

Sitting atop this mountain, city lights gleam,
Faint echoes of laughter drift soft in a dream.
Grandma's love counted by the gifts she supplied,
Mom and the dark man, their love also tied.
Grandpa's came from the swap meet, patient, and true,

Moments that mattered in ways he never knew.
Their season is hollow, all sparkle, no heart,
While my emotions crash and tear me apart.
Material wealth could not anchor or stay,
Only love unforced could carry the way.
I watch the waves roll, both bitter and wide,
Learning real love cannot ever be denied.

Through evolution hard lessons are learned,
A brown thumb turns green, a hunger returns.
Before all their eyes, the shell I had made;
The mask for the public begins to decay.
It splinters and falls and from pieces take flight,
A wild butterfly, unafraid of the sky.
Her wings bear the scars of the songs that still sting,
Of knowing too deeply why caged birds still sing.
Truth is my compass, adventure my guide
No longer chained by what others decide
This awakening climbs, unbound and free,
Threading my soul, reclaiming all of me.

On this silent eve, beneath the moon's soft light
This peace that I've found finally feels right
But how do I balance this calm that I keep,
When evil still stirs and refuses to sleep?
Be grateful they say, "Just exist in your tier"
Yet duality whispers and lingers all year.
Starving children and death from the glow in my phone,
Their screams reach places I once called my own.
We share a heartbeat that pounds through the ground
In unity's echo, humanity is found
If love is the rhythm, hate cannot stay,
It pops and it crackles and it fizzles away.

Some people celebrate the same way each year,
Families expand, contract, marking time clear.
All for a surprise, tucked in a lone little sock,
This Yule I spend with my small chosen flock.
No big meal, no fanfare, just simple and true,
A small dinner set for three, a soft, tender hue.
The candles burn low while the world softly weeps,
Its sorrow runs quiet, in shadows it sleeps.
The world riddled with violence, yet here we remain,
Threading our peace through the fabric of pain.
A quiet, somber warmth in the soft winter light,
Happy Yule to all, and to all a good night.

24
Oh, Culty Night

Ivy Graves

Trigger Warnings
Supernatural Themes
Sexual Themes
Death
Occult

THE FAMILY ESTATE

The looming, renovated mansion-castle dominates the property as my handsome new boyfriend's car winds up the hill.

I watch Christopher's sexy hands on the wheel, those veins rising, and a glint of light reflects off his expensive cuff links.

"Sheesh," I say. "Looks like something out of a Hitchcock film. Where are the birds?"

I smile and watch his angular poker face and wonder whether he's heard of Hitchcock.

I sigh and stare out the window as we find a park on the circular drive, next to a bunch of vintage WW2 era cars.

Church steeples dot the turrets on the house, and something about this place just doesn't feel right. Huge, beautiful windows welcome the outside in, dozens of candles inside the mansion cast a warm glow, and nerves shoot through me as the car comes to a stop.

His very rich and potentially pompous family are standing at the entrance, waiting for us.

Ugh. Here we go!

The matriarch is slim, statue-straight. Teetering on high heels, she makes her way across to us with open arms.

"Christopher, oh darling. How was the drive?" She kisses him on both cheeks then turns to me. She takes my hand in hers, and I flinch when I realise how cold she is.

A shudder runs up my arm as she squeezes my hands.

She's attractive, but there is ice behind her eyes, too.

"And you must be Valarie Vickers!" Her accent is clipped.

I cringe and add, "So lovely to meet you!"

Did she tell me her name?

His father is hugging me now, and I fight the urge to shove him off me.

Chris is in the car, unloading our luggage.

"Come inside," his mother says. "Let Argyle get the cases. Come and have a cocktail."

I hate this bitch already.

She has giant diamond earrings dangling in the shape of snowflakes. Her hands sparkle with multicoloured gems.

I'm estimating the value in my head. More than I'd earn in six years.

I want to ask, "Where did your old money come from?" But I manage to bite my tongue.

I'm wide-eyed as they usher us into the house and show us to the fucking library which has a wheely ladder and everything.

The cucumber cocktail makes me wince, but I drink it anyway, looking around at this family of the boyfriend I don't actually know much about.

"So, Val, has Christopher dear told you about the family games?"

I look at him. He shrugs.

"No Mother. I thought I'd ease her into the weekend. Don't want to scare her away, do we?"

He chuckles, but there is a dark undercurrent to his joke.

What the fuck have I got myself into here?

I check my phone and see no reception.

Fuck. I never leave the city, so I never worried about changing my phone carrier over.

I hate Christmas, and I want this to be over already. I wish I'd stayed home.

After choking down the hideous cucumber drink, we make our way through the house to the lavish backyard.

It's set up as a fancy Shakespearean midsummer soiree, and the sexual tension between the group is palpable.

The guests in the sunken garden are strangers to me, and the music pulsating from hidden speakers sends arousing shivers.

It's so mysterious, and I feel so out of my league.

I've never partied with people this rich before, and I'm starting to wonder exactly what we are celebrating here.

I look up to see tinsel dangling from the trees and the reindeer sculptures aglow with their lights.

But, there is a strange, erotic undercurrant.

I wonder who is fucking who.

And whether they are related.

But that strange thought sends another illicit shiver.

And I turn to speak once more to Christopher's mother.

If he's going to keep proving himself to be a giant scoop of vanilla ice cream, perhaps I can set the mood by seducing his mother.

And fucking her in a spare room.

I look at her elegant neck, the diamond choker highlighting her status. This will be a fun weekend. I can't wait to enjoy the festivities.

"I'd love to see some more of the estate, if you'd like to give me a tour," I say to her.

MUMMY, DEAREST

She leads me with her clacking gold heels, and as we arrive in a grand ballroom, she turns, the red silk dress skimming lightly across her obvious bra-less bust. Her nipples form peaks, and she's not subtle about it either.

Again, I wonder what kind of weird family shit goes down in these rich houses.

She shows me art, furnishings, and history lessons on the region.

I move quickly as I kiss her, and her tongue pushes against me desperately, like we're going at it in an illicit bathroom in a shady dive bar.

She tastes like cinnamon and booze. She smells like vanilla and Mrs Robinson, but I don't care.

I don't love Christopher. I'm still undecided as to whether I actually like him.

And this night is too weird not to indulge in some slutty behaviour. Especially with an estate and a cast of freaks as perfect as this lot.

No, something sinister is in the air, here, and I want to be inhaling it first hand.

"What's the password, honey?" she coos into my ear.

"Password? For what?" I ask.

She just smiles, and leans forward to take my nipple between her teeth. The bites playfully.

"I guess Chris hasn't decided whether you're invited to the games."

I shake my head, and arch my back. I don't care what she's talking about when her experienced mouth makes me feel so damn good.

Better than her son ever has, that's for sure.

She glances across to a gold bookshelf.

"That's a secret door, takes you into the initiation room. If you don't have the password, this is as far as you get. With the password, you could discover every pleasure."

"Ugh, sorry, but this has killed the moon. I'm going to look for Chris. Thanks for the fun. See ya down there!"

THE FEAR

After my upstairs tryst with my boyfriend's mother, I returned to find Christoph—oh shit. I just realised his name has 'Christ' in it.

At Christmas. He does have a dash of God complex. And Oedipus too, come to think of it.

I snort as I remember how his mother's lips taste, and join him again outside with his friends.

"Val, there you are!" he says. "Come, meet twins Jim and Sandy. We've been friends since we were born the same day in the same hospital."

"And the night just gets more peculiar," I say, as I shake their hands.

Now first drinks spiral into fourth and fifths, we find ourselves swanning through grand corridors and up flights of stairs, until we arrive in the East Wing, with a four poster bed and view of the tiered garden before us.

A small natural pine tree stands aloft in the corner, the scent mingling with the eucalyptus trees outside the window.

I open the door and make my way to the balcony. Chris follows me and wraps his firm arms around my waist.

"So, what do you think of my childhood home?"

I roll my eyes.

"Not bad. Could do with a few more servants," I say, bluffing.

He nips me on the neck, which sends a carnal shiver down my body.

I lean into him, and his kiss grazes my jaw, and before I know what's happening, we're undressing each other and flopping around on the oversized bed.

We're in the heat of the moment when an ear-piercing howl rings out through the castle.

"What the fuck?" Christopher says, jumping up and stuffing his feet into his jeans.

That uneasiness I felt earlier makes a reappearance as I watch the back of my boyfriend rush out the door. He stops before he goes and says, "Probably best to lock this from the inside after I'm gone."

I stare at him.

"What?"

And then the door shuts with a click, and he's gone, the sound of a woman, or an animal, continues to terrify me.

I scramble to lock the door behind him, then reach for my phone.

"Please have reception. Please have a bar."

Nothing.

Just SOS.

And at this point, it's not an emergency.

But something makes me want to call a ride and get the fuck out of here.

I climb under the covers, suddenly not horny at all.

The screaming has stopped, but now there are people out on the lawn, calling to each other.

Where did that scream come from?

Suddenly, the sound of Christmas carols begin to wind their way around the castle, oldy world sounding, like it's coming from an old record player. That only makes everything that came before it even more surreal.

I clutch the blanket to my chest and hop out of bed again, anxiously pacing, and I peep out the window.

The party people have gone, but now I just see lots of torch flames, and bonfires, and people with masks and robes and all kinds of coloured smoke coming from a burning effigy.

What does this all mean?

And should I be making a run for it?

This is scary as fuck.

Who the hell is Christopher?

And who the hell are his parents anyway?

THE TRAP DOOR

I shove the heavy curtains aside, dust filling my nostrils. How long has this room been used? Does anyone actually live here? It's like a fucking museum.

Who actually owns it?

A scratching from the floor. I drop to my hands and knees, pulling a rug aside to discover a trapdoor.

A knock from below now, the wooden floor, fear in my throat, I dash toward the door.

"Help me, please! Is that you, Valarie?"

It's locked from the inside. Nails scratch from below. A wail.

I'm not trapped; I can run away at any second. Open the door and run. But what's worse, unknown scratching from hell, or an obvious cult sacrificing virgins under the fucking blood moon.

Jesus.

I pace back and forth, panic swirling. Bonfires and chanting outside.

Out the window, more screaming. Then from under the trapdoor, a woman's voice.

"Valarie, it's me. Josephine. Chris's sister!"

"Who? He never mentioned a sister!"

What the fuck? He never mentioned any siblings. Is this some weird supernatural thing?

Oh my god, of course!

His mother said something about games.

This is a fucking panic escape room! This is planned!

I laugh, stand up and look around for hidden cameras. I grab a fire poker and start hitting the smoke detector off, springs and batteries flying as I search for red flashing lights.

Nothing.

"Of course he didn't," comes the voice below, followed with a haunting laugh. "I'm captive here, their precious virgin sacrifice. Never allowed to leave Valarie, oh no. I've been living here for all my life. Locked in this room with all my toys and fancy dress. With the doctors and teachers and priests with their crosses and their holy oil. I'm scared of my family, Valarie, please help me! They keep me locked in my fancy bedroom because they're afraid of what I'll say to the public if I'm let out. Every time I run away, they bring me back and torture me even worse."

She begins to cry, then her haunting voice sings, and the hairs on my arms stand on end.

"Polly put the kettle on, Polly put the kettle on ..."

"Oh shit, please stop singing! Can you unlock the door from below? I can't see a handle up here! I'll help you, but ... I don't know how!"

I look around the room, hoping to see an axe or a crowbar. I run for the fire poker and come back.

Trying to use it for leverage, I managed to jam it into a thin crack.

But I stumble back, breathless.

"Oh God, I'm so scared!" I cry. "I don't want to play this game anymore. Christopher, please stop the game. I'm scared, and I want to go home."

I collapse in a heap, sobbing my eyes out, when the trapdoor pops up right next to me, and her pale face is inches from mine.

She stares deep into my eyes with her dark grey orbs.

"Valarie, come with me. They're going to sacrifice you on the stake. They're going to give you over to the dark gods in return for power. You're nothing but a pawn. Me too, but I'm a bigger piece on the board. I'm the fucking Queen's bitch daughter. And the Queen is the boss. She can lock her own kids up in a house for their entire lives. Pretend that I died at birth. This house is evil, please, help me escape!"

"Escape?" I ask, suspicious. "This is a game, right? You're a hired performance artist? You're really good."

I say this, but I'm not sure. Either I'm very drunk or this bitch is a shadow. A ghost. A spectre.

"Are you ..."

"Alive?" she asks, giggling darkly.

THE ROOM

I climb down the ladder after Josephine, clutching my phone just in case my provider decides to give me a bar. My bare feet land on a wooden floor, the heat dripping down my back.

"When was the last time this room was aired?" I ask, covering my face. "It smells like death."

Josephine stands before me, white linen nightdress. Black hair. Gaunt features. Sunken eyes.

"It is my death. I'm over there in the corner. Covered in a white cloth."

I gasp, spinning to look in the corner of the room. Sitting on a princess chair is a taxidermy doll. A woman sits, her delicate ruffled dress and hair ribbons decorate her empty vessel hair curled and styled under a lace veil.

"That's you?" I ask, spinning from the taxidermy corpse with the huge blue sapphires where eyeballs once were.

"Yes, that's me," says the phantom. "They killed me this night last year."

"May I?" I ask her.

"What? Touch me? Go for it. Take the fucking sapphires,I don't give a shit. They were stolen, anyway. Stolen from the Jews. Give them back. Take them back to the family that owns them!"

"What the fuck? I'm not touching a haunted doll with stolen Jewish gems for eyes? Are you kidding me right now? I've had enough of this horror Christmas death game, whatever the fuck is going on. I want off this ride. I'm being so real right now. HELP ME! I do not consent!"

"But what's the password, Valarie?"

My gut shoots through my mouth.

"The password? What password?" I scream.

THE PASSWORD

Hinges creak, and a figure appears coming down the ladder, first feet and and a shaft of candlelight shines through. First an arm, draped in long velvet, and then the face.

"Christopher, oh my God! It's a game, isn't it? Tell me it's a game."

"Babe, are you okay? Oh god Val, how did you get in here?"

He looks up, sees the ladder and trapdoor.

Josephine stands next to me, but he looks right through her.

"Your sister Josephine here, she got the ladder for me."

His jaw drops.

"Val, this room has been locked for twenty years. The girl that lived here died, and they never cleaned it out."

I look back to the lifesized taxidermy doll with gigantic deep sapphires for eyes. They glinted from the light of his hand held candelabra. The candlelight flickers.

Josephine's shadow turns to smoke.

"Have you been smoking weed? Or have a few too many cucumber cocktails?"

"No, I haven't! I'm terrified. And who was screaming?"

I jump up and run to the curtain, and look outside.

Darkness.

No one. Nothing.

No burning effigies.

No ghosts. No giant doll, just a small porcelain one, its creepy face staring at me with painted blue eyes.

"Where were you?" I ask. I'm shaking from shock. From fear. For my life.

"Am I having a heart attack? Oh my God. I thought I was dead!"

"I was right next to you," Chris says, his dumb pretty face smiling. "Never left the room! You were asleep, shouting, screaming, shoving me off you. So I left you alone."

"No! You ran out! I paced around, looked outside, talked to Josephine, and she gave me the ladder!"

"Babe, I don't know where you got that ladder from, but there is no one called Josephine in this house and there never was. We fucked, you fell asleep, so did I. I woke up and you were gone. The trapdoor was open. Here you are."

What scream? No one was screaming.

Oh shit, what the fuck.

This is the most terrifying night of my life.

What the fuck was in those cocktails?

I don't know, but please take me home.

I hate Christmas.

After this, when I get home, I think I need to book myself into a spa and take a very long nap on the couch.

Tears streak my cheeks.

I reach into his pockets, grabbing his key fob. Rushing from the room, I bolt through the house, down more steps and out onto the drive. Scanning quickly for his car, I press buttons wildly.

"Valarie! Fuck me! What are you doing?"

"I'm getting out of here. You are all fucked!"

The sun is coming up now. The sky is hues of orange and pink, and the gentle moo of cattle can be heard from across the hill.

Jumping behind the driver's seat, I adjust the position and rear-view mirror, and start the car.

Without letting it warm up, I leave Christopher standing in the driveway, jeans and shirtless, shouting at me as I drive down the long entrance.

"I told you they're evil," a voice says from behind me. A whisper of cold shivers over my shoulders.

"They killed me, Valarie. Tell the police!"

I can't help spinning around, looking behind me. Not surprised to see the apparition from earlier, but now, sitting directly behind me, staring at me with a wicked grin.

The car swerves, and glass tinkles as I lose control. Trees slowing down the vehicle, lurching into a ditch and then up the other side.

The last thing I hear is the scraping of metal and timber, and Josephine's chilling voice calls over my shoulder.

"See you on the other side. The password is Tinsel."

THE NEXT LIFE

Dark matter lures me in and spits me out in another fucking wormhole.

I came. And I'm sitting in the passenger seat of Chris's car again.

We're driving toward his house.

The Hitchcock house.

I never asked if he liked Hitchcock. But I've done this before. A moment ago I was behind the wheel going the other way. Out of here.

I've done this before.

I crashed the car.

The ghost in the back seat.

The password is Tinsel.

What does that mean?

"Christopher, I'm going to call an Uber when we get inside. I need to go home straightaway. I just remembered something important."

THE FAMILY AGAIN

The weird cult family is standing at the entrance again. Waiting for us.

Here we go again.

The matriarch, who I previously had my tongue inside, welcomes her son.

"Christopher, oh darling. How was the drive?" She kisses him on both cheeks.

"And you must be Valarie Vickers!"

I will change what I say this time. Short and sweet.

But while I'm here, instead of going home just yet, I might kiss that sweet lady again.

Then I'll be out of here.

I look at her, smile knowingly, and say in a velvety voice, "Hi there, so lovely to meet you."

My heart hammers. Is this the right decision? I'm supposed to be getting the fuck out of here. I don't want to see that fucking ghost again. She scared the fuck out of me.

The father is hugging me again, and this time I do push him away, gently.

Chris is in the car, unloading our luggage.

"Come inside," his mother says. "Let Argyle get the cases. Come and have a cocktail."

I hate this bitch, again.

But this time, I know the password.

I swallow the compulsion to blurt out, "The password is TINSEL! NOW WHAT?"

But I don't.

I repeat everything as though I've seen a rip in time. I should be getting away, but I need to taste her. To know what all this means. To see whether I'm having a psychotic break, or whether this is how I die. Never to be found by my family, the police, or the police divers.

I carry on through the party in a daze.

Until I reach the part where I'm necking with my boyfriend's sexy mother, and she whispers the magical words.

Soft and smooth in my ear.

Exactly as has already unfolded.

"What's the password, honey?"

I pull back, lock eyes with her.

"Well, I believe the password is Tinsel."

A micro-expression gives away her surprise before she smiles, stands, and strides across the room to the gold bookcase.

"Come," she says, beckoning me over with her gesture.

Earlier, before the crash, when I drove away, everything was going quickly. Like it was speeding up.

Now everything slows down.

She's still; nothing moves. Not a breath of breeze on this hot and balmy Australian Xmas Eve.

A floatiness washes over me.

I'm not drunk yet. I'm only one drink in.

This isn't real.

"Oh yes it is," says Josephine, her chilling voice behind me. "This is very real. How else would she be showing you what is behind that wall? It's the truth. And you're the sacrifice. They're about to send you to slaughter, Valarie. Run."

25

Jeffrey's Cookout

Laneie Lestrange

Trigger Warnings
Graphic Violence and Gore
Cannibalism
Death and Murder
Psychological Horror

The desert stretched out like a graveyard of heat and bone, and on Christmas night, it was quiet enough to hear the wind chew through the sand. The neon sign for Jeffery's Cookout buzzed and flickered, half the letters burnt out, leaving only Jeff Cook glowing red like a wound in the dark. Even the grinning Santa sign wore a smear of grime that turned his smile into a snarl.

Inside, the diner looked embalmed in time. Cracked red booths, the smell of rancid, overly-burnt grease, a jukebox that hadn't worked since the '80s stood like a testimony of eternity. Harold wiped the counter with a cloth already dingy from hours of use. He wore his Santa-red, faded-to-rust apron, its once white trim yellowed with age, fabric stiff, deep with history.

He hummed Silent Night off-key, eyes glassy with reflection. The radio by the window played a static, half-carol, breaking in and out like a dying breath. Over the pie case, a strand of dollar-store tinsel sagged in a tired smile.

Headlights cut through the windows, throwing a splash of light into the otherwise dead room. Tires crunched on the gravel and came to a stop. Then came laughter—too loud and too eager. Four travelers walked through the door, their voices spilling in with the desert chill. They looked more like they belonged on screens, not in a place like this: faces shaved to angles by phone lights and jackets too theatrical for the cold. That particular brightness of people who wanted the world to look back at them.

"Yo, check this place out," said the one in the leather jacket, pointing to the cracked neon Santa that buzzed over the door. "Total horror-movie setup."

The woman with glitter eyeliner leaned against the pie case, her breath fogging the glass. "If we vanish out here, at least it'll get views," she said, half-laughing.

The third, rail-thin and jittery, with eyes like camera lenses, drummed his fingers on a booth as if testing for hidden microphones.

The last one was the quietest of the lot. He kept looking past everything, toward the windows and the long, plain darkness beyond.

Harold smiled from behind the counter, the expression stretching too far, like a rubber mask pulled taut. "Evenin', sweethearts. Cold night to be out. Coffee?"

"Four hot cocoas," Glitter-Liner said, already spelling the order to nobody in particular. "If it comes in chipped mugs, that's bonus points."

Harold set out four chipped mugs, each with a different state name partly rubbed off. Steam curled up like breath in cold air. The four fanned out through the diner, peeking, prodding, collecting angles. The quiet one stopped by the snow globe, tapping it once. The glitter inside lifted and swam around like ash in a flurry, then settled into calm.

Harold set down the chipped mugs, steam winding like ghosts in the cold. "Four cocoas," he said. "Menu's there if you're hungry."

He watched their young hands wrap around the warmth of the cups. Their wrists appeared too thin.

Without a rule, and in no particular order, the four slid into the booth under the flickering Santa light. The neon red flashed over their faces in a hellish glow.

Leather Jacket flipped open the laminated menu. "Wait, where's the chili?" he snorted. "I thought this was the place with the chili."

Glitter-Liner frowned. "Yeah. Didn't the old guy at the other diner say this place had the best chili in the state? Said we'd never forget it.'"

"Maybe it's on the lunch menu or something," Rail-Thin muttered, swaying the camera on his phone over the cracked tile and the faded ketchup bottles. "We just need a hook. 'Desert diner mystery chili' and... boom! Viral."

From the next booth, a man with sun-leathered skin and eyes like road dust turned his head slightly. "Ain't on the menu," he said without looking at them. "You gotta ask."

The group froze, the air between them suddenly heavy with possibility. "Ask for what?" Glitter-Liner asked, half-smiling. The man smiled into his coffee. "The chili. Trust me, you'll want it. Just... make sure you can handle it."

Harold appeared from behind the counter, wiping his hands on the sad apron, eyes already knowing too much. "Somebody tellin' tales again?" he asked, voice as calm as cooling grease.

Leather Jacket smirked, leaning back in the booth. "Guess so. They said you've got the best chili. Some kind of a secret family recipe?"

Harold's hand stilled mid-wipe. The rag stalled, and the time lagged around the table. His gaze swept over them slowly, deliberately, gauging like a butcher selecting cuts.

"Secret recipe..." he finally said, voice a low rasp, full of gravel and smoke. "Now... how'd you hear about that?"

Rail-Thin lifted his chin, performing for the camera that wasn't even recording. "Rumors on the road, man. Said it's the best meal of your life if you know how to ask."

Glitter-Liner chuckled, swirling her cocoa. "We chase stories, not food. People love a legend they can taste."

Harold's reflection warped in the window behind them, his smile stretching a bit too wide. "Figures. Someone couldn't keep their mouth shut," he grumbled, tone like a knife dragged over stone, and he continued louder, "Well now ... wouldn't be right to let Christmas pass without servin' the family recipe. But I'll warn you once you taste it, you'll never be the same."

THE KITCHEN

The kitchen was Harold's church. The hum of the freezer was the organ, and the hiss of simmering chili his hymn. Strings of feeble Christmas lights blinked above rows of meat hooks. The old walk-in cold room was tucked in the far corner, its door scarred with deep gouges the way a tree remembers lightning. He ran his fingers across them as if reading the braille of old prayers.

His hands trembled slightly, but he managed to unlock the padlock and looked inside: parcels wrapped in brown butcher paper—some small, some human-sized—stacked like sleeping animals. A smudge of something dark stained the bottom, where it had seeped through the paper. A breath of cold air brushed across his face.

Harold picked up a bundle as carefully as a grandmother selecting fruit. He unwrapped it slowly, peeling back twine and paper until the flesh revealed itself: deep-red and fine-grained marbled tenderness. He pressed a thumb and checked its give, as if gauging ripeness. Under his breath, he hummed *Deck the Halls* as he laid it on the cutting board.

His fingers tightened around the handle of the old, loved knife. The blade carrying memories kissed the meat and parted it the way a teacher parts hair for lice checks. Clinical and thorough, he cut with surgical precision and kept humming while working. Blood slicked his hands, not warm anymore but still adhesive. It freckled the white tile in soft constellations and painted the Christmas lights pink. The smell of copper filled the air and his nostrils. He almost tasted it, as if it were a penny on his tongue.

Behind him, on the stove, a pot the size of a grave burbled low and steady, steam coiling like dancing spirits over its rim. With calculated moves, Harold scraped the diced flesh into it. The meat sizzled, swallowed by the bubbling mass. The chili was already thick with beans and slow-cooked meat from earlier in the week, but the new addition changed its smell entirely. Richer. Sharper. Almost holy.

The wooden spoon left red trails that vanished beneath the surface as he stirred it, with slow, wide circles. More onions were added to the mix, along with a scoop of brown sugar, and his own blend of ground desert herbs that whispered sage and creosote after rain.

From the walk-in came a thump, then another. The weak insistence of a fist against steel followed right after.

Harold tilted his head toward the sound the way you listen to a kettle. "Almost there," he said, and the pot hissed back like a background supporting choir.

He slurped from the spoon, tasting it. Steam burst past his teeth: salt, smoke, sweetness; the ghost of something he could never name without spoiling it. Eyes closed, he savored it.

The flavor reached backward through him. Through Harold, his father, and Harold's father's father, until it reached Jeffrey at the root, apron clean, hands new to sin. Until the first Christmas played like a movie in front of his eyes: linseed oil and lamplight, travelers in frock coats, the meat... A miracle that no one questioned. Then the recipe was born. Like any recipe, it becomes a tradition if it lasts long enough.

He ladled the chili into four heavy bowls, each steaming and lumpy. A dollop of sour cream, a sprinkle of shredded cheese that melted into ribbons, and a square of cornbread perched like a halo on the edge.

When he returned to the diner, the heat followed him, just like blood scent clings to a hunter.

THE FEAST

"House special," Harold said, setting the bowls down with pride. "Jeffery's chili family recipe has been simmerin' since 1847. Older than good manners."

Glitter-Liner laughed, leaning over the bowl. "Smells like the devil finally learned how to cook."

They dug in, spoons clinking, steam fogging the air between them. The chili was thick, dark red, almost black in places, with chunks of meat so tender they fell apart at the touch.

"Holy shit," Rail-Thin muttered through a full mouth. "That's insane. It just... melts in your mouth."

"Tender as sin," Leather Jacket said, and he laughed, already digging another spoonful.

Glitter-Liner hummed, licking a bit of sauce from her thumb. "Tastes like smoke and... something sweet. What is that?"

Harold smiled. "Patience," he said. "It takes a long time to get it that soft."

They ate. Not in silence, but making noises people usually save for private grief or sex.

The girl's glitter eyeliner bled with the steam. Rail-Thin coughed a chunk of meat that went down wrong and wheezed with laughter through a red face. The quiet one wiped his mouth with his sleeve and peered past Harold toward the still-swinging kitchen door, as if he'd heard something move that wasn't the fan.

"You cook a lot on Christmas?" the quiet one asked.

Harold stirred his coffee, eyes distant and almost void. "Christmas cooks itself," he said softly. "I just help."

The quiet one smiled a little and didn't like how it felt on his face. "You mean holiday traffic."

Harold looked up, the corners of his mouth twitching. "I mean ..." he said, and let the rest cool between them like steam fading off a grave.

They didn't stop after one bowl. They didn't know how. It wasn't hunger anymore. It was something else. It was deeper, more like a craving.

Harold had always counted on how the first taste stirred new appetites. He walked back to the kitchen and returned with bowls of beans glossy as lacquer, another ladle of meat for the boy with the burning furnace inside, and a dessert that looked like apple pie, but tasted like a sermon about hunger.

The radio found the right station for a full minute, just long enough for a choir of children to sing *All Is Calm, All Is Bright* before the static swallowed the sound.

"Okay, but ..." Glitter-Liner said, scraping gravy with her plastic knife, "... real talk. Is it pork? For real?"

The quiet one didn't look away from Harold when he answered. He wanted to see it in his eyes.

Harold smiled. "It's what you asked for."

Rail-Thin laughed too loudly. "Dude, if it's roadkill, don't tell me. I'll cry."

Harold leaned back, elbows on the counter. Up close, the Santa on his apron grinned as if he knew a joke the room didn't. "You know, folks always say the same thing when they eat the recipe for the first time," he nearly whispered. "They always ask what it is, as if knowing would make it taste less like heaven."

"Does it?" the quiet one asked.

Harold took it in, as if it were the first time anyone had posed the question.

He let his eyes linger over each of them. "No," he said. "It only makes it taste more like home."

The quiet one's jaw worked. The jukebox blinked to life in the corner, though no one had fed it. One of its lights pulsed once like a heartbeat, then dimmed.

Before anyone realized, the bowls in front of them were empty. The heat sat heavy in their stomachs, slow and almost narcotic. The chili's sweetness clung to their tongues like something that refused to dissipate.

Rail-Thin's temple throbbed, bright as if lit from within. Glitter-Liner's laugh stuck in her throat, syrupy and faulty.

Leather Jacket leaned back, sighing, drunk on flavor. "Damn," he said softly. "That's... unreal."

Harold smiled faintly, his hand reaching beneath the counter. He found the cleaver with the same ease you find your own pulse. The lights flickered with a loud buzz, but immediately steadied. The radio crooned a soft line of *Silent Night.*

You don't start a cut against the music—the line played in Harold's mind. The family learned that early on. Harold wasn't sure if it was his own thought or some other voice he'd heard in his head.

The quiet one's spoon halted halfway to his mouth. He stared into the bowl, at what looked too red, too fibrous. A pulse of understanding passed through him—small and cold. Complete in a way that made his stomach churn.

With slow and careful moves, he folded his napkin. "I need the restroom," he said, but his small voice didn't match his expression.

"Back through the kitchen," Harold said without blinking.

The door swung open with a squeaky sigh, letting out a breath of freezer air that rolled over their ankles.

Leather Jacket giggled. "Bro's gonna spook himself."

"Film the hallway!" Rail-Thin called after him. "If there's a ghost, make it do a thumbs-up!"

Glitter-Liner leaned toward Harold, her voice syrupy and unsure. "Do you ever get lonely out here?"

Harold smiled, but it didn't reach his eyes. "Never on Christmas," he said, and somewhere behind him, a metal door squeaked shut.

CAT AND MOUSE

The kitchen welcomed the quiet one with its soft hums and clean, sharp knives standing in line. He didn't touch anything, but just looked. He let his eyes clock the hooks, the cutting board, the padlocked door with the scars running down its weathered surface.

He listened. From the other side of the walk-in cold room, a sound as faint as a hand learning to make a fist emerged, followed by the breathy complaint of someone who had tried to scream too many times before, but reached the bottom of it.

The quiet one crouched as if to tie his shoe and examined the floor. The scuff at the base of the freezer wasn't from feet, but was from something heavier being dragged and lifted over its edge. The groove told a story you only get by reading it with your gut.

He reached for the padlock.

The swing door gave a sombre whisper. Harold's figure filled the doorway, Santa apron grinning like a red-mouthed witness to something that didn't happen yet.

"Bathroom's the other way," Harold said, voice just above a mutter.

The quiet one straightened up, his hands empty and calm. "Sorry. I got ... distracted."

Harold's eyes darted to the lock and back. "Happens," he said, not unkind. Without flinching, he took two steps sideways, standing between the boy and the door. "You and yours came a long way for a story. You want to hear mine?"

The quiet one nodded. "I think I'm eating it." His genuine honesty surprised them both.

Harold's smile widened slowly. "You're the first whose mouth knew before his head did," he said, voice almost gentle. "Feels different, doesn't it? Knowing and wanting at the same time."

The boy's throat worked. The freezer made its little sorrowing sound, and the knives along the magnet strip reflected Christmas lights like stars shining in a dark winter sky.

"Go back," Harold said, and the kindness in his voice was the worst thing in the room. "Wouldn't want your friends to think you got lost."

The quiet one left, and Harold watched the swing door breathe after him, then put his palm flat on the freezer, closing his eyes as if in prayer. "Shush," he told whatever was inside. "We're feeding the living."

Back in the diner, the leather jacket dude had discovered the bell near the register and was ringing it with devotional joy.

Glitter-Liner filmed the snow globe while narrating a little fiction about the ghost of Santa trapped inside.

Rail-Thin had stopped eating only to pull a pocketknife and pick at something wedged between his teeth. He didn't notice how his hand trembled until the blade slipped and nicked him. A bright crimson bead welled up on his fingertip. He popped it into his mouth and laughed at his own clumsiness.

"That's iron," he said, surprised. "Tastes like coins."

"Blood tastes like blood," Harold said, resuming his place. He set a fifth plate on the counter, just a little leaner than the rest. A little fresher. "Compliments of the house."

"What's the occasion?" Glitter-Liner asked.

"Christmas," Harold paused. "And gratitude."

"For what?" the leather jacket dude asked through a mouthful.

"For keepin' an old tradition fed."

The radio lost the choir and found an organ. The lights stuttered again. Rail-Thin's laughter broke into hiccups.

"Hey," the quiet one said gently, laying a hand on his friend's back. "Slow down."

Harold's hand slid beneath the counter and found the cleaver's handle with the same ease as if it were just another bone in his body.

"Wait," Glitter-Liner said suddenly, blinking fast as if water had gotten into her lenses. Her voice turned small, barely audible. "What meat did you say it was?"

"I didn't," Harold smirked.

And because every ritual needs a bell, the leather jacket dude struck the counter bell one last time, and that was the signal.

The Butchery

The first blow landed on the bell-ringer's wrist. A crack like a snapped icicle, and the bell skittered, chimed, and fell silent. Harold plunged over the counter like a snowplow. Flat and inevitable. The cleaver rose again, and the world turned red.

The second blow took the leather jacket dude at the neck—the cut wasn't clean, but hungry. The blade chewed through the tendon and slowed at the spine. He made a sound that wasn't a scream yet, but more of a squelchy question. Harold answered with weight and leverage, finishing what he'd begun. The head thudded on the formica and turned to look at its own body with the calm surprise of a fish.

Rail-Thin bolted, legs forgetting what their job was. He took three steps before the rug betrayed him, and the booth tripped him in the shins.

Harold wondered whether the cleaver was the right tool for this angle. Without a tinge of hesitation, he dropped it and quickly switched to the boning knife, sliding it between ribs with the tenderness of a lover removing a splinter. The fine blade rotated until cartilage sobbed, cracking into separation.

Rail-Thin's breath left him in a cheerful 'oof,' that shifted into a horrible wheeze, followed by a stretched inhale as if he tried to breathe around the blade.

As if awoken from a nightmare, Glitter-Liner ran for the door, rattling it in despair. Locked. As if he had done this many times before, Harold's hand moved faster and slid the bolt without even looking.

She shouldered it once, then again, and turned to grab the first chair within reach. She swung it, hoping the glass would break with the right momentum and belief. Prompt again, Harold's hand gripped the chair and yanked it from her, his moves full of grace, like a dance instructor correcting form. Just as poised, he placed it down.

His fingers cupped the back of her head, and he whispered, "Shush," before swinging the meat tenderizer, which somehow appeared in his hand. The first hit was a near-fail. The forehead cracked, and an eye flower opened wider.

Harold changed hands, adjusting his hold on the bludgeoning instrument. The second blow turned off the lights in Glitter-Liner's eyes. She folded where she stood—a puppet who'd learned gravity halfway through a trick.

The quiet one didn't run. He stepped into Harold's shadow and put his hands up empty, palms out. "Don't," he said. Not begging, but advising.

"You knew," Harold said, with a nearly pleased sneer.

"I didn't want it," the boy parried, and Harold almost believed him.

"I did." Honesty sounded like mercy in Harold's voice. He gestured toward the kitchen with the tip of the knife. "Let's not make a mess where people sit."

They went through the swing door together like colleagues punching in for the night shift. The kitchen welcomed them in, stainless steel workstations waiting, like an altar ready for offerings. Harold set the meat tenderizer down with care, then picked a different tool—a fillet knife thin as a rumor.

The quiet one watched him with the same interest as if he studied a craft he hated, but admired at the same time.

"What's your name?" Harold asked.

The boy appeared to contemplate for a moment. "Does it matter?"

"It does to me," Harold said, the words landing truth-heavy between them.

"Joshua." The boy's voice barely reached the walls.

Harold repeated it slowly, savoring the word. "Joshua," he said, and smirked. "Every recipe starts with a name. Come here."

The boy moved closer. Harold grabbed his wrist like a father at a skating rink and pressed the arm flat on the cutting board. The first slash barely pierced the meat beside the thumb. Letting out a surprised gasp, the boy steadied himself, pushing his free hand against the counter. The second cut was deeper, a thin gush of blood flowing in a red seam. Harold's breath fogged softly in the walk-in's ghostly draft.

"You can fight," Harold said. "It'll be uglier. Or you can give in, and I'll make it quick."

The boy shut his eyes. "Is any of it quick?"

"It is for the living parts," Harold said, and he meant it. With just two fingers under his chin, he guided the boy's head to turn, beady eyes evaluating the tendon map along his neck. "You'll taste good," he added, not out of cruelty but for himself. Because the sentence had to exist in the world where the rest of it already did.

The boy opened his eyes. "If I asked you not to, would you?"

Harold believed in mercy the same way a butcher believes in waste. "No," he said, and he turned quiet.

He continued, slow and proper. The first cut? Clean and deep enough to end fast. Controlled enough to spare the walls. He murmured the old words under his breath, half prayer, half inventory, each one a name that didn't belong to him anymore.

The boy's knees buckled, and Harold's hand gently guided him down, as if lowering someone into bed. It wasn't theatrical or cruel. Instead, it was sad and efficient, like cleaning up after a party that had ended when no one wanted to end.

Harold stayed there for a moment, holding the body the way you cradle a sleeping child in a booth so they didn't fall. Then he set him down carefully, folded his hands, and closed his eyes for the length of a single note from the radio's din.

The Legacy

He 'worked' for hours after that, using the word the way his grandfather had, meaning grace with a knife. He separated the shoulder from the arm, found the seams with a fingertip, and ran the blade between joints. Portioned hips, and tenderloin, and wrapped every cut in brown paper that absorbed the map of him.

He labeled the bundles in a cursive style no one alive knew anymore: *prime, tender, choice.* The fat, trimmed into little white comets, was pushed into a jar of what looked like ordinary lard, holding the history of a hundred meals.

He reserved the heads for broth and the faces for something special. Bones simmered until the room smelled like time. He moved like a man cleaning a church after midnight Mass, tired but satisfied. A necessary task.

Out front, the neon sign kept vigil, red and white on repeat as if Santa were winking slowly. The jukebox's only remaining bulb pulsed in sync with the freezer's heartbeat. On the counter, the snow globe sent down glitter the way a shaken sky might decide to snow.

He dragged the mop in patient infinity symbols. The water shifted from pink to red to rust and back to clear again. He changed it three times. Finally, he passed a white-gloved hand over the edges of the pie case and smiled when he found no smear. Before setting the bell back by the register, he dinged it once. For tradition. In the hush that followed, the sound reverberated with a sense of holiness.

He wrapped, stacked, and tucked until the walk-in cold room exhaled in contentment. Somewhere inside, a sound shifted, settling the way houses settle when the last guest leaves.

At dawn, the diner sparkled, spotless. The booths gleamed, and the scent of iron lay low, concealed under coffee, cinnamon, and breakfast flavors. The wind blew up the highway, rattling the windows in a friendly way.

Ignorant, a random coyote trotted across the parking lot as it passed the only car parked there.

Harold poured himself a cup and sat at the counter.

His hands shook just a little, but enough that he had to steady the mug with the other. He listened to the building talk to itself: heat in the vents, the thin click of cooling metal, the radio giving up and becoming pure static.

He thought of Jeffery and the first Christmas, the first travelers, the way a recipe becomes a religion when stirred enough times into a hot pan. He thought of the faces he had fed and the ones he had made into food.

The shake faded, and his hands steadied. No guilt ate at him. Not for the way the stories liked to dress it. Instead, he thought of it as continuity, legacy, and the quiet satisfaction of a job done right.

Harold paced to the window and stood there, watching the road. The desert never stayed empty for too long. Someone always came in. Hungry.

With one practiced flip, he turned the OPEN sign to CLOSED because that simple gesture gave the morning a different shape.

Restless, he felt his hands shaking again, demanding more work, so he gave the counter one final wipe, then tapped the snow globe and watched the flurry decide to fall.

From the freezer came a soft thump, as if someone just remembered to answer in a passcode.

Harold bent, reverently, and lifted the mug in a little toast to the ghostly reflection in the glass. "Merry Christmas, Jeffery," he said.